HERE WITH ME

AN ADAIR FAMILY NOVEL

SAMANTHA YOUNG

Here With Me

An Adair Family Novel

By Samantha Young
Copyright © 2021 Samantha Young

Edited by Jennifer Sommersby Young
Cover Design By Hang Le

ALSO BY SAMANTHA YOUNG

Other Adult Contemporary Novels by Samantha Young

On Hart's Boardwalk (a novella)

Hart's Boardwalk Series:

The One Real Thing
Every Little Thing
Things We Never Said
The Truest Thing

Young Adult contemporary titles by Samantha Young

The Impossible Vastness of Us

The Fragile Ordinary

Young Adult Urban Fantasy titles by Samantha Young

War of the Covens Trilogy:
Hunted
Destined
Ascended

Warriors of Ankh Trilogy:
Blood Will Tell
Blood Past
Shades of Blood

Fire Spirits Series:
Smokeless Fire
Scorched Skies
Borrowed Ember
Darkness, Kindled

Other Titles

Drip Drop Teardrop, a novella

Titles Co-written with Kristen Callihan

Outmatched

Titles Written Under S. Young

Fear of Fire and Shadow

True Immortality Series:

War of Hearts

Kiss of Vengeance

Kiss of Eternity: A True Immortality Short Story

Bound by Forever

To Dad,
Not a day goes by that I don't feel proud and grateful to be your
daughter.
I love you to the moon and back.

PROLOGUE

ROBYN

One year ago

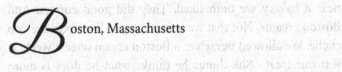

oston, Massachusetts

THE RAIN LASHED our patrol car as we sipped our coffees, waiting for a crackle on the radio.

I was enjoying the peaceful lull created by the sounds of raindrops on metal when a pop of color in the overwhelming gray beyond my window caught my attention.

On the sidewalk, a woman in a navy coat, one hand holding a black umbrella, the other a leash, was halted by the dog on the end of it. From here, it looked like a Lab. The dog wore a bright red raincoat. And he'd sat his ass down on the sidewalk as if to say, "I'm done with this shit. Make it stop."

1

I laughed under my breath as the woman gesticulated wildly, as if to reply, "What the hell do you want me to do about it?"

Her arms thrown wide, head bent toward the dog staring back up at her, became a snapshot in my head. I wished I had my camera. I'd use a wide aperture and my 150mm lens to blur out the gray, movement-filled background and focus on the woman and her stubborn dog.

"Jaz thinks you should dump Mark." My partner, Autry Davis, yanked me out of the mental photography processing in my head.

Smirking at the comment, I ignored the uneasiness that accompanied it. "Oh, *Jaz* thinks that?"

Jasmine "Jaz" Davis was pretty outspoken, but Autry had made it clear he didn't like my boyfriend Mark from the moment he'd met him.

"Sure does." Autry stared out the window at the passing traffic. We were parked on Maverick Square in East Boston, near a bakery we both liked. They did good coffees. And Boston creams. Not that we were trying to live up to the cop cliché. We allowed ourselves a Boston cream once a week. It was our treat. "She thinks he thinks what he does is more important than what you do and that he never prioritizes you."

That did sound like something Jaz would say.

Mark was a prosecutor and very good at his job. His success was appealing because I found hardworking guys sexy. But lately he'd been pushing me to make a change. He thought I should work my way up, apply to become a sergeant detective and then move up to lieutenant.

He didn't understand I didn't want that because he was the most driven son of a bitch I'd ever met. Like I said, that was hot until he tried to make me into someone I wasn't.

"Well, you can tell Jaz I'm breaking up with him."

Autry tried not to look too happy about that and failed. "Yeah?"

"Yeah. He's too much like hard work."

"Not that I want to talk you out of dumping the guy, but you do realize relationships *are* hard work. Right?"

I snorted. "Says the man with the wife and kids he adores."

"Doesn't mean it isn't hard work."

"I know that. But you've got to *want* to work hard at it, and I don't want to with Mark. Last weekend, he blew up at me for buying a fish-eye lens for my camera. Told me an expensive 'hobby' was a waste of my mediocre income, and he wasn't about to *indulge* me in a pastime." My skin flushed hot with anger at the reminder. I'd emotionally and verbally shut him out ever since.

"He said what?" Autry frowned. "Yeah, you need to dump his ass, pronto. Shit, can you imagine Jaz if I tried to condescend to her like that? He's lucky he's dealing with you and not my woman. He wouldn't have come out of it alive. And I'm not telling her what you just told me, 'cause he still might not. Damn, Penhaligon. Life is too short for that bullshit."

"The sex is pretty good, though." I said it mostly to be funny. No sex was worth being with a guy who made me feel small and unimportant.

Autry cut me a warning look. "Don't want to hear it."

I laughed under my breath and sipped my coffee.

Straight out of the academy at twenty-one, I was introduced to Autry Davis, my beat partner. A tall, good-looking man seven years my senior with a quick sense of humor and a warmth that could melt even the coldest soul. I'd developed a crush on the man. A crush that soon faded into friendship and trust. Especially when I met his wife Jaz and their two young daughters, Asia and Jada. In the last six years, the Davises had welcomed me into their family. Autry now was like an older brother. Like any brother, he didn't want to hear about his little sister's sex life.

And like any little sister, I deliberately ignored his pleas to stop torturing him with the details.

"I mean, there's room for improvement, but he's definitely better at it than Axel." Axel was the guy before Mark. A musician. Self-involved. Selfish in bed. And out of it. When I was sick with a bad head cold, he didn't opt to check in on me or offer to buy me groceries so I could stay in bed. Nope. He disappeared and said he wouldn't be back until I was well again. Jaz and Autry took care of me. Axel didn't come back when I was well again because I told him not to. Mark wasn't that giving in bed either, to be fair, but at least with him, I reached climax.

"I can't hear you." Autry scowled out the window. "I am no longer in the car. I am someplace where the world is good and right and the Celtics are winning the season."

"So the land of make-believe, then?"

"Don't you come at the Celtics."

I chuckled, opening my mouth to continue teasing him when the radio crackled.

"Domestic disturbance. Lexington Street, apartment 302B. Neighbor called it in."

Autry reached for the radio. "Gold 1-67. Three minutes out."

"Roger that."

I'd already started the engine and was swinging the car into traffic.

"What do you think it is this time?" I asked.

"Affair."

"You always guess that."

"Because I'm nearly always right."

"Last time you were wrong."

"What was last time?"

"Oh, Davis, you're getting old," I teased. "Girlfriend found out boyfriend had gambled all her savings. She beat the shit out of him."

"Oh yeah. That was a nasty one. That man will never be able to have children after what she did to him."

Unfortunately, probably true. I winced at the memory.

Only a few minutes later, we pulled up to the apartment building on the corner of Lexington. It had the same architecture as all the buildings in this part of Boston—narrow with wooden shingle siding. This one was painted white years ago and was in dire need of a repaint. It had two entrances, one for the downstairs apartment and the other for the upstairs. A woman in bright yellow pajamas, her hair covered with a matching bandana, stood outside the first-floor apartment door. She approached us as we got out of the car.

"They've been yelling up there for the last thirty minutes, and then I heard things crashing and she started screaming and crying." The neighbor looked shaken. "He's shiesty as fuck, that one. Think he's into drugs. Thought I better call it in."

I gave her a reassuring smile and was about to speak when a terrified shriek sounded from above. Autry hurried to the door. Turning back to the neighbor, I ordered, "Please return to your apartment, ma'am."

As I watched her do this, Autry banged on the door to the upstairs apartment. "Boston PD, open up!"

An angry male voice could be heard yelling obscenities upstairs. I caught "fucking bitch" in among the rambling, followed by loud sobbing broken by intermittent, garbled screaming.

Autry looked at me, face grim, and my hand went to my holster.

I nodded.

He turned the handle on the front door and it opened.

As we moved into the cramped hall, to the stairs leading steeply up to the next floor, I followed Autry and took out my gun. The occupants of the apartment no doubt couldn't hear us over their argument. As we climbed the stairs, it became apparent, from what I could make out, that this altercation was about drugs. He seemed to think she was skimming money off the top while selling his product. Not an average domestic disturbance call after all.

I steeled myself.

The stairs led to a hallway with two doorways opposite each other. We peeked in one and saw it was the bedroom; it appeared empty. Then we moved just beyond the door into the other, which took us into a small kitchen/living space. The place was trashed. Coffee table on its side, TV smashed, photographs falling out of broken frames and glass littered in their midst. A stool at the mini breakfast bar lay on its side.

A young woman huddled on the sofa, face streaked with mascara, fear in her liquid eyes as she stared up at a tall, skinny guy who held a handgun in her face.

We raised our guns.

"Boston PD. Lower your weapon," Autry demanded.

The man looked at us without doing as warned. He scowled. "What the fuck are you fuckin' bastards doing here? This ain't your business. Did that nosy cunt downstairs call the cops?"

His pupils were dilated, his speech slurred.

The guy was high.

This situation just got better and better.

I repeated, "Sir, lower your weapon."

"Or what?"

"If you do not lower your weapon, it will be construed as a threat and I will shoot you," Autry warned.

"I didn't understand half that shit." The gun wavered dangerously in his hand.

"Davis," I murmured and turned my head ever so slightly to look up at my partner—

Movement flashed in my peripheral. Adrenaline shot through me as another guy came charging into the room, handgun raised and pointed at Autry's back, finger on the trigger.

There was no time for anything but to move in front of my partner.

To shield him.

With threats front and back, I had no choice but to fire at the threat from behind. Two gunshots sounded, louder than a clap of thunder above the building. The sound ricocheted through my head at almost the same time that the sharp, burning sensation ripped through my chest.

Another bang. Another burn. And another.

I slumped into Autry as more gunfire sounded above my head.

There was noise. Groaning. Screaming.

Autry's voice calmly telling me I would be okay.

"Three people with gunshot wounds. We got an officer down. She's been shot multiple times. I need ambulances to 302B Lexington Street."

The pain in my chest seemed to spread through my whole body as I felt pressure on my wounds. "Shit, Robyn, shit," Autry murmured in my ear. "Why, why?"

I understood what he asked.

I wanted to answer, but I couldn't make my lips move, and there was something wrong with my vision. Black shadows crept around the edges, growing thicker and faster.

"Stay with me, Robbie. Stay with me."

I wanted to.

I did.

I wanted to reach out and grip tight to him and not let go.

But my body and mind felt disconnected, my mind pulling me farther and farther away …

1

ROBYN

PRESENT DAY

*A*rdnoch, Sutherland,
Scotland

FOR ONCE, I wasn't thinking about my camera or the scenery or the perfect shot. Amazing, really, when I was in one of the most beautiful places I'd ever been in my life.

Yet, it was difficult to see it right now when I was minutes away from meeting my father.

A man I hadn't seen since I was fourteen years old.

People called the nervous flutters in their stomach butterflies. Butterflies didn't cut it. Surely butterflies were when you were excited-nervous? What was happening in my gut right now made me feel physically ill. Even my knees shook.

And I hated that my birth father, Mac Galbraith, had that power over me.

I got out of my rental and forced my shoulders back, taking a deep breath as I strode down the gravel driveway toward the enormous security gates built into brick pillars.

Those pillars flowed into a tall wall. On the other side of the gate, the drive continued, fading into the darkness of the woodland that shadowed its edges.

As I grew closer, I searched for a call button or cameras. Nothing. Stopping at the gate, I gave them a shake, but they were made of solid iron and immovable. Eyes narrowing, I searched beyond into the trees, trying to listen past the chirping of birds and the rustle of leaves in the wind.

A slight whirring to my left drew my attention, and I caught the light glancing off the movement of a lens. Ducking my head to look closer, I saw the security camera camouflaged in a tree.

I saluted the camera with two fingers off my forehead to let whoever was behind it know I'd seen them.

Now all I could do was wait.

Just what my nerves needed.

I turned, leaned against the gate, and crossed my arms and legs in a deliberate pose that said, "I'm not going anywhere until someone comes out here."

Not even a few minutes later, I heard an engine and the kick of gravel. Pushing off the gate, I turned and watched the black Range Rover with its tinted windows approach from the other side.

My nerves rose to the fore with a vengeance.

Why oh why did my father have to be head of security at one of the most prestigious members-only clubs in the world?

Oh right.

Because of Lachlan Adair.

Jealousy and resentment that I hated I felt burned in the back of my throat. Ignoring the sensation, I crossed my arms over my chest and tried to look nonchalant as the Range Rover stopped. The driver door opened, and a man wearing black pants, a black shirt, and a leather jacket approached the gate.

I noted the little wire in his ear.

He was security.

But he was not my father.

"Madam, this is private property," the guy said in a Scottish brogue much like Mac's.

"I know." I stared him down through the gate bars. "I'm here to see my father."

"I'm afraid only members and staff are allowed entrance onto the estate. I'll have to ask you to return to your vehicle and leave."

Like I could give a rat's ass that Ardnoch Castle and Estate was home to actors and movie and TV industry types who paid a fortune in annual fees just to say they were a member. "My name is Robyn Penhaligon. My father is Mac Galbraith. Could you let him know I'm here?"

The security guard was good—he didn't betray his reaction to this news. "Do you have identification?"

Knowing they'd ask for it, I'd stuck my driver's license in the ass pocket of my jeans. I whipped it out and handed it over.

"One second, please." The guy returned to the vehicle and opened the driver's door. He got in without closing it, and I heard him murmuring.

While his conversation with whoever went on, I returned to my car to get the sweater I'd thrown in the back seat. I'd been too hot with nerves when I'd left the hotel, but the chilled spring air now made me shiver.

A few minutes later, the guy returned to the gate. "Ms. Penhaligon, I must ask you to hand over any recording devices you have on your person, including any smartphones."

"Excuse me?"

"Nonmembers are not allowed onto the estate with recording devices. This ensures the privacy of our guests."

"Right." At least that meant Daddy Dearest didn't intend to turn me away.

Shit.

A little part of me almost wished he had.

I grabbed my phone out of my car, glad I'd had the sense to leave my camera in my room. I trusted no one with my baby.

"Is that everything?"

"Yup."

"Please return to your vehicle. The gates will open momentarily, and you will follow me onto the estate."

I nodded and got back into my rented SUV. A four-by-four had seemed like the right choice for spending time in the Highlands, and this one was affordable. Deciding to fly to Scotland without booking a return ticket gave my savings account serious palpitations. I had to be careful with my money while I was here.

As soon as the security guy couldn't see my face anymore, I let out a shaky exhale and waited for the gates to open. While I did this, the guy turned the Range Rover around and drove up the gravel drive to give the gates room. They swung inward seconds later, and I drove forward.

The driveway led through woodlands for what felt like forever before the trees disappeared to reveal grass for miles around a mammoth building in the distance. Flags were situated throughout the rolling plains of the estate—a golf course. Tiny distant figures could be seen playing.

Eyes back on Ardnoch Castle, I sucked in another breath.

I'd never felt more out of place.

It was a feeling I was used to when it came to Mac.

I never felt a part of his world.

He'd never let me.

The castle was a rambling, castellated mansion, six stories tall and about two hundred years old. I knew from my research that while it was the club's main building, there were several buildings throughout the twelve-thousand acre estate, including permanent residences members paid exorbitant amounts to own. According to Google, the estate sat on the coast of Ardnoch and was home to pine forests (which I could attest to), rolling plains (again, saw that), heather moors (really wanted to see those), and golden beaches (really, really wanted to see those). While I wasn't sure how this visit with my father would go, I kind of hoped it went well enough for a tour of the estate.

Even if I did feel like a fish out of water.

As I followed the Range Rover up to the castle, I mused over the security here in general. While there was a great big gate and walls at the main entrance, how did they ensure members privacy when there were twelve thousand acres to manage?

Something to ask Dear Old Dad if we ever got past the awkward, "Why didn't you love me enough to stay in my life, leaving me with rampant abandonment issues that have impacted me to almost fatal levels?"

There went my stomach again, roiling like a ship caught in a storm.

"Jesus Christ," I whispered as I pushed open the driver's door. The castle was like Downton Abbey on steroids. There were turrets, and a flag of the St. Andrew's Cross flew from one of the parapets. Columns supported a mini-crenellated roof over an elaborate portico that housed double iron doors.

As I got out, the wind blew my ponytail in my face and battered through my sweater. It was much windier here without the protection of the trees. And it had an icy nip that surprised me, considering it was almost April. The smell of saltwater hung in the air despite the fact the castle sat two miles inland.

I loved the air here. Crisp and fresh. It filled me with energy.

Neck craned, I stared up at the flag and heard the creak of the iron doors opening. A man wearing a traditional butler's uniform, including white gloves, stepped out as if to greet me.

But then he was halted by the appearance of another man.

Drawing a breath, I stepped out from behind the driver's door and closed it, forcing myself to look at the very tall, broad-shouldered figure heading my way.

A mixture of overwhelming emotions flooded me as I recognized the man. He wore a tailored gray suit that didn't quite civilize him. His thick, salt-and-pepper hair needed a trim and curled at his nape. His cheeks were unshaven.

He appeared to be in his late thirties but I knew him to be forty-four years old.

Expression neutral, he strode toward me with determination. As he drew closer, I realized how much I looked like my father. His hair was darker. But I had his face shape and his eyes.

Those were definitely my eyes. The same light brown around the pupil, striations of gray and green bleeding into the brown from the edges of the iris.

Mom always said at least my father had given me something good.

Mac Galbraith stared at me stonily. That bland countenance disappeared as he swallowed hard. "Robyn?"

"Mac." I held out my hand to shake his.

He stared at it for a second as if not quite sure what to do.

Manners compelled him to shake it finally. He squeezed my hand before seeming reluctant to release me. The action caused a complex response I hadn't expected. Tears threatened, and I glanced away, as if casual, unaffected. Staring at the castle, I said, blasé, "This is some place you have here."

"It's not mine," he replied. "It's Lachlan's. The Adairs."

Yeah, like I didn't already know that. There was that awful resentment again. I forced myself to look at my father. "I guess you're wondering why I'm here."

"Aye. Not that it isn't a nice surprise."

Was it?

I narrowed my gaze, trying to discern the truth in his statement. "It's not something I can just blurt out on the driveway of a castle with a man I barely know hovering at my back." I referred to Security Guy who was still with us.

"Sorry about that. Protocol."

I nodded. I knew all about protocol.

"You'd know all about that," Mac said, as if plucking the words from my head. "Last I heard, you were a police officer."

He looked pleased about this. As if it connected us. I hated that it did. After all, he'd been a cop once too. But so was my stepfather, Seth Penhaligon. "Family business, I guess," I replied. "Wanted to be like my old man, Seth." When I was 16, I'd decided to change my name legally from Galbraith to Penhaligon. After two years of no contact with Mac, I'd wanted to sever our connection as well as have the same name as the family who were in my life daily.

While Mac was very good at hiding his reaction, there was a flicker of something in his eyes that suggested I'd hit a sore spot.

Hmm.

"I'm not a cop anymore."

"Oh?"

"Like I said, I don't want to chat on a driveway. I know this place doesn't cater to riffraff, so can you get away?"

Mac frowned. "My daughter isn't riffraff. Come inside. We'll talk and then I'll give you a tour."

I thumbed over my shoulder. "Is this guy going to babysit us the whole time?"

Mac glanced at his colleague. "Jock, why don't you take the vehicle back to the mews and return to your duties."

"Yes, sir."

"Shall we?" Mac said to me, gesturing to the castle entrance.

"Isn't there a servants' entrance that would be more suited to my position?"

"There's a delivery entrance, but we're usually prepared for *those* packages." He shot me a sardonic look and walked toward the castle.

"What about my car?"

"It's fine there. We'll move it later if we need to."

I studied the back of Mac's head as he strode in front of me. My father had to be around six feet four and was physically fit. He made an intimidating figure. At forty-four, he had the physique of a man half his age. He looked great. Ruggedly handsome. Successful. He didn't look old enough to be my father. But for a kid who got his older girlfriend pregnant when he was only sixteen, he'd done okay for himself.

But I guess a person could when they went out into the world to succeed by sacrificing their relationship with their child.

So lost in my thoughts, it took a second for my surroundings to hit me.

Holy shit.

I stopped just inside the door and gaped.

Yeah, I definitely felt like a fish out of water.

"Wakefield, this is my daughter Robyn." Mac stopped next

to the guy in uniform. "Robyn, this is Wakefield, the butler at Ardnoch."

A butler. Of course. "Nice to meet you."

The butler bowed his head, expression stoic. "Welcome to Ardnoch Estate, miss."

I nodded vaguely, my attention returning to the space beyond us as we stepped inside.

"Impressive, aye?" Mac said, grinning at my expression.

It was mammoth.

Polished parquet flooring underfoot made it appear even more so. The décor was traditional and screamed Scottish opulence. The grandest staircase I'd ever seen descended before me, fitted with a red-and-gray tartan wool runner. It led to a landing where three floor-to-ceiling stained glass windows spilled light down it. Then it branched off at either side, twin staircases leading to the floor above, which I could partially see from the galleried balconies at either end of the reception hall. A fire burned in the huge hearth on the wall adjacent to the entrance and opposite the staircase. The smell of burning wood accentuated the coziness the interior designer had managed to pull off despite the dark, wood-paneled walls and ceiling. Tiffany lamps scattered throughout on end tables gave the space a warm glow.

Opposite the fire sat two matching suede-and-fabric buttoned sofas with a coffee table in between. More light spilled into the hall from large openings that led to other rooms on this floor. I could hear the rise and fall of conversation in the distance beyond.

In one of those doorways appeared a man as tall as my father. He paused at the sight of us and then made his way across the humongous reception hall.

As he drew closer, I recognized him.

Millions of people across the world knew this guy's face.

Wearing a fitted, black cashmere sweater that caressed his

muscular physique and black dress pants, the man wore casual chic beautifully. He had the body and swagger that fashion magazines loved in their Hollywood actors.

And that's what he'd once been.

An A-list Hollywood actor.

Lachlan Adair.

Normal women would swoon at his dark blond handsomeness, his lovely blue eyes and brooding mouth, the short, almost dark brown beard. While obviously good-looking, there was a rough edge to his masculine beauty that made his face substantially more appealing. And he was well known for the wicked twinkle in his eyes. From what I could tell, he hadn't been a bad actor either, although typecast in mostly action movies.

I didn't swoon as he approached.

I was nervous, but not because his charisma and fame intimidated me.

Beneath my calm facade, I held a deep reserve of resentment toward this guy. It wasn't his fault. Not really. But this was the man my father abandoned me in favor of.

When Lachlan Adair broke out in Hollywood at twenty-one with a huge action blockbuster, he hired my father as part of his private security. Perhaps it was that they were both Scots that drew them together. I wouldn't know. I only knew they became close. So close, Mac went everywhere Lachlan did, even if that meant missing out on my teen years. My birthdays. Graduation. And then they moved back to Scotland when Lachlan retired to turn a family-owned estate into this exclusive, members-only resort.

Mac was head of security and lived in the village.

"I heard you had a visitor," Lachlan said. His attention moved beyond us and he addressed the butler. "Wakefield, there seems to be a problem with a guest in the Duchess's Suite. Would you mind assisting?"

The butler strode past us. "Right away, sir." He disappeared up the grand staircase, moving with efficient speed without looking like he was in a hurry.

Adair focused his stony gaze on me even as he addressed my father. "Mac, it seems an introduction is in order."

"Lachlan, this is my daughter, Robyn. Robyn, this is Lachlan Adair."

Neither of us reached for the other's hand. Awkward tension fell between us.

I didn't know what his problem with me was.

I wasn't the one who'd stolen *his* father.

"I know who he is," I said, unimpressed.

Lachlan's eyes narrowed ever so slightly. "I've heard a lot about you. It seems strange to have been in Mac's life for almost twenty years and never have met his daughter."

"Yeah, that tends to happen when a father abandons his kid to follow an *actor* around the world." I didn't dare look at my father. Despite my complicated feelings, I hadn't come here to attack him. There was a small part of me that understood why Mac hadn't been around.

"Excuse me?" Adair's tone had a dangerous quietness to it.

I ignored him and turned to my father. "Can we have some privacy?"

"Of course," Adair answered. "Forgive me for intruding." He gave Mac a look of concern. "Just wanted to make sure everything was okay here?"

Mac nodded, his expression guarded. "If you would prefer us to go off the estate, we can."

"Don't be daft." Adair took a step back. "Give Ms. *Penhaligon* a tour."

Did he just emphasize my surname?

For a moment, Mac pressed his lips together in a tight line and seemed to give Adair a warning glance. The lord of the castle lifted his hands in a gesture of surrender and without looking at me, turned on his heel and walked away.

Overall, he'd been as rude to me as I was to him.

But I had an excuse for my rudeness, even if it was unfair to blame him for my father's actions.

What had I ever done to Lachlan Adair?

2

ROBYN

*M*inutes later, I found myself in a room tucked away at the back of the first floor—Mac's office. It had been decorated much simpler than what I'd seen of the castle so far.

A shallow window behind his desk offered a barely there glimpse of the estate grounds. Dark and gray, the room was saved from grimness by the multitude of lamps, comfortable antique furnishings, and the surprising collection of books on the shelves.

Two armchairs sat across from his desk. He offered one to me. "Can I send for tea or coffee?"

Suddenly feeling more nervous than I did when Mac first approached me, I nodded and muttered, "Coffee, thanks."

I took a seat, hoping the tremble in my knees didn't show.

Mac picked up the telephone on his desk and pressed a button. A few seconds later, he said, "Stephen, can you arrange for coffee and refreshments to be sent to my office, please? For two."

I heard the murmur of a voice down the line.

"Thank you." Mac hung up and then sat on the edge of his desk.

Perhaps it was finally being alone with him, but when our eyes locked, a crushing ache in my chest overwhelmed me. Silence fell between us. It lasted agonizing minutes.

At least it seemed to.

"So"—Mac finally broke the painful tension—"I gather you came to visit for a specific reason?"

Everything that had percolated in my mind for months since my therapist suggested I visit Mac for closure at once seemed too much. If I told this man, this near stranger, everything I felt, I'd make myself vulnerable to someone who'd already hurt me beyond bearing. That hadn't sunk in until I looked into his eyes and felt the pain of longing for a father I barely knew.

Mac waited patiently for me to speak. The words caught in my throat, choking me.

Concern furrowed his brows. "Robyn, has something happened?"

"I ... uh ... I quit my job."

"You said. Is there a reason?"

Wrenching my gaze from his, I stared unseeingly at his bookshelf. "Decided it wasn't for me, I guess." Frustrated with myself for failing to be honest, I ground my teeth.

"Is that the only reason?" he pressed.

"Yeah," I lied and glanced back at him. "I started a photography business. Mostly the usual kind of work. But I started selling shots of Boston through my Instagram, and they're doing well. I've always wanted to see Scotland, since I'm part Scottish, and thought photos from here might be a big hit ... And, well, I thought I should stop in and see you since you *gave* me the Scottish part."

His lips twitched. "I'm glad you did come to see me. And

congratulations on your new business." His eyes brightened. "I gave you your first camera. Do you remember?"

Stupid tears burned in my throat and I abruptly stood. "You know what, I'm not ready to do this after all—"

"Robyn—" Mac stood too.

"I'm going to go."

His expression fell. "Please stay. Have a coffee with me."

I couldn't. I was seconds from bursting into tears. It was mortifying and seemed to come out of nowhere. "Later. I need to go."

Hurrying toward the door, I wrenched it open and marched out, narrowly missing the young man in a uniform similar to Wakefield's, holding a tea tray with our coffee on it. "Sorry." I rounded him, determined to get away from Mac.

"Christ!" Mac bit out. "Stephen, sorry. Please put the tray in my office." And then he fell into step with me as I followed the narrow corridor toward the reception hall.

"Please stay and talk," he pleaded.

"Not now, okay."

"But you're staying here? I will see you again?"

I nodded. Yeah, I wasn't ready to leave quite yet. I just needed to regroup. Obviously seeing him again after so long an absence affected me more than I'd anticipated. "I'm staying in Ardnoch. At the Gloaming."

"Aye, good."

We fell into silence again.

"Do you know what *the gloaming* means?" Mac asked.

"Yeah. Gordon, the owner, explained it means *twilight*."

"Of course." Mac grinned. "I'm sure Gordon explains it to everyone."

"You know him?"

"It's a wee place. Everybody knows everybody."

"Right." I considered that as Mac held the main door open

for me. "Does that make it easier or harder to keep this place private for members?"

"Believe it or not, the villagers aren't interested in the comings and goings of the rich and famous. The members go in and out of the village without any worry about finding photos of themselves online afterward—unless the paparazzi are around during the summer. The people here understand the members will return and spend money in a place that affords them privacy and a sense of normality. You'll find more gossip among the villagers about each other than you'll ever find about the club and its members."

"I guess that makes sense." My rental sat in the drive where I'd left it. Feeling more than a little embarrassed by my abrupt departure, I couldn't look at Mac. "Sorry about the drama. I just …" I shrugged, unable to finish my sentence.

"Mr. Galbraith!"

Mac turned as I looked beyond his shoulder to see a man dressed much the same as Jock hurrying toward us. "What is it?"

"Sir, you're needed urgently at the delivery entrance." His eyes widened ever so slightly, as if trying to communicate a message.

A message my father seemed to understand. He cursed under his breath and said to me, "I have to go. But perhaps we could do dinner at the Gloaming tonight?"

So soon?

"Um … how about tomorrow night?"

He nodded and lifted a hand as if to touch me but dropped it quickly. "I'll come by around seven."

I'd barely agreed before he hurried across the gravel after his employee.

Once he'd disappeared inside the castle, I looked up at its crenellated roofline and sighed. Disappointment filled me. What had I expected in coming here? A miraculous sense of connection? That I'd be able to unload all my hurt feelings of rejection in the hopes of what? Filling this emptiness inside me?

I huffed and pulled open my driver's side door.

"Wait!"

I stiffened, recognizing that voice.

Taking a deep breath at the sound of gravel crunching behind me, I turned to face Lachlan Adair as he drew to a stop.

He seemed bigger, more intimidating in the bright daylight. His eyes, a striking azure blue, were steely upon me. No sign of that famous wicked twinkle.

"Can I help you?" I asked coldly.

"What are you doing here?"

A hot aggravation came over me as fast as a flame on the strike of a match. My voice softened with it. "I don't know if you got the memo, but I'm Mac's daughter."

Adair studied me impassively. "If you're here to cause trouble for Mac, I'd advise against it. He has a lot on his plate, and the last thing he needs right now is you coming along and fucking with his head."

Who was this asshole? The audacity was unbelievable. "Me, fuck with his head? He abandoned me, not the other way around."

"Aye, I know that's the story your mother likes to tell."

Furious, I slammed my car door and faced him. An uncharacteristic desire to yell at him came over me, and it took all my self-control to modulate my tone. "Who the hell do you think you are? Don't you dare talk about my mother. You know shit."

Adair cast me a pitying look that begged to be smacked off his face. "I dare say I know more about it than you do." He took a step closer, forcing me back against my car. A chill entered his eyes. "Mac is like a brother to me. Family. I won't let anyone, not even you, screw him over, so I'm politely suggesting you put your arse back on a plane and get the hell out of here."

"You think you scare me?" I pushed off my car, pressing my body into his, forcing *him* to take a step back. "I've faced bigger and badder things in the world than an ex-actor, so I'm not so politely suggesting that you stay out of my business with my *father*. I think I can say with some certainty that he wouldn't be too happy to learn of your interference."

A muscle ticked in Adair's jaw as he took another step back. It seemed he'd been expecting me to crumble under his intimidation.

"I think we understand each other now." I smirked and yanked open my car door.

But as I slid into my seat, Adair said in a soft, menacing tone, "You hurt my family, Ms. Penhaligon, and I'll make sure you pay for it."

With the hard sincerity of his words ringing in my ears, I watched the big bastard stride into his castle and cursed him for getting in the last word.

3

LACHLAN

Still seething from the encounter with Mac's so-called daughter, Lachlan decided he was no company for his club members. It was better to hide in his real office than his stage office until he got his irritation under control. Hearing laughter from one of the social rooms off the entrance, he skirted past and strode toward the door that led into the staff-only area of the castle.

Robyn Penhaligon's face floated across Lachlan's vision. Smug, conniving witch, threatening to tell Mac on him. Like they were five-year-olds on the goddamn playground.

Still, a niggle of unease gnawed at him.

Perhaps he had stepped over the line.

As much as he wanted to protect Mac from a woman who might be just as unforgiving as her mother, it was her father's place to decide whether Robyn stayed at Ardnoch.

But Mac had a lot on his mind. They all did. The last thing they needed was an estranged and resentful daughter getting in their way.

To be fair, Lachlan was already in a shitty mood that morning before Robyn surprised Mac. His publicist had called him; she also happened to be his brother's publicist. Gwen shared a link to a US tabloid that had published photographs last night of his brother, Brodan, in a drunken brawl with doormen at a Los Angeles nightclub.

Lachlan didn't know what to do with him. When he'd warned Brodan about following his big brother to Hollywood, Brodan promised he could handle the pressure and notoriety.

Lately, his antics suggested otherwise.

On top of their other situation, Lachlan felt like he was failing. That feeling of powerlessness may have contributed to his behavior toward Robyn Penhaligon. That, and something about the arrogant tilt of her chin, had set him off.

Lachlan's phone rang in his back pocket, and when he pulled it out, Mac's name lit up the screen. Christ, had she made good on her promise already? "Mac," he answered, drawing to a stop in the narrow hallway that led to their offices.

"Delivery entrance. Now."

Dread filled him. "Not another?"

"Just get here." Mac hung up.

Case in point.

He ground his teeth. And then hurried down the corridors that led through their busy kitchen and into the hallway to the delivery entrance. Staff hovered in the kitchen doorway, murmuring to one another. Worry and tension hung heavily in the air.

"Haven't you all got work to do?" Lachlan demanded. Their expressions turned sheepish in response. "Well?"

"You heard Mr. Adair!" his sous chef, Raffaella, yelled in her Italian accent as his kitchen staff skittered away from the door. "Back to work!"

Leaving her to deal with them, he followed the cool

breeze blowing up the hall as daylight streamed in from where the delivery entrance door was shoved wide open.

Mac stood outside it with Pete and Jock, two of their security men. Lachlan's head of security looked up as he slowly approached. "Prepare yourself. It's not pretty."

The smell hit him first, and he swallowed hard against the urge to gag.

"Fuck," he muttered as his eyes lowered to the ground.

A once-beautiful, small doe lay slaughtered at the door entrance, her entrails spilled onto the gravel, a bunch of red roses nestled by her carcass. Lachlan looked up at Mac.

He held out a white card. Noting Mac wore gloves to touch it, Lachlan didn't take it from him.

But reading it, his concern increased tenfold.

You were once so very dear to me.
But now so very dead to me.
Xoxo

"Again, it's not specifically addressed to anyone."

Mac sighed. "We're going on the assumption here, like the others, the message is for you."

"I don't care about me." He glowered. "But I do care about the safety of my staff and my members. The last incident was the start of something darker here, Mac. This, however … it's time to call the police."

Mac cut his men a look before addressing Lachlan. "Just give us a little more time to figure it out. It's better to go to the police with a culprit so that when it does hit the news, the estate members are assured it's dealt with and they're safe."

"We shouldn't keep this from them. They already know something is amiss. And Lucy is well aware." Though she'd promised to keep it to herself. "Not to mention, we can't guarantee a staff member won't let this slip."

"If they talk about *anything* on the estate with a member or outsider, it's breach of contract." Mac told him something he already knew. "Unless they want a lawsuit on their hands, they won't talk."

Lachlan scowled. Those contracts were drawn up with the thought of gossip and scandal, not some unknown person leaving sick messages for the estate's owner.

"Just give me time," Mac said. "I don't want you to lose everything over this. My men and I can do it."

"We can," Jock and Pete spoke in unison.

Lachlan wasn't convinced. "How did this happen?" He gestured to the carcass and then looked up at the camera angled above the door. There were cameras at every entrance. "Do we have footage of the culprit?"

Mac's frustration was palpable, and Lachlan knew the answer before he spoke.

Cutting Jock and Pete a look, he gestured to the grounds. "Would you give us some privacy, gentlemen?"

With abrupt nods, they turned on their heels and moved to leave.

"Be back in two to take this bonny beast to McCulloch. See if Collum can salvage her. Make her death worth something."

"McCulloch?" Lachlan raised an eyebrow. Collum McCulloch's family had farmed the land north of Ardnoch for generations. He and Lachlan's father had a bitter history, which had trickled down into his interactions with the younger Adairs.

"I'll risk owing him for the sake of this poor beast." Mac shot the deer a saddened look before gesturing Lachlan inside the castle.

"No footage?" he asked Mac as soon as they were alone.

"No. It has to be someone from the estate, Lachlan. The evidence is irrefutable."

"Not a stalker, then?"

"No, this is definitely stalker behavior."

"And it's coming from someone on the estate?"

"Has to be."

It wouldn't be the first time he'd been subjected to stalker-like messages, but nothing like this. Or within his own circle. "I'm giving you two weeks to resolve this, Mac. Then I'm going to the police." He simmered with anger. They'd had destruction of property and threatening notes, but this was the first time a living being had been harmed. "This is escalating. Now I'm *worried*."

Mac fell into step beside him. "I know. I am too. But let's try to stay focused. I'll have Tracey run prints on the card."

Lachlan's head of security had a contact in forensics who'd been running prints on anything left behind by the Ardnoch stalker. So far, nothing. But it was worth trying.

"The last thing you needed today was your daughter turning up."

"I wouldn't say that," Mac disagreed. "It was a shock, but I can't say I'm not glad to see her."

Lachlan grunted.

"She's my daughter." Mac's voice held a warning note. "And I'm the one who wronged her."

"You tried. Her mother is the one who wronged her."

"I should have tried harder." His friend frowned. "I think something might have happened to her."

"Like what?"

"I'm not sure. She's …" He shrugged.

That earlier unease Lachlan had felt returned. "I might have said something to her I shouldn't have."

"When? How?"

"Before she left, I told her to go home. Back to the States."

31

Mac drew to an abrupt stop. Lachlan sighed inwardly at the anger on his face. "You what?"

He held up his hands in apology. "It was wrong. I'm sorry. I'm just worried about you. But I shouldn't have done it. Not that she seems to be easily intimidated."

A smirk of pride cut through Mac's annoyance. "Well, she wouldn't be, would she? That girl has more of me in her than she realizes."

"Woman," Lachlan reminded him. "Woman, Mac. She's not a girl anymore. She's twenty-eight. Remember, she's here on her own agenda, and that might not be in your best interests."

"But it is my business. I appreciate the sentiment behind why you said what you said ..." Mac took a step toward him. "We're family. But she's my family, too, and if you drive her away before she and I have the chance to talk, that's not something I'll easily forgive."

Lachlan gave him a curt nod. "Understood."

"Now." Mac stepped back, giving him a wry, unamused look. "If you'll excuse me, I've got a sick stalker to find."

The reminder put his teeth on edge. "I'll have another think on any slights I might have caused to staff or members over the years."

"Aye, well, you might be thinking awhile." The cheeky fucker walked away before Lachlan could retort.

4

ROBYN

he village of Ardnoch shared Boston's pride for history, except the Scots' history went even further back.

Otherwise, Ardnoch was unlike any place I'd ever visited.

For a start, it was tiny.

The nineteenth-century hotel and restaurant I was staying in sat on the square with a huge parking lot for visitors. But from what I'd gathered during my wanderings around the place yesterday, the shops, restaurants, and bed-and-breakfasts were scattered throughout the village on quaint row streets.

The historical architecture and design of the village was beautiful. Everything predated the mid-twentieth century, and dominating it all, not far from the Gloaming, sat a medieval cathedral. I'd taken a ton of photos and spent the night uploading them to my laptop for a little editing before adding them to my Instagram. Once I returned to Boston, I'd resume printing and selling.

Another reason I couldn't stay in Ardnoch too long. To

my delight, I had just over fifty-thousand followers since my work started circulating the social media platform nine months ago. It was great advertising for my online store, but once I uploaded the Ardnoch shots, customers would complain if I didn't get them up on the store soon after.

Planning on losing myself at the beach for a few hours with my camera, I took Gordon's advice and walked west down Castle Street (the main road off the square that led right out of Ardnoch toward Ardnoch Castle and Estate), an avenue of identical nineteenth-century, terraced houses with dormer windows. Most of the homes had been converted into boutiques, cafés, and inns. In among them was Morag's, a small grocery store. According to Gordon, Morag ran a sandwich counter where she sold delicious, fresh homemade sandwiches.

I was an early riser, so Morag's had barely opened when I stepped inside. Stands at the window displayed beach products, such as kids' sand buckets and shovels. Neat rows of shelves stocked with groceries were situated up front, and a refrigerator containing dairy products and a freezer with all manner of frozen foods lined the back walls.

A bright-faced, middle-aged woman with pink-rinsed hair stood behind a counter at the back of the shop. Inside the chilled case were fresh ingredients for custom sandwiches, along with preprepared ones.

"Morning," she called to me.

"Good morning," I replied, offering her a smile as I paused at the refrigerator for bottled water. My eyes flicked between her and the sandwiches as I approached her counter. "Wow, those look great."

"Thank you. We have ..." She rattled off the different fixings. I could listen to her talk all day. I'd noted the villagers spoke with a slightly more anglicized accent than

Mac who was originally from Glasgow. The locals had more of a lilting brogue, like Adair's.

When she finished, I asked, "Could you make me one? I'd just like a plain tuna and mayo with red onion."

"No problem at all." She moved around the mini deli section. "Any grand plans today? May I recommend places to visit?"

"I'm just heading to the beach."

"Oh, we're a good month or two away from good beach weather," she warned. "The water is cold even in the summer."

Grinning, I nodded. "I've been duly warned by Gordon."

"You're staying at the Gloaming. Very nice. Here long?"

"Probably not."

She shot me a bemused look, presumably at my vague answer. "Well, it's nice to have you here. I'm Morag Sutherland."

"Like the area?" Ardnoch was in the county of Sutherland.

"Yes. My family has been here a long time. Dating as far back as the twelfth century. I'm distantly related to the current Earl of Sutherland. *Distantly*, mind you. Still ..." She beamed proudly.

"That is very cool," I replied sincerely. "Imagine knowing your family has been here as long as medieval times. I don't know anything about my family before the twentieth century."

"You should look into it. It's fascinating stuff learning where you come from and who you're related to."

The shop door opened, and Morag peered past me. She wrinkled her nose as if displeased by the newcomer. At the sound of heavy footsteps walking toward us, I glanced over my shoulder. A man almost as big as Mac, wearing a thread-bare cable-knit sweater, worn jeans, and mud-splattered boots, came to a stop at my side. He smelled of … well … animal. In all its forms.

I took in the grizzly, gray beard and deep wrinkles around his dark eyes. A wool hat covered his hair, but I estimated he was much older than Mac.

And a farmer, if the smell was anything to go by.

"Usual, Morag," he demanded in a gruff, gravelly voice.

Morag gave him a pained smile. "The corned beef didn't come in with my delivery, Collum. Is there anything else you'd like?" She gestured to the sandwich counter.

Collum glared at her in obvious annoyance and then down at the counter. "The ham instead."

"With all the usual, though?"

He grunted.

Morag seemed to take that as a yes and then gave me an apologetic look. "Are you in a hurry, dear? It's just Mr. McCulloch is our local farmer, and I usually have his sandwich ready so he can just collect it and go."

"I can wait."

She set aside the tuna-mayo mix and worked on the farmer's sandwich.

There was a moment of awkward silence as we watched Morag.

Until the left side of my face tingled.

The farmer was staring at me.

I raised an eyebrow at him.

He stared impassively down at me and then looked at Morag. "Another one?"

She frowned and then glanced at me, her face clearing. "Oh, I don't believe so. Just a tourist."

"Robyn," I offered. "My name is Robyn." Staring up at McCulloch, I asked bluntly, "What do you mean by 'another one'?"

Our eyes met. "So-called actor from that godforsaken club."

Realizing he meant one of the Ardnoch members, I shook my head. "No, I'm not one of them. I'm a cop." Or I *was* a cop. I needed to stop introducing myself as such. Habit.

The farmer studied me closely. "Aye, you don't look like you stick poison in your face."

I let out a confused snort. "What?"

He sighed, as though aggravated our conversation had gone on this long. "Sarah, my granddaughter, she says they all stick poison in their faces to smooth their wrinkles. In their lips to make them fuller." He eyed me again. "Not that you need that."

"No. I don't need Botox in my lips."

His brows drew together.

"That's what you call the toxin. Or at least the treatment. Botox."

"Fascinating."

I couldn't help a bark of laughter at his dry sarcasm.

"Really, Collum," Morag tutted. "You could try to be a little more welcoming to our tourists."

"Why?"

She flushed. "It's … well, it's the decent thing. The friendly thing."

"Bullshit," he muttered. "You're all only nice to them because of the money. Well"—he cut me a sardonic look —"not Morag here. She actually *likes* people."

His disbelieving tone made me laugh harder, and his eyes sparkled with amusement.

"Oh, you." Morag tutted again, but a smile teased her lips as she wrapped up his sandwich. McCulloch gave her money, and Morag handed over his lunch. "Tell Sarah I was asking for her."

He grunted again and turned to leave.

"It was nice to meet you," I said.

McCulloch shot me a look of disbelief before glancing back at Morag. He gave a slight shake of his head but tipped his sandwich at me in acknowledgement before striding out.

As soon as the door closed behind him, Morag said, sounding surprised, "I think he thought it was nice meeting you too."

I grinned. "He's not the friendly sort, huh?"

"No. You got more conversation out of him than I have in the last ten years," she cracked.

"I liked him."

"You like cantankerous, do you?"

"I like honest."

Morag smiled and returned to my sandwich. When it was done, she handed it over after accepting payment and said, "Have a nice day at the beach."

I left Morag's and walked east to the parking lot on the square across from the Gloaming. I'd parked there, and I planned on driving a few minutes east to Ardnoch's beautiful, golden sands. It wasn't a particularly sunny day. There was a chill in the late spring air, but the belly of the clouds weren't dark enough to suggest coming rain.

Strolling down the quiet street toward the square, I noted a Range Rover drive past and watched it pull into the parking lot near my rental. As I approached my car, the doors of the Rover opened, and a couple rounded the trunk to lace their hands together. Surprise moved through me, and I'll admit a little thrill.

It was Gabriella Ruiz and Sebastian Stone. Stone was a three-time Oscar-winning actor, and Gabriella was his popstar fiancée. She was ten years his senior—he was thirty-five, she was forty-five—but she looked his age, if not younger. And not because of Botox either. Good genes and a healthy lifestyle did that. She was inspiring; he was beyond talented. As a couple, they were constantly hounded by the press.

Again, I wondered how Adair kept the media away from Ardnoch.

Gabriella offered me a gorgeous grin, and I was proud of the friendly but cool smile I returned. I wasn't the type to fangirl, but I was also extremely aware that the estate members loved Ardnoch because it offered them some normality.

Pulling open the door to my rental, I shot a look over my shoulder as the couple strolled hand in hand down Castle Street. I shook my head in disbelief, smiling to myself. Rock music was my thing, not pop, so seeing Gabriella wasn't what it might be to some other folks, though I admired her obvious work ethic. And I had to admit, Sebastian Stone was a great actor.

I'd just walked past them both.

So surreal.

It occurred to me as I drove toward the beach that it hadn't felt surreal to meet Lachlan Adair, even though he'd once been as famous as Stone and wasn't exactly unknown now.

No, it hadn't been surreal.

It had just been painful.

The thought of the meeting reminded me of the dinner I'd promised tonight.

Me and Mac. Alone at the Gloaming.

After my embarrassing near breakdown the day before, I hoped I could keep it together tonight.

I was thankful the road to the beach was straightforward because learning to drive on the left was discombobulating; there seemed to be rotaries (though the Scots called them roundabouts) everywhere. Rotaries alone weren't the problem; rotaries on the left side were the problem!

As the beach came into view, my anxieties melted away.

After parking the car, I grabbed my camera out of the back seat and followed the footpath down onto the beach. A sense of calm washed over me. The sea air held a soothing aroma, heightened by the sound of flying gulls and the gentle waves lapping at the shore. I'd never have believed sands this smooth and golden could be found in Scotland.

The water reflected the color of the sky, a muted dark blue, but I was curious what the sea was like in summer, if the clear sky made its waters as blue as the Mediterranean. Strolling along the beach, I took snapshots of the grass-covered hills that jutted out over the sea or sloped down toward the sand. There was a wild order to the beauty here.

Just like that, my worries about tonight, those irritating butterflies in my belly, disappeared as I hid behind my camera, walking the coastline, trying to capture the essence of this rare tranquility and knowing I wouldn't completely succeed.

This place had to be experienced to understand its magic.

* * *

THE LARGE GRANDFATHER clock in the corner of the restaurant at the Gloaming read 7:20.

Mac was twenty minutes late.

I was angry.

Worse, I felt hurt and humiliated.

I'd spent hours getting ready for our dinner, trying on every piece of clothing I'd brought because nothing seemed like the right outfit for my first adult conversation with my father.

I'd even ignored a call from my mom because I knew she'd just repeat what a bad idea she thought this was.

And apparently, she'd have been right.

Heat burned my cheeks as I stared at the empty place settings of our table tucked at the back of the restaurant. I'd asked Gordon for a table that provided some privacy.

Furious tears pricked my eyes as I avoided looking at the other diners.

I cursed the effort I'd gone to for a man who'd forgotten to show up.

For once, my thick hair wasn't pulled back in a casual ponytail, but I'd blown it out and left it down. And I was wearing heels with my cigarette pants and a green silk shirt that I'd bought for the trip. I repeat: I was in high heels.

Mac was such a bastard.

Watching the clock as it crept toward the half-hour mark, I pushed back from the table and stood to leave, but just then, a concerned, pale-faced blond burst into the restaurant. Something about her contained panic made me freeze as she scanned the room.

Our eyes met.

Recognition lit hers, and I tensed in surprise as she hurried toward me.

As she grew closer, I recognized her from my research.

Arrochar Adair. The only female sibling and the youngest of the Adairs.

What on earth?

"Robyn?" Arrochar asked, sounding out of breath as she stopped at my table.

She'd drawn the attention of the other diners.

Despite the messy ponytail, the oversized sweater, worn-out skinny jeans, and hiking boots, Arrochar had an ethereal quality. Her irises were a paler shade of blue than Lachlan's, almost icy, and the anxiety and fear within them transferred to me.

"Yes?"

She released a shaky exhale as tears brightened her eyes.

"I'm Arrochar Adair." She didn't pronounce her name like I'd expected—it was pronounced Arro-car. "Something has happened to Mac. He's been rushed to the hospital. I'll explain on the way."

Horror flooded me, but my inner cop moved into action. I grabbed my purse off the table and hurried after Arrochar.

"Ms. Penhaligon?" Gordon called out as I passed.

"I'll explain later. I have to go."

A green Land Rover Defender sat parked on the yellow lines outside the Gloaming. Arrochar jumped into the driver's side, and I rounded the hood and hopped in beside her.

"Talk to me," I demanded as she tore down Castle Street.

Arrochar's hands tightened around the wheel, her distress so palpable, it felt like a weight on my chest. "Someone attacked Mac. A neighbor witnessed the attack and chased off the perpetrator. It all happened on Mac's front door. He's been stabbed. They think multiple times." Her voice broke.

My mind reeled. "What?"

"There's stuff going on here you don't know about, Robyn." Her fearful gaze met mine for a second before she turned back to the road. "Someone means to harm Lachlan, and it looks like they've decided to ramp things up by taking out his former bodyguard." Silent tears rolled down her cheeks. "Oh God, Mac," she whispered. "I don't know what ... no ... he has to be okay. He has to be okay."

That's when realization dawned.

My father had just been brutally attacked.

I might lose him before I even got the chance to know him.

"How far is the hospital?"

Arrochar wiped hastily at her tears. "They airlifted him to Inverness."

"Inverness? Isn't that pretty far?"

42

"About an hour by car."

Shit.

"How fast can this thing go?"

In answer, Arrochar put her foot down on the accelerator.

5

LACHLAN

The waiting room chair bit into his back.

It wasn't the first time Lachlan sat in one and questioned why they made hospital waiting room chairs so bloody uncomfortable. Was it to keep you alert so you'd be ready for when the doctor came to give you the best or worst news of your life?

His nerve endings frayed. Launching out of the chair, needing to move, he ignored his brother Thane's concerned look.

"He'll be all right, Lachlan," Thane assured. "This is Mac we're talking about. It's not even the first time he's been stabbed."

"But that was a bar brawl. This … was a premeditated attack." Christ, how long had they been here? It felt like ages. That couldn't be a good sign.

"Lachlan!"

He spun around to see Arrochar racing across the waiting room toward him. The fear on her face only made his worse. But he hid it and braced himself as she threw herself against him. Wrapping his arms tight around his sister, Lachlan whispered there was no word yet but everything would be okay.

As he said those reassuring words to her, his gaze remained locked on the person Arrochar had insisted on retrieving.

Mac's daughter.

Robyn looked different as she approached. He didn't know if it was the strained concern on her face that surprised him or how much the simple act of wearing her hair down transformed her.

Both.

Robyn drew to a stop before him.

Lachlan hadn't noticed how big her eyes were. Not round. They were large and oval. Unusual. Lashes that went on for miles. There was no way to discern her exact eye color, only that the cool steel in them yesterday had disappeared.

Robyn Penhaligon was worried about Mac.

"No word," he repeated to her as Arrochar pulled her head out of his chest. He didn't release her because she trembled.

They all loved Mac.

It was hard to picture him as a father to Robyn who looked her twenty-eight years, but seemed older. Mac was just a kid himself when he'd fathered her.

"Do you think they'll release more information to a family member?" Robyn asked.

"Perhaps," Thane answered, moving to Lachlan's side. He ran a comforting hand down Arrochar's arm to let her know he was there. She reached for his hand and held it tight, still holding on to Lachlan too.

Robyn studied Thane, her attention drifting down to where Arrochar held his hand and then to where her head rested on Lachlan's chest. Some kind of realization crossed her expression, and her jaw clenched as she looked away.

"I'm Thane Adair," his brother introduced himself. "You must be Robyn."

She nodded. "Hey."

"Mac told us you were here. I'm sorry we're meeting under such terrible circumstances."

"Me too," she murmured absently. "I'm just gonna ..." She gestured to the nurses' station and strode away, her heels clicking against the floor.

"It's hard to believe Mac is old enough to have a daughter Arrochar's age."

"Not my age," Arrochar whispered. "She's a few years younger than me."

"Still. She's what ... twenty-nine?"

"Twenty-eight," Lachlan supplied, watching as she talked with the nurse behind the desk.

"And a police officer," Thane muttered. "She didn't fall far from the tree."

"As far as we know, she's nothing like Mac."

Arrochar tensed in his arms and reminded him, unnecessarily, "She's his daughter, Lachlan."

"Imagine having a kid at sixteen," Thane continued in awe. "I can barely look after my two as it is. I can't imagine being a father at that age."

"One, you're a great dad," Lachlan replied. "Two, that's my point. Mac was sixteen when Robyn was born. He was a kid. And her mother"—he gestured to Robyn—"made him into a villain. Somehow Mac's the bad guy for going off to make some money for them? Mac's the bad guy even though *she* stopped him from seeing his daughter. He's lying in a hospital bed right now, and if Robyn even thinks of starting—"

"Whoa, calm down." Arrochar pushed away from him.

"Lachlan, you're angry at whoever did this to Mac. At whoever is doing this to you. Not at Robyn. So don't take it out on her while Mac is fighting for his life."

Her words calmed the aggravation building inside him.

She was right. This wasn't Robyn's fault. Just like it probably wasn't her fault her name was Penhaligon when it should be Galbraith. But he remembered when Mac found out she'd legally changed it. He remembered how hurt his friend had been.

Still, he nodded, and Arrochar relaxed just as Robyn's heels sounded again.

Lachlan studied her as she neared, and when he noted the vulnerability in her eyes, the rest of his anger toward her deflated.

"No word yet," Robyn informed them. That vulnerability he'd seen just seconds ago disappeared under flint. "Where are the police? Shouldn't they be here?"

"They've already been," Lachlan informed her. "They questioned Mac's neighbor, Jim, and left."

"Where is this neighbor?" She looked determinedly around the waiting room.

"I sent him home. He had quite a shock."

Her eyes narrowed. "And what did he have to say?"

Lachlan tried not to react to her demanding tone. "That he was walking home from the pub when he saw Mac ..." He took a breath. "Mac on his knees while someone, a man, stood over him. Jim thought he was punching Mac in the gut. When he shouted, the perpetrator took off. That's when Jim got to Mac and realized he'd been stabbed."

She didn't flinch at that news. "Did he see the perp's face? Any discernible qualities that stuck out to him about the guy?"

He shook his head, frustrated. "The man wore a ski mask.

All black. All Jim could determine was his height. Around five ten, five eleven. Stocky build."

"How did he catch Mac unaware?" Robyn asked in disbelief.

"It was right on his doorstep. He was dressed in a suit for dinner with you. The police reckon he'd just stepped outside the door when it happened. He obviously had no time to react."

She nodded, processing this. Her gaze moved to the floor, and Lachlan contemplated her face, trying to uncover a resemblance to Mac. He couldn't see it. Mac had dark hair. She had a mass of long hair that spilled past her shoulders and didn't seem to know what color it wanted to be. Was it brown or blond or red? It was an undecided shade of all three.

But her manner ... she had the same forthright quality as Mac. The thought barely formed when Robyn's head snapped up and she glared at Arrochar. "What did you mean when you said someone meant to harm Lachlan, and they'd decided to take out his former bodyguard?"

Lachlan stiffened.

Arrochar shot her brother an apologetic look.

Oh, that's just fantastic.

* * *

ROBYN

ADAIR TOOK hold of my elbow to lead me away from the waiting room, and it took a lot of restraint not to shake off his touch. The man couldn't make it any clearer that he despised me.

I let him lead me to an empty corner of a hospital corridor. "Well?" I finally shook off his hold, and he dropped his hand like I'd burned him.

Staring stonily down at me, I became much too aware that he had me pinned to a wall while he towered over me. His height and build, plus those eyes and that rugged face, had made him Hollywood's perfect action hero.

In reality, his physique was perfect for intimidating people.

I didn't appreciate it.

Slipping out from the wall, I put my back to the corridor, and Adair turned with me. I had an issue with putting my back to an entrance or open space, but after working through it with my therapist, I was determined to overcome the anxiety by forcing myself to stay put. To not encourage the fear by always placing myself with my back to a wall. Besides, I didn't want my back to a wall in his presence.

Adair raised an eyebrow at my deliberate repositioning but didn't remark on it. Instead, he offered, "There have been incidents at the estate."

"What kind of incidents?"

"Not ones I'm willing to discuss with an outsider."

Anger flared, but I kept it buried. "If it has something to do with what happened to my father, then I have a right to know."

"Then it'll be up to Mac to tell you himself. If he wants to. For now, all you need to know is that his attack is most likely tied to these incidents."

His vagueness frustrated me. Instead of engaging in an immature spat, I opened my purse and retrieved my phone.

"What are you doing? Who are you calling?"

"My mom. I have to tell her Mac's in the hospital."

"No, you don't." To my shock, he grabbed my phone out of my hand.

Indignation roared through me. "What are you doing?"

Adair leaned into me, all pretense of politeness gone. His face was a mask of controlled fury. "The police have agreed to keep the incident with Mac quiet. As fucked-up as it may be, no one cares about a random man being stabbed. What people do care about is a man being stabbed in one of the safest villages in Scotland. A man who happens to be head of security at Ardnoch Estate. If you tell your mother, it'll be all over the news."

"You're protecting your club?" I sneered. "My father is in surgery with multiple stab wounds, and you care about your goddamn club?"

"Don't." Adair slipped on an obdurate countenance. "Don't take that high-and-mighty attitude with me. I've been by Mac's side for seventeen years. You don't know the first thing about him, but I do. And he was the one who wanted to keep all this from the police and the public. I'm just trying to obey his wishes."

Keep all of what from the police and public? "Funny how his wishes coincide with your best interests."

"Believe what you want. But you're not calling your mother." He held up my phone, captive in his big fist. "It would be hypocritical to say she'd give a shit."

I flushed. Because he was right. "Give me my phone back."

"Are you going to call her?"

"No."

To my surprise, he returned the phone but followed it with, "Are you here because of obligation or because you care about Mac?"

I scoffed, ignoring the hurt his question elicited. "I don't owe you that answer." I marched away, cursing my heels for slowing me down. Just as I rounded the corner that led out into the waiting room, a doctor approached from the opposite direction and called out, "MacKennon Galbraith's family?"

"Here!" I hurried to him and felt the heat of Adair at my back. "I'm his daughter."

The doctor lowered his voice, his expression neutral and therefore unreadable. "Ms. Galbraith, I'm Dr. Chiu, your father's surgeon. Your father suffered three stab wounds to his abdomen."

I attempted not to flinch at the imagery those words conjured.

"By some miracle, no major organs were hit, but an artery was. I had to perform surgery to stop the bleed, and I'm glad to say it was successful. Your father has been taken to a private room to recover."

Relief flooded me. "He's going to be okay?"

"Yes." Dr. Chiu gave me a polite smile. "Your father is young, healthy, and fit, and I expect a quick recovery, considering. You can visit, but it might take him some time to wake up, and when he does, he'll be groggy."

"Thank you, Doctor."

"You're welcome. Nurse Bukhari"—he gestured to a woman in scrubs standing off to the side—"will show you the way."

Once the doctor had gone, I approached the nurse and felt all three Adair siblings move with me.

The nurse lifted a hand. "Two at a time, for now."

I heard Arrochar make a sound of frustration in the back of her throat, but I couldn't focus on the Adairs. I just wanted to see Mac and make sure he was okay.

Unfortunately, the eldest Adair decided to follow me in.

The whole time, I'd been fixated on the cause of the situation. Why had Mac been stabbed? By whom? What was going on at Ardnoch Estate that had led to this?

But stepping into that hospital room, memories flooded

me. Waking up with tubes coming out of me. Feeling real fear for the first time in my life. The nightmares and perpetual sensation of being in peril, a feeling that had taken months of therapy to work through.

Staring at Mac, I took a shaky breath.

This wasn't about me.

It was about him.

Processing the IV inserted into Mac's hand, the wires connecting him to the machines, the steady beeping of said machine that told me his heart rate was good, I tried to relax, and failed.

Mac was such a big guy. They said people looked diminutive in hospital beds, but not him.

The only change to his appearance was the paleness of his usually olive-skinned face. There was strain around his mouth even in his sleep.

I reached for his hand that didn't have the tube in it.

My hand looked tiny in his.

Tears pricked my eyes as I thought of all the years I'd missed holding my father's hand. A memory hit me out of the blue. Me, just a little kid, up on his shoulders, my hands in his as we walked through Boston Public Garden together. We strolled over the bridge, and Mac sang loudly, not caring that people looked, a song by Billy Connolly, a Scottish comedian he liked.

Something about Glasgow, the city of Mac's birth.

"Robyn?"

Adair's voice brought me out of the memory, and I glared at him, hating his presence, that he was witness to my obvious vulnerability around Mac.

Adair's expression softened. "I'll give you a moment."

To my shock, he left the room with the nurse.

Covering Mac's hand with mine, I slid into the seat by the bed. "Where did you go?" I whispered, choking back the tears. "Why did you leave me?"

* * *

HOURS LATER, I sat in the same chair by Mac's bed, my eyes never leaving my father's handsome face.

I'd stayed outside the room with Adair as Arrochar and Thane paid a visit. They'd emerged awhile later, Thane's arm around Arrochar, her eyes red and bloodshot from crying.

"I'm taking Arro home," Thane said to Adair. "I need to get back to the kids. Are you staying?"

"Yes, I'll keep you posted." Adair hugged his sister and then his brother. I gave them both a tight nod and thanked Arrochar for bringing me to the hospital before I slid past them into the private room.

Mac's boss and friend wasn't far behind me.

Adair sat on a chair opposite the foot of the bed.

We'd stayed in silence for what seemed like an age.

That silence broke abruptly when a young nurse came into the room with a clipboard in hand. She halted at the sight of us, her attention moving to Adair. Her cheeks flushed pink with recognition as their eyes met. "Oh, Mr. Adair ..." Her eyes flicked to me, then back to him, and her cheeks turned scarlet red. "I'm sorry, sir, but it should be family only outside of visiting hours."

I tensed for his reaction and saw the frustration pass over his features before he controlled it. He stood slowly, and the nurse took a step back.

"I am sorry, Mr. Adair."

Guilt niggled at me. "Don't," I blurted out. "I might as well be the product of a sperm donation. He's"—I gestured to Adair—"he's like a brother to my father."

The young nurse blushed again at my bluntness, but

nodded. "All right, then. Let me just check Mr. Galbraith's vitals."

A renewal of the awkward silence filled the room as she went about her duties and Adair retook his seat.

I could feel him staring at me, but I kept my focus firmly on Mac's face.

The nurse left.

"You honestly believe that?" Adair asked as soon as she was gone.

Knowing he referred to my last comment, I turned to him. Despite Mac's attack bringing back terrible memories, I already knew it wouldn't send me running. It wasn't in my nature. I'd quit being a cop not because of what happened to me but because I wasn't happy. Fear didn't shut me down. It fueled me. It made me want to overcome it. And I could only overcome this particular fear by sticking around.

"I don't know what to believe. I guess I'll have time to find out." My expression hardened as stubborn determination gripped me. I had to find out who did this to my father. "Because I won't be going anywhere for a while."

My statement hung in the air between us like a threat.

6

ROBYN

*H*e came out of nowhere. The man. Handgun raised, pointed at Autry. My heart exploded into action as I saw his finger on the trigger. Eddie. This guy was Eddie Johnstone, a known drug dealer in East Boston.

I didn't know that. How did I know that?

"Eddie, no!" I yelled, diving in front of Autry, gun raised. "Don't make me shoot."

His expression darkened. "Take your best shot, bitch."

I pulled the trigger.

Eddie's eyes widened. There was a hole in his forehead. Blood and brain matter splattered the wall behind him.

Then he fell, hitting the apartment floor with a loud, decisive slam.

Relieved, shocked, I turned to Autry to make sure he was okay.

"Robbie," Autry whispered, looking grief stricken.

"What is it? We're okay, we're okay."

"Robbie, no." He looked down at my chest.

Frowning, I followed his gaze and terror paralyzed me. There was a huge hole where my heart should be. A person could see right through me.

55

"He shot you, Robbie. You're dead."

It can't be, *a voice whispered in my mind as the floor came toward me.* Robyn, you're dreaming. It's not real. It's not real. It's not real—

My eyes slammed open, and I gasped for breath. The sight of the cracked ceiling of my hotel room brought reality crashing in and with it, a huge wave of relief.

It was just a nightmare.

"Fuck," I muttered as my heart rate slowed. Pushing the heavy duvet off, I tried to cool down. Light perspiration coated my skin, and I cursed the lack of air conditioning in the Gloaming. Spring nights in Scotland were cold, so Gordon kept the hotel heated at a certain level, a little too warm for my liking. Especially after a sweaty nightmare.

Swinging my legs out of bed, I rested my elbows on my knees and my face in my hands.

I hadn't had a nightmare about the shooting in months.

Pushing my hair off my damp forehead, I stared unseeingly into the connecting bathroom. It didn't take a professional to explain that Mac's attack had triggered the nightmare.

It wasn't just that I'd almost died for a job I wasn't passionate about. There was more to it than that. But I'd promised myself to stop living for other people and start doing what I wanted. Build a photography business. Travel the world to take pictures I could sell. It wouldn't be easy, yet it would be worse not to try.

Somehow, however, I found myself back in cop mode.

When Mac had awoken in the early hours of yesterday morning, my flood of emotions took me aback. I did not want to cry in front of Lachlan Adair, but as Mac opened his eyes and slid them to the left—as if he'd felt me there—all my words caught in my throat as the relief, fear, confusion, and frustration strangled me.

"My wee birdie," he whispered hoarsely.

Just like that, the tears spilled down my cheeks. There was no stopping them.

I hadn't heard my father call me "wee birdie" since I was fourteen. "Hey, Dad." I smiled through my tears.

I hadn't called Mac "Dad" since I was fourteen either.

At the memory of yesterday, I swiped at my tears. I didn't want to forgive Mac just because of his attack. But I also couldn't deny the fact that as much as he'd hurt me, I still felt an undeniable connection with him.

I still loved him.

Thankfully, Adair hadn't made a comment on my emotional slip. We both left not long after Mac shared a few words of reassurance. His eyes closed, and the nurse suggested we return home to rest. I'd gone back to the hospital the next morning, but Mac drowsed in and out of sleep, so I returned to Ardnoch when Adair and Arrochar showed up to sit with Mac.

Arriving back at my hotel emotionally and physically exhausted, I'd fallen asleep early and quickly last night with renewed determination that I wasn't going anywhere anytime soon.

Yes, I wanted to get to know my father ... but I also wanted to get to the truth about why someone had nearly taken away our chance to reconnect. If I had to put up with a few nightmares along the way, then so be it. I wasn't leaving Ardnoch until whoever did this was brought to justice—until I knew Mac was safe.

"Which means finding somewhere cheaper to live," I muttered, pushing up off the bed. First stop was a visit to Mac at the hospital. Later, I'd think about my next move for accommodation.

* * *

To be honest, I was surprised to walk into Mac's private room that morning to find Adair already there. I knew he and my father were close, but I'd assumed his responsibilities on the estate would keep him away.

That he'd prioritized my father was incongruous to the information I'd gleaned the night Mac was rushed in. It had seemed to me then that Adair cared more about protecting his business than my father.

Still, I'd kept my word and I hadn't told Mom that Mac had been attacked. She'd tried to video call me a few times, and I'd shot off quick messages saying I couldn't talk. I knew she was probably hurt, and I hated the idea of hurting Mom's feelings, but I'd just have to deal with that later.

Relief moved through me to see Mac sitting up, awake, with a little more color in his cheeks. "Hey," I greeted him quietly as I stepped into the room. I ignored Adair but was extremely aware of his presence. "How are you?"

"Better." Mac gestured to the chair on his right. "Come sit."

That would put me directly opposite Adair who sat in a chair at Mac's left.

I hesitated briefly.

Adair stood. "I better get going."

He was dressed more casually than I'd seen him, wearing a fitted cashmere sweater and dark jeans. The sweater did great things for his physique. I'm sure he made nurses and doctors swoon as he walked through the hospital corridors.

Asshole.

Adair focused on Mac. "I'll come back later."

"Don't," Mac said, waving him off, seeming a lot more exhausted than I'd first thought. "It's an hour here and then back. I'm fine. You need to be at the estate. Now more than ever."

Another cryptic comment about the estate.

"I'll come back later," Adair insisted.

Stubborn asshole.

I found myself caught in Adair's impossibly blue gaze that continued to lack that wicked, mischievous twinkle from his movies. "I hope you're not here to interrogate him. He still needs his rest."

"I guess I should abandon my plans to waterboard him then, huh?"

My father snorted.

Adair narrowed his eyes. "I'm serious."

"I noticed. You should reconsider how serious you are. It's interfering with the heroic efforts of the Botox in your forehead."

I was pretty sure Adair didn't use Botox. And I was also pretty sure I was being immature.

Yet I couldn't help myself.

He cut my father an exasperated look. "I'll see you later. No shoptalk until you're fully recovered."

Mac didn't agree. "We'll talk later."

Adair lifted his chin at him and then strode out of the room without acknowledging me, though he couldn't hide the way he bristled as he departed.

I smirked.

It was petty, but I liked that I had the ability to irritate him.

Mac noted my smugness and shook his head, though amusement glittered in his eyes. "You're baiting him."

"He makes it so easy." I finally sat down, relaxing back in the chair. "So really ... how are you?"

"I feel lucky." Mac surprised me. "It could have been much worse."

That was true. He could have been like me, fighting for my life for days in the ICU.

Guilt pricked me more than ever.

Mom hadn't called Mac when I got shot.

She later told me she'd had no intention of calling him unless I'd died.

I hadn't thought much about that until now. Now that our situation was reversed. Knowing that if I hadn't been here, the Adairs wouldn't have contacted me unless Mac died.

And that would have really hurt.

Damn it.

"I feel like a fool," Mac whispered, glowering at the wall. "A trained bloody bodyguard, and I let the fucker blindside me."

I leaned toward him, touching his arm in comfort. "You don't have to tell me, but if you're up to it, I'd like to know what happened."

"I've told the police and Lachlan. Why shouldn't I tell you?" He turned his head toward me. "I'd just stepped out the front door, on my way to meet you for dinner. And it was like a black blur, he came at me so fast. He must have been waiting at the side of the door. I felt the pain of the blade going in. Three quick jabs."

Police training assisted my maintained neutral expression. Inside, however, I flinched at the thought of Mac's attack. It just seemed unreal. When I was a kid, Mac was this invincible presence.

"There was no time to react, to defend myself. Then my neighbor, Jim, started shouting, and the guy took off. I managed to show Jim my wounds before I lost consciousness."

I was going to legally eviscerate the fucker who'd done this. "And you have no idea who it was?"

Mac shook his head. "Head to foot in black clothing, gloves, and a black ski mask. I looked into his eyes—the bastard wore purple contacts."

"Contacts? Are you sure? Some people have a purple tinge to their eyes."

"Definitely contacts. It was an unnatural hue of purple. And something about the way they sat on his irises. They were contacts."

"Mac." I sat forward. "That suggests you know this person. Why go to the effort of concealing his eye color if he didn't think it might identify him?"

"Aye." He smirked wearily. "I came to that conclusion myself."

"I want to know more, but we'll wait until you're feeling better."

"There's no need, Robyn. The police have been informed, and my men are still investigating. You don't have to stay, sweetheart. I know you probably only intended a short visit."

"That's true. But I also didn't expect my father to get stabbed and almost killed, for Arrochar Adair to tell me someone had tried to hurt Lachlan Adair and decided to take you out in order to succeed. I'm staying. I'm staying until I find out who did this to you. I'm staying until I bring them to justice."

"You're not a police officer anymore. And even when you were, you weren't a detective."

His comment stung my pride. "I could have been if I'd wanted."

"I believe it. I meant no insult."

Silence fell between us.

Then he smiled, that handsome, roguish smile I knew had fooled my mother, a twenty-year-old college student, into believing Mac was three years older than the sixteen-year-old he actually was. "You're not going anywhere, are you?"

"Not a chance in hell."

"Then let's work together."

"You can't." I gestured to the bed.

Mac's expression turned obstinate. "And you can't expect me to lie here and do nothing. We work together on this, or I tell you nothing."

That made me grin even as I shook my head at him. Shit. I was more like my father than I'd realized. "I can't believe you're bargaining with me."

"Aye, you can."

"Fine. But here's the deal ... I do all the legwork. Your only role in this is helping me put the pieces together. You will rest up as long as the doc says you need to."

He considered this.

Then ... "Fine."

"Okay. Let's start with the club. What the hell has been going on?"

7

LACHLAN

*H*e'd just taken a sip of coffee when the piercing cry of a bagpipe's opening note split through the office, startling him. The coffee missed Lachlan's mouth and landed on his white shirt.

"Fuck."

His bagpiper, Malcolm, played as he sauntered around the castle at 3 p.m. every day to signal afternoon tea was now being served. Lachlan's members loved the tradition.

He, however, somehow managed to continually forget that Malcolm started outside his office at the same time every bloody day.

Striding out the door, Lachlan tried to hurry through the castle without being seen by members. Occupancy was relatively low as his members preferred to stay in the summer and winter months. However, his staff still went about their duties, trying not to look at the boss quizzically as he sped through the castle with a big, dirty brown stain on his shirt.

Of all people, he encountered Sebastian Stone on the gallery.

"Have you seen Gabriella?" Stone asked, referring to his

fiancée. The club admitted only TV and movie industry professionals and their spouses. While Gabriella was in the music industry, she gained guest entry through her relationship with Stone. He was an arrogant prick who everybody knew was fucking around on a woman he didn't deserve, but he was a bloody good actor with a stellar reputation. Stone was good at hiding how much of an arrogant prick he was, and they didn't admit anyone into Ardnoch who would cause trouble.

Lachlan inwardly huffed at the thought of the mess they currently faced; at least they did what they *thought* were thorough checks before granting a member admittance.

By we, he meant his board, made up of himself and three Hollywood stars: Lachlan's friends, fellow actors Lucy Wainwright and Luther Ameen, and Hollywood legend, director Wesley Howard. Wesley had directed Lachlan's biggest blockbuster, a sci-fi action movie along the lines of *Terminator*. They'd gotten along so well, they'd stayed in touch. Wesley invested in Ardnoch and owned the largest multimillion-pound holiday home on the estate. The irony of that was he also visited the estate the least of all its members, though his wife visited annually during the summer.

"No," Lachlan answered as he moved past Stone. He glanced over his shoulder at him. "The Spa?" Two buildings, a five-minute walk from the castle, erected in a contemporary style at odds with the castle's architecture but in complete harmony with the woodlands surrounding it housed a gym and a spa and salon. Both were very popular with his members.

"I'll have Wakefield call the spa to check. Hey, Adair?"

Lachlan stopped, turning to him.

Stone smirked. "Did I see Camille and Barton leaving yesterday?"

It took effort, but he kept his expression neutral. Another

reason the resort was quiet was because he'd informed his guests about the incidents. Mac hadn't wanted him to, but Lachlan couldn't put his members' lives in danger. And there was the small matter of the detective inspectors showing up and insisting they might have to question the members. Lachlan had shown them around the estate where the incidents occurred and handed over the evidence Mac had collected. When they'd said they might have to return to interview the members, he knew it was time to inform them of the truth.

Lachlan hunted down all his guests and explained what had happened to Mac and that there'd been threats made on the estate. Lachlan made it clear the threats were obviously geared toward him and that their security team was working around the clock to keep everyone safe. Half the members left, anyway. More than just Camille and Barton, which Stone would soon realize. Those who stayed valued the privacy the estate offered over the danger. That might sound crazy to some, but sometimes peace was worth any cost.

Lachlan hoped those who left the estate respected their membership enough to remain quiet about the situation. If his reputation was tarnished, if Ardnoch lost its reputation as one of the most prestigious members-only clubs in the world, Lachlan faced selling it.

An estate that had been in his family for centuries.

He shrugged noncommittally at Stone.

"You'll notify me immediately if anything else occurs." It wasn't a question. It was a demand.

Lachlan bristled.

"I have to keep my fiancée safe."

"You're perfectly safe here."

"Well, your head of security was stabbed, so I'm not too sure about that."

"You're welcome to leave."

Sebastian raised an eyebrow at Lachlan. "Shouldn't you be groveling to keep us all sweet so we'll stay?"

He strode toward Stone, towering a few inches above his six feet. Stone was a good actor. He didn't flinch a bit as Lachlan bent his head toward him. "I don't fucking grovel. Stay or don't stay."

"Nice attitude toward your members, Adair. Guess Gabriella and I will be leaving first thing in the morning. And I don't think we'll be back."

"Do what you want. No refunds on your annual fee," he reminded Stone as he walked away. And knowing how much Stone liked being top of the food chain, he threw over his shoulder, "And good luck finding a club with a reputation as illustrious as Ardnoch."

Only the best of the best became members at his home.

And Stone knew it.

Lachlan doubted he and his pop-star fiancée were going anywhere.

Still, this day was turning into an absolute shit show.

First, Robyn Penhaligon showed up at the hospital and gave him cheek. The woman couldn't make it any clearer how little respect she had for him.

Irritating woman.

And then he'd returned to the estate to discover word had reached Roman Bright about the incidents and he'd canceled his annual "May Stay" at the estate until further notice. Roman was Hollywood royalty. His membership was important to Lachlan.

Stone's little dig had pricked his insecurities. But if he let any of these people smell blood in the water, they'd go in for the kill. Lachlan had to make them feel like *they* needed *him* and not the other way around. They admired strength, popularity, and prestige, especially if it came with that elusive thing called privacy. But they also weren't morons, and

Lachlan didn't blame Roman for not wanting to be at Ardnoch.

They needed to solve the case of the mystery stalker.

Fuck. His life sounded like a bloody Nancy Drew novel.

* * *

ALTHOUGH LACHLAN OWNED a house on the edge of the Adair land just outside Ardnoch, sitting on the firth next to Thane's home, he rarely stayed there. Lachlan kept a room at Ardnoch, one of the smaller suites on the third floor. He liked to be on-site as much as possible.

"You need a life outside of this place, Lachlan," Arrochar had said more times than he could count. She'd repeated the same words only yesterday. *"You need more to your life than Ardnoch. I'm worried about you."*

There was no reason to worry.

They would figure out who was causing all the trouble, Robyn would go home, and everything would return to normal.

The door to the Countess's Suite opened, and Lucy Wainwright stepped into the corridor. The suite was not far from his and was one of the best in the castle. It would be. As a board member, Lucy got dibs. Whenever he knew she was coming, he made sure the Countess's Suite was available.

She gave him the glamorous smile that made her fellow Americans fall in love with her. "Hey, you."

Lachlan slowed to a stop. "Afternoon. Heading down for lunch?"

"Yeah." Lucy closed the gap between them and touched the stain on his shirt. "What happened here?"

"Malcolm."

She chuckled, her blue eyes glittering. "Again?"

He gave a huff of laughter. "Yes."

"*You* hired him."

"*You* said it was a good idea."

"It is. The members love all things Scottish. That's one of the reasons they come here." She wrinkled her nose. "Well, maybe not for the haggis."

"That's a matter of opinion." Personally, he enjoyed a bit of haggis. "How are you about all of this?"

Lucy heaved a heavy sigh as she pushed a hand through her red hair, holding it back from her stunning face. "I was okay until Mac. Do you think it would be weird if I visited him today?"

"Why would it be weird? I'm sure he'd appreciate it."

Lucy Wainwright was a name synonymous with Hollywood. She'd gotten her break eight years ago starring alongside Lachlan in one of his last action films. While he would go on to retire, Lucy took on more serious roles and became the latest Hollywood sweetheart, bagging herself an Oscar within three years of breaking out. They'd remained friends because Lucy understood what was important in life. She hadn't gotten swept up in the fame game and all the bullshit that came with it.

So Lachlan asked her to become a board member. She loved Scotland and adored Ardnoch. Their friendship swerved for a while two years ago when they began a casual affair. They'd had sex for months before Lachlan decided any longer would be dangerous to their friendship. Lucy was one of those rare people who, like him, didn't want anything more serious; she agreed that to continue might ruin their friendship. They amicably broke off the affair. Lucy started seeing another actor, and Lachlan returned to casual dating. Not long ago, he'd begun a long-distance, casual thing with Leighanne, a makeup artist he'd met during a visit to Glasgow.

Having Lucy in his life for almost a decade meant Mac

was well acquainted with her. He wouldn't find it strange that she cared enough to visit him.

"Arrochar said his daughter is here," Lucy prompted.

Lachlan's earlier agitation rose to the fore. "She's here."

"You don't sound too happy about that?"

"She's a pain in the arse. And her being here ... I just ... he doesn't need that right now, you know."

Lucy patted his chest. "Lachlan, maybe she's exactly what he needs right now. Don't you want Mac to spend time with his daughter, finally? I know if it were me and I had a chance to work things out with my dad, I'd want to."

That surprised him. Lucy came from a crappy home life. Her father had abandoned her when she was a kid, leaving her with a selfish mother and a stepfather Lucy wouldn't even talk about, she hated him that much.

"So you're saying I should just let them get on with it."

She grinned. "I know your need to manage people comes from a good place. I've never met anyone as protective as you. But yeah ... you need to let them get on with it without any interference."

Lachlan thought about Robyn's tears when Mac opened his eyes yesterday morning.

Those were genuine.

As much as she grated, she might actually want to have a relationship with Mac. He sighed. "Fine."

"Good chat." Lucy laughed as she walked past him. "I'll let you know if I need a car for Inverness later."

"Sure." He continued to his room, but just before he could swipe his key card over it, the door opened and Sarah McCulloch appeared.

"Oh." She blushed beetroot. "I'm sorry, sir, I was just ... tidying up."

He narrowed his eyes. "All housekeeping duties should be done by now."

Lachlan had been wary of hiring Sarah McCulloch as a housekeeper because her grandfather hated him. He thought it was a deliberate attempt to spy on Ardnoch. Thane said he was being paranoid, that Sarah just needed a job, and everyone knew Lachlan paid his staff above-average wages. Considering she'd worked at the castle for a year without incident, Thane had been right.

Yet Lachlan felt her eyes on him now and then, and she blushed and stammered around him until even he was uncomfortable.

Her crush was obvious.

Lachlan could put up with it.

But not with her in his rooms when she shouldn't be there.

Cheeks hot red, Sarah couldn't meet his eyes as she bent to collect a bundle of sheets.

He hadn't seen them.

Lachlan relaxed as she muttered, "Sorry, sir, we had to clean the guest rooms of those who left early, and we fell behind. Mrs. Hutchinson thought you wouldn't mind if we left your suite until last."

Mrs. Hutchinson—Agnes—his head housekeeper.

Feeling remorseful for snapping at her, he stepped aside. "Of course not, Sarah. My apologies. Do you need help with the sheets?"

"Oh no, Mr. Adair." She looked horrified by the thought as she scurried by, her face almost hidden behind the bundle. "I've got them. I'll just take them to the laundry chute."

"Fine. Thank you." He escaped into his room, away from her nervous energy, and closed the door behind him.

His rooms looked in order. Nothing seemed to be touched.

He was growing paranoid.

Or was he?

No, it couldn't be Sarah. A *man* attacked Mac. Unless they were dealing with more than one person?

But little Sarah McCulloch? Lachlan couldn't imagine her hurting a fly, let alone a doe and a grown man.

Head beginning to pound, Lachlan quickly changed his shirt and was about to leave when the phone in his room rang. Only staff members had his room number. He picked up. "Adair."

"Sir." It was Jock. "I'm sorry, but there's been another incident."

Lachlan felt adrenaline rush through him. "Who is it? What's happened?"

"No one is hurt, sir. But Ms. Willows is pretty shaken up. Can you meet us at her studio?"

"I'll be right there."

* * *

EREDINE WILLOWS WAS HIS PILATES, yoga, and mindfulness instructor.

More than that, she was Lachlan's friend.

Not in the same way as Lucy; he cared a great deal about Lucy.

But Eredine was different. Lachlan felt as protective of her as he did of Arrochar.

Knowing what he'd helped her escape from, Lachlan felt furious that someone used her to get to him in this way.

The studio was a modern building on the edge of a private loch on the estate. Loch Ardnoch was small and could be found by following a path that cut through the golf course from the castle, a mere ten-minute walk. The wall of the studio facing the loch was made entirely of glass, and Eredine led her classes from there so members had a view of Loch Ardnoch as they worked out or practiced mindfulness.

When Lachlan built the place, he didn't have anyone in mind for it.

Then he met Eredine by chance in LA.

She was looking for a new start, preferably somewhere remote, and Lachlan offered her the position at Ardnoch. Knowing how private she was, he'd helped her find a cabin to rent north of the village, far from the estate, with no other neighbors around. You would have thought he'd handed her a million dollars, she loved that place so much.

She loved her studio too.

Someone had violated her space.

The rage he'd felt when he heard of Mac's attack came burning back.

Why was this fucker going after everyone he cared about?

The coward needed to come at Lachlan so he could end him.

Lachlan was more than aware of the shredded yoga mats, the damaged walls, the broken windows, and the spray-painted words across the cracked mirrors, but his priority was Eredine. She sat with her back to the wall, knees drawn to her chest, not looking at anyone.

"She won't let us near her." Jock fell into stride with him as he crossed the room.

Lachlan warned him off with just a gesture.

"Eredine, it's all right." He lowered to his haunches and tentatively touched her knee.

Large, haunted eyes looked up at him, and he cursed this stalking bastard to hell all over again. Guilt suffused him. "I'm so sorry, sweetheart. But this isn't about you. You know that, don't you?"

Arrochar and Eredine were close, so she'd confided in the skittish young yoga instructor early on about the threatening messages they'd found around the estate, knowing Ery could be trusted. As such, she'd been aware of the situation well before now. Lachlan hadn't sensed she was frightened beyond her concern for him and Mac.

But now her fear was obvious.

"Come here," Lachlan whispered hoarsely, pulling her into his arms.

Thankfully, she came willingly, clinging to him. She trembled in his embrace.

"Nothing is going to happen to you."

"I'm worried about you," she whispered. "Look what happened to Mac."

"I'll be fine. Mac is fine. We're going to figure this out. Can you tell me what happened?"

She shook harder. "I just … I found it like this. M-my afternoon classes are s-supposed to start a-a-at three thirty."

"We'll take care of that." He looked up at Jock. They needed to take photos, deal with members, and call the police. However, he didn't want Eredine to be alone. Arrochar was a forest engineer, currently on site at Blairnie Forest, and probably unreachable. The only person on the estate Eredine liked and trusted was Lucy. "Get Ms. Wainwright."

He sat with Eredine, just holding her, staring at the threatening message spray-painted across the mirrors as they waited for Lucy.

Lucy's eyes widened as she stepped into the studio and saw the destruction—and the message. Her expression darkened with anger and then softened with sympathy when she saw Lachlan holding Eredine.

"Eredine." Lachlan cupped her pretty face in his hands, swiping her tears away with his thumbs. "Luce is going to take you to one of the empty cabins." He'd built the extra accommodation along the loch. "I'm sending a security member with you, but he'll stay outside."

"Come on, angel." Lucy held out her arms. "I'll make you a strong cup of tea and keep you company for a while."

Relief moved through him as Eredine melted into Lucy's embrace. She was almost as tall as Lucy, but she still somehow managed to look small and fragile in her arms.

As soon as they were gone, Lachlan studied the message.

"Cameras?" he asked, referring to the security cameras placed outside the studio. "Eredine had classes this morning, so this had to have happened between noon and three."

Jock scowled. "Cameras are wiped."

"This is bloody ridiculous. I take it the cameras into the security room have been wiped too?"

"Aye, sir."

"From now on, only you, Pete, and Kyle, and whoever you *absolutely* trust, have access to the security booth. If that means paying overtime, I'll do it. Understood?"

He nodded grimly. "Understood."

Exasperated, he gestured to the mess. "Just ... call the police."

A murmur sounded from Jock's earpiece. He turned to his boss. "Mac's daughter is here. And apparently Mac just called from the hospital to say we're to allow Ms. Penhaligon access to his office and his laptop."

Understanding dawned. Mac kept copies of all the evidence and his notes on his laptop. He wanted her in on this investigation.

Christ Almighty.

The mere thought of Robyn poking her nose into his life and estate exhausted him.

But he wouldn't defy Mac's wishes.

"Hold off on calling the police." He gestured to the message. "Not until Ms. Penhaligon has had a look. Get one of your boys to escort her here."

Not ten minutes later, Robyn walked into the room. She

had a large camera draped around her neck that looked like something a professional reporter used. How did that get past security?

Mac, he realized.

To Lachlan's increasing irritation, he couldn't tear his eyes off Mac's daughter. He would have felt her presence even if he hadn't been watching the door.

She had an undefinable energy. Robyn wasn't a typical beauty, but something Lachlan couldn't quite put his finger on made a person look at her. In Hollywood, an actor didn't have to be physically perfect to be successful. They just needed to have that *thing*. Charisma. It couldn't be taught. Years ago, his agent had tried to talk Mac into auditioning for work as an actor. Because he had it.

His daughter had inherited it.

Robyn's gaze moved through Lachlan, washing over the wrecked studio. Her booted steps echoed off the damaged wooden floors as she strode across the space to stop at his side. A musky, floral scent surrounded her. She stared at the message:

I'll make you see me.
And I'll be the last thing you ever see.
xoxo

Robyn read the message out loud. She glanced up at him. The sunlight streamed in through the shattered glass doors and made her changeable irises seem a grayish green. "Well, that makes me feel better."

Lachlan frowned. "What does?"

"Knowing I'm not the only one you piss off."

8

ROBYN

*L*achlan's expression turned so cold, I almost shivered.

"Do you think this is funny?" He motioned to the threat spray-painted on the studio mirrors. "Do you think finding my staff member trembling in a corner, terrified out of her mind, is funny?"

Remorse slapped the sarcasm out of me. "No. I apologize. Sometimes I open my mouth without thinking."

A muscle ticked in his jaw as he glared at the mirrors.

"Is she okay? Your staff member?"

His gaze returned to me. Guarded. Wary. "Eredine." He pronounced it *Ery-deen*. "Yoga instructor, among other things. Finished classes this morning and returned for her afternoon sessions to find the place like this."

"And is this definitely about you, not her?"

"No. I'm certain it's another attack on me. The other messages were also found in random areas of the estate, except for one."

"Have you called the police?"

"I'm just about to."

76

"Can you hold off?" I raised my camera, which hung heavily around my neck on its strap. "Do you mind?"

Lachlan took the last step that separated us, so I had to tilt my head to meet his cool gaze. "Mac sent you?"

I could tell by his tone that he wasn't happy with the prospect of me taking over for Mac.

"Yeah. He wants to continue investigating. I made a deal with him. He rests up, and I do all the legwork. We figure out the case together."

Adair bit out a curse. "The man should be convalescing."

"Would you?" I raised an eyebrow. "If some asshole, most probably one you know, stabbed you and threatened the people you cared about, could you just sit back and do nothing?"

Releasing a heavy exhale, Adair retreated and waved to the room. "Have at it. But be quick. I need to let the detectives see this so we can make repairs as quickly as possible."

"Yeah, wouldn't want your club members to miss out on their yoga." I snapped pictures of the vandalized room.

"I don't want Eredine to be afraid of this space. It's her space. I want it returned to that immediately."

I looked up from my camera. Adair was furious about this. But more so for this mysterious Eredine. I wondered if they were in a relationship. "Can I talk to her? I'd like to piece together what happened here."

"No."

That was emphatic. "Adair, I'm investigating a crime scene. I need to speak to the witness."

He narrowed his eyes, practically shooting hate fire at me. "Only if Eredine agrees."

"Well, yeah." I wouldn't bully anyone into talking to me, for Christ's sake.

The man grunted and strode out of the studio while I continued to take photographs of the space. I had to admit, I could see the appeal in coming to work out in a place like this. The sliding windows, when they weren't cracked, looked out over the tranquil loch. I could imagine this was the perfect place to meditate, when it wasn't wrecked to shit with red spray paint and a creepy message.

Jock and the security guy accompanying him moved out of my way as I catalogued every piece of damage I could find. Then I zoomed in on the spray paint to take photographs of the message. I wanted to match them up with the other messages, see if the graffiti was by the same person.

Adair's voice startled me. "Eredine will speak to you."

I lowered the camera to find him scowling again. "Great. Lead the way."

"Before I do ... if she starts to get upset, you back off."

I was sympathetic to his yoga instructor and what she'd been through, but he needed to be sensible. "You do know the police will want to talk to her when they get here?"

He didn't reply. Just stalked out of the studio.

It was hard not to roll my eyes as I followed him. There should be a picture of him next to the word *brooding* in the dictionary.

Broody was never my thing. I liked a guy with a sense of humor. Which was one of the many reasons me and Mark did not survive past the six-month point.

"Lose the camera," Adair threw over his shoulder.

Lose it where? My camera was expensive and precious.

Sighing, I noted that although Jock was on the phone to the police, he watched us, so I whipped off the camera and handed it to him. "Be careful with that," I mouthed.

He winked, and that sign of life—of humor—at Ardnoch made me smile.

Adair led me down a gravel path that followed the lochside. We passed a couple of small cabins with great views of the water until we came to one situated farther away from the others on its own at the western side. I followed him up the decked porch and waited behind him as he knocked.

The door swung open, and I hid my surprise.

Lucy Wainwright stood before us.

Lucy "America's Sweetheart" Wainwright.

"Luce." Adair squeezed her shoulder as she stepped aside to let us in. He didn't look back as he begrudgingly introduced me. "This is Mac's daughter, Robyn."

To my bemusement, Lucy's stunning, cat-shaped blue eyes widened as I stepped inside. She held out a flawlessly manicured hand. Thin gold rings covered nearly every finger. From her jewelry choices to her monochrome outfit of black silk shirt and white wide-leg pants that no ordinary human being could make look good, Lucy Wainwright screamed chic style and money.

Not surprising.

"Nice to meet you," I said.

"And you." She peered closely at me. "Wow, you have Mac's gorgeous eyes."

"No, she doesn't," Adair emphatically denied as he stopped in front of a young woman seated in the living room.

"Yeah, I do." I crossed my arms over my chest, shocked by his belligerent denial.

"She does," Lucy insisted. "I doubt you would have noticed. Heterosexual guys don't go around staring into each other's eyes, right?"

Adair's answer was to squint at me. I could feel him studying my eyes. His intense perusal made me uncomfortable, so I focused past him.

The young woman sitting on a small sofa was a beauty.

It shouldn't surprise me that Adair, an ex-Hollywood god, would be surrounded by the most stunning women in the world. But seeing them all in one place was kind of unnerving. Was this what living in LA was like?

"You must be Eredine," I said, keeping my tone light.

A tormented expression in her large green eyes made me realize Adair hadn't been exaggerating about her reaction. Either she was especially sensitive, or there was more to her reaction than merely being upset by property damage and a creepy message meant for her boss. Perhaps she and Adair *were* together, and she was terrified for him after what happened to Mac.

Eredine nodded, her mass of dark brown curls shimmering with the movement. Her age wasn't clear. She had smooth, golden brown skin that made her eyes seem unusually light. No signs of a certain age in her skin and definitely not in her long, lithe body delineated by her workout bra and yoga pants.

I'd put her in her twenties, but I didn't know which end of the scale.

If I went by how gorgeous she was and how Adair hovered protectively, I'd say there was definitely something going on between them. That would make her the perfect target for his stalker. If that was what we were dealing with.

Realizing all three of us stood over her, I gestured to Adair and Lucy. "Maybe we can all just sit and have a chat."

I took the sofa across from Eredine without asking as Adair sat beside his yoga instructor and Lucy sprawled casually on the window seat near the front of the cabin. I almost laughed at how effortlessly elegant she looked—like she was ready for a photo shoot.

I was in a cabin with two-time Oscar-winning actor Lucy Wainwright hours after visiting my father in the hospital where he was recovering from multiple stab wounds.

My life had taken a very surreal turn.

"So, Eredine, I'm Mac's daughter, Robyn."

"I know." She leaned forward, her elbows on her knees, her graceful fingers twisting together as she stared at the coffee table between us.

"I'm helping Mac with the investigation. I'm a cop. Well, I was a cop. Back in Boston."

"Okay."

"You teach Pilates and yoga here?"

"Yeah. And mindfulness."

"I've studied mindfulness." It was something my therapist had suggested. It was a type of meditation, and to my surprise, I really got into it. During moments of stress, I practiced it. "It works."

I ignored Adair's intense stare because Eredine had finally lifted her eyes to meet mine.

"Yeah, it does." She was American. I couldn't place a specific accent. With a name like Eredine, I'd assumed she was Scottish. False name?

"So, when did you discover the break-in at the studio?"

Her hands twisted tighter together. "About 2:45. I-I'd finished my morning classes. There are only a few members who come to those at this time of year. Occupancy is higher during the summer. But my afternoon classes are a little busier. They start at three thirty."

"But you discovered the studio was wrecked."

"Yes."

"Did you touch anything?"

Eredine shook her head. "I called security and waited."

Adair covered her hands with one of his, drawing my attention. Genuine concern and distress etched his rugged features.

"I … uh … I'm still trying to get a picture here of what's going on, but I know from Mac's findings that he's pretty certain the messages are all for you, Adair. That it's mostly

81

likely a stalker, and it's more than likely someone you know who has access here."

"Your point?"

I ignored his harsh tone. "Is Eredine a deliberate target because of your relationship with her?"

"For fuck's sake," he gritted out. "A man holds a woman's hand to comfort her and suddenly they're in a relationship?"

"No need to get defensive."

"We're not in a relationship. Eredine is a longtime friend of the family and a valued member of our staff."

Eredine nodded in agreement. Such sadness in her eyes.

"Okay. Then I guess we can assume the stalker is just making the rounds. And, Eredine, you didn't see anyone leaving the studio before you got there?"

"No one. I'm sorry I can't be more helpful."

"Thank God she didn't see anyone," Lucy spoke up. "Can you imagine what might have happened if she'd turned up while that person was there? Look at what happened to Mac."

Eredine inhaled sharply.

"Lucy," Adair admonished.

The actor winced. "I'm sorry. I just meant it was a good thing Ery didn't see anything."

I studied the way Eredine seemed to fold in on herself, frowning angrily at the coffee table.

Call it a cop's instinct, or a woman's instinct, but she was definitely afraid of something. Possibly frustrated by that fear too. Maybe I was projecting.

Whenever I was afraid, it pissed me off, and I'd find a way to arm myself.

When I was fifteen, I'd gone on a fifth date with a junior I'd been crushing on forever. That night in his car, he'd pushed me to go to third base. When I'd said no, he'd fought me and touched me without my permission. I was furious, humiliated, violated ... and scared.

But instead of letting the little shit win, I told my stepdad what happened. Seth dealt with the boy's parents, but he also enrolled me in a mixed martial arts class. Because his parents came down hard on him, that boy and his friends taunted me for months. Then one day, near the end of the school year, he came at me in the parking lot.

I took him down with what I'd learned, and he was so humiliated, I never heard a peep out of him again.

It empowered me.

And it had given me more confidence as a female cop to know I could handle myself against stronger perpetrators.

It wasn't the answer for every woman.

But it could be.

"Eredine." My softer tone drew her eyes back to mine. "I know when something like this happens, we feel violated. It's not just our space that's violated, it feels like *we* have been." Her eyes narrowed, and I could feel her drawing away so I hurried on. "I do mixed martial arts. I started training when I was fifteen after some shithead got the better of me." Her expression relaxed into understanding. "I'm going to be here awhile, visiting my dad, figuring all of this out. I could teach you self-defense."

Her surprise was obvious.

Adair butted in, "Teach her?"

I didn't look at him. This wasn't about him. "Teach you some self-defense moves that actually work in real-life situations. I know it made me feel better prepared going out on the streets of Boston every day. It's not just about self-defense. It's about the confidence it gives you. I took back my power when I started training."

Interest lit her eyes but was just as quickly shut out by mistrust. "Thank you, but I'm okay."

I kept my expression neutral, my tone relaxed. "Well, you know we could train in your studio between your classes. It'll be fun."

She scowled ferociously.

I was losing her.

"Eredine ..." I leaned forward. "Let me help you take that space back. We'll make it yours again in no time."

There was that flicker of fire in her eyes again. Her chin jutted stubbornly—she reminded me of me. "The studio *is* my space. I don't need to take it back."

"You heard her." Adair's tone had a slight bite to it. It was then I recognized his expression. He looked at Eredine much the same way he did Arrochar. Like a sister. My curiosity pricked. How had they come into each other's lives?

"If Eredine won't train with you, I certainly will," Lucy said.

All three of us looked at her in surprise. "You want to learn MMA?"

"Sure. I'm taking a year out from working after an exhaustive eight years of nonstop filming, and Ardnoch is my favorite place." She smiled sweetly. "I'm going to be here, so why not? It might come in handy for future roles. I could play a badass with authenticity. And what's more authentic than a real-life badass female cop teaching me how to defend myself?"

Something told me Lucy only offered to train with me in an effort to convince Eredine too.

In that moment, I decided I liked Lucy Wainwright. A lot. And not just because she'd called me a badass. Though I loved the sound of it.

"Maybe Ery would be kind enough to let us use the studio when her classes are out?"

Eredine, for her part, looked thrown by Lucy's decision to

train with a complete stranger. "Well … it's not technically my studio." She glanced up at Adair.

"It *is* your studio. Your decision."

"Then it's okay with me."

"You should stick around to watch." Lucy grinned at her. "I'd like you there."

I kept my smile to myself when Eredine silently agreed.

* * *

LEAVING Lucy to look after Eredine, I followed Adair. I'd collected my camera from Jock who left to greet the police. Knowing the cops would probably take umbrage to a "civilian" nosing around, Lachlan and I made sure we'd left the studio before they showed.

After I'd brandished the key card that opened the desk in Mac's office, Adair reluctantly led me back to the castle. We walked the entire way in silence, both of us lost in our thoughts.

I'd had to retrieve the key card from Mac's house. His place surprised me. He lived in one of the cute row houses near the quieter end of Castle Street. It was small and cozy inside, the house tastefully decorated in a masculine palette with hints of tartan here and there.

I hadn't stayed long. It felt weird and invasive to be in Mac's house—for the first time—without him.

I'd stayed awhile at the hospital in Inverness, and we'd talked about the Ardnoch stalker case and joked and made small talk. But we hadn't delved into our relationship. It would have to wait until he was well enough. I didn't look forward to it. Despite the horrible circumstances, it was nice just hanging out with Mac, and I was afraid our issues would come between us permanently once we aired them out.

It took me a moment to realize we were at a door opposite Mac's office. "What are you doing?"

"The key to Mac's office is in my office."

Ah.

Adair retrieved the key card while I stood outside in the hall, noting his space wasn't much bigger than Mac's and almost a mirror image in design. I would've thought Adair would have a huge office with a roaring fire and wall-to-wall bookshelves. As if he'd read my mind, he smirked as he moved past me, closing the door behind him. "This is my real office where I work when I don't want to be interrupted."

Adair swiped the key over the pad on Mac's office door, and it lit up. He pushed it open, glancing back at me with that twinkle in his eyes I'd only ever seen in his films. "Mac and I call my other office my stage office. It's where I go when I'm happy to be interrupted by members."

"And where is it?"

"Just off the members' library. It's more in keeping with the rest of the castle."

I could picture it—said roaring fire and wall-to-wall shelves. I wanted to see it just to see if I was right.

"Why do you need a stage office?" I asked as I veered past him into Mac's space, avoiding touching Adair.

"Ardnoch is a product. The members are here because they love the traditional aspects of the escape we offer."

"And to them, you're not just the owner, you're the lord of the manor, so to speak?"

"Exactly. That's the environment they want to see me in."

I nodded because it made sense. But it sounded exhausting. "So it's a retreat, but it's still a show. I guess you never gave up acting after all." I rounded Mac's desk.

At Adair's silence, I glanced up. He looked caught off guard, stopping me in motion.

"Adair?"

He blinked quickly, a blank mask falling over his features. "Did you find his laptop?"

Going with the change of subject, I found the slot in the desk that matched the key card and slid it in. It beeped and a drawer in the middle of the desk popped out. Mac's laptop sat neatly inside it. I chuckled. "How very James Bond."

"Mac is a private man."

My humor fled and I muttered, "Understatement."

"What happened to you when you were fifteen?"

Now it was my turn to be caught off guard. But Adair's blunt question deserved a blunt response. I picked up the laptop and slid the hidden drawer back into place. "I was assaulted by a boyfriend."

He looked stunned as I rounded the desk toward him.

"What is it?"

"Mac doesn't know about that, does he?"

"It wasn't worth trying to track him down. And my stepdad took care of it."

Anger glittered in Adair's eyes. For a so-called actor, he wasn't very good at hiding his feelings. "Mac would have wanted to know."

"Why? So he could feel bad but not bad enough to come to Boston to check on me?"

"He would have been there in a heartbeat."

The old hurt flared. "You don't know shit."

Adair stepped into my space, his spicy cologne distracting as the heat and size of him threatened to surround me. I tilted my chin up, refusing to back down.

"If you think so little of Mac, why are you here? We don't *need* your help."

"Well, you have it," I snapped, losing my cool. "I'm helping my father. What is your problem with me? Because you've been a bastard from the moment I got here. I'm the one who should hate you, not the other way around."

His nostrils flared. "Hate me? For what? You don't even know me."

"Because of you, I rarely saw my father. He missed birthdays and graduations and all because he was protecting your ass while you gallivanted around the world as Mr. Big Shot Hollywood Actor. Guess a skinny, boring little kid from Dorchester couldn't compete with that."

Adair stared at me in utter disbelief. "How can you even think that?"

I shrugged, trying to cover my pain with nonchalance. "Whatever. It's done now."

"It's done? Clearly, it's *not* done." He studied me like it was the first time he'd really seen me. "It's not my place ... but I suggest when he's up to it, you have an honest conversation with Mac about your relationship. And about your mother's part in the lack thereof."

It was automatic to want to defend my mother. But this wasn't the first time he'd mentioned her. Uneasiness shifted through me. "I ... I plan to. But for now, I have a new case to work on." I motioned with the laptop.

Adair nodded and moved toward the door. But before he opened it, he looked back at me. "I don't hate you, Robyn. I don't know you."

"Then what's with the attitude?"

"I don't trust outsiders. And I'm protective of my family."

Aggravated, I nudged past him and opened the door myself. "Not a good-enough excuse for being an asshole. Now ... have you got places to be, or do you have time to take me around the estate? I want a tour of every crime scene."

9

ROBYN

"*A*nd this is why Mac's convinced the messages are for you?" I bent over the laptop as it rested on the small desk in Adair's private suite.

We'd spent the last hour walking around the castle. There'd been five incidents in the past eight weeks. That actually wasn't a lot considering how quickly it had escalated to Mac's attack.

There was a dead deer, mutilated and left outside the trade entrance, along with a threatening and creepily cutesy message. A housekeeper had discovered Lachlan's "stage office" trashed two weeks ago. The message, "Why won't you see me?" was handwritten on hundreds of Post-it Notes and placed around the office. According to Mac's findings, there were no prints on any of them, so the person wore gloves.

A few weeks before that, the mews (an old-fashioned word for the castle garage) was broken into, and three of the Range Rovers vandalized. Painted across the body of one was the message, "You aren't you without me."

And finally, roughly two months ago when Adair had returned from a trip to Glasgow, he'd found his suite filled with wilting roses. Someone had removed his clothes from the closet and scattered them over the bed in a way that made it appear as if they'd rolled around on them.

I studied the photographs on Mac's laptop, trying not to think about anything but the case and not how surprised I was that Adair's suite was fairly humble, or how reluctant he'd been to allow me into it.

The wall behind his bed was recently re-wallpapered because a message had been painted across it. I stared at the message in the photos Mac had taken: "You're everything to me. I have to be everything to you."

Adair bent over the desk, too, staring at the photos. My breath caught as I turned my head to find his face next to mine. He scowled at the photograph. "It was the first message. The first violation. I think we can be pretty certain this is about me."

As he spoke, I found myself unable to tear my gaze from his lips.

A flutter in my stomach shocked me, and I abruptly stood, moving away from him and the computer.

He slowly stood, frowning.

Grateful that hot, embarrassed cheeks never translated to *red* cheeks for me, I pretended to study his suite again. "According to Mac's notes, there were no prints. Nothing else in the room seemed broken or touched."

"That's right." Adair sat on the desk, crossing his arms over his chest, his long legs sprawled out, one ankle over the other. "There are no cameras in the hallway here, so no footage of anyone breaking in. We checked the cameras in the security booth where all our extra key cards are housed, and no evidence of anyone stealing a key card for my suite either."

"Tell me about security on the estate. How do you ensure privacy at Ardnoch?"

"We have antidrone technology, which is our biggest defense against the tabloids or threats. A large security team who patrol the twelve thousand acres. Cameras in and around the estate … even some hidden in the woodlands. The security booth is manned twenty-four seven."

I frowned. I'd only read some of Mac's notes as we wandered around the castle, but surely it flummoxed him how someone could gain access to their security system. "Cameras have been wiped, turned off …" I mused over this. "While we have to consider there might be an issue from within your security team, we also should consider that we might be looking at a hacker."

"A hacker?" Adair stood, his brows pulled together in concern. "A stalker who is also a hacker?"

"Or a stalker with access to a hacker. If I were you, I'd talk with whoever installed and maintains your security system. They should be able to tell you if your security system has been hacked. Increased data usage will be a big giveaway." I exhaled slowly—what I had to ask next would likely not be well received. "What you and I need to do is narrow down a list of suspects from within the club. Because it has to be someone who can move freely around the estate."

"I've already given a list to Mac and to the police. It's a short list. I'm not in the habit of making enemies."

This comment surprised me. "Haven't you been the subject of stalker-like behavior before?"

"It comes with being in the public eye."

And being major eye candy.

"And what did all those people have in common?"

Adair gave a slight shake of his hand.

I gestured to him. "They didn't actually know you."

His expression hardened as understanding dawned. "It could be someone I don't even realize I've snubbed or pissed off."

"Exactly. But I'm not saying it's someone you don't know or who doesn't know you. In fact, most stalkers know their victims and have formed an unhealthy obsession with them. I think in your case, we can say due to the high level of security around Ardnoch, this is someone from within the estate or inner circle of your family and friends."

"No one in my family, not one friend of mine, would do this to me. It has to be someone on staff or one of the members."

I gave him a pitying smile even though I knew it would piss him off. "Your loyalty is sweet, but I have to leave no stone unturned."

"You will if I tell you to."

"No." I took a step toward him. "See, all this became less about you the moment my father was attacked. So every stone will be turned, and I couldn't give a rat's ass if you fight me or hate me for it." Before he could reply, I strode to the desk and nudged him aside so I could open a new document on the laptop. Now that I'd started this conversation, I intended to get what I wanted from it. "The most obvious suspect is a scorned lover."

"No."

I glared over my shoulder at him. "I'm absolutely positive that it is."

"I'm not discussing my private life with you."

"Did you discuss it with Mac?"

"There was no reason to. I don't have an angry ex running around the estate."

"Oh, we are confident in our ability to charm the opposite sex, aren't we?" I straightened, my expression mocking. "Believe me, Adair, women can be good at hiding when we're hurt or angry."

"Contrary to your example."

"I'm not an angry woman. You're just intensely aggravating."

He curled his upper lip. "Pot, meet Kettle."

I turned to face him fully but pushed the laptop toward him with the document open where Mac had compiled the messages in chronological order.

1. You're everything to me. I have to be everything to you.
2. You aren't you without me.
3. Why won't you see me?
4. You were once so very dear to me. But now so very dead to me.
5. I'll make you see me. And I'll be the last thing you ever see.

"Look at the pattern." I pointed to the screen. "Mac's noted it too. The messages start off kind of lovelorn and obsessive. The third is starting to sound desperate and hurt. Then it abruptly changes with the dead deer carcass to a threat. What happened there? Did you have an altercation with anyone on the estate between the time of the third and fourth messages?"

"No, I wasn't even on the estate. Mac suggested I leave him to run things and take a break. I went to Glasgow."

"Why Glasgow?"

Adair looked so put off by my questioning, I actually enjoyed it. "There's a woman there. It's a casual thing."

Oh.

Right.

Of course.

The guy probably had a woman in every city.

Something occurred to me. "Did anyone know that's where you were?"

93

He shrugged.

"Who?"

"Why?"

"Because some obsessive stalker who, up until that point, was trying to get you to 'see them' suddenly turned violent after you got back from spending time with whom I'm inferring is a woman you're in a sexual relationship with. Was this the first time you'd seen any woman sexually in a while?"

Anger brightened Adair's eyes. "Again, I am not discussing my private life with you."

"Oh, give me a break, Adair. I'm investigating a stalker, not compiling gossip to sell to a tabloid."

"That doesn't mean I trust you."

"Considering you're the most uptight, mistrustful son of a bitch I've ever encountered, I'm not going to take that personally. But Mac trusts me, so you're going to have to unshrivel your balls and share."

He spluttered comically. "Unshrivel my what?"

"This is getting us nowhere." I slammed the laptop shut and picked it up. "When you realize I'm right and there may be a correlation between you leaving for Glasgow and the acceleration of events, call me. I'm staying at the Gloaming until I can find cheaper accommodation."

I'd just touched the door handle when Adair bit out, "Everyone knew about Glasgow. Everyone in Scotland, that is."

I turned to face him, surprised he'd given in so quickly.

His tone rang with bitterness. "Someone sold photos of me and Leighanne kissing outside a coffee shop on Buchanan Street. The photos were all over the Scottish tabloids the next day. I made sure Leighanne was okay, that the tabloids had left her alone, then I cut short my stay and returned to Ardnoch. You showed up the next day, and so did a dead deer carcass."

"I'll assume that last sentence wasn't meant as some kind of tonal comparison for that particular day."

To my utter shock, Adair's lips actually twitched.

Was that humor in his eyes?

Who knew?

Then I realized what he'd relayed meant we were no closer to narrowing down our suspects. Frowning in thought, I spoke. "Like I said, we have to focus on people with access to the estate." Our eyes met, and I hated to dispel his unusual moment of almost being friendly, but I continued, "Is there anyone here who you've engaged in a relationship with or had bad business dealings with?"

Just like that, the guard slammed shut over his face. "No one who could do this."

"Lachlan ... I'm just trying to help. I promise."

I didn't know if it was because I'd used his first name or if my softer tone worked wonders, but he let out a long, weary sigh and slumped into the armchair near his bed. "There are only two people on the estate I've slept with. Gabriella Ruiz is one of them. But it was years ago."

My brain ticked over. "Isn't she here because Sebastian Stone is a member?"

"Yes."

"And does Stone know about your past relationship with his fiancée?"

Adair smirked. "It was hardly a relationship. But yes, he does."

"And his attitude?"

"Shitty." He gestured to the laptop in my hands. "But Mac has noted that, and his security team have been keeping a close eye on Stone."

"Okay. And the other person?"

His expression clouded over. "It's not her."

"Who?"

95

I could see the muscle flexing in his jaw. Jesus, he really didn't want to tell me. It was a shock, then, when he admitted, "Lucy."

My eyebrows nearly hit my hairline. "Lucy Wainwright?"

"You sound surprised."

"It's just … Lucy Wainwright. Wow. I wouldn't have thought you were her type."

"What does that mean?"

"I just … I mean, she's very … I don't swing that way, but if I did, Lucy Wainwright would be the home screen on my phone, you know? She's smokin'. And you …" I was just messing with him, but oh my God, it was so worth it to see him affronted.

"And I'm …?" He held out his hands, palm upward, openly offended by the unsaid insinuation that he wasn't attractive enough to sleep with Lucy Wainwright.

"I'm sorry." I swallowed my laughter. "I shouldn't have said anything. I'm sure plenty of women find you attractive enough to forgive the lack of sense of humor. I mean, Gabriella Ruiz obviously did, and she's gorgeous, so why not Lucy?"

"I have a sense of humor. I have—for fuck's sake." He scowled up at the ceiling. "Why the hell am I letting her bait me?"

Covering my grin with my hand, I watched Adair as he finally returned his eyes to mine.

Realization dawned on his face. "You're awful, you know that?"

Yet his tone suggested otherwise.

Awareness zinged between us and just like that, my smile slipped. Discomfited by the moment, I straightened from the door and cleared my throat. "I, uh … I take it from how Lucy was with you today that things ended well between you? Or haven't they ended?"

Adair was all business again as he pushed up off the armchair. "Things ended with Lucy over a year ago. It was amicable, and we're still very good friends. You saw how she was with Eredine. There's no way she would put Eredine in that position today."

"Something happened to her, didn't it? To Eredine. In the past."

Lachlan stared stonily at me.

Protecting her.

I got it.

Still, I said, "My offer to teach her MMA is genuine. It might help her."

"If anyone can talk her around to it, it'll be Lucy."

The mention of Lucy again reminded me we were still no closer to a list of suspects, although Stone was the beginning of one. He had the motive, however flimsy, and the money to acquire a hacker. He wasn't a strong suspect, though.

Deciding I needed to have a deeper look at Mac's files, I motioned to the door. "I'm going back to the village. I'll return tomorrow for my training with Lucy. If you have time, it would be great if you could write up a list of all your current staff, all the members who have stayed here in the last eight weeks, and notes about anything personal between you and them that you can think of."

"Oh, is that all?"

Ignoring his droll tone, I sighed. "I need to be thorough."

"Fine." He marched across the room to open the door, motioning for me to exit first.

"You don't need to walk me out."

"Yes, I do."

I'd like to think it was because he was a gentleman, but I got the distinct impression it was because he didn't want me to wander the castle alone.

Adair still didn't trust me.

I couldn't expect it. I rarely trusted anyone until I'd gotten to know them better.

However, I had to admit, if only to myself, that Lachlan's determination to treat me as an outsider stung.

It stung more than I'd like.

10

LACHLAN

*H*e and the board selected their members carefully at Ardnoch, which meant they tried to avoid A-listers with a reputation for being difficult, people who believed the world revolved entirely around them.

That meant issues with members' bad behavior were few and far between.

Mostly because Lachlan made it his business to anticipate the needs of his members.

It didn't mean problems, no matter how silly they might seem, didn't arise.

"I don't think I'm understanding the issue, Agnes." He stared impatiently at his head housekeeper.

Lachlan was informed half an hour ago that Robyn was on the estate, this time to train Lucy in self-defense. This information agitated him. He vowed to stay away from the source of said agitation, but to his utter irritation, he itched to make sure she wasn't up to any nonsense while his back was turned.

That meant Lachlan had little to no patience to deal with

99

Angeline Potter, British actor and current darling of a mammoth streaming service, insisting on extra shortbread in her room. They filled a crystal jar of locally made shortbread every day as part of the housekeeping service. In the evening for turndown service, they left locally made chocolates in little gift bags on the members' pillows and a hot toddy on their bedside table.

It was little touches like this the members loved. Ardnoch was the ultimate hotel experience. A home away from home where everything was taken care of.

Agnes had been with Lachlan since they'd opened Ardnoch. She'd been head housekeeper at a five-star hotel in Glasgow when he'd stolen her away. "Sir, it is not that Ms. Potter has requested extra shortbread. Of that, we are happy to oblige. It is that Ms. Potter has accused my housekeepers of stealing her shortbread instead of admitting she has eaten it all herself."

It was extremely hard to keep a straight face. "I see."

"Och, don't you dare laugh. It's not a laughing matter."

Only Agnes could get away with admonishing him like a schoolboy. "I apologize. And I am sorry that Ms. Potter has accused the housekeeping of stealing. If her accusations continue, then I will discuss it with her. However, for now, add a second jar of shortbread to her room each morning and see if that helps."

"I can already tell you, it won't. She'll eat both jars and be even angrier at herself for it and then blame us."

Lachlan would like to claim obliviousness to such thinking, but he'd seen people behave bizarrely when it came to food and body image. His attention caught on the grandfather clock in Agnes's office. Robyn had been on the estate for thirty-five minutes. She'd leave soon. Then he'd feel less agitated. "I'm sure you can think of something to handle it, Agnes. For now, I have a pressing matter to see to." He gave her an abrupt nod, ignored her glare of annoyance, and strode out of her office and through the castle.

Cutting through the drawing room that led to a side entrance, he nodded hello at a director and his wife who sat near the exit and ignored everyone else because that's what they preferred. If they wanted to talk, they approached him. Otherwise, he left them to it, as if this was their home too.

As he passed into the short corridor between the drawing room and the library, he caught sight of one of his waiters stealing an hors d'oeuvre and cramming it into his mouth.

He saw Lachlan at the last second and blanched.

Trying to quell his impatience to march down to the studio at the loch, he made sure none of the five guests in the drawing room watched as he approached the young man.

His name was Andrew, and he was a permanent member of staff. Lachlan hired extra staff during the summer months and often in the early winter months too.

"Andrew," Lachlan murmured.

"Sir," he squeaked out.

"Do I not pay you well enough, Andrew?"

"Sir?"

"To feed yourself?"

He paled. "Sorry, sir."

Lachlan straightened Andrew's cravat. His butler, under-butler, footmen, and waitstaff, all genders, wore the traditional uniform—cravat, waistcoat, coat tails, and white gloves. The members loved it. Lachlan doubted his waitstaff loved it, though the girls seemed to get a kick out of it. Or that's what Alfred, his maître d'hôtel, told him.

"While I see no harm in swiping leftovers once they're taken back to the kitchen," Lachlan said, giving him a pointed look, "I do not want to see you eating the members' food in plain sight of them ever again. Are we clear?"

He swallowed. "Yes, sir."

"Mr. Adair."

He turned to see Alfred approaching. The maître d'hôtel wore the same uniform but his waistcoat, like Wakefield's, was dark green instead of white to differentiate them from the rest of the staff. Alfred glanced between Andrew and his boss, eyes glinting hard at the thought of one of his staff displeasing Lachlan. While Alfred was the best maître d'hôtel in the country, he was so because he was dedicated and disciplined.

Once he was close enough not to be overheard, he murmured, "I do hope there isn't a problem, Mr. Adair."

"No, Mr. Ramsay." Lachlan always used Alfred's full name in front of the staff and members. It was his preference to be as formal and professional as possible. "I was just asking Andrew how he likes the job so far. I do believe he's only been with us for a few months."

Andrew looked surprised he'd covered for him but hid it quickly.

"And what did Andrew reply?" Alfred asked his waiter directly.

The young man straightened like a soldier. "I like it very much, Mr. Ramsay, Mr. Adair."

"Well, if that'll be all." Lachlan nodded to the men and hurried away before either could stop him.

Escaping out the side entrance that led onto the path that cut through the golf course and down to the loch, Lachlan thought he was home free. Someone had to make sure Robyn didn't cause trouble while she was here.

Mac's words from earlier that morning came to him.

"You're treating her well?" Mac asked from his hospital bed. His pallor had improved significantly. "Robyn?"

"Treating her well?"

"Accommodating her. She wouldn't tell me much this morning. Just wanted to talk the case through."

"She's not exhausting you, is she?"

"No." He gave a sharp shake of his head. *"But I feel useless lying here while she's out there investigating. If anything happens to her, Lachlan, because of this case ..."*

Stupidly, it hadn't occurred to him that Robyn might be putting herself in danger. *"Shit, Mac ... ask her to stop, then."*

"Nah. She's as stubborn as her old man. Just ... watch out for her. Please."

It was the last thing he wanted to do.

In fact, he vowed to stay away from her. She was intrusive and brash and he always felt like she was quietly mocking him.

No woman had ever dared to quietly mock Lachlan.

No one, for that matter.

At least not to his face.

"Lachlan!" a man shouted from behind him, gravel crunching underfoot.

"Oh, for fuck's sake," he muttered under his breath. Was he to never get to the damn studio? Reluctantly turning, Lachlan found Fergus hurrying across the estate grounds from the direction of the mews.

He wore overalls and a massive grin.

That was Fergus. You always got him the same way. Cheerful and accommodating.

Lachlan tried to shrug off his impatience. Fergus didn't deserve it.

"Fergus, what I can do for you?" he asked.

"I saw you heading toward the loch?"

He nodded.

The mechanic grinned. "Great. I'll come with you. I need to speak to Ery about her Defender."

Lachlan knew Fergus was working on a Defender Eredine had saved from the scrap heap. He was doing it during his downtime, between his work on the estate cars.

Together they walked to Eredine's studio, Fergus prattling on about the Defender, his words going in one ear and out the other. Lachlan nodded and made noises of agreement now and then, but he had absolutely no clue what the mechanic was talking about. His mind was on Robyn Penhaligon and the stalker threatening the peace at Ardnoch. His mind seemed to be on very little else these days.

Climbing the porch of the studio, he could hear Robyn's husky voice. Lachlan held a hand up to Fergus to stop him from entering the studio, and he quietly pulled open the door to look inside.

While the broken windows were taped up as they waited for the new ones to arrive, the mirrors were cleaned, and all damage had been repaired as quickly as possible. The studio was usable again.

Something Lachlan couldn't quite understand moved through him when he saw Lucy and Eredine locked in a grapple while Robyn stood beside them, hands on hips, calling out instructions.

Eredine trained with her.

Eredine, who trusted no one but his family.

Lachlan's attention drifted from his pseudo sister's expression of concentration, past Lucy, to Robyn. She'd performed a miracle.

"That's it!" Robyn called out, clapping. "You've turned Lucy's strike against her. You have her trapped. Now, if she were a man, you would pull her forward—pull her forward, Eredine—that's it, and this is where she, or more likely he, is open to a knee strike. Do you see? Yes, like that. If Lucy were a dude and you'd actually hit him, he'd be in extreme testicular agony right now."

He heard Eredine's chuckle and Lucy's snort, but for some ludicrous reason, he couldn't take his eyes off Robyn.

She wore workout gear, much like the other ladies, except she wore a full tank covering her slender torso. No cleavage on display, though the tank was tight enough to reveal she had an ample bosom. And she was tall for a woman. Maybe five seven, five eight. Her legs went on forever.

She turned and bent down to grab a bottle of water, providing him with an excellent view of a perfect, heart-shaped arse.

"Lachlan!" Eredine called.

Robyn whirled, and he yanked his gaze away, locking eyes with Eredine. He gave her what he hoped wasn't a guilty smile. "Just wanted to check on things."

"Can I go in yet?" Fergus said at his back. "Or are you done ogling?"

Lachlan cut him a dirty look over his shoulder. "I wasn't ogling. And do you want to be fired?"

He grinned, dark eyes bright with mirth, because he knew there was no way Lachlan would fire him. *Little fucker.*

Fergus pushed by and into the studio. "Hullo, ladies."

Lucy and Eredine broke their grapple to stride over to them. Lachlan avoided Robyn's eyes.

"You decided to train." He cuddled Eredine into his side.

"It's fun." Her gaze cut to Robyn. "Robyn's a great instructor. I told her if she stays, she should open a class."

"Hear! Hear!" Lucy tapped her eco water bottle against Robyn's. "And I told her if she ever wants to come to LA, I will pay her good money to turn me into a badass."

"You're already a badass," Robyn returned, flipping her long ponytail over her shoulder. "You don't need me for that." Her eyes met his. They were so large, filled with so much expression. This morning, he'd taken time to look at Mac's eyes and he'd realized, Lucy was right. Robyn had his eyes.

But they looked different on her.

Robyn's were ever changing.

Unpredictable.

She was unpredictable.

"So, why are you here?" Eredine nudged him. When he looked down at her, she wore a knowing smirk that confused him.

"I'm here to check on you, and Fergus is here ..." Lachlan gestured to him.

"About the Defender. I have paint and interior samples for you to see. But first, I feel I should introduce myself to our lovely guest." Fergus stared at Robyn with open admiration. It was a bit much. It wasn't like he wasn't used to women more beautiful than she was roaming the estate.

They were in a room with two of them.

Then why the fuck can you not stop staring at her?

Disgruntled, Lachlan focused on Fergus. "This is Robyn, Mac's daughter." He might have emphasized that last part with an unspoken "off-limits." Mac wouldn't want men sniffing around his daughter while he wasn't here to keep her safe. That job had unfortunately fallen to Lachlan by default.

"Robyn, I'm Fergus, the mews mechanic." He shook her hand vigorously, and she offered him an amused grin.

Then something changed in her expression. "The mechanic who found the message painted across the Land Rover?"

Jesus, she was a bulldog. "Robyn—"

"The very one." Fergus stepped into her space. "I didn't know we were telling people about that."

"Robyn isn't people," Lachlan cut in. "She's police. And investigating on Mac's behalf."

"I thought the DIs from Inverness were investigating it?"

"They are." He heaved a sigh. "But Mac would feel better

about it if Robyn investigated too. That means we're still not talking about it with anyone off the estate, Fergus. Understood?"

At his biting tone, Fergus stepped back, arms raised in defense. "You know I wouldn't spread gossip."

Eredine gave Lachlan a little shove in admonishment and stepped out of his hold toward the mechanic. "Come on, Fergus. You can show me the samples."

"I'll come too," Lucy said, following them out. "You know I love giving my opinion even when no one's asked for it."

The three of them left the studio without even saying goodbye.

Leaving Lachlan there.

With her.

He shoved his hands into his pockets and met her confident stare. "Fergus is a family friend."

Robyn crossed her arms over her chest, drawing attention to it. He kept his focus firmly on her face. "Oh?" she asked.

"He was my brother Brodan's best friend growing up. He was also Arrochar's first boyfriend, but it fizzled out when she went to Aberdeen Uni. She broke things off. Brodan and he stayed friends, but they don't see each other much now that my brother lives in LA. Still, Fergus feels like family." Even if he acted a bit of a prat now and then.

"So you offered him the mechanic's job?"

He took a step toward her. "His dad used to own the only garage in the area, but he sold it, and the person who bought it renovated and turned it into an inn. Fergus didn't want to leave Ardnoch, so I decided the estate should have its own small fleet of cars for chauffeuring members to and from the airport, or for those who wanted to explore the Highlands. The mews required a mechanic and valet."

Robyn's eyes narrowed as her gaze slid away from him to the studio exit.

She considered something.

How did he know that about her already?

"What is it?" He took another step toward her.

Her eyes flickered back to him, down his body and up again upon the realization he'd moved closer. When their eyes met, he saw now that hers looked browner today than they had yesterday. "We need to put Fergus on our suspect list."

It was like someone slammed open the studio door and an icy spring wind ripped through him. He retreated physically and mentally. "Excuse me?"

"Arrochar dumped him. And then Brodan left him behind. Who's to say he isn't taking that out on you?"

"That's a thin argument, Robyn. And you can't go around accusing good people of heinous crimes. People *I* care about."

"Look, I'm sorry." She didn't sound sorry at all. "But I have a dad lying in a hospital bed recovering from three knife wounds perpetrated upon him by a man who fits Fergus's physical description. I'm not accusing him. I'm just … considering all theories."

He could feel his anger brewing steadily hotter.

Robyn seemed to sense it. She held up a hand as if warding him off. "You're allowed to be mad at me. But you also have to cooperate." He watched her, unable to speak for fear he'd insult her and thus piss off Mac, as she strode across the studio to grab a shoulder bag and her camera.

"Why do you take that thing everywhere?" He gestured in irritation at the camera. He wasn't a fan of cameras. Lachlan connected them to an invasion of privacy.

Robyn shrugged. "I own a photography business."

The urge to ask her why she gave up police work was strong, but becoming curious about this woman was not a path he should let himself go down. "Why do you need the camera on the estate? You know there's no way I'll give you permission to print any photographs you take here."

"I'm going to take some shots outside the estate once I'm done here. I didn't see the point in driving back to the Gloaming for my camera when I'm going in the opposite direction. Is that okay with you, oh lord and master?" She threw him a dry smirk as he held open the studio door for her to exit.

Ignoring her sarcasm, Lachlan followed her down the porch steps. Before he could think of an appropriate and cutting response, she spoke again.

"Tell me about the village."

He looked down at her as they walked up the path toward the castle. "What do you want to know?"

"You can guarantee your members privacy on the estate, but how can you guarantee them privacy in the village?"

"I can't."

Her eyes widened. "Lachlan Adair just admitted to something he can't do."

He flashed her a dark smile. "You say that like you know me."

Robyn's eyes narrowed, her thick lashes almost concealing them from him entirely. Her full lips made a moue in thought. "You're right. I don't know you. I only know you through what the internet says, and we all know that's a place truth goes to die."

Lachlan snorted. She grinned up at him.

Then she tripped on a crack in the path he'd been on maintenance to fix for a week. She let out an *oof* as her body launched forward.

Instinctively, he reached out, hauling her against him to steady her.

He could feel every inch of her curves.

Could feel her heat.

Smell that musky floral perfume that suited her perfectly.

She pushed against him with a strength that belied her slender build, and he quickly released her.

"Are you okay?" he asked gruffly.

Robyn wouldn't look at him as she brushed strands loosened from her ponytail behind her ears. "I'm fine. I just need to watch where I'm going."

"The path will be repaired. I'll make sure to mention it to maintenance again."

"It's fine. I would have stopped myself from face-planting even if you hadn't caught me."

His lips twitched at the stubborn tilt of her chin.

Lachlan had a feeling it would take a miracle for this woman to admit she ever needed someone.

"You were saying," she continued, "about the village. You can't guarantee privacy?"

Deciding to give her what she wanted, he replied, "No. But it's quiet there during the off-season, like now. During the summer, however, tourists pile into Ardnoch for the award-winning beaches and in the hopes of seeing a famous person. With them come the tabloids. Most of the club members stick to the estate during the summer, or they take vehicles out and drive farther afield."

"Still, it must bring in quite the revenue for the village?"

"Tourism is a huge industry here in Scotland, but I can think of no other village that sees the kind of business we do during the summer. Everywhere is booked months in advance. A traveler comes through on the off chance, looking for a place to stay, they'd be shit out of luck."

"The people here must love you."

"My family has been here for centuries. We had a good relationship with the villagers before I launched the club."

"Well, that's not strictly true, is it?" She glanced up at him before returning her gaze to the path.

Irritated by the insinuation the villagers didn't like the Adairs, he growled, "What does that mean?"

"Oh, don't take offense, Adair." She threw him an exasperated look. "I'm talking about McCulloch."

Understanding dawned. "You've been reading Mac's notes."

"Yeah. But I want you to tell me why McCulloch is on Mac's list of possible suspects. Though, he's too tall to be the man who stabbed him."

"Mac has him on the list for a reason." He thought of that bitter old man and his hatred of Lachlan's family.

"What happened there?"

"Ask anyone in the village and they'll tell you."

"I'm asking you."

"It's not a long story. In fact, it's a tale as old as time. McCulloch was raised to believe that my great-great-great-great-grandfather stole McCulloch land and incorporated it into Adair land. He says there was nothing his ancestor could do against the might of the Adair family. The Adairs had wealth and social standing, were landed gentry. In fact, my great-great-great-grandfather's sister married the younger brother of the Duke of Sutherland."

"Is it true? That your family stole the land?"

"I don't know," he admitted. "My father looked into it, and there's no documented evidence that McCulloch is right. But McCulloch has never let it go. It didn't help that my father had an affair with McCulloch's sister and broke it off when he met my mother." The story was not a happy one. Certainly not for McCulloch. And what had happened afterward had left a wound in his dad Lachlan knew scarred over but never faded. "McCulloch's sister killed herself a few weeks later. He found her hanging in one of the barns."

"Oh my God," Robyn gasped, her expression tight with sadness.

"McCulloch blamed my father, but we all know there had to be more to his sister's decision than a broken heart. McCulloch has never let it go, which only added to my father's guilt. As I said, a tale as old as time. Love and land. It's always the thing people go to war over, isn't it?"

"It's a sad story. And fascinating too." Robyn frowned at the path. "But what of this housekeeper, Sarah? Why would Mac list McCulloch's granddaughter as a suspect?"

Discomfort moved through him at the thought of Sarah. "It was a surprise that she wanted to work here or that McCulloch would allow it. At first, I was wary. In case he'd lost the plot and was actually sending her in as a spy—"

"A bit dramatic, no?"

"And what would you call the events of the last eight weeks?"

"Point taken," she conceded easily. "So, Sarah?"

He grimaced. "She has a very obvious crush on me. And I've found her coming out of my suite outside housekeeping hours."

Robyn stopped on the path to face him, obviously surprised. "Well, that's damning."

Shaking his head, he sighed. "You haven't met her, Robyn. This is a young woman who can barely say boo to a goose."

"You mean a ghost?"

"I mean a goose."

"Why would you say boo to a goose?"

"Because that's the saying."

"The saying is boo to a ghost."

"Goose. Google it."

"I think I will." She turned away, that chin in the air again.

"Fuck, but you're stubborn."

112

"Uh, Pot meet Kettle." She threw his words from yesterday back at him but with a sultry smile.

Lachlan shook his head but continued as they neared the castle. "Sarah is timid. I can't imagine her being a part of all this."

"That may be, but I'd like a chance to talk with her. In a way that she has no idea I'm investigating, of course."

"Of course."

Robyn raised an eyebrow at his sarcastic tone.

"How are we supposed to manufacture that meeting?"

"I'll think of something," she insisted.

Silence fell between them as gravel crunched underfoot. They strolled around the outside of the castle toward the front entrance.

"So," she asked, her tone softer than before, "your mom passed away a few years before your dad, right?"

The question destroyed any humor or warmth that may have crept between them. He rounded the castle and saw her SUV waiting at the entrance.

At his silence, Robyn sighed. "I'm very sorry for your loss, Lachlan."

Her use of his name cut through the cold. He was acting like a bastard. He nodded at her. "Thank you."

"That's why I'm here, you know." She stepped toward him. He could feel her heat, and she hadn't even touched him. "I know you look on me as some kind of outsider—maybe even an enemy—because I don't understand the trials and tribulations of the rich and famous. But I'm not here to hurt or exploit anyone." Her expression suddenly grew unguarded in a way Lachlan hadn't expected. Those extraordinary eyes were green, gray, blue, and brown all at once, and filled with feeling. "I just don't want to get a phone call one day telling me *my* dad died and then I'd have to bury him along with all my regrets. That's why I'm here. For him. For him and me. The possibility of it."

With that, she spun, kicking up gravel with the speed of her movement.

Before Lachlan knew it, she was in her vehicle and driving away.

Leaving him stunned and disoriented by her confession and the sincerity he'd heard in it.

11

ROBYN

Seven days had passed since Mac was attacked, and they were finally discharging him from the hospital in the morning. Staring at the cork pin board I'd ordered online, my eyes darted around the evidence I'd collated, trying to make sense of it. The problem was, there were several people in Ardnoch with motive.

At the sound of a car pulling up next to the trailer, I reached over and turned the board around to hide it from plain sight. A Range Rover drew up outside, and I knew it must be Lucy.

Gordon was a friend of Mac's, and he offered me his rental trailer in what the Scots called a caravan (not a trailer) park by the beach. He rented it to me for peanuts, which eased my financial concerns. It was a little cramped and gloomy on cloudy days, but I'd take it. At least it was one thing I didn't have to worry about on top of the stress over Mac, the stalker, and my mom calling nonstop. I'd brushed off her calls with emails, but I knew I'd have to pick up the phone soon. I hated lying to her and knew I'd have to for Mac's and Adair's sakes.

"Hey," I greeted Lucy as I stepped out of the trailer. Like me, she wore yoga pants and a T-shirt. When I told her I'd started running the beach in the morning, she jumped on the chance to join me. I wasn't sure why she wanted to spend time with me, but I enjoyed her company so why question it?

She threw me her glamorous smile as she rounded the SUV, and I marveled at her ability to look constantly flawless. "Hey, yourself."

We fell into companionable silence, walking down the grassy edge of the dunes and onto the beach. The sand was soft and golden, resistant to our footfalls until we neared the shore where it was compacted by the water's continual caress.

Lucy stopped and took in a deep breath as she looked out across the sea. "There's nothing like it here. The fresh sea air. The sound of perfect silence." She eyed me with a soft smile. "I always thought perfect silence was nothing. But it's not. It's the world devoid of *human* noise. It's waves lapping at the shore, gulls crying in the sky, the breeze whistling over clifftops and soaring down valleys."

I smiled at her as I started warm-up exercises. Lucy followed suit, and I observed, "I think there's a writer in you, Lucy Wainwright."

"Do you? Because I'm writing a script."

"About what?"

"It's a character story. Rags to riches. No clichés. Kinda … autobiographical. Though that's just between me and you. I would never sell it as that. My business is my business."

Hearing the hard edge in her tone, I nodded in agreement. "I thought you were taking time off?"

"Oh, I am. And I've been offered amazing material, too, but you have to listen to your body, you know."

I definitely understood.

Falling into silence, we jogged. It wasn't surprising that

Lucy kept up with me. I knew from our relaxed mixed martial arts lessons that she worked with the personal trainer at the estate every day. Being in shape was a prerequisite for the action roles she enjoyed between her more character-driven work.

After five miles, we turned and made our way back.

We were still about a mile from the caravan park when it started raining, and my muscles burned with the strain of running on sand. I slowed, breathing hard, hands on knees as sweat trickled down my spine.

"That was ... that was great." Lucy puffed out. "Why ... why haven't I—I been doing that ... the whole time?"

"Beach running?"

"Yeah."

"Good, right? Tougher on the muscles. And invigorating."

"It is." Lucy straightened to join me in cool-down exercises. "Though I'd prefer later in the morning. I need my beauty sleep."

I shrugged unapologetically. "I'm an early bird."

"Then I guess I'm up early for the foreseeable future. It'll do me good."

"If this is how you look early in the morning, I don't think you have to worry about it affecting your beauty," I assured her.

"You're sweet." Lucy beamed. "When you say stuff like that, I know you actually mean it. There's no insincerity or jealousy behind it. It's refreshing."

We were silent as we finished our cool-down and then moved again. The drizzle felt great against my hot skin as we ambled down the beach. "Is that what it's like? Envy and fakeness all the time? Hollywood, I mean?"

"Not everyone. Obviously. Lachlan isn't like that. There're lots of actors not like that, although there are lots of actors who are ... it's more about LA. Everyone is constantly in competition. For everything. It's exhausting. Sometimes you don't know who your real friends are, and when they say you look beautiful, there's this look in their eyes like they wish you'd fall off a cliff and die."

Shocked, I raised an eyebrow.

At my silence, she gave me a sad shrug. "I'm not exaggerating. Don't get me wrong, I have some good friends in the industry. But I have some girlfriends in LA who started out in the business at the same time as me and hate that I've had success. They try very hard to hide it but can't. I'm just one more pretty face standing in their way."

"You're more than a pretty face. You're a damn good actor."

"Thank you, Robyn. I mean it. You're a good person. I could tell that right away about you. But it makes sense. Mac is too."

The insinuation that I was anything like Mac caused a twist in my gut. It wasn't that I was blind; I could see there were similarities between us. But I still didn't know how to handle my emotions when it came to my father.

Reading my silence, Lucy admitted, "I have a shitty relationship with my father too."

I glanced at her sharply, surprised she trusted me with personal information. "I didn't know that."

"No one does. I don't talk about my personal life in interviews. Drives the journalists batshit." She chuckled. "I'm very good at evasive maneuvering. Adds to my mystery. Anyway … my dad ran out on us when I was eight. Mom remarried a real dick, and my dad never came back. I hated him for a long time, and I know I would benefit from hashing out my issues with him. You're brave."

"You think I'm brave?"

"Coming all the way to Scotland to face the man you feel abandoned by? Yeah, I think that's pretty damn brave."

Her words were a balm; I hadn't been feeling very brave since arriving here. "I haven't spoken to him about anything but this case. I don't want to upset him while he's recovering, so everything is still up in the air between us."

"That's fair. Just because you don't want to push him right now doesn't mean you're avoiding the issue. Right?"

"I don't know about that. It feels like I'm putting it off. You should've seen me when I first arrived. I sat down in his office and honestly thought I was going to start sobbing my guts out right there and then. I couldn't leave fast enough."

"Robyn, I don't know the ins and outs of what happened between you two, but give yourself some slack. Parents have this ability to cripple us emotionally. Trust me. You're doing good. I mean, look"—she gestured up the sand dunes to my trailer as we approached—"you've turned what was a flying visit into an indefinite stay so you can find the person who did this to Mac. Give yourself some credit."

I snorted. "I would if I were any closer to figuring out who's behind the attack."

Concern strained her features. "You don't have any clue?"

"There are a few people who have motive, but there's no evidence to support it's any one of them."

"Shit." Lucy drew to a stop at the hood of the Range Rover, her arms crossed over her chest. "I'd hoped you were getting somewhere." Her stunning blue eyes met mine. "At least Lachlan discovered the security system was hacked."

Surprised moved through me. "He did?" Why didn't I know about that? I felt a sting of emotion I didn't want to name.

"Yeah. He just got word last night. His security guy found all kinds of evidence the system was hacked, so now he's trying to hack the hacker to see if they can trace who it is."

"Did Lachlan inform the police?"

Lucy shook her head. "He's pretty irritated with them.

119

They came around a few times this past week to interview members and informed Lachlan they were out of leads. He's supposed to tell them if anything else happens, but—"

"He thinks he's more competent than the cops?" I sneered. Arrogant asshole.

"No." Lucy grinned. "I think he thinks *you're* more competent because you have a reason to be invested in it. That's why I hoped you might have figured something out by now. Don't tell Lachlan, but it's why I'm sticking around. I'm supposed to be in the South of France with this guy I'm casually seeing, but I didn't want to leave Lachlan, or Eredine, for that matter, in the middle of all this."

The thought of Lucy taking off disappointed me. While we'd only known each other a week, I'd miss her if she left. She was the opposite of everything I thought a famous actor would be in real life. Down-to-earth, funny, considerate. Plus, she was the most confident woman I'd ever met, and while some might think her arrogant, I found it refreshing how much she owned the fact she thought she was the shit. More people should be like Lucy.

But I didn't want her to feel unsafe. "I don't think Eredine or Adair would want you to put off plans for them."

"That's what friends do." She nudged me with her shoulder. "Besides, wouldn't you miss me?"

I chuckled. "I would, actually. I don't have a lot of female friends back home. My closest friend is married to my old partner."

"Your cop partner?"

"Yeah. We drifted apart when I gave up the job, but we're still good friends. The job kind of became my life, though, so I don't have friends outside of it."

"Well, you have me and Eredine now. And I'm not going anywhere. Sex with a guy in the South of France is easy to come by. Friends I actually connect with? Not so much.

Which is why I'm staying, even though"—a cloud darkened her eyes—"this person is starting to give me the willies. Not knowing what's going to happen next ... especially since it looks like it's someone close to Lachlan."

Protectiveness surged inside me at her display of vulnerability. "Lucy, I won't let anything happen to you."

Her expression lightened. "I believe you."

"And I promise, I'm constantly thinking about this case. I will figure out who is behind it." At the moment, I was leaning toward McCulloch and his granddaughter, Sarah. They seemed the most obvious choice. Occam's razor: the answer that requires the fewest assumptions is usually correct. "How much do you know about Sarah McCulloch?"

Lucy braced against the hood of the SUV, seemingly as uncaring as me about the drizzle dampening our respective hairdos. "The housemaid. I mean ... housekeeper." She grimaced. "Lachlan admonishes me for calling them housemaids." Her voice lowered to a gruff brogue. "They're house*keepers*, Lucy. How many times do I have to remind you that you can't call them maids?"

Smirking at her impression, I nodded. "Yeah, the housekeeper."

Lucy gave me a *look*. "I'd say you're on the right path if that's the way you're thinking. She has a serious thing for Lachlan."

"How serious?"

"Like every time I'm with him and turn around in that castle, she's scurrying out of sight like she was watching us. She blushes and stammers around him, all googly-eyed and adoring."

I grunted at the idea of anyone acting that way around Adair.

Lucy chuckled, apparently reading me like a book. "You don't like him, huh?"

"I'm not going to disparage your friend."

"But ...?"

I couldn't help myself. "He gives off this vibe like he thinks he's better than me." I winced, hating how juvenile I sounded. "It's ... I'm not good with people who lord their superiority over others. Considering I'm pretty epic, I take offense to someone thinking I'm not good enough." Beneath my bravado, there was that kid who'd been abandoned by her father, who worried that maybe she *wasn't* good enough.

"Girl, you *are* epic, and I love that you know it." Lucy pushed off the hood and gave me a coaxing smile. "So few of us are brave enough to admit our awesomeness out loud. But be nice to Lachlan. He's my friend, and my friends should be treated well."

Hearing the edge of admonishment in her voice, I looked away.

Lucy prompted, "I take it Lachlan told you that he and I ..."

I shifted uncomfortably, hoping me knowing wasn't a problem between us.

"I get that for this case, you had to ask him about past relationships with anyone on the estate. Easy to work that one out, and I am more than a pretty face."

I turned back to her. "I know that."

The teasing sparkle was gone from Lucy's eyes. "It was strictly casual, my thing with Lachlan. Great sex with someone I felt safe with. But not at any point did I let my emotional guard down because I knew I'd get hurt. When he suggested we end things, it surprised me how relieved I was."

"Why are you telling me this?"

She snorted. "Because one, I don't want you thinking I'm moping after him and leaving dead deer carcasses in my wake."

"Fair enough." I chuckled.

"And two, it wouldn't surprise me if his inability to let someone in, truly in, is why he's in this mess. Lachlan is charismatic, kind, and patient—"

The huff of disbelief burst out of me before I could stop it.

Thankfully, Lucy just laughed. "He is. And if you aren't smart, like me, a person could find themselves longing for something they can't have, reading him wrong, thinking there's more between them than there is, and getting pretty pissed about it when Lachlan doesn't fulfill the fantasy they've created in their heads."

I edged closer to her. "You think this *is* a scorned lover?"

"Or someone who *wants* to be his lover." Her expression was pointed.

Sarah McCulloch.

It was about time I found a way to talk to the young housekeeper so I could get a sense of her myself.

* * *

WITH THE PROMISE of seeing one another tomorrow for another MMA lesson with Eredine, Lucy and I parted, she to the estate and I into a quick shower before my daily drive to Inverness. The shower stall in the trailer was so narrow, I banged my elbows against the walls every time I turned. Trying not to remember the luxurious bathroom I'd spotted in Lachlan's suite days ago, I hurried through the routine I usually enjoyed and reminded myself the trailer was temporary.

Mac told me not to come to the hospital until tomorrow for his discharge because it was a two-hour round trip. But I had to see him every day.

My worry compelled me to see for myself he was alive and well and healing.

Somehow I'd managed to avoid Lachlan, not just at the hospital but at the estate, these last few days too. Lucy had shown me around Ardnoch Castle and Estate, giving me a real tour of the place. It teemed with luxury. The wine cellar in the basement seemed to go on forever, and the Michelin Star restaurant was run by Arrochar's boyfriend chef, Guy, whom I had yet to meet. And five minutes from the castle, two larch-clad contemporary buildings, designed by Thane Adair, housed a spa and salon (Lucy explained Lachlan had hired professionals from all over the globe to run it) and a state-of-the-art gym. There were a couple of boxing bags inside the gym that I eyed longingly. I had one in my apartment at home, and a workout on it was a great stress reliever. Finally, the heated indoor pool made a person want to dive right in.

My envy of the club members only grew when I saw the large but cozy castle library. I wasn't a big reader but I didn't need to be to find the space alluring. Wall-to-wall dark oak bookshelves, a large, open fireplace, comfortable armchairs, footstools, and sofas. Floor-to-ceiling windows on either side of the fireplace let light in so it didn't feel too dark. The plethora of table lamps aided in chasing off the gloom too. Luxurious velvet curtains at the windows pooled on the wooden floors, most of which were covered in expensive Aubusson carpets.

I'd caught a glimpse of Lachlan's stage office, which was a smaller version of the library. Lucy also grabbed a golf cart and took me across the large course and into the woodlands to tour the private residences.

"One of these days, I'm going to buy one of these beauties," she'd said as the woods disappeared behind us and we emerged onto an open clifftop overlooking the water. Sand dunes fell dramatically toward the beach, making it a steep jump to get down to it. I'd gaped at the four large homes

dotted along the coastline. "And it's going to be one of those."
She'd continued and then pointed, "See the second closest
to us?"

"Yeah?"

"That's Wesley Howard's summer home. Well, his
summer house in Scotland. He has homes all over the world."

"The director?"

She'd nodded and again I'd been reminded I was visiting
another world here. Wesley Howard was on par with the
Spielbergs and Scorseses. "He's a board member. He and
Lachlan are friends."

Wow.

"But he rarely uses the house. Someday I'm going to be
able to afford to buy it off the bastard." Lucy grinned at the
thought. "And I'll live here anytime I'm not working on
location."

"You love it here, don't you?"

"You get why, though, right?" She'd motioned to the soft
but wild scenery.

I did get it. Lucy enjoyed a semblance of normal life here
in a beautiful place.

It was not surprising that Lachlan was scarce that day,
and the next day, and the day after that. He was most definitely avoiding me, and I couldn't care less.

Shoving the irritating man from my thoughts, I stopped
outside Mac's hospital room and paused at what I witnessed
through the window panels.

Arrochar Adair. Sitting beside Mac, her hands clasping
one of his as she leaned over the bed.

Mac sat up, the color back in his cheeks, and he looked at
Arrochar ...

My breath caught as they laughed together, staring deeply
into each other's eyes.

Then Arrochar pressed her lips to the back of Mac's hand,

and this pained look crossed my father's face. He tugged gently on his hand to release it, and Arrochar reluctantly let go.

Whatever she'd said to him, however, brought his gaze to her mouth.

A flush of heat scored my cheeks.

I pushed into the room and watched as they both jerked away from each other. "Hey."

At the awkward silence, I decided not to jump to conclusions about what I'd observed and pretended I hadn't interrupted anything. I smiled at Mac and then Arrochar. "Hey, it's nice to see you again."

Her pale cheeks flushed as she stood. "You too. But I was just leaving. I have to return to work."

"I'll walk you out." The words fell from my mouth before I could stop them.

She gave me a tight smile and then said to Mac, "I'll see you later."

He nodded, expression carefully blank.

Arrochar narrowed her eyes ever so slightly and then walked away. I followed her, throwing over my shoulder at Mac, "Be back in five."

Falling into step with Arrochar, I asked, "How is he today?" At her questioning look, I continued, "Sometimes I wonder if he's not telling me how he really feels."

She nodded in understanding, and I studied her. Arrochar Adair wasn't a typical beauty, but she was certainly striking with her unusually pale-blue eyes, high, sharp cheekbones, and slightly pointed chin. Her lips were heart-shaped, adding to her overall fay features.

I imagined she had no trouble turning heads.

I just wasn't expecting that one of those would be Mac's. I struggled to remember her age but thought it was close to mine. Perhaps a year or two older? That made the age difference between them fourteen to sixteen years. I knew my dad was young when they had me, and forty-four definitely wasn't old, but still—

Robyn, stop.

I could absolutely be jumping to conclusions.

"Mac is hardy." Arrochar yanked me out of my troubled thoughts. "He's healing well," she assured me. "He's happy you're here."

"Why do I get the feeling you're not?"

"Oh, I am." She hurried to say, flushing slightly. "I just ... I worry about him."

Yeah, everyone was worried about Mac's feelings. I got it. But a little understanding for the kid he walked out on might be nice. "You're dating the chef at Ardnoch, right?"

I think she was as surprised as me by the question. "Uh, yes. Guy. We've been dating for the past few months. Why?"

Scrambling to think of a reasonable reason for asking, I blurted, "Does it bother Fergus?"

"Fergus? Fergus Ray?"

I nodded.

"Why would it?"

"Because you dated him." I lowered my voice. "I'm helping Mac investigate the stalker at Ardnoch."

"And you think Fergus is the stalker?" She laughed, a musical, sparkly sound that made her eyes darken to a warmer shade of blue. "God, no. Fergus wouldn't hurt a fly."

"But you dated?"

"Yes. When we were kids. He was my first boyfriend. My first ..." She raised her eyebrows. "Well, you know. But as sweet as he is, he's immature."

"That's why you broke up?"

Arrochar made a face, like she couldn't believe I was this nosy, but I genuinely did want to know about Fergus. "Um ... that, and he had a gambling problem."

That was new. "Gambling problem?"

"Online gambling."

"Does he still?"

"I don't think so. I think if he did, he'd have nothing left financially, and he's got his flat that he rents and a good job on the estate ..."

Still, I tucked that little note about him aside to put on my pin board later.

"Fergus isn't behind the attacks. He's like family. He and Brodan are best friends. He'd never hurt any of us."

I also noted that, but he was still on my list. "Okay."

Arrochar studied me like I'd just studied her. "You have Mac's eyes."

"So I've heard."

"We should have dinner together."

I raised an eyebrow at the abrupt change of topic. "We should?"

"Absolutely. Eredine has been talking about you nonstop, and you *are* Mac's daughter. We should get to know each other."

Considering what I may or may not have walked in on between her and Mac, I decided she was right. "Sounds great."

Once we'd exchanged numbers and promised to arrange something, I returned to Mac's room.

He gave me a soft, tender smile that caused an ache deep in my chest.

"Hey. How are you feeling?"

"Like you didn't already ask Arro?"

I chuckled, sliding into the seat she'd vacated. "Okay, I did."

"I'm fine." He assured me. "Feeling much better and ready to get the hell out of here. Tomorrow can't come soon enough. You have no idea how awful it is to be in here this long."

"Actually, I do," I blurted out.

Mac's eyes sharpened, his face clouding over. "Robyn?"

I hadn't come here that morning with the intention of telling him the truth. That conversation was supposed to happen later. But after talking to Lucy about how cowardly I'd felt ever since I'd arrived in Scotland, the words just spilled out before I could stop them. "I'm not a cop anymore because last year, I was shot in the line of duty. I almost died."

My father turned a worrying shade of chalk.

12

LACHLAN

The Cromarty Bridge sat low on the firth, and on a cold, dreich spring day where the water reflected the weariness in the clouds, it felt almost as though the wheels of his SUV were touching distance from it. The softly rolling farmland on the opposite side of the water was a lush green or hay gold on a warm summer's day, yet today, Lachlan could barely make out the land through the constant misty haze that hovered over the banks of the Cromarty Firth.

Mac was finally being discharged from hospital, and Lachlan was on his way to collect him. He wanted to bring Mac to the estate where his staff could look after him, including the security team. But, as always, his friend was a stubborn bastard, and he wanted to be taken to his cottage, where he had no help while he recuperated.

Lachlan hadn't given up trying to convince him otherwise. He'd give it another go once he reached the hospital. Part of him just wanted to drive the mule to the castle despite his inevitable protests.

The drive from Ardnoch to the hospital in Inverness was

a straightforward journey following the A9 road almost the entire way. Still, Lachlan would be glad to have Mac back at Ardnoch. Not just for the convenience of it but because it unsettled him to have the man so far away with no protection. Mac would chafe if he knew Lachlan worried about him. Until now, Lachlan thought sourly, he'd never had any cause. Part of him had almost believed his ex-bodyguard was invincible.

A little under twenty minutes from the hospital, Lachlan's phone rang through the car system. The screen in the middle of the dash told him it was Leighanne. For a second, he considered not answering because he was so distracted. Then it occurred to him that he'd been distracted for weeks, and if he was abiding by that rule, he'd never answer the phone again.

He hit the answer button. "Leighanne."

"Hi, you. I haven't caught you at a bad time, have I?" She had a light, high voice that always sounded on the verge of laughter.

"I wouldn't have answered if you had," he replied honestly.

"True. I was just calling to see if you had time to visit this weekend? It's been awhile, and I … well, I'm horny as hell." She laughed.

Lachlan smiled. "As much as I'd like to help you with that, I can't leave the estate anytime soon."

"Oh? Problems?"

His hands tightened around the steering wheel. Their relationship was casual. Sex only. They'd both gone into it knowing that. And Lachlan barely trusted anyone with the personal details of his business, or his life, for that matter, let alone a woman he only met up with to fuck in a five-star hotel on weekends. "No. Just busy."

"Too busy to get off with something other than your right

hand?"

"Who said I'm not?" He wasn't, but that wasn't the point.

Leighanne hesitated and then chuckled. It sounded fake. "Right."

Irritation and guilt filled him. The guilt only made him feel more irritated. Why did women do this? They agreed to the rules and then got hurt when he stuck to them.

"I'll just go out on the prowl," Leighanne said with forced levity. He knew it was forced because her voice rose an octave. "Find someone else to keep me company this weekend."

Tone friendly, reflecting that he had no issue with her doing so, he replied, "You should do that. Be safe, though. Go with some friends."

Her burst of laughter sounded disbelieving. "Right. Of course. I guess … I guess I'll call you later, then?"

"Have a good weekend. Bye."

"Bye, babe." She hesitated again.

Lachlan frowned at the awkward silence and then tapped the button on his wheel to hang up.

He could do with some stress relief, and sex was his favorite tension reliever. Wasn't it for most men? There was no one he could fuck at Ardnoch except Lucy, and he would never go back down that road. Her friendship meant too much. Every other option was too close to home, and a liability. Especially now.

Robyn's face flashed in his mind, and Lachlan tensed. The woman had been on the estate every other day for the past week, either working out with Eredine and Lucy or touring the place. Everywhere he turned, he caught glimpses of a defiant chin and hair of indiscriminate color. It bothered the fuck out of him that he was being chased around his own castle, hiding from a mere slip of a woman.

But he was doing it for Mac's sake. Robyn agitated Lachlan, and he was likely to say something to upset her that would get back to Mac and cause problems between him and his friend.

The woman wasn't worth that.

However, she was worth something to Mac. So Lachlan would continue to avoid her, even in his own home, if it meant playing nice for his friend. No one could blame him for finding her abrasive. She was cocky and superior and looked down her nose at him.

He sighed. Heavily. Okay, so sometimes she wasn't all that. She could be funny. And the last time they'd spoken, she showed a side of herself Lachlan wasn't expecting.

A vulnerability.

If he was honest with himself, that's when he'd decided to avoid her.

So lost in his thoughts, Lachlan realized he was already on the Kessock Bridge and a mere ten minutes from the hospital. Shoving thoughts of large, hazel eyes (Were they even hazel? Why was everything about the woman so bloody contradictory and changing?) out of his mind, Lachlan considered the best way to convince Mac to stay at the castle.

By the time he arrived, he'd still thought of nothing that might persuade Mac. All he had left was brute force and the fact that he was the one driving the damn vehicle.

A woman strode out of the main entrance and gave him a double glance, her lips parting in surprise. Used to people recognizing him, Lachlan offered her a tight-lipped nod of acknowledgment while her cheeks flushed with the thrill some people seemed to get at crossing paths with a famous person. Before she could whip out her phone and ask for a selfie, Lachlan marched inside the hospital. He was lucky to call Ardnoch home. It was a place where people thought of him as an Adair rather than an ex-Hollywood actor.

Venturing farther afield wasn't so bad these days. Not like

it was at the height of his career. Back then, he couldn't go anywhere without being recognized. Now he could. But the fame still lingered like a vulture he couldn't shake off.

Nodding to the hospital staff who had come to expect his visits this past week, Lachlan almost missed her.

Robyn.

He slowed to a stop. Mac's room was straight ahead. Robyn stood at the bottom of the corridor to his left, back to him, phone pressed to her ear. She kicked a foot gently at the wall, her head bent so her ponytail hit between her shoulders instead of the middle of her back. She had a fuck ton of hair.

His breath quickened for a moment before he controlled it.

There was something about her posture that was off. Her shoulders were hunched. Robyn was usually straight-backed, her body language betraying her innate confidence and sense of self.

If she were any other woman, he would think her sexy as hell.

Lachlan strolled toward her, drawn despite himself. He hadn't seen her in days.

Should have anticipated she'd be here, though.

Maybe he already had.

"I told you." Robyn's voice carried to his ears, and he heard the defensiveness in her tone. "It was a heart scare ... Mac's doing okay. I just want to stick around a little longer ... I know. I know, I should have called sooner ... Mom, I told you I'm sorry. How many more times do you need to hear it?"

Lachlan stopped a few feet away. She'd lied to her mum? Good.

"I'm not taking a tone with you ... no, it's not Mac's influence. I'm here, I'm on the phone, aren't I? ... Oh, so now we actually get to the reason you're pissed ... No ... Absolutely not … Because she's a grown-ass woman, and she can do whatever she wants … I'm not acting like a child. I have my own stuff going on, and you're her mother … As far as I'm concerned, she can do whatever she wants. I'm done running after her. Look, I have to go … no, I have to. Talk later." She hung up and growled, "Fuck!"

"That sounded like a fun conversation."

Robyn whirled, those big eyes round with surprise. "Jesus, you scared me."

He smirked. "Sorry."

"Oh, you sound it."

He gestured to the phone clasped in her hand. "Mum?"

"Yeah." She slipped the phone into the ass pocket of her jeans. "Don't worry. I didn't tell her anything. Made up some stuff about Mac having heart issues."

Seeing how disgruntled she was about lying, Lachlan found himself offering, "Well, it's appreciated."

"I gave you my word, didn't I?"

She had.

And she'd upheld it.

His gaze dropped to her mouth. She had a natural pout that lent itself to her current discontentment. Dragging his attention to her eyes, he said, "Sounds like you're needed at home."

Her upper lip quirked before she replied, "Trying to get rid of me?"

Maybe.

He shrugged.

Robyn crossed her arms, studying him as she might an opponent. "I'm not going anywhere."

"Never said you were."

"You didn't tell me you discovered someone hacked your security system."

Lachlan didn't know what to be more bemused by: the

randomness of the subject change, or her belligerence. "I would have eventually. I haven't seen you."

"I've been on the estate plenty."

He shrugged.

Her arms dropped to her sides in obvious irritation. "I swear if you shrug at me one more time ..."

"You'll what?" he taunted.

Her eyes narrowed, her lashes flicking dramatically out at the corners. "Why didn't you tell me about the hacker?"

"I was going to when I saw you next."

She relaxed marginally. "Any leads?"

Lachlan shook his head. "My man is working on hacking the hacker. And I had Lucy spread it around the estate that the system can no longer be compromised."

Robyn considered this. "So whoever it is knows that whatever they do on the estate, it *will* get caught on camera now."

"Exactly."

"That will only run them to ground for so long."

"Long enough to figure out who it is. Hopefully."

Frustration etched into her features as she blew out a shaky exhale and placed her hands behind her head. She turned slightly away from him. The gesture caused her Henley to rise, showing off the taut skin of her stomach.

Lachlan glanced quickly up at her face. She'd been hiding it before now, but he could see how stressed she was. It was in the pinch of her mouth, the deep furrow between her brows, the way her fingers clenched into the hair at the back of her head.

"Are you required at home?" he asked in all seriousness. "Mac will understand if so."

She shot him a look of surprise as her arms flopped down at her sides. "No. It's fine."

He raised an eyebrow.

Robyn let out another long exhale. The woman was wound tighter than a watch. "My sister. Regan. Mom's worried about her."

Sister?

Right. The half sister.

Lachlan had forgotten Robyn had a sister. Regan Penhaligon was the daughter of Robyn's mum and stepfather. Something occurred to him. Something strange, considering she'd mentioned both her mother and Seth Penhaligon in previous conversations. "You haven't talked about your sister."

Robyn looked away, expression carefully blank. Had being a cop taught her to control her deeper emotions? Mac always hid his feelings when it mattered too. "Not a lot to talk about. Regan is a bit of a loose cannon. We were close when we were kids ... not so much now." She raised that arrogant, stubborn chin of hers. "I let her get on with her life, and she leaves me to get on with mine."

Lachlan could relate and surprised himself by admitting, "I have one of those."

"Oh?"

"Arran. My youngest brother. He's second youngest after Arrochar."

"I knew that, actually. He's thirty-four, right?"

"Yes?" His tone was questioning. How did she know that?

Robyn met him stony stare for stony stare. "My father works for your family. I did my research."

Fair enough.

"Didn't find out much on Arran, though."

"There's not a lot to find. He took off years ago. Drops me an email now and then to let me know he's okay. Stops by for Christmas every second year or so and leaves just as quickly." Because Lachlan couldn't help but lecture him about what he was doing with his life. His youngest brother was a hellion at school and a petty criminal as a teen. Lachlan had used his contacts to get Arran out of trouble more times than he could count, and after one explosive argument, Arran had left his family behind. Lachlan lived daily with the fear he'd receive a call that Arran was either in prison or dead.

While he was close to Arrochar, Thane, and his niece and nephew, Eilidh and Lewis, there was no denying Lachlan had failed Brodan and Arran. He just didn't know how to bring them back into the fold without pushing them further away.

"Hey, you okay?" Robyn took a step toward him, her perfume lingering between them.

Lachlan retreated physically and emotionally. "I'm fine," he clipped. "But I can't stick around being interrogated by you all day, Ms. Penhaligon. I'm here to collect Mac."

A coolness leaked into her expression. "Yeah, about that … that's why I'm here. There's no need for *you* to be here."

Indignation fired his blood. "I'm Mac's oldest friend. Who else would be here?"

"Uh … I don't know. His *daughter*?"

"A familial label has to be earned, in my opinion."

She cut him a dark look as she pushed past. "No one asked your opinion."

He hurried after her. "My vehicle is bigger than yours. It will be more comfortable for him."

"My car is comfy enough. And my company is far superior. I'm not leaving him stuck in a car with you for an hour."

"Some people would pay good money to be in my company."

"I don't need to know how you paid for college."

It took him a moment to understand the gibe. He growled at her back as she pushed into Mac's private room.

"Inferring I was a whore. How mature."

He was vaguely aware of Mac dressed and sitting on the bed, eyebrows raised to his hairline at their entrance. But

Lachlan's attention was captured by Robyn. Laughter danced on her lips, but her eyes filled with anger. "You just handed it to me."

He seethed. Why was she so bloody aggravating? "Mac is coming with me."

"With me." Her hands flew to her hips, drawing his gaze there.

"You'll take him back to his cottage."

"That's where he wants to go."

"I don't bloody care what he wants."

"Of course you don't, Mr. I Have to Control Everyone and the Universe."

He bared his teeth. "Who will look after him if he goes back to the cottage, alone?"

Her mouth slammed shut, her lips pouting lushly.

Lachlan's hands curled into fists at his sides.

Robyn turned to face Mac. "Who *is* going to look after you?"

Mac glanced between them, and something in his searching expression made Lachlan uncomfortable. "I'll be fine."

"No." Robyn shook her head. "You won't. The doc says you need to rest for a few weeks. Gentle exercise only. You'll need taking care of. I could do it."

Hearing the uncertainty in her voice, Lachlan stepped toward Mac. "No, if Mac will be reasonable, he'll see that the best idea is to stay at the castle where staff and his security team can look after him."

"Staff? No." Robyn bit her lip, brows furrowed in thought. Finally, she said, "Family should take care of him."

Something softened in Lachlan. "You can visit as often as you please, Ms. Penhaligon. But the staff at Ardnoch *are* Mac's family."

Just like that, her expressive face closed down. She again

139

donned what Lachlan had come to think of as her cop face. "Fine."

"Not fine." Mac glared at Lachlan. "I told you, I'll be okay."

Exasperation exploded out of Lachlan. "Mac, for fuck's sake, give me one less thing to worry about, please."

Mac glowered. Silence filled the hospital room.

And then, "Fine. I'll stay at the castle," Mac grumbled under his breath. "Jesus Christ."

"I'm going to find the nurse and see when we can get out of here." Robyn cut him a dark look. "Try not to yell at my still-injured father while I'm gone."

He rolled his eyes, throwing his hands in the air as he turned away from the irritating father and daughter.

Not long later, Mac bristled as the nurse forced him into a wheelchair that barely fit his large physique.

"Is it necessary?" Lachlan asked the nurse, knowing he'd feel just as mortified being wheeled out of the hospital like an invalid.

"It's policy." The nurse remained unmoved.

He flashed her the smile that had gotten him laid many a time. "Can you not let it go, just this once?"

The nurse smirked. "Not even for you."

"Let's just go." Robyn took hold of the wheelchair handles.

"I'll do it." Lachlan tried to brush her aside.

"I'm already here. Hey, get off. My God, you are unbelievably controlling." She pushed Mac toward the exit.

Lachlan wanted to throttle her. "It's not about being in control. I thought your father might appreciate me wheeling him instead of his bloody daughter."

"Mac is fine."

"And I'm controlling? I've never met a more aggravating ballbuster in my life."

"Ugh, men like you always call women like me ballbusters. Just because I don't melt in a puddle at your feet every time you flash that stupid-ass grin doesn't mean I'm a control freak or a ballbuster."

"Men like me?"

"Afraid of strong women."

"I'm not afraid of strong women, Ms. Penhaligon. In fact, I rather enjoy fucking them. A strong woman isn't afraid to let a man be a *man*."

Her cheeks flushed. "Men. You always make it about sex."

"I meant in life. You mentioned something a while ago about me unshriveling my balls. Perhaps if you didn't make men feel small, and treat them like they were unintelligent and useless, you wouldn't make their balls want to climb inside themselves. Maybe then you wouldn't be almost thirty and still single."

It was a low blow. And a sexist one at that.

He knew it.

But she frustrated him in a way he couldn't remember any woman ever doing.

"Lachlan." Mac's voice cut through the air like a whip.

Robyn had rolled him to a stop at Lachlan's Range Rover.

Fuck.

He'd forgotten his friend.

Mac scowled up at him in warning.

Robyn refused to make eye contact with Lachlan.

Double fuck.

So much for avoiding her these last few days so he wouldn't say something shitty that might get back to Mac.

He'd said it right in front of him.

A terrible silence fell among them as Mac eased out of the chair and into the passenger seat of Lachlan's SUV, his hand pressed to his stomach as if to hold himself together.

"I'll see you at the estate," Robyn said softly to her father.

Mac gave her a tender smile. "Okay, wee birdie. See you

soon."

Something devastating flashed in her eyes at Mac's pet name. She covered it quickly with a tight smile, and Lachlan closed the passenger door.

He followed Robyn around the hood of the car as she wheeled the chair toward the hospital to return it. An apology caught in the back of his throat as he stared at her back.

Then she halted, leaving the chair to stomp back to him.

Anticipation thrummed through him at the stubborn tilt of her chin.

"Not that I have to explain myself, but I'm single because *I* want to be single." She drew her eyes down his body and back up again in disgust. "It's just downright low of you to turn whatever bullshit this is between us into what you just did. I don't need you to think a certain way about me. In fact, you've made it pretty clear how little you think of me. I don't care." She shook her head, her fierceness electrifying the air between them. "I am epic, and if a guy plays his cards right, I know how to make him feel like a goddamn *king* ..."

She straightened, casting him one last disdainful look. "So don't you think for one second your opinion has any effect on my self-esteem."

Lachlan was stunned silent.

Not just because of her words.

But because of how they made him feel in places he had no right feeling with regard to Robyn Penhaligon.

As he watched her stride away pushing the wheelchair, tight ass swaying with her swagger, he cursed under his breath.

It took him a minute to gather himself before he could turn back to the Range Rover and get in. Avoiding Mac's eyes, he started the engine and swung the car out of the parking space.

More awkward silence hung between them.

"You do let her get to you, don't you," Mac broke in, sounding half amused, half unimpressed by Lachlan's lack of self-control.

"I can't help it." His hands squeezed the wheel. "She's irritating. No offense."

He could feel Mac's penetrating, relentless stare.

"What?" he snapped, throwing the man an aggravated look before returning his focus to the road.

"Nothing."

"Not nothing. You're thinking something."

Mac sighed. "The two of you remind me of me and Donna Ferguson in the playground when we were eight years old."

"Excuse me?"

"I'd pull her pigtails to get her attention. She'd trip me when I was running past her."

"I'm still not getting it." It was a lie. Lachlan knew exactly what Mac was getting at. His stomach churned at the thought.

"Let me be clearer," Mac said, his voice hardening. "I have no right to interfere in Robyn's life ... but be careful, Lachlan. Be very careful."

Tension tightened his shoulders, and he threw Mac another look.

His friend wore a taut expression of warning.

Lachlan expelled another exasperated breath. "Oh bloody Nora, Mac, you know you have nothing to worry about on that account."

Mac's answer was a disbelieving grunt.

The silence fell between them again, tense and uneasy.

Damn the woman, Lachlan thought hotly. He wished she'd never shown her face at Ardnoch.

13

ROBYN

*C*all your sister.

I stared down at the message in the email app on my phone.

It was from my mom.

I'd expected another call after I hung up on her yesterday in the hospital. This short, to-the-point email instead was unexpected.

And somehow worse than an angry rant.

It practically dripped with the disdain of disappointment.

Guilt kept me company all day and night. And worry. Mom wouldn't tell me what was going on, only that Regan was home and acting shady. As much as I'd hounded her for details, Mom wouldn't give them to me, and she'd shut Seth up so he couldn't either. It was Mom's way of making me imagine all kinds of shitty things so I would step up and help. As much as I tried not to, and as much as I'd tried to break the chains of the role I'd been given in my sister's life, I found myself cursing under my breath and calling her.

It went straight to voicemail.

Hey, you've reached Regan. I'm otherwise engaged at the

moment, but leave a message after the beep and I'll get back to you if I feel like it.

Brat.

"Change your voicemail, you sound like a dick," I said after the beep. "And get back to me. If it's too pricey to call, email me. I mean it, Regan. I have Mom on my ass about whatever it is you're getting up to back home." I hung up angrily because I hated that she made me worry when she seemingly couldn't give a damn about me.

Shoving my phone in my ass pocket, I pushed into Morag's trying to shake off the guilt I shouldn't feel. Why did parents have the ability to do that? For some reason, it had fallen to me to be Regan's guide, guardian, protector, or whatever. She'd always been a little wild and impulsive as a kid, and I'd been the only one able to temper her. My mom, in particular, had come to expect me to be the one who made Regan toe the line. And it was just crappy of Mom to withhold details of my sister's escapades to manipulate *me* into toeing the line.

Despite the four-year age difference, we'd never needed anyone else to be our best friend when we were kids. When I was fourteen and going out on my first date, it was ten-year-old Regan who sat in my room and talked about what I would wear. When Mom argued against me joining the force after college, Regan and Seth were the ones who supported the decision. Regan was there to pick up the pieces the first and only time I'd had my heart broken. I was nineteen, Josh was my college boyfriend, and while he promised he'd never cheated on me, he fell in love with a senior and dumped me.

At seventeen, Regan had a pregnancy scare when a test kit turned positive, and it was me who took her to the doctor. It was me who held her while she cried with relief when the doctor said she wasn't pregnant, and it was me who told the doctor to mind his own business when he tried to lecture my sister on "promiscuous behavior."

When our parents got into it with Regan about having no life direction after college, I was the one there supporting her and telling her she had plenty of time to figure out what she wanted to do with her future.

Always me and her against the world.

Until she took off with a group of friends she'd met online to backpack around Asia. That was around four weeks after I'd been shot.

My best friend.

Turned her back on me when I needed her most.

Kind of like Mac.

It made it hard to trust people when the ones you trusted most proved to be the most unreliable. It didn't mean I wasn't worried about Regan and what might be going on with her, but I was in the middle of a pretty big life situation myself. Instead of running after Regan, like Mom obviously wanted me to do, for once, I was putting myself first. Mom and Seth could deal with my sister. As for my abandonment issues, I refused to let it poison any possible friendships or relationships in the future.

Well, except with Lachlan.

The guy gave me whiplash. One minute I thought we'd attained a level of civility, and the next, he ignited an inner anger and fire that confused the heck out of me. Just the thought of my immature argument with him at the hospital in front of Mac was enough to make my cheeks hot.

"Robyn," Morag greeted with a warm smile, pulling me out of my mortifying memories of yesterday. Had I called myself epic in front of Lachlan?

So what? You are epic.

I nodded to myself.

You couldn't walk into dangerous situations like I had as

146

a cop without confidence in your abilities. There was a balance. If you thought you were invincible, you'd get hurt (though sometimes that happened, anyway), but if you struck just the right chords of self-assurance and self-belief, it made dealing with the worst parts of the job, and the worst kinds of people, possible.

"Hey, Morag."

"Same today?"

I'd visited every morning to buy a sandwich since that first day. "Yeah, please, times two, though."

"How's Mac?" she asked as she worked.

"At the castle, recuperating." I smirked as I remembered helping him get settled into a suite that was much bigger than even Lachlan's private rooms. "Frustrated with the idea of bed rest."

Morag chuckled. "Oh, I can imagine." Her gaze flickered over me. "I still can't believe Mac has a daughter your age. Gosh, he must have been so young."

I'd heard the same thing repeatedly over the last eight days, mostly from nurses at the hospital who clearly had whopping crushes on my father.

An image of him and Arrochar in his hospital room floated across my mind.

It was strange to me—surprising—but from an outsider's perspective?

Not so much.

I grimaced. The idea of my father dating a thirty-some-thing woman wasn't actually weird, but it was weird for me. Mac never brought women around when I was a kid, and I had no idea if he'd had any serious relationships over the past twenty-eight years.

I'd always held on to the fact that his age was a huge factor in him abandoning me ... but it was never clearer than it was now that I was grown up, thinking back on myself at sixteen, that Mac was a *kid* when Mom had me. An actual kid.

Look how scared Regan and I were when she had a pregnancy scare at seventeen.

But would you have taken off, left your kid?

No.

Then again, neither had Mac. Not at first.

That came later, when he was older. When I was a little older. No longer his "wee birdie," even though he'd started calling me that again.

And fuck, did it hurt every time he did.

A deep, aching tension pressed against my skull.

"I'm sorry, Robyn, I didn't mean to say anything out of turn."

Blinking in confusion at Morag, I realized by her expression and my sudden headache that I was practically scowling at her. "Oh. No. You didn't. Sorry ... I drifted. That was rude."

Her face cleared. "Not at all. Are you off to visit Mac?"

"Yeah, the other sandwich is for him."

"Oh, you should have said. Mac likes my roast beef and pickle sandwich the best."

Another reminder that I didn't even know what kind of sandwich my dad liked. "Then I'll take one of those instead."

"He always buys two. Big, strapping man like Mac." She tittered like a schoolgirl.

God, was there anyone who didn't have a crush on my father?

It is not Morag's fault I am estranged from Mac, I vehemently reminded myself as I gave her a tight smile and nodded for her to make two.

Morag's bell rang, and I glanced over my shoulder. McCulloch trudged toward us. I hadn't seen him in the shop since that first day. Then again, I hadn't been in this early on my other visits. But I was eager to get more of a measure of the man now that he was on my suspect list.

He had an intimidating presence, not just because of his size. It was the way his dark eyes zeroed in on me; his icy focus was surprising. I straightened as if I'd been smacked on the ass.

"Morning, Collum, I have yours here," Morag said, turning to retrieve his daily order.

His eyes remained on me.

I raised an eyebrow, refusing to be intimidated. "Good morning."

"You're Galbraith's daughter."

I didn't like his disparaging tone. In fact, I felt positively defensive. "I am." *Got a problem with that?*

The farmer grunted. "Never understood his alliance with the Adairs."

"Alliance? You mean friendship?"

"It isn't friendship when you're being paid, lass." He narrowed his eyes. "I always warned your father to watch his back, getting caught up with the likes of Lachlan Adair. I guess I should have warned him to watch his front."

That sounded suspiciously ominous and threatening.

"Collum." Morag, face taut with irritation, skirted the counter to hand him his sandwich.

He snapped it out of her hands and handed over the money. Then his dark eyes returned to me. "Lachlan Adair isn't worth protecting. Just like his old man, he's a thieving, money-grubbing bastard. Turned this village into a sideshow with his useless Hollywood followers. Anything that happens to him, he most likely brought on himself. I wouldn't get in the way of that if I were you, lass. Like I said, he's not worth making yourself or your father collateral damage."

"Collum!" Morag snapped.

But the farmer was already striding out of the shop.

My hands fisted at my sides so tightly, my nails bit into my skin.

"He didn't mean anything by that, Robyn. His issues with the Adairs go back a long way."

Yeah. They sure did. But that sounded a lot like a threat to me. Either he didn't see me as someone he needed to watch his words around, or he actually didn't care if he was a suspect. I knew from Mac that the police had interviewed McCulloch, and he'd staunchly denied having anything to do with the events at the estate.

If I were McCulloch and I wasn't behind the crimes but I wanted revenge on Lachlan, I'd leak the situation to the press, right?

But he hadn't.

Because he *was* behind the crimes, and that was a much more satisfying revenge?

If I found out Collum McCulloch had paid someone to attack my father …

"Oh, Robyn, I see what you're thinking," Morag said. "But Collum wouldn't hurt anyone."

Yeah?

We'd see about that.

* * *

THANKFULLY, it was Jock, and not Lachlan, who let me onto the estate and then escorted me to Mac's second-floor suite.

"How is he this morning?" I asked as we climbed the main staircase.

"Frustrated. Mac wasn't built for bed rest," Jock said with an amused twinkle in his eye.

I remembered what I was like on bed rest. "Yeah. I feel for him. But he has to stay put for now."

At my warning tone, Jock smiled. It was an incredibly

attractive grin that transformed him from ordinary to handsome. "Don't worry. Mr. Adair is pulling out all the stops to make sure Mac stays in bed and is taken care of."

"That's reassuring," I muttered.

The security guard chuckled as if he knew exactly how much his boss and I bothered each other. I realized Jock referred to my father by name while his other men called him Mr. Galbraith. It revealed a familiarity and friendship that perhaps the others didn't have with Mac. Curious, I asked, "How long have you worked here?"

"As long as Mac. I hadn't long joined Mr. Adair's private security team when he ..." His voice trailed off, his expression solemn for an instant before becoming neutral again. "When he decided to quit Hollywood and turn the estate into a members-only club."

"And he retained your services."

"Exactly. Mac and I have a rapport, which is essential as part of a team. It transferred to life here at Ardnoch."

"Still, there's a big difference between traveling around the world and being stuck in a tiny village in the north of Scotland."

"Aye, right enough. But I missed her. Scotland. I liked the idea of being able to do my job here."

"Are you from Ardnoch?" His accent sounded more like Mac's.

"No, no. I'm originally from Paisley. Near Glasgow."

"Wife? Kids?"

He eyed me. "Is this an interrogation?"

I gave a huff of embarrassed laughter. "No, actually. I was just curious. Guess I'm not so good at the small-talk thing. I didn't realize I sounded like a cop."

"Och, I'm just teasing." We stopped at double doors that required a key card. Mac was in one of the best suites in the castle, in the east wing, which had added security for privacy.

The card unlocked the doors, and Jock pushed one open, gesturing for me to go ahead.

"Thanks."

As we fell into step again, he said, "I have a wee boy, Adam, and a fiancé. William."

Lucky William. "I shouldn't have assumed 'wife.' Sorry."

"Don't worry about it," he assured me.

"Did you guys adopt?"

"No." We drew to a stop outside Mac's door.

"I'm being nosy. Again, I'm sorry."

"Not at all." Jock stood, his hands behind his back, stance wide. It was the alert-bodyguard pose that seemed to be his natural resting position. "When we moved to Ardnoch, I met my ex, Kayla, on a night out in Inverness. We dated, she got pregnant, she had Adam, we broke up ... and Will moved to Ardnoch. He's an artist. I fell in love with his work first." Jock shrugged with that lazy, gorgeous smile of his. "Then I couldn't deny how I felt about *him*."

He was being lighthearted with a woman he barely knew, and I understood. However, there was a slight shadow behind his happiness that made me wonder how hard the road to admitting he was gay had been for him, and why.

"Does your little boy stay with you?"

"Full time." Jock's eyes glittered with utter love. "He's amazing. Hilarious. I highly recommend procreation."

I laughed but didn't ask why he had Adam full time. None of my business. "Maybe one day." Who knew? I always imagined I'd have kids, but only if I was as madly in love with a guy the way Jaz loved Autry. Not everyone got to have that, though. In fact, as far as I could tell, lots of people settled for less than what they wanted, deserved, or needed.

Even my mom with Seth to an extent. While he'd been a wonderful stepfather, their relationship had been tumultuous over the years. As I grew older and put the pieces together, I often questioned if my mom lost a piece of her heart to a boy who'd seemed so much more like a man than he actually was. A boy who'd broken her heart in a different way from how he'd broken mine.

"It's good you're here." Jock surprised me. "I'm glad you're here for Mac."

Unexpected emotion prickled my eyes.

He was the first person since I'd arrived to say those words to me. Everyone else, except for Lucy, had regarded me with suspicion; their concern for Mac trumped the feelings of a strange woman, an outsider.

"Thank you, Jock."

"Thought someone should say it." There was a note of censure in his voice, and I liked to imagine it was aimed at Lachlan.

I beamed at my father's colleague as he knocked on Mac's door and waited for him to call us in.

Jock didn't follow me. Just nodded at me as he opened the door, and I gave him another smile in thanks. The door closed and I found myself standing in Mac's suite, offering a different smile to my father.

He was here and alive and safe.

A massive bed sat in the middle of the room and didn't even begin to take up space. Light spilled through an enormous bay window into the king-size room. Pale velvet curtains draped the window, and a light oak desk was situated beneath it.

There was a living area on a lowered level of the floor several steps down. More light spilled in from more windows on the same side as the bay window. A TV once sat in the living area, but Lachlan had a few guys come in and move the TV cabinet up into Mac's bedroom so it was directly opposite the bed.

The color palette was different in this room than in Lach-

Ian's. More feminine. But I could see why he'd put Mac in here. All the silvers and champagnes gave the room a much more tranquil, restful feel than the heavy, traditional reds and golds found elsewhere in the castle.

"Are you just going to stare at me?" Mac teased.

"You look well." I approached the bed, holding up the brown bag in my hands. "Roast beef and pickle sandwich from Morag's. Times two."

His expression brightened. "Hand it over, you darling girl."

I chuckled. "Should I call for refreshments?"

"Mini fridge." Mac pointed to the sideboard adjacent to his bed. "Inside the cupboard closest to me."

I pulled up an armchair next to his bed, kicked off my shoes, and propped up my legs. Once settled, we ate in companionable silence.

During our last real conversation, I'd confessed about the shooting and that I technically died on the operating table and had to be resuscitated.

While I still had a lot to learn about Mac, I knew he wasn't hiding his distress or anger that he hadn't been informed. He didn't voice his emotions, though. He'd just clamped his lips tight and seethed.

It seemed neither of us was very good at admitting how we really felt, even though it was pretty damn obvious.

Thankfully, Mac didn't seem to hold a grudge. I'd asked him not to share what I'd told him with anyone. It wasn't something I could easily talk about, and I didn't want someone like Lachlan, for instance, throwing it into conversation.

I swallowed the last of my sandwich and settled my hands on my stomach. "I ran into McCulloch at Morag's."

Mac raised a questioning eyebrow, so I relayed the icy conversation with the ill-tempered farmer.

"That's nothing. He's said similar to me and everyone who would listen for years."

"Well, I found it threatening."

My father scowled. "Then I'll be having words with the old bastard."

"No." I shook my head, lifting my legs off the bed to lean toward him. "I mean, the exact wording, the tone … it was very suspicious."

"McCulloch didn't stab me. The guy was at least five inches shorter than McCulloch. And younger."

"How can you tell he was younger?"

"The way he moved."

Understanding, I nodded, contemplating this. "Does McCulloch work alone? Or does he have farmhands? Grandsons? Anyone who might fit the description of your attacker?"

"I think he's estranged from his only grandson. He's worked his farm with Ross Inch for years, and Ross is closer to his age."

I sighed and sat back in my chair. "Now that the estate's security system is secure, the likelihood of another incident here is slim. And we have no concrete evidence from the other ones."

Mac snorted. "You want something else to happen?"

"No, of course not. But without another incident, there is no chance for this person to slip up, and our chances of finding them grow slimmer."

We contemplated each other in silence for a few seconds.

Then Mac asked, "Have you ever seen a stalker case before?"

"I was called out to a situation that turned into a case. Obviously, I wasn't on it, but I kept an interest in it. A Boston socialite, Erica Reeves. A stalker. Turned out it was a shop worker in her favorite boutique in Back Bay. Developed an obsession with her. Did all kinds of nasty shit. Took months before he slipped up and left evidence. Got a warrant to run his DNA. Forensics matched him to sperm deposits he'd left inside gifts for her. Was arrested, got a few months. Waited awhile after he was out … eventually attempted to kidnap her. Thankfully, her security team caught him, but what they found in his car …" I shuddered just thinking about what he'd planned to do to her.

My father nodded. "He waited. He bided his time. But his obsession didn't allow him to stop."

Understanding, I sighed. "This person will strike again. It might not be now or next week or even next month … but they're not going anywhere."

"No, they're not."

"You know what I don't get? You weren't any closer to finding out who it was than I am right now. So why attack you like that? It doesn't make sense. The level of anger and violence feels different from what we found around the estate. The incidents on the estate … I can't put my finger on it. It feels wrong to say feminine, but …"

Mac plumped the pillows behind him, sitting up straighter. "I understand what you mean. My attacker was male. And he might have worn contacts, but he was furious. I could feel his rage, and it was definitely directed at me."

Fear exploded through me at the thought of what might have happened if that knife had hit an organ. I lowered my eyes so Mac wouldn't see how disturbed I was.

"Right …" I blew out a breath to steady myself. "But the incidents here on the estate directed at Lachlan, while growing increasingly agitated and angry … the threat level is completely different."

Before Mac could respond, another loud knock sounded on the door before it swung open.

"Mac!" Two children exploded into the room, a boy and a

girl. Neither paid any attention to me as they headed straight for my father with concerning enthusiasm.

"Don't jump on Uncle Mac," Thane warned as he followed them into the room.

Thankfully, his booming voice stopped the kids in their tracks at the foot of Mac's bed.

"Och, they're fine." Mac leaned forward, gesturing to them. "Come see me. Up and up."

"Okay, but be careful." Arrochar burst through the door, running to catch up with the two kids I assumed were Thane's as they scrambled onto the bed. "Not near Uncle Mac's stomach." Arrochar reached to pull the girl back.

"She's fine, Arro," Mac chastised softly.

Arrochar glared at him. "I'll decide."

He chuckled, giving her a soft look before turning to the little girl. By the size of her chubby limbs, the cherubic face, huge blue eyes, and the mass of dark curls, she was probably only four or five years old.

The boy who kneeled at his sister's back also had a mass of thick curls, but he looked a little older. Perhaps six or seven.

As if he'd felt my stare, he turned and looked at me. Curiosity brightened his blue eyes. "Who are you?"

The little girl who giggled as my father tickled her went to fall into Mac as she turned to see who her brother was talking to. I lunged to stop her, but Arrochar beat me to it, pulling her off the bed and into her arms.

"I want Mac!" she cried, outraged.

Mac caught her foot in his hand and gave it a little wiggle. "Right here, Bonny Blue."

"Robyn."

I turned to Thane and found him watching me almost as closely as his son was. "Hey."

He gave me a small smile, and I realized for the first time

what a good-looking son of a bitch he was. While I'd seen plenty of Lachlan and Brodan because they were famous, I'd only seen *a* photo of Thane, Arran, and Arrochar Adair before coming here.

The brothers all shared the same coloring. While Brodan had more classical features than his brothers, they all had dark blond hair, blue eyes, and something boyishly wicked in their eyes that was undeniably attractive. Lachlan and Arran, despite the age difference, from what I could tell from photos, looked the most alike. Thane's eyes were slightly grayer than Lachlan's, his hair a bit longer, and he had a thick beard that was darker than his hair. While Lachlan had a short beard, it was neatly trimmed. Everything about him was put together, as if he were ready to be photographed by the paparazzi at any moment.

Thane had a very appealing unkemptness to his appearance, like he was too busy living his life to care what he looked like. I knew he was younger than Lachlan by two years, but he actually looked a little older. It might have been the attractive lines at the corners of his eyes, or it might have just been the air of responsibility that hung around him.

Maybe it was a single-dad thing.

Whatever it was, it looked good on him.

He raised an eyebrow at me, and I realized I was staring. "You all right?"

"Yeah. How are you?"

Thane sighed heavily. "Fine. The kids have been asking to see Mac all week." He turned to his son who sat at the foot of the bed, watching me closely. "Lewis, Eilidh, this is Mac's daughter Robyn." He looked at me again. "Robyn, these are my children, Lewis and Eilidh." He pronounced his daughter's name *A-Lay*.

"Nice to meet you," I said to the kids, unsure how to interact with them, to be honest.

"Mac's daughter?" Lewis frowned. His attention turned to Mac. "How can you have a daughter the same age as you?"

There was a choked, awkward silence.

Which I broke with a wince. "Well, that hurt."

Mac, Arrochar, and Thane burst out laughing. Through her chuckles, Arrochar allowed Eilidh back onto the bed beside Mac and said to me, "Oh, pay no attention, Robyn. You know kids have no concept of age. Everyone over the age of eighteen is ancient to them."

I nodded, but my ego was somewhat bruised. I half laughed, half grimaced at Thane who gave me an amused but apologetic look. "Do I really look his age?"

"Oi, watch it," Mac threw at me with a twinkle in his eyes before he turned to speak softly with Eilidh.

Something painful pierced my chest at the sight of their heads bent together.

"Of course not," Thane assured.

But I didn't care anymore.

I watched Mac with Eilidh and then Lewis who'd clambered up to his other side. They asked quiet questions about his injuries, and Mac made up a story about how he'd annoyed a wee fairy and she'd exacted her revenge. As he wove a whimsical story for them, it reminded me of the stories he'd told me.

How he'd come to see me every Saturday, and we'd spend the whole day together. How he'd spin the most magical fairy tales. How, as we both got older, I was allowed to stay entire weekends with him. How every second of those weekends, I had all his attention.

And for the first time in years, I allowed myself to remember how much I'd loved him, to the depths of my soul.

As much as I'd loved my mom, there was no one in the world like my dad.

Then one day … one day, he just wasn't there anymore.

He'd broken my heart in two.

Here he was now. As close to the Adairs as if they were family. These kids called him Uncle Mac. They knew him in ways I no longer did. They loved him and were clearly adored by him.

At once, it was like the air had been sucked from the room. My face prickled, and the room swayed. I needed air. I needed gone from here. Moving swiftly, I brushed past Thane and hurried out, vaguely aware of Mac calling my name.

Hurrying out into the hall, I tried to gulp air but couldn't. The walls seemed to close in on me, the carpet moving as I rushed toward the double doors. Bursting out of them, Lachlan was suddenly there, cursing and jumping back so as not to get hit in the face.

The stairs wavered beyond him.

"Robyn?" His voice was muffled in my ears as I shoved him out of my way.

He wrapped a hand around my wrist. "Robyn, what's wrong?"

I wrenched out of his hold, hurrying down the staircase.

Air. I just needed air.

"Robyn!"

By the time I made it out of the castle, I was about to pass out.

I tried to gulp oxygen, but it didn't help. I couldn't catch my breath. What the fuck was happening? Leaning against the brick exterior, my fingers clawed at the stone as I tried to breathe.

And then Lucy's voice was in my ear, gentle, reassuring. "It's just a panic attack, Robyn. Stop. Relax. You're okay." I felt her hand on my back. "Breathe in and then breathe out. Nice and slow. You're okay. Look at me, gorgeous." I turned my head to find Lucy at my side, eyes locked to mine. She gave me a kind smile. "That's it. Slowly." She took a deep breath in and let it out, and I began to mimic her.

Not long later, the world stopped spinning, and the prickling sensation left my face.

But I felt exhausted.

I slumped against the wall. "What the hell?"

"Adrenaline crash." She tucked a loose strand of hair behind my ear. "It can happen after a panic attack. You might feel exhausted for hours."

"Panic attack." I lowered my eyes, another memory returning. Me, fourteen years old, at school. Having a panic attack when the teacher asked me to read out a poem I'd written about Mac leaving. By that time, I'd seen him only once since I was twelve years old.

The initial panic attack was followed by a string of others, and the doctor told my mom it was probably just a mix of stress and teenage hormones. They abruptly stopped not long after, when Mac had shown up for Christmas that year and we'd spent four days together. I'd never thought of them again.

I'd never had one again.

Not even after the shooting.

Shit.

"Do you want to tell me what happened?" Lucy asked.

I sighed and pushed off the castle, nodding to my SUV. "Not here."

I wanted as far away from Mac and the Adairs as I could get.

14

ROBYN

he first thing I should have done was check in on Mac.

Instead, I told the security guy, Pete, who'd let me onto the estate the next morning, that I wanted to use the gym. Pete, whose British accent I couldn't quite place, had clearly been told I had the run of the estate because he offered no objection to me driving my SUV to the gym.

Lucy let it slip how much it cost to be a member at Ardnoch, and it made sense that Lachlan went all out with the facilities. The joining fee was £35,000, and members had to pay an annual fee of £7000 after that. He'd also sold several of the houses and lodges on the estate to members and rented out the others. Those staying in the castle paid for their rooms like they would in a hotel. The annual fee covered the exclusivity, privacy, security, food, drink, and all the facilities but not accommodation fees. There were a thousand members. The owner of Ardnoch Castle and Estate made millions every year but employed a lot of people to keep his members happy.

It still seemed ludicrous that someone would be willing to

spend what was a year's annual salary in joining fees, just to say they were a member of some elite club in the Scottish Highlands.

Lucy had seen the look on my face and admonished me. "You don't know what it's like being hounded constantly. To never have privacy. To always feel on display. Ardnoch offers a break from that, where we get to hang out with people who understand. And make no mistake, it's also the place where business is done, where movies and television shows get green-lighted and actors get a chance at the roles of a life-time. For those of us who have it, that £35K and the annual fee is a drop in the ocean for what it provides us over the long term. The waiting list to get into Ardnoch is in the thousands. And while many of those people do just want in so they can say they're a member, a lot of us are here because it makes us happy, and it's a sound business decision."

"I'm sorry," I apologized. "I didn't mean to judge."

Lucy shrugged. "It's hard for outsiders to understand."

Outsider.

Lucy hadn't meant any harm in using the word; in fact, she'd been nothing but sweet to me yesterday, escorting me around the village after my panic attack. We visited boutiques I hadn't had time to go into yet and introduced me to the owners who all seemed to be on a first-name basis with her. Janet from the tourist shop sold a weird mix of what Lucy called "tat"—cheap "Scottish"-related items, such as mugs, key rings, scarves, hats, magnets, shortbread, and this amazing sugary treat called tablet—and more expensive and exclusive items, like whisky locked in a glass cabinet and handcrafted jewelry.

We also visited the affable and funny Moira Siddiqui and her husband Suveer, confectioners and owners of Moira's Chocolate Box. And their chocolates were amazing! I bought a box for Mac and a box for myself and cursed Lucy for bringing me into the store because I was pretty sure I was addicted to the expensive treats.

Then we'd had lunch at a café tucked down one of the side streets and chatted for hours.

She hadn't pushed about what had spurred on the attack.

But that word ... outsider ... I guess that's what caused it.

Lachlan had called me an outsider, but watching Mac with Thane's kids, with them all, had shown me that's exactly what I was. And it reduced me to an insecure, unwanted teen. It chafed to have anyone make me feel that way again.

The fact that I'd embarrassed myself in front the Adairs was icing on the cake of mortifying myself in front of Mac. There was no way he wouldn't want to know what had prompted my melodramatic departure, and as it turned out, I still wasn't ready to confront him. I avoided him instead. It was so unlike me, and my failure grated.

I'd promised Lucy I'd be on the estate for our session with Eredine, but I showed up a little early because I'd remembered the boxing bags in the gym. Nothing sounded better than punching and kicking that bag as an outlet for the emotions I didn't know how to deal with.

When I arrived at the gym, it was still early, and I wasn't surprised to find there was only one other person there, a guy I couldn't quite make out was on a bench press at the back of the large, well-equipped room.

There were no trainers around. Lucy said members had to book appointments in advance if they wanted to meet with a trainer since they didn't work only on the estate. They had other clients elsewhere too.

I zeroed in on the boxing bags on the opposite side of the room and put my back to my sole companion.

Boxing gloves hung on a nearby hook, but I didn't need them. Instead I warmed up with some stretches and then grabbed the fingerless gel gloves I'd ordered, express delivery, after I'd seen the boxing equipment during my estate tour. Gordon said I could have anything I needed delivered to the Gloaming, so I'd collected the gloves last evening.

Perfect timing.

I strapped them on and moved into position.

Then I ripped into it.

The bag moved but only in increments—my punches came so fast, they contained it in a tight sway between each jab. Then I stepped back and did several sidekicks, pivoting my right hip and knee into the movement with full force. The bag swung with a satisfying drag on the chain holding it to the ceiling, and I had to reposition after each blow. I kicked with alternating legs, but the power in my right leg was far superior. When I kicked with the right, the bag yanked against the chain with harder satisfaction.

I imagined the bag was the fucker who knifed Mac.

Then I remembered yesterday.

The embarrassment of it.

Everyone knew I was messed up. They also probably were smart enough to guess it was because of Mac.

Mac.

"Hey, wee birdie."

"Right here, Bonny Blue."

"Uncle Mac, how did you get hurt?"

"Well, it was a wee fairy, you see ..."

"Dad, tell me a story about the fairies!"

"Another one, wee birdie? All right, let me see ... did I tell you the one about the faerie queen and the moment she heard a song by a musical wizard called David Bowie?"

"No, tell me that one, tell that one."

My own memories mingled with yesterday's scene with the Adair children and were a burn in my throat. I wanted them gone. I wanted this ridiculous childish hold on the past gone!

THUMP, THUMP, THUMP!

I launched it all into the bag with my fists until my body was damp, my hair sticking wherever it touched skin. Sweat trickled down my bare stomach and my biceps burned; my hands throbbed, and it propelled me. Stepping back, I spun and landed a rear hook kick on the bag, sending it rattling on its chain again.

Breathing heavily, I rested my hands on my hips and stared unseeing at the bag as I tried to catch my breath.

"I could watch you do that all day."

I jolted at the American-accented voice, having completely forgotten I wasn't alone.

Glancing over my shoulder, I started.

Sebastian Stone stood a few feet from me, wearing nothing but a pair of track pants. His T-shirt was tucked into the back of the pants so I could see every muscle of his slender but tightly ripped physique.

His words and the obvious come-on in his eyes annoyed the shit out of me. I hoped I was reading him wrong. "Excuse me?"

Stone took a couple more steps toward me so I faced him. He gave me what many women would consider a sexy-ass smirk as he lowered his eyes down my body and back up again. I wished I weren't wearing only a sports bra with my yoga pants. "You. Pounding the hell out of that boxing bag. You've got a lot of fight in you." He dragged his teeth over his bottom lip as his gaze zeroed in on my breasts. "An excess of energy."

Yeah, I definitely wasn't reading him wrong.

Feeling my skin crawl, I crossed my arms over my chest and radiated "back off" vibes. "Can I help you with something?"

He didn't read me. Instead he stepped into my personal space so I had to tilt my head back to hold his gaze. "You must be the guest of a member."

I looked over his shoulder to check the room.

We were still alone.

But my eyes snagged on the security cameras in the corner near the ceiling.

That made me relax slightly.

"Guest of the owner, then?" Sebastian reached out to tuck a loose strand behind my ear, and my arm snapped up, batting him away. His expression darkened even as he maintained that stupid smirk. "I'm just being friendly. You do know who I am, right?"

The urge to snort was real.

He was one of those. And he was seriously ruining his movies for me. He was so likable in them. Now he just came across as sleazy and like his fame entitled him to be in a stranger's personal space without permission. "Sebastian Stone. Could you step back, please?"

He raised an eyebrow. "You don't have to be intimidated by me. Are you an aspiring actress?"

"I'm not intimidated, and no." I motioned for him to move back.

To my growing disquiet, he took another step toward me, forcing me to retreat.

Shit.

"Really?" He contemplated me, a hard edge in his eyes. "You have the energy for acting. You've got something about you. I've seen you around the estate but didn't know quite who you belonged to."

"I belong to me." Asshole.

"Right. All women say that, but the truth is, you want to belong to a man. It turns you on to be owned."

"You did not just say that."

He grinned like a shark. "Protest. They all do. But I know the truth." He studied me with hot eyes. "You're very sexy in

167

a Lara Croft, Black Widow kinda way. Great mouth. Eyes. Tits are good too. Your nose is a little long but a nose job can fix that." The urge to smash his face in grew as he leaned in to whisper in my ear, "I have a lot of influence in the world, and I'm very happy to help out my *friends*." That's when I felt his tongue touch my neck.

I pushed him off, but he was solid and barely moved. "Back off," I warned.

His eyes flashed in disbelief, and suddenly I was pressed to the gym wall and had an angry, petulant, miscreant of an actor flush against me, caging me in. "Who the fuck do you think you are?"

"Someone who is about to do permanent damage to your dick if you don't get the hell away from me."

Stone laughed, but it didn't reach his eyes. "You don't get it." He was almost whispering. "In my world, if I see something I like, I take it. And there's not a lot you can do about it."

Fury rose in my gut. How many women had this slime cornered? How many had he assaulted?

Just because he could get away with it.

He reached for my breast and squeezed it hard.

I snapped.

Grabbing his wrist with both hands, I kneed him in the balls. Satisfied with his roar of pain, I took advantage as his legs gave way with the agony. Moving away from the wall, I took hold of his arm at the shoulder and wrist, straightened it, and twisted until it was close to dislocating.

Knees on the floor, Sebastian let out another yell of pain and glared up at me with absolute hatred in his eyes.

Something cold moved through me as we stared at each other. This guy cared about power. He got off on having it. To say he was displeased to be beaten by a woman was an understatement.

"Let me go, you fucking bitch!" he yelled, spittle flying.

I put pressure on his shoulder, twisting just enough to make him flinch with fear. "Oh, you don't want to be friends anymore?"

His eyes flew over my shoulder and his face reddened even further. "Adair, get this bitch off me!"

Glancing behind me, I found Lachlan striding toward us, his face a thundercloud. "What is going on?" he demanded.

Suddenly, I was aware of my racing heart.

I pushed Stone toward the floor, releasing him with force so his face nearly hit the ground. "Just teaching Mr. Stone here a lesson about how being a famous person doesn't entitle him to sexually assault any woman who strikes his fancy."

Lachlan was helping Stone to his feet but now gripped him by the jaw, bringing his face to his. Emotion swelled out of Lachlan, so palpable, it caused my stomach to roil.

He was angrier than I'd ever seen him, yet his words came out deceptively soft. "Did you accost a woman in my home, Stone?"

"She's fucking lying!" Stone flailed in Lachlan's grip, trying, and failing, to push away. "Get off me. The bitch is a whack job, and I'm suing you for letting her loose on your members!"

Adair pushed him away with such strength, Stone stumbled, tried to right himself, but still landed on his ass. As he struggled to his feet, vibrating with his rage, Lachlan took a menacing step toward him. "I have cameras in this gym, Sebastian. All I have to do is check them to verify Ms. Penhaligon's claim."

Stone's chest heaved, but the rest of his body tensed.

Adair didn't miss a beat. "That's what I thought ... you dirty piece of scum. Pack your bags and get the fuck off my estate. Consider your membership terminated."

My would-be attacker's face slackened with disbelief. He looked like a teenager whose parents had finally backed up threats with some consequences. "You can't do that."

"You signed a contract, and in that contract it clearly states that any untoward behavior in or outside the estate will lead to the immediate termination of your membership."

"For that nobody cunt?" Stone gestured to me.

An almost animalistic growl rumbled in the back of Adair's throat, and he lunged toward Stone before drawing himself up short. His hands clenched into fists at his sides. "Ms. Penhaligon, would you like me to call the police so you can press charges against Mr. Stone?"

Stone's lips quirked into an "I dare you" sneer. Because he knew.

I was trapped.

We had security footage to prove he'd accosted me, but there was no sound on that footage, and I knew enough from my experience as a cop to know how defense attorneys could twist anything to blame the victim. Especially those like the attorney Stone could afford. Furthermore, we were in the middle of our own investigation, and charges against Stone would bring tabloid press from all over the world to Ardnoch, which was the last thing we needed. And finally, did I want to see my face splashed across tabloids and feel the full weight of hatred from Stone's fanbase? Because that's what would happen. I would be victim-blamed because he was so loved.

He would get away with this and whatever else he wanted to do in the future because women like me didn't really have the power. I could beat the shit out of him, true, but I'd never win in a court of law. Or maybe I could. But that fight would drain the life out of me.

And I'd never hated anyone more for making me feel powerless. "No," I bit out.

Lachlan's voice was rough as he said, "If I hear even a whisper of you doing something like this again, Stone, I'll ruin you where it hurts. You might think you're a big man in this industry, but you're a bug, and I will take you out like that." He snapped his fingers.

Sensing the truth behind Adair's warning, Stone cut us both one last look of disgusted rage before he stormed out of the gym.

Adair pulled his cell from his ass pocket, tapped the screen, and held it up to his ear. "Jock, there's been an incident with Stone ..." Adair looked at me, his expression tightening. "Oh, you did. You were ... okay. Then you'll understand that Mr. Stone and his fiancée require an escort off the estate. Good." He hung up. "Security saw Stone accosting you on the cameras and were on their way. I just happened to get here first." His eyes drifted over my body, but it didn't feel like Stone's perusal. It was a concerned once-over. And unbelievably, I found I quite liked *him* looking at me.

Oh boy.

"Are you okay?"

Irritation with my awareness of him put me over the top. "I don't even know what happened!" I angrily removed my gloves. "One minute I was working out, and the next he's up in my space like he's God's gift to women, touching me, and threatening to take what he wanted." I threw my gloves at my bag, unable to look at Lachlan, hating that he'd seen me vulnerable again. "I'm not a stranger to a guy acting like he's entitled to me, but that happened on a date in an escalating situation. This ... was out of nowhere. I saw a lot of that shit in my line of work, cases where men attacked women they didn't know ... but actually experiencing it is surreal. That there are men like that who—"

Lachlan touched me, and I whipped around, almost clocking him as I tried to move away.

He raised his hands as if approaching a wild animal. "I'm sorry. I was just … I wanted to make sure you're okay."

Grabbing my bag off the floor, I hooked it over my shoulder and nodded. "I'm fine."

Adair studied my face as if trying to discern the truth. "Men like Stone are so used to women throwing themselves at them that they start to think sex is something they no longer have to ask for. That they can take it whenever they feel like it. I knew he was a bit of an ass, but I didn't realize he was one of those men until now …"

It wasn't Adair's fault. I said so. Then I huffed, "He's engaged to one of the most beautiful, talented women on the planet. What a dick."

"He sees Gabriella as a reflection of himself. A trophy. That's all she is to him. Fucker."

I studied him, detecting his genuine anger on Gabriella's behalf and remembered he'd had a thing with her. Evidence suggested Adair was a protector through and through. "I can't ever imagine you treating a woman like that, not even at the height of your career."

His lips twitched, something like surprise in his expression. "Why, Ms. Penhaligon, did you just say something nice to me?"

"Don't get used to it." I threw him a smirk and moved to walk around him.

Adair fell into step beside me. "Are you okay?" he repeated.

"It's not the first time a man has attacked me. I can take care of myself, Adair."

"Oh, I saw that."

Something in his tone drew my gaze. He was looking at

me with what I'd consider heat in his eyes, if he'd been any other man.

I shivered and looked away. "I'm late for Eredine and Lucy."

"I'll walk you."

"You don't have to."

"No, but I will."

As we stepped outside, the sight of my SUV drew me up short. I'd forgotten I'd driven it to the gym. Something insane like disappointment filled me. "I guess I can drive."

"Not to the studio, you can't." Adair reminded me that there was only a footpath to it. "Keys?" He held out his hand.

Perhaps it was because of what he'd just revealed of himself, but I handed them over.

"One of the men will drive it to the mews." He started walking again, and I moved to keep pace with his long-legged strides.

"I'm sorry," he blurted out.

"For what?"

Adair shot me a dark look. "For what just occurred in the gym. It should never have happened."

"You made certain it won't again. Not many people would have thrown him out, Adair, or offered to call the police." There was an honorable, principled side to him.

It was annoyingly attractive.

I felt his eyes on my face, but I couldn't look at him. Instead I kept my view on the castle as we walked up the road between it and the gym.

After a stretch of silence, he said, "Will you pop in to see Mac?"

"If I have time." I had to force my shoulders not to hunch around my ears.

"That's why I came to the gym. Jock told me you were

here, but you'd gone straight there. Mac is asking for you. He's worried ... after yesterday."

Hearing the question in his voice, I shook my head. "Well, I'm fine. Just wasn't feeling great. Needed some air."

He wrapped his hand around my upper arm and gently drew me to a stop. I reluctantly met his searching gaze. "You came here for Mac. Don't shut him out now that you're here."

I tugged on my arm, and Adair released it immediately. Agitated by him in more ways than I could count, I snapped, "Why don't you just stay out of my relationship with my father? Your interference has done enough over the years." With that unfair comment stinging the air between us, I stalked off, calling over my shoulder, "I can see myself to the studio."

This time, he didn't argue or follow me.

15

LACHLAN

*L*ight rays spilled across the wooden floor in Mac's suite, the first sign of sun for days in this part of the country.

Unfortunately, it didn't seem to make a difference to Mac's mood.

Like the weather, it, too, was foul.

"How much bloody longer do I have to stay in here?" he snarled.

Refusing to react to his friend's tone, Lachlan calmly took another sip of coffee as he sat on the edge of the desk at the bay window.

Mac's head whipped toward him. "Well?"

"You're not trapped in here," Lachlan reminded him. "We just went for a walk."

Mac scoffed. "Around this floor and the one below."

"Doctor says gentle exercise. You work your way up to more."

"I'm perfectly capable of more. I'm not a slight wee thing that can be blown over by a stiff wind. I'm strong and recovering well, and being cooped up in here with Rob—" He cut off, shoulders bowing.

He knew what Mac was about to say.

This wasn't just about being stuck in the castle for days on end. This was about Robyn.

Of course, Lachlan had told Mac what happened between her and Stone. He was always going to because he didn't keep secrets from his friend, but if he hadn't, the security team would have. The men had watched the footage of Robyn's takedown of Stone from the security cameras, and it was clear they were all impressed by her. Curious, Lachlan watched it. Jock showed him the footage running up to the event with Robyn beating the shit out of a boxing bag with a power and energy he had to admit was sexy as fuck.

But the part with Stone got his blood boiling again.

He hated seeing Stone approach Robyn as he had. Even though she'd handled it, Lachlan could tell it had shaken her up. By allowing that bastard on his estate, he'd inadvertently allowed that to happen to her. And now he couldn't help but worry Stone might have cornered female members of his staff in the past without his knowledge. Ones who might not have been able to fend him off.

After his warning to Stone, as Lachlan had known there would be, there was quiet on that front. However, thinking of the mistreatment his friends (of all genders) had faced at the hands of powerful men, Lachlan wasn't satisfied with merely ending Stone's membership.

He wanted to end the bastard's power, power he wielded over women. His sense of power came from his fame. A few whispered words in the right ear, and work might just start drying up for Sebastian Stone.

"What are you thinking so hard on?" Mac asked.

Shaking off thoughts of Stone, Lachlan considered his friend and decided to put what was pissing Mac off out there. "Just thinking you're acting like a grumpy shit because of Robyn."

Mac scowled. "She's not been to see me in days."

"She's not been on the estate in days." Lachlan frowned. Not since Stone.

"Lucy says it's because she's working. Driving around Sutherland, taking photos." Mac didn't sound convinced.

Lachlan wasn't entirely either. Although it could be true that she was out taking photos for her business. Arrochar found Robyn's photography site and Instagram account. She showed both to Mac. Lachlan, being a nosy bastard, looked too. To his shock, he discovered Robyn's work was exceptional. No wonder she had so many followers on her Instagram account. He thought of her as a cop, not just because she was investigating the stalker/attacker case but because of her manner. But there was no denying where her true talent lay.

Her shots were interesting city perspectives on Boston and New York. And lately, incredible scenic shots of Ardnoch and Sutherland. So beautiful, in fact, Lachlan considered commissioning work from her that he could display on the estate.

"Lucy's probably right."

"She's avoiding me." Mac ran an aggrieved hand through his hair. "I'm not a stupid man, Lachlan. She was fine one second and then the next, I'm Uncle Mac with Eilidh and Lewis, and Robyn can't get out of here fast enough."

His brows furrowed as he remembered the moment. Robyn looked so panicked, Lachlan had instinctively reached for her. When she'd eluded him, he'd chased after her, bumping into Lucy on the way. Lucy had gone after her in his stead, but it had surprised Lachlan how concerned he'd been for Robyn. Later, when he'd inquired about her to Lucy, his friend was closemouthed. She assured him, however, Mac's daughter was okay.

It didn't occur to him that what was wrong with Robyn was watching Mac interact with Lachlan's niece and nephew. Belatedly, he pieced together what Mac had perceptively already done. "She found it hard to see you being parental?"

Mac gave a slight lift of his chin in answer. Lachlan noted the way the muscle in his friend's jaw ticked. And ticked, ticked, ticked.

Sympathy moved through him as he stood from the desk to approach the bed. "Mac, you need to give her the letters."

"I don't want her to think her mother is to blame for this. I'm in the wrong too."

"I never said you weren't. But things might have gone differently if her mum hadn't made it so bloody hard for you." He thought of Robyn again, looking so young and alone that morning she'd run from Mac's suite, like savage ghosts of the past were chasing her. He found the idea of cocksure, tough Robyn Penhaligon so easily broken by Mac's behavior oddly disconcerting. While he still wanted to protect Mac, Lachlan knew it was in Robyn's best interests, too, to discover the truth. "Who got hurt the most in the end? Clearly Robyn. And she should know that losing you isn't just *on* you."

Mac's eyes narrowed as if he heard something in Lachlan's voice. "It is. I hurt Stacey." Mac referred to Robyn's mother. "And she hurt me back through Robyn."

"Only to hurt Robyn too."

"Well … it'll be up to me to tell Robyn. *If* I decide to tell her. She already hates one parent. She shouldn't have to hate two."

"She doesn't hate you, Mac." Her big, wounded eyes flashed in Lachlan's mind. "She wouldn't be here if she hated you. She wouldn't be gunning for the person who attacked you if she hated you."

Mac studied him closely. "You won't tell her. I mean it. There are things I will forgive you when it comes to Robyn..." He gave Lachlan a pointed look he pretended not to understand. "But telling her about her mother is not one of them."

"I wouldn't dream of interfering," Lachlan semi-lied, even as he crossed the room with that purpose in mind. He wouldn't tell Robyn about her mother, but he'd certainly give her a kick up the backside to come visit Mac and sort out their shit. "I'm going back to work. Arro should be here soon. Said she'd pop by to have lunch with you."

"I don't need to be babysat," Mac grumbled.

"Then I'll tell her not to bother."

"Well, I never said that. She's probably already on her way here. Would be silly to stop her now."

Lachlan hid a grin as he pulled open the bedroom door. "Enjoy lunch."

As for work, he technically hadn't lied about returning to it. He needed to ask Robyn about commissioning those photographs.

And if he happened to remind her while he was there that she had a duty to look after her father's well-being, then so be it.

***

ROBYN

"Isn't it still early there?" I held my phone up to my face so Autry and Jaz could see me in the dim light of the trailer.

We'd exchanged DMs on social media since my arrival in Scotland, but this was the first time we'd all had a chance to video chat. When I'd gotten Jaz's text a few minutes ago about the call, I'd been surprised but delighted. Once upon a time, these two people were my closest friends, but ever since I'd left the force, I'd felt them slipping away.

"It's nearly seven in the morning," Jaz replied and pulled back the phone so I could see her silk robe. "Still in my pj's."

"If that's what you call pj's," I teased. "Do I even want to know what's under there?"

"For my eyes only." Autry wrapped an arm around Jaz and pulled her back into his chest.

A twinge of jealousy moved through me.

How wonderful would it be to have what my friends had together?

"I miss you guys," I said honestly.

The last few days had been a test on my emotions. More than once, I'd considered packing up and going home. Yet, it wasn't in me to admit defeat. And I still wanted to find out who had attacked Mac.

"We miss you too." Jaz narrowed her gorgeous dark eyes. "Are you okay? You look tired, Robbie."

"Gee, thanks."

"I'm serious."

I glanced between Jaz's and Autry's concerned faces. "I haven't been telling the truth about what's going on here." I went on to explain what happened to Mac, what was happening at the estate, and that I didn't want Mom or Seth to know. While they weren't close to my parents, Autry might have occasion to see Seth now and then, considering my stepfather was a detective at our precinct.

"Shit, is your daddy okay?" Jaz asked.

I nodded. "He's strong. Recovering. Though I've avoided him this past week."

"Why?"

I then explained my meltdown after seeing him with Thane's kids.

Autry listened patiently, and I knew he was processing and would have an opinion on the matter, but it was Jaz who spoke first. "Robbie, you might as well come home if you're going to hide out in what looks like the most depressing trailer I have ever seen."

I chuckled. "You can barely see any of it."

"I can see some nasty-looking, poo-colored floral sofa situation going on, and that is enough."

I laughed harder. "Okay, the trailer is bad, but it's cheap rent."

"It's money you don't need to spend if you aren't going to face your dad and your problems."

As always, straight to the heart of the matter with blunt precision. It's kind of why I loved her.

"Am I right?" she asked her husband over his shoulder.

Autry gave her squeeze and said to me, "My shift starts in five, so I'll say this quickly: You did not travel three thousand miles to turn back at the first hurdle. You knew this would be tough, Robbie. But you've been through worse. I watched you go through worse. I'm here today because of the worse you've gone through. If you can survive that, you can survive anything. You don't want this hanging over your head for the rest of your life, wondering if you could've fixed things with your dad."

"Pretty much what I said but with more words," Jaz joked.

Autry took her teasing as he always did, killing her with kisses to her neck that were intimate in a way that was more than just physical. I lowered my eyes, offering them some privacy. Jaz, however, quickly shooed Autry off, with great reluctance, and I thanked my friend for his advice before he had to leave for his shift. I didn't miss the job, but I missed working by Autry's side day by day. I said so to Jaz once he'd left.

"Robbie, he misses you too. They got him working with that dumbass Colin Bolton."

"Oh God, Autry never said." Colin was one of those cops who got off on "the power" and strolled around the city streets like a puffed-up peacock making an ass out of the uniform. One of these days, I had no doubt he'd screw up so badly, he'd lose his job, but for now, I hated that Autry was stuck with him. "Is it permanent?"

"You know Autry. He'll only take shit for so long."

That would be a no, it wasn't permanent. Still. "I'm sorry."

"What for?"

"For leaving him in the lurch like that."

"You didn't." Jaz scowled at me. "You nearly died saving his life. Do you think a day goes by when we ever forget that? Because we don't. We want you to have everything you want in life. You deserve that, Robbie, after what you gave us that day. So, the job is not an issue. It's not why we barely see each other anymore. I say this with love ... but it goes both ways. Effort needs to come from both sides, and you can't say we haven't tried."

I felt my cheeks heat at her blunt admonishment. Maybe I had pushed Jaz and Autry away. "I'll do better."

"Good. Because Jada and Asia miss their Aunty Robbie, and I ... well, I just miss my friend."

"I'm here," I promised.

She smiled and then true to Jaz form, forgave by continuing on, "Did I tell you I'm up for promotion? Deputy managing editor for local news."

Jaz worked at the *Boston Sun*. She'd worked her way up to assistant managing editor of Projects, and now this. It didn't surprise me. "One day, editor in chief," I predicted.

She nodded. "Baby, you know it."

"I don't know how you do it—juggle the kids, Autry, the house, and a career."

"Not easily," she assured me. "Some things fall by the wayside, but I have to be an example to my girls of what is possible. Even if I only sleep three hours a night."

"I hope you're kidding and that you're sleeping more than that."

Jaz shrugged. "Gotta do what you gotta do, right? Tell me more about this club. You said in your texts that you're hanging out with Lucy Wainwright. That was a joke, right?"

I opened my mouth to respond, but the sound of a car kicking up gravel next to the trailer stopped me. "Wait a sec, Jaz." I pushed up off the floral couch she hated so much that turned into a guest bed and peered out the tiny kitchen window. The sight of a black Range Rover furrowed my brows. Lucy had left this morning after our run on the beach—

Lachlan Adair got out of the driver's side, scowling at the trailer.

"What on earth?" I muttered.

"What is it?"

I stared, dazed at my phone. "Jaz, I have to go. Someone is here."

"Yeah, okay. I better enjoy the Saturday quiet before the babies wake up."

"You do that. We'll talk soon." I hung up, irritated that I'd been forced to end our conversation.

What was Adair doing here?

A hard knock rattled the trailer door and I spun around, making sure I didn't have underwear or anything embarrassing lying around. Running my hands through my hair, I checked my body. It had been raining all week, adding to my depression, but the sun came out today, so I'd switched out my damp yoga pants and T-shirt from my run this morning for a fresh pair.

"Penhaligon, open up!" Adair yelled.

I yanked open the door. "What are—hey!" I cried out in annoyance as Lachlan pushed past me into the trailer. His huge form dwarfed the small living space, and he had to hunch his shoulders to stand up. He glanced around, eyes catching on my evidence board, before coming to rest on me.

Crossing my arms, I glared. "Come on in, why don'tcha."

He ignored my sarcasm. "Where the hell have you been?"

My spine tensed at his tone. "Wherever the hell I've wanted to be."

"Mac is recovering from knife wounds, and he hasn't seen you in a week."

The censure in his voice ignited that now-familiar anger where he was concerned. "Point?"

Adair's azure eyes flashed with emotion that mirrored my own. "My point is, go see your father."

Well, shit!

After my talk with Autry and Jaz, I had every intention of sucking it up and going to see Mac. But now it was going to look like I was only doing it because of this fiend!

"Why don't you mind your own business?" I seethed.

"Mac *is* my business," he growled, leaning into me.

Heat flushed the back of my neck. "Mac *and me*, however, is *our* business. Not yours. Does he know you're here?"

"No. But he does know Stone tried to assault you this week, he's restless as fuck, and he's worried about his daughter."

Dismay filled me. "Why would you tell him about Stone?"

"Because you're his daughter and he deserved to know."

"You are an interfering bell-end, do you know that?" Lucy had taught me British insults she'd learned from a fellow actor. Who better to practice them on than Lachlan?

His chest heaved as the air in the trailer turned thick and hot with his palpable anger. "Do you even know what that means?"

"I can guess."

"It's better than being an immature, selfish brat."

His words hurt. But I wouldn't let him have the satisfaction of knowing it. "Says the overbearing, egotistical man-child who has been gunning to get rid of me since I showed up. Now you're here, trying to bully me into visiting Mac. What is it you want, Adair? Me gone, or me here ... because your mixed signals are giving me a non-vehicular version of road rage!" I rarely yelled, even when I was mad, and he was making me yell! "I had every intention of going to see Mac on my time. Not yours! Mine! You can't manage me like you manage—"

Adair's mouth crushing down on mine abruptly cut me off.

I made a noise of shock in the back of my throat as I tried to process what was happening.

Strong, firm lips pressed to mine.

Beard tickling my face.

The smell of expensive cologne.

Heat. So much heat surrounding me.

The sound and feel of him breathing heavily into me.

Adair's hands wrapped tight around my biceps, the heels of my feet lifted from the ground. Pulled up into his kiss.

Adair was kissing me.

His lips moved against mine with a grunt of feeling, and that noise, on top of all my other senses, caused lust to pool low and deep between my legs. I gasped at the thrilling awareness that electrified my very nerve endings. Adair took advantage and licked his tongue against mine.

Aroused beyond thinking, I reached for him, feeling his beard prickly soft on my palms. Suddenly his arms were around me, hauling me against his hard body, his kiss turning wild and voracious.

We stumbled against the kitchen counter as he wove some kind of spell over me. I forgot everything but how good his body felt pressed to mine, how exciting and intensely sexual the stroke of his tongue against mine was, eliciting an answering throbbing in my breasts and between my legs. I'd never been kissed like this. While it tasted of anger and frustration, there was a savage desperation to it that turned me the heck on.

His lips finally left mine, and they stung with the release, swollen by his fervent kisses. My eyes flew open, a sense of reality on the verge of returning—

Until I felt his tongue on my neck.

Oh God.

I arched into him as he scored a fiery trail of kisses down my neck while one of his hands pushed beneath my shirt. My back bowed, envisioning him ripping the neckline of my shirt so he could cover my breasts in kisses too. I gasped at the thought, my fingers pushing into his hair to pull him down. "Lachlan," I panted, wanting him everywhere at once.

He tensed, freezing against the rise of my breasts.

Heart racing, I held still as that moment allowed reality to hit home.

Oh my God.

Adair exploded back from me.

There was no other word for it.

One minute he'd been sucking on my cleavage while caressing my stomach, and the next he was across the small space, standing at the trailer door, chest heaving.

Oh my God.

I'd just made out with Lachlan Adair. Like … *really, really* made out.

We glowered at each other like enemies on a battlefield.

"That shouldn't have happened," Adair bit out.

Rejection burned.

Refusing to let him see it, I lifted my chin. "You kissed me first."

It was childish. I knew it even as I said it.

His eyes narrowed. "You didn't exactly push me away."

"Call it a moment of deep insanity."

A muscle twitched in his jaw. "Visit your bloody father," he demanded and then spun and pushed out of the trailer, seemingly taking all the air with him.

I sucked in a breath, my hand resting against my racing heart.

My skin was on fire.

Dissatisfaction was a bitter sting. The bastard aroused me to inflammatory levels within seconds, and now my body was a tightly wound coil.

"Wanker," I bit out as I strode into the small bedroom at the back of the trailer.

Forced to take care of the tension by myself, I tried to block Adair out of my thoughts.

But I could still feel his hard kiss, his hot lips, his beard tickling my skin in a way that was surprisingly stimulating. I cried out in climax, the sound an empty echo around the small bedroom. As I tried to catch my breath, I felt strangely vulnerable.

Why him?

I didn't even like him.

"That shouldn't have happened."

Then why did it?

Squeezing my eyes closed, I tried not to think about the next time I'd see him.

16

LACHLAN

*A*rdnoch Castle and Estate ran like a well-oiled machine. The management team was beyond competent and dealt with the daily running of the place so that Lachlan had the freedom to put his energy elsewhere. Like securing famous musicians to play at the castle throughout the summer period and installing Michelin Star guest chefs for special weekend dining events.

That one bothered Arrochar's boyfriend somewhat. Guy Lewis had been an Australian culinary star working as a sous chef in a two-hatted restaurant in Melbourne when he and Lachlan met. Lachlan offered him more money than he could refuse, and he was one of the best investments Lachlan had made for Ardnoch in recent years. The members loved the food.

However, it was always smart to shake things up a little by bringing in chefs from the world's top fifty list to add some excitement. It pricked Guy's pride, but Lachlan was a businessman and couldn't afford to pander to a chef's ego. Especially one dating his little sister. Guy worked long hours and was obsessive about food. Lachlan didn't understand how he could possibly give Arrochar the attention and focus she deserved.

As a big brother, he was particularly protective of his youngest sibling. He constantly had to remind himself she was thirty-one years old and perfectly capable of handling her own life. But that didn't mean he had to like any of her boyfriends.

Mac flashed to his mind.

Guilt quickly followed the thought.

Fuck. He could still taste Robyn in his mouth.

Groaning, he sat back in his chair in his real office as he felt his body tighten with the memory of yesterday in her caravan. Seeing her in that run-down piece of shit of Gordon's had irritated him to no end, reminding him that as Mac's daughter, Lachlan should have offered Robyn a room or a cabin on the estate. Rent-free. Agitated at her living quarters, irritated with himself, and bothered constantly by her, he'd lost his goddamn mind.

There she'd been, yelling at him, and the only way he could think to stop her was to kiss her.

"Great plan," he muttered, throwing his pen across his desk.

She'd lit up under his hands.

He tasted her fire on his tongue and, goddamn, it ignited something inside him.

It made no sense.

She was Mac's daughter.

She'd given Lachlan nothing but hell since she'd arrived and treated him with disdain.

"Tell that to my dick."

The sound of bagpipes pierced the room, jolting him. "Jesus!" He glared over his shoulder, out the small window

189

where he could see the sway of Malcolm's dark green, black, red, and white kilt. He wore Sutherland tartan; they all did if an event called for traditional attire.

"Every time." Lachlan pushed back from the desk, needing distance from the pipes and a chance to clear his head. Wanting to escape the castle without bumping into any members, he took the side entrance off the staff quarters and walked toward the path that led to the beach. It was around a thirty-minute walk, past Loch Ardnoch and the second loch near the coast, Loch Evelyn, named after his great-great-grandmother.

He'd only just passed the footpath that forked toward Loch Ardnoch and Eredine's studio when he heard someone calling his name over the bagpipes. Trying not to be irritated by the interruption to his solitude, he stopped and turned.

Lucy, dressed in workout clothes, hurried toward him. "Hey, you!"

"Hi." He nodded toward the castle and raised his voice to be heard. "Not going in for afternoon tea?"

"Not today. Where are you going?"

"Just a walk down to the beach."

"Can I join you?"

Lachlan didn't want anyone to join him, but he'd never say that to Lucy. "Of course."

They fell into step together, the breeze particularly strong as they walked through nothing but rolling, wild fields that would eventually lead them to the water in the distance. As Malcolm ambled around the other side of the castle and he and Lucy moved farther away, the pipes became a distant wail.

"Are you okay?" his friend asked.

"Fine."

He could feel her eyes on his face. "Did something happen between you and Robyn?"

"Why would you ask that?" It seemed unlikely that Robyn would say anything about the kiss. Right? Though she and Lucy had grown close these last few weeks.

"Robyn is off today too. But it could be because she's gearing up to see Mac."

"She's here?" He glared. No one had told him Robyn was on the estate.

"Yeah. She's with Ery. She said she's going to see Mac after their session."

"About bloody time," he muttered, satisfied that his visit yesterday had yielded a result. Though, considering he'd gone there with the intention of commissioning photography from her and instead pissed her off, kissed the hell out of her, and pissed her off some more, it wasn't much of an accomplishment.

He'd never gotten off on needling a woman before in his life, but there was just something about her—

"You're scowling so hard, it's a wonder your face doesn't crack."

Lachlan turned that scowl on his friend.

Lucy just laughed. "What is going on with you?"

He considered confiding in her. If there was one person he could trust with his personal life, knowing it would go no further than her ears, it was Lucy. But what was the point? It was never going to happen again.

Lucy's laughter died. "Seriously, Lachlan. What is going on? You're wound so tight these days."

"I kissed Robyn," he blurted out, rubbing a self-conscious hand through his hair.

At her silence, he looked at her, and to his annoyance, Lucy was quite obviously struggling not to laugh.

"Oh, it's funny, is it?" he huffed.

Her reply was a long snort that turned into laughter. "Oh baby, what have you done?"

"It was an accident."

"What? You tripped into her mouth?"

"For Christ's sake, you know what I mean."

"No, actually, I don't."

"It shouldn't have happened."

"Why?"

Lachlan's answering glower was incredulous. "Have you met the woman?"

"Yes, and I happen to think she's almost as great as I am."

He sighed, ignoring her teasing. "She's Mac's daughter."

"True."

"She's immature."

"Ah, no, I quite rightly disagree. You just happen to provoke an immature side. And vice versa."

"I'm immature?"

"You two go at each other like kids at recess."

The comment was scarily similar to something Mac had said.

Fuck.

This whole time they'd been snipping and snarling at each other, attracted to one another and resenting the other for it.

"It makes no bloody sense." He picked up his stride, as if moving farther from the castle—and from Robyn—would somehow help.

Lucy hurried to keep up. "Why? Because she's not one of us?"

"Not that. You know me better than that."

"Then what's the problem?"

He stopped abruptly. "Luce, you know me. I'm never going to settle down with one woman. My family are the Adairs and you, Ery, and Mac. It's one thing to be attracted to a woman who drives me up the bloody wall, it's another that she also happens to be my best friend's daughter."

"It's still so weird Mac is old enough to have had Robyn," Lucy opined.

"It doesn't matter. She's Mac's. She's ten years younger than me. And I don't do serious. So she's off-limits. I just need to avoid her."

Lucy made a choking sound. "Are you saying that you can't control yourself around her?"

A memory of yesterday flashed before his eyes. He hadn't expected the electric sexual chemistry between them.

"I can control myself. It's just an itch."

His friend patted his shoulder. "Baby, you and I are the same. And I agree. It's just an itch. An infatuation heightened by the need to get laid."

"Leighanne," he murmured.

The thought of channeling his sexual frustration into Leighanne left him feeling beyond dissatisfied.

"You'd go all the way to Glasgow to get laid? That sounds like escaping to me. Does that mean … you honestly can't control yourself around Robyn?"

That almost sounded like a taunt.

He eyed Lucy, but her expression was neutral. No evidence of the goading he'd been sure he'd heard in her voice.

"I can control myself. I have never been unable to control an attraction to a woman in my life."

* * *

THE RAIN CAME on before he and Lucy could make it to the beach, so they turned back. By the time they neared Loch Ardnoch, it was lashing down. Lucy yelled that she'd see him later and dashed toward Eredine's studio. Lachlan hurried toward the castle. His white shirt was soaked through and water dripped off his beard and hair. He pushed the latter back off his face as he entered the side entrance near his office and froze in the doorway at the sight of Robyn leaning against the wall, trying to catch her breath.

Her gorgeous big eyes met his. They were a moss green today.

Strange, unpredictable, changing female.

As he closed the door behind him, the tension between them was thick, palpable.

Robyn pushed off the wall, her wet ponytail trailing over her bare shoulder.

Yesterday was bad enough ... the tight T-shirt and yoga pants showing off every curve of her strong but feminine body.

Today was worse.

A sports bra her breasts strained against. Her nipples were hard. From the cold rain ... or him? *Wishful thinking?*

Heat flushed through him, arousal heightening as a trail of water trickled down her toned stomach.

Lachlan's mouth felt dry. All his blood rushed south.

Damn her.

"I hope you don't mind I used this entrance," Robyn said, breaking the tense silence. "It was the closest point of shelter."

Rain moistened her lush lower lip.

Images of licking it off, of pushing her up against the wall and possessing every inch of her exploded through his mind, and he moved.

"Adair—" Robyn cut off as he grabbed her by the arm while roughly pulling his office key card from his back pocket. "Adair, what are—"

He hauled her into his office and used her body to close the door.

Chest heaving, desire for her fogging up every rational

thought in his head, Lachlan braced his hands on the door at either side of her head, caging her in. "I don't do relationships."

Robyn looked baffled. "O … kay."

"If we fuck, that's all it will ever be."

Understanding dawned.

Her face flushed as she glared up at him. "I think there's been a misunderstanding."

"Oh?" He leaned into her, letting her feel what she did to him.

Arousal flared in her eyes, and it was a wonder, with them both soaked to the skin, that steam didn't rise from their clothing in reaction to the heat they generated.

Then Robyn pushed at his chest with force, anger clouding whatever lust she felt, and Lachlan let himself stumble back with an aggravated curse under his breath.

"One, I don't need to know you don't do relationships. It might be hard for you to believe, Adair, but you're the last man I would want to be in a relationship with."

Pride pricked, he glared at her. He wasn't imagining things. This wasn't one-sided. "You want to fuck me as badly as I want to fuck you."

Her breathing grew a little shaky. "I can control myself. Better yet, I can find someone else to take the edge off. Anyone would be better than you."

The thought of her taking what he'd provoked and giving it to some other man snapped Lachlan's patience. He hooked a hand around her nape and hauled her against him, crushing his mouth over hers. *Tell me you don't feel this.*

Her hands went to his arms as if to push him, but instead her fingers curled around his biceps and she melted into him.

Satisfaction roared through Lachlan, and they stumbled against the door as the kiss gave way to unbridled lust.

The taste of her, the feel of her, her smell, her electricity … he couldn't remember the last time he'd wanted someone this much. As their tongues mimicked what their bodies needed to do, Lachlan thrust his hips against her, the heat of him throbbing at her core. Robyn gasped into his mouth, and he felt her arch into it, their bodies moving together until he was almost mad with the need to be naked.

To be inside her.

She sucked on his tongue, and he felt the last of the blood rush out of his brain. Grunting with want, his hands slipped down her slim back and beneath her yoga pants and underwear. The feel of her bare ass in his hands turned his kiss more desperate. He groaned into it, squeezing her firm, smooth cheeks and pulling her up against his erection.

Robyn gasped, breaking the kiss. "Lachlan."

He kissed down her throat, licking, teeth scraping skin, wanting to devour every goddamn inch of her. Trailing his lips across her chest, he felt a change in its texture, like raised skin, and the sensation pulled him out of his fog. Lifting his head, Lachlan stared down at her chest, near the wide strap of her sports bra, and saw something he'd missed before. Curious, he removed his hands from inside her pants to pull at her strap to see better.

"Adair!" Robyn grabbed at his wrist, but it was too late.

He'd seen the scar.

That looked suspiciously like a scar from a bullet wound.

His head whipped up as he glared at her in question.

Robyn flushed, this time not with arousal, and she shoved at him. "Get off me."

As he backed away slowly, drinking in the awesome sight of her trembling with unsatisfied desire—desire he'd be happy to sate if she'd let him—his eyes caught on something else he'd missed.

Another scar, not quite but almost hidden by the hem of the sports bra.

Jesus Christ.

She'd been shot.

Multiple times.

The thought was like ice water over his arousal.

"Does Mac know?" His voice was hoarse.

Instead of an answer, she threw him another dirty look and dashed out before he could stop her.

"Robyn!" He followed her into the hall and caught her by the waist.

She squirmed in his arms, full of fight that exhausted him now. "Let go of me."

Instead he kissed her again.

He kissed her hard and almost punishing, wanting to remind her how she'd felt only seconds ago, before he'd discovered her scars.

The reminder of the scars gentled him, his kiss softening, almost coaxing, and she kissed him back. Her supple body relaxed into him, giving way to this bloody madness between them. Lachlan wanted to know about the scars. But he wanted her like this more. Needful and wanting and hot magic in his searching hands.

They fell against the wall, this time his back to it, while Robyn pressed her whole body into his.

He gripped her ass, pulling her deeper against him.

"Dear God!" The squeak of surprise separated them with the impact of a clap of thunder.

Trying to catch his breath, Lachlan turned his head to the right. Standing frozen in the staff corridor was Agnes, his head housekeeper, and Sarah McCulloch.

Damn.

Robyn wriggled, and he realized belatedly she was trying

to escape his hold. He let her go so abruptly, she stumbled back. Lachlan reached to steady her, but she waved him off.

She wouldn't meet his eyes.

"I have to go see my father." She hurried from him before he could protest.

Once Robyn was out of sight, Lachlan became fully aware that he'd just been caught practically humping Mac's daughter.

Deciding to pretend nothing had happened, he strode toward his head housekeeper and McCulloch's granddaughter. "I got caught in the rain. I need to change."

"Of course, sir." Agnes grimaced. "I'm so sorry, sir, we didn't—"

He cut her off with a stern expression that warned her not to say anything else on the subject.

Then he swiftly made his way to his suite before any of the members could find him. The door slammed shut behind him as he marched into his room. Hands on hips, he stared unseeing out the window as the events of the last fifteen minutes filled his mind.

Robyn had been shot, and Mac might not know about it.

Goddamn it.

It wasn't the only thing Mac didn't know about.

Groaning, Lachlan slumped into his armchair, elbows to knees, head in his hands.

His attraction to Robyn was not within his control.

He could admit that.

But maybe if they both understood the rules, it wouldn't be a problem. They could fuck until they'd exhausted the attraction between them, and everything would eventually return to normal.

Mac didn't need to know.

Guilt stirred in Lachlan's gut.

He shouldn't touch her again.

It was the right thing to do.

The loyal thing to do.

And yet he couldn't get the damn taste of her off his tongue.

Worse ... he wanted more.

So much more.

17

ROBYN

hankfully, Mac seemed to accept that I was flustered from being caught in a torrential downpour and had no idea what just occurred between me and his boss/friend.

Since it had been over a week since I'd seen my father, it shouldn't have been a surprise to find him walking around his suite, but it was. He was recovering fast, which shouldn't have been a surprise either. He'd answered the door, taken one look at the state of me, and dug out an oversized T-shirt for me to change into. He'd then called housekeeping to collect my clothes to dry them as fast as possible; they'd brought tea too.

Since I was eight inches shorter than my father, his T-shirt almost hit my knees. I used his blow-dryer for my hair, and he insisted I tuck a throw across my lap. He then shoved a hot mug of tea into my hands. I wanted to tell him not to bother because my blood was still on fire from the hottest make-out session of my life.

Why Lachlan Adair?

I barely liked the man.

In fact, I wasn't even sure I *barely* liked him.

And now I was facing Mac, the tension thick between us, and I felt exhausted and overwhelmed by ... well, my freaking life.

Mac was settled in an armchair across from me, his feet on a stool. We stared silently at one another. Every lamp was switched on in the room to fight the gloom of the dark clouds over Ardnoch.

"It rains here a lot," I muttered inanely.

"Welcome to Scotland, sweetheart," Mac replied dryly.

"Do you miss LA?" It had been his semipermanent residence for years while Lachlan was making bank in Hollywood.

"Sometimes I miss the good weather. I don't miss LA."

"Do you get bored here?"

He shook his head. "No. I like the peace and quiet. And I travel during my annual leave for a change of pace."

"I haven't traveled much."

"No?"

"Regan and I always said we'd go backpacking together." I smirked unhappily. "She went with some friends instead. I had my job. I couldn't just take three months off." Maybe if I had, our relationship wouldn't be in tatters. I wouldn't have gotten shot. But then if I hadn't gotten shot, Regan wouldn't have had the chance to prove how selfish she is.

"How is Regan?"

Remembering how Mac used to be Uncle Mac to my little sister, I shrugged, my bitterness probably clear to hear and see. "I wouldn't know. She walked out of my life after the shooting. Like I said, took off backpacking. Mom called to say she's worried about her, but she won't tell me why, and Regan won't call me back."

Mac's eyes narrowed. "It's not up to you to chase her. Your sister is a grown woman."

"But that's what you do for family. You never give up on them, even if they give up on you."

Dismay filled Mac's expression. "Oh sweetheart ... I never once gave up on you."

This was it.

We were doing this.

Blood rushed in my ears. "Funny, it felt an awful lot like it."

Mac leaned forward in his chair, winced, and sat back.

Reminded of his wound, I said, "Maybe we shouldn't do this now."

"We're doing this. You came all the way here so we could do this. And I want you to say everything you came here to say. No matter how difficult it might be to hear."

Emotion clogged my throat. Where did I start? How did I do this? My mouth made up my mind for me. "I didn't see you for nearly a year after my twelfth birthday. And then you missed my thirteenth and my fourteenth before you showed up again."

"I know," he replied hoarsely, his guilt clear.

Tears filled my eyes. "I shouldn't care. I'm twenty-eight. I've lived my entire adult life without you, and I'm lucky because I genuinely like myself and who I am ... but after I got shot, I realized I'd never stopped wondering what it was about me that wasn't lovable to you."

"Oh, Robyn, no—"

"I didn't become a cop because of Seth. I thought I did. But when they told me my heart stopped in surgery, it hit me that I would've died for a job I only pursued to feel closer to a man who didn't even know I was on an operating table, fighting for my life."

Mac's eyes were bright, his devastation clear and confusing for me.

I gestured to him. "See ... I don't get it. I don't get how

you could leave me all those years if you feel something for me."

"I love you," he whispered harshly. "You are my daughter, and I have loved you from the moment the doctor put you in my arms as a wee bairn."

"Then where were you when I needed you!" It exploded out of me like I was a slow-burning stick of dynamite, much closer to detonating than I'd even realized. With the hurt and resentment came painful sobs I yelled through. "Where were you when my boyfriend assaulted me when I was fifteen? Where were you when Josh Horner broke my heart when I was twenty? Where were you when I graduated from the police academy? Where were you when I was shot three times in the chest? Where were you every time Mom gave me a hard time? Every time she made it clear I had to work my ass off to prove to her that I wasn't you? Where were you every moment I felt unbearably alone!"

My father cried, silently, his hand covering his mouth as my pain swelled inside the room.

I breathed hard, shocked not only by my lack of control but by the force of my anger. It had been buried so long, I hadn't even acknowledged how mammoth it was.

Like a dragon finally unleashed.

It was out there.

Breathing fire.

No taking it back.

"Mom never made me feel good enough. Don't get me wrong, she's told me she's proud of me in the past. But it always comes with a 'but.' I can always do better. And you leaving me just proved her right. No matter how many times Seth or Regan tried to tell me different, tried to love me enough for the both of you, I've spent my whole life fighting the feeling of being not good enough, not lovable enough. Because of you. And because of her. But you were worse,

Dad." The tears fell anew. "Because she has *always* made me work hard for her love, but when I was little, you didn't. I thought there was no one like you. You were my hero, and no kid could have loved you harder than I loved you."

He moved. Quickly. Was at my side, pulling me into his arms.

We shook against each other, my soft sobs, his wrecked breathing, and I tried to let him take my hurt, my pain, but I was afraid it was so much a part of me, I'd never be rid of it.

* * *

THE ROOM WAS QUIET. It was a different kind of silence from before. Less angry. But still tense.

Mac cried.

I'd never seen my dad cry before.

It was beyond disconcerting to see a big, tough guy like Mac weep.

I wanted to understand. I wanted to believe him when he said he loved me. More than I'd ever wanted to believe anyone who'd said it to me.

Worried about his injuries, I'd forced him to sit back in his armchair. I'd brought my chair closer to his, so it didn't feel like we had a massive stretch of space between us. We studied each other. I was probably a mess. I didn't care.

"Before I tell you this"—Mac broke the silence, making me a jolt a little—"you have to know that I take the blame too. I should have tried harder. I should have taken your mum to court and fought for my parental rights."

I stiffened, wondering where this was going. Lachlan's words about my mom flitted through my mind and made my pulse skitter.

Mac released a shaky exhale. "I was so sure that because of my job, I would never get joint custody. And I didn't want to quit my job as a bodyguard because I made the kind of money that not only paid child support but it paid for your college education."

I knew that. Mom hadn't kept that from me. But I had an awful feeling she'd kept something else.

"However," Mac said, leaning toward me, "I'm not going to lie to you, Robyn. You've had enough of that, and if I'd even thought for one second you felt the way you felt …" He shook his head, taking another shaky breath. He met my gaze directly. "I won't tell you I wasn't a scared-shitless kid when we had you. Or that I loved your mother. I didn't. I've always been a big guy. Even as a kid, I was bigger than all the other kids, grew up in a tough part of Glasgow, and I looked and acted older because of it. I won't go into the details, but I made a habit of going after older girls, older women. I was only fifteen when I met your mum."

"And you lied about your age."

He nodded. "I told her I was eighteen. She was nineteen. Not only did I lie to her about my age but I was an arrogant wee shit, and I admit, I assumed she felt how I felt. That it was just physical, and that she didn't mean it when she said she loved me—it was just something people said …" Mac's gaze intensified. "You have no idea how much you changed me. I had no one. My dad died of a heroin overdose when I was eight. I found him."

"Jesus." I hadn't known that about my grandfather. I didn't know much at all about my dad. More sadness seeped through me. "I'm so sorry."

"We were close. My mum took off just after I was born, so I didn't know her. But Dad couldn't shake his addiction, and it got worse over the years. He wanted to kick it. We tried to get him help, but drugs are a massive problem here. Anyway, the withdrawals were so bad, he couldn't stand it. When he died, his mum took me in, but she was already caring for my aunt and her two kids. We were crammed in a small high-rise flat, and I was left to my own devices. I fell in with the wrong crowd, and we did some not-very-nice things."

He lowered his eyes, but I'd caught the shadows in them. "Gran eventually stepped in, knowing I would eventually either end up in prison or dead. She contacted my uncle who'd moved to the States years ago. He had a garage in Boston, did all right for himself. He agreed to take me in but told me if I started any nonsense, I'd be out on my ear. Not long after arriving there, I got your mum pregnant.

"I knew as soon as she told me that I wouldn't run. I wouldn't do to my kid what my mum had done to me." He grimaced. "But I did it eventually, to my utter regret."

"Mac ..."

He shook his head. "Anyway, my uncle said I had to get my shit together, needed a goal, a proper career. He had a friend on the police force. Told me if I went to community college, worked for my GED, that I could eventually apply to the academy when I was twenty-one and he'd help me get in. So I worked in the garage for my uncle, and I studied part time. Then you were born." His eyes filled with a light that took my breath away. "For the first time in my life, I had purpose. You, Robyn. I have never loved anyone the way I love you. Those have never been easy words for me to say, except with you."

I remembered.

He used to tell me all the time he loved me.

Renewed tears slipped down my cheeks.

His sad eyes tracked them. "I tried to make things work with your mum, but we were just too different. And she never forgave me for lying about my age."

"*Did* she love you?"

"Aye, I eventually realized that she did. But she was also caustic and argumentative and controlling. I brought out the worst in her. And I … I was still so young. While I'd never been allowed to be a kid, looking back, I realize emotionally, I was. I was just a kid. Still, as scary as it was, I loved being your dad. But I wasn't ready to be a husband. Stacey and I didn't last long. We were only together for about a year after you were born, and then I got you every other weekend and alternating holidays."

"I remember."

"I met Seth a few years before I joined the police academy and introduced him to your mum and everything was better for a while. They got pregnant with Regan quite quickly, but Stacey was different. Happier." His features tightened as he looked over my shoulder, lost in his memories it seemed. "I'd been training in jiujitsu since I was eighteen, and I started RBSD during my time on the force. I was pretty good at the former—I don't know if you remember?"

I remembered. Dad was being modest. He'd won the US national championship in jiujitsu three years running and had wanted me to learn, but Mom was against it. Said I was too young. As for the RBSD training, I hadn't known about that. Reality-based self-defense was a style of martial arts originally developed by a soldier turned cop for close combat situations. I was sure it, Mac's police training, and his championship wins looked good on a résumé for someone in need of a bodyguard.

Mac continued, and I understood why he was telling me all this. "I realized I didn't want to be a cop, but I felt suited to protecting people. When a security position came up for a senator, I applied. I got it. From there, I worked as a bodyguard for a few wealthy clients. I was on a work trip in Los Angeles and quite by chance was introduced to Lachlan. His first big film was a huge hit, and his face was everywhere. He was looking for a permanent security team. At first, we were just two Scotsmen happy to be in the company of a fellow

Scotsman, but then we realized we got along well, and I accepted his offer to join his team."

Mac sighed again. "Robyn, I won't lie to you and say I left Boston just for the money. I loved my job, and I liked traveling. In the end, I was a selfish prick."

I didn't know what to say. Mostly because I didn't disagree.

"But I did try. I promise you, I tried." He reached for my hand, squeezing it tight. "Something happened between your mother and me, and … when I told her I was taking the job with Lachlan and that we'd need to figure out a new custody arrangement, she told me that she was still in love with me and she didn't want me to leave."

I think my jaw might have hit the floor. "When … I was … but I was twelve. Regan was eight. Mom and Seth had been married almost as long."

"It came out of nowhere for me."

"I can imagine." Jesus Christ. No wonder Seth and Mom had argued so much back then.

"I suspected she was just going through something and was fixated on the idea that whatever was making her unhappy was losing me. I didn't believe that was what was wrong with her, and I told her to stay with Seth who loved her. To talk to him. Figure things out. But your mum … och, I don't know, Robyn. I don't know if part of it was that she was a wee bit jealous of my new job, my new life …"

"And the way I hero-worshipped you," I added.

"Aye, maybe that too." He released my hand but only to slump back in his chair. He looked exhausted, and I was just about to open my mouth to suggest we leave it there and talk later when he continued. "She started making it impossible to see you. Anytime I had time off and could fly back to Boston, it wasn't the right time for her. When I asked if you could spend a few weeks in LA with me during the summer, she said no. It went on like that for a while, until you were about fourteen, I think, and out of the blue, she called and told me I needed to come to Boston, that you needed me, you missed me."

When I was fourteen?

Oh my God.

The panic attacks. The doctor's appointments.

She must have felt guilty for keeping him from me once she realized how badly his abandonment affected me.

I told Mac about the episodes at school.

Mac looked furious before he quickly cleared his expression. "Right. Well ... that makes sense. I don't know what happened after that, but ... that was the last time I saw you. Every time after that, your mum made it harder to see you. We'd argue on the phone until my ears almost bled. She threatened to take me to court, to take away my parental rights. Warned me that no court would grant custody to a man whose job meant he traveled at the drop of a hat. She wasn't wrong, Robyn." He glared. "And I'm a selfish bastard because in that moment, I should have just gone back to Boston."

"And let her bully you into it?" I knew how I'd have felt about that. My stubborn ass hated to be pushed into anything.

"Pride should not have come before my daughter."

There it was.

"Nor the love of a job."

"But it did."

"I wrote to you," he blurted out, expression almost desperate. "Real letters," he huffed with unamused laughter. "It was alien to me to do something like that, but I needed a connection with you, and she wouldn't even give me your email address."

"Couldn't you have hacked me or something?" I half-heartedly joked.

"I could have reached out to you without your mum's knowledge, yes. But I didn't want to do it that way, no matter how desperate I was. I didn't want you to know you were caught in a war between us."

Shocked, I shook my head. "I didn't get any letters."

"Your mother returned them unopened. I wrote until you were nineteen, and I sent you birthday and Christmas presents. And Regan too."

"We never got them." My hands curled into fists on my lap. Was this true?

"No, I know. I kept hoping Stacey would see I was sincere about wanting to see you and that she'd give the letters, the gifts, to you. She never did. But she'd return them with her own letters, updating me on your life. She sent me photographs, bits and pieces of work you'd done at school. Copies of your high school and graduation certificates, a photo of you at your graduation from the academy. The last photo she sent was four years ago, on your twenty-fourth birthday. You were in a bar somewhere, big, giant yellow cake in front of you, a guy covered in tattoos had his arms around you."

Oh my God. She *had* sent him photos. "Axel. My ex-boyfriend. He was a musician. We had a birthday dinner at my favorite Irish pub. The whole family. Regan too."

"I still have everything," Mac said. "My letters and your mother's. In my cottage. You can have them."

Something hot and furious built inside me. "Why didn't you tell me about them sooner?"

"Because I didn't want you to think I was using them to put the blame on Stacey. She and I are *both* at fault. I didn't even think I would tell you about them because I didn't want to harm your relationship with your mother, but that was before I knew your relationship with her isn't perfect."

"No relationship is perfect." I pushed up out of the chair, needing to walk, restless rage surging through me. "But this is worse than I imagined. She lied to me? I … I have to see the letters." I had to know if it was true.

Mac cautiously got out of his chair and crossed the room to the bedside table. He rummaged through its drawer, grabbed something, and then made his way back to me. He held out the key in his hand. "The key to my house. The letters, mine and your mum's, are in a box under my bed."

I stared at the key. It wouldn't be the first time I'd gone into his house without him. But searching under his bed? "Your privacy …"

"I've nothing to hide. Take it."

I did, the metal warm from Mac's hand.

We stared warily at one another.

Then he whispered, "I can't undo the damage I've done, as much as I wish I could. You have no idea how much I wish I could. My only excuse is that I truly believed you were better off without me. And I'm so sorry for how wrong I was."

I didn't think I had any tears left, but they slipped down my cheeks now. "I want to move on. I do. I just don't know how to let go of the past."

"Then read the letters. If, after that, you can't, I won't hold it against you, Robyn. No matter what you decide to do, I will love you. I will always love you, wee birdie."

18

ROBYN

$\mathcal{I}$t was still raining when I pulled away from Mac's cottage that night. Wearied, I drove ploddingly out of the village, my windshield wipers squeaking with every stroke. It was annoying. I'd have to get them fixed if I decided to stay longer.

I glanced down at the large container filled with letters and gifts I'd found exactly where Mac said I would. My staying would all depend on what I discovered in there. The fact that it existed made my head hurt. I'd come here to figure out my issues with Mac, not to create issues with my mom.

Focusing on the road that led to the outskirts of Ardnoch and my trailer, part of me wished I'd stayed in Mac's cozy, two-bedroom cottage. I hadn't wanted to stick around long because it felt weird and wrong to be in his house without him again. Last time when I'd retrieved his office key card, I'd just done a quick sweep of the place. This time, I studied it. While there was a definite masculine edge to the interior, it was comfortable and inviting. The front door led into the sitting room, with the staircase against the wall, directly opposite the entrance. A wood-burner sat in the corner of the living room, and Mac had dark, worn leather sofas, one pointed toward the fire, the other toward the huge television mounted in the middle of the wall. There were tartan cushions and throw blankets, footstools, and a battered wooden coffee table.

A doorway at the back of the room led into a small kitchen. It had been renovated and was übermodern, sleek white cabinets, white tile flooring, and a gray quartz countertop. A door off the kitchen led to a small downstairs bathroom.

Upstairs, I'd found a tidy guest bedroom and Mac's master. It wasn't massive, but it was cozy. There was an original fireplace that Mac clearly still used and a basket of firewood next to it. His bed took up most of the room to accommodate his size, and the frame was made of solid dark oak.

His bedding was a simple gray with a dark tartan blanket strewn across it. A small window looked down over Castle Street.

I could imagine his cottage with the fires on, how cozy a retreat it would be.

Instead of the dismal, cold trailer I was headed back to.

Realizing the trailer hadn't bothered me until now, I decided it was because I was in a weird mood. Today was exhausting. First with Lachlan and then the emotional drain of the confrontation with Mac.

And now those, I thought, glancing quickly at the letters.

Driving through the park, I noted the warm yellow lights glowing from a few trailers. Scottish spring weather hadn't chased people off.

Gordon's trailer was situated at the farthest end of the

park, a little away from its neighbors, with fantastic views of the water. That's how I'd gotten through the last week— sitting at the dining table, watching the waves lap at the shore. Still, there was something depressing about approaching the dark trailer that night. Pulling the SUV up beside it, I decided to open the trailer door first and then come back for Mac's large box.

The rain lashed angrily at me, and I could hear how rough the sea was, the sound of it rushing the beach, the waves crashing, the wind moaning like hovering ghosts. Shivering against the fierceness of it, I hurried up the little porch to the trailer and shoved my key in the lock—

I froze, instantly alert.

The door was already unlocked.

Maybe you left it unlocked.

No. I definitely hadn't.

I glanced over my shoulder, peering into the dark of the park.

There was nothing but shadows and long grass dancing frantically against the weather.

For the first time since I'd arrived in Scotland, I wished I could carry a firearm. Mac told me all handguns, pump-action rifles, and semiautomatics were illegal. Even most police officers didn't carry guns here. Mac and his team had special permits, but they didn't carry daily.

Without a weapon, I'd have to rely on my body as one.

I weighed what to do next. If someone was in the trailer, I could be walking into a trap.

The rain battered my skin, and I trembled against the cold. My gaze moved to the kitchen window. I could barely make out anything. Stalking quietly along the porch, I looked into the main window of the trailer that overlooked the beach. Eyes adjusting to the shadows inside, I could just make out the mess.

Someone had trashed it.

Anger flooded me, and I marched in, hitting the light switch at the door. Ignoring the mess, I grabbed the large kitchen knife out of the block by the sink and moved through the small space. There were only two places someone could hide: in the minuscule bathroom or the micro bedroom.

Heart racing, I pushed open the bathroom's rickety accordion door to find it empty. The bedroom was empty, too, except for my clothes dumped and scattered all over the bed. Just like Lachlan's in the first incident.

Knife by my side, I charged into the main trailer. The few cabinets in the kitchen had been opened and emptied onto the floor. Cereal, bread, pasta, scattered everywhere.

All the evidence pinned to my corkboard had been ripped up and thrown around the sofa and dining table.

I neared the board propped against the back wall.

Written across it in big black marker was a threat:

Kiss what's mine and I'll kill what's yours

THE ADRENALINE that had spiked through my body as soon as I realized the trailer was unlocked peaked, and even as I moved out onto the porch to check the trailer perimeter, I shook.

Soaked for the second time that day, I was cautious as I approached the SUV to retrieve Mac's box and my camera equipment. Once safely inside the trailer, I locked it and then rolled my suitcase out from where I'd stacked it in the tight bedroom wardrobe. I wedged it against the trailer door, along with the heavy plastic container I'd just collected from Mac's.

With the lights blazing inside, I felt marginally better. Yet my hands still trembled as I snapped photos of the mess and the threatening message. I thanked God I'd kept my camera equipment in the car and not the trailer.

Then I cleaned it up.

Except the threat.

It wouldn't come off.

I stared at it, thinking of Mac's knife attack, unable to deny I was rattled.

If I told Mac about this new incident, it was more than likely my dad would ask me to return home for my own safety. If I told Lachlan, he'd tell Mac.

As much as I hated it, and as much as it wasn't the smartest plan, my emotions won out.

I didn't want to leave Mac. Not now.

So I'd keep this to myself for the moment, but I'd find a way to make sure security was still tight around my dad. The threat could be directed at him. The thought made me pause. To protect Mac, I *would* have to tell him and Lachlan about this.

Something else occurred to me. What if I told him, and Mac was angry at me for kissing his best friend and boss? What if it caused problems between him and Lachlan?

Shit.

I narrowed my eyes on the black marker threat. This was a breakthrough in the case, though.

The stalker saw Lachlan and me kissing outside his office. Anyone on the security team might have seen us on camera ... but there was one person who saw us up close and personal.

I spun the corkboard around and recreated what was

destroyed. It took me awhile. When it was done, I wrote out the latest threat.

Then drew a big fat circle around Sarah McCulloch's name.

No more putting it off. It was time I had a little chat with the shy housekeeper.

19

LACHLAN

The sun glinted off the sea, somewhat lightening Lachlan's strange mood. The spectacular view across Ardnoch Estate toward Ardnoch Firth, the inlet that drained into the North Sea, was the reason he'd chosen the smaller apartments for his personal use.

Hands in his pockets, he contemplated his family's estate, and wondered (not for the first time) if creating the club had been the right route to preserve it. There was no question something had to be done. Estates of this size were a fortune to run, and he'd known if he didn't transform it into some kind of business, he'd end up having to sell it bit by bit. He'd already sold off Adair land to provide his siblings with some form of inheritance.

That land hadn't been their home, though. The thought of being the Adair who lost Ardnoch was unbearable.

Yet, even with its success, Lachlan admitted to a feeling of discontent. He'd put it down to the strange and dangerous stalker situation that had grown ominously quiet since the security system was no longer a liability. However, he'd been feeling this way before the stalker started messing with the lives of the people he cared about.

His phone abruptly rang, vibrating on the desk beside the window. Lachlan reached for it, relieved to see Brodan's name flashing across the screen. He answered, "It's about time."

His brother chuckled. "I thought I better call you before you drive my agent mad with your constant harassment."

"If you'd answer your bloody phone now and then, I wouldn't have to harass your agent."

"You're right. I'm sorry. It's been a busy time."

"Yes, brawling with club bouncers will certainly keep you busy."

Brodan huffed. "Lachlan—"

"What's going on with you?"

"Nothing's going on with me," Brodan answered tightly. "And don't speak to me like I'm a child. I got into a fight when I was drunk. Big deal."

"It is a big deal. One, you're thirty-five years old. Maybe, I don't know … grow the hell up?"

"I don't need this—"

"Two, you wanted to act, and you said you could handle the fame. It comes with the responsibility of maintaining this family's reputation when you're out there. That means not giving those tabloid vultures fodder."

His brother was deadly silent.

Lachlan sighed. "Brodan, you promised me when I got you into that life, it wouldn't change you."

"How has it changed me?" he snapped.

"You're never home. You don't call your family. You have no idea what is going on with them most of the time, and you're out there living it up as this drunken, wild party boy that wasn't you even when you were a boy."

"I'm not the only one who doesn't know what's going on with his family half the time."

Lachlan tensed. "And what does that mean?"

Brodan hesitated. Then, "Arran. At least I know where our brother is."

Wincing at the reminder that he'd failed his youngest brother, Lachlan leaned against the desk and bowed his head. "Is he okay?"

His middle brother's tone softened. "He's fine. He's in Thailand, working at a bar on the beach and having the time of his life."

Not sure Brodan was telling the truth, Lachlan didn't respond.

Brodan exhaled heavily. "I'm sorry I haven't been keeping in touch. I'll do better. As for the brawl, it was just me letting off steam. That role in Dick's movie was brutal, Lachlan. I had to go to some dark places."

While Lachlan had been typecast in action thrillers and romantic comedy action movies, Brodan was a far better actor than his big brother. He'd started out in those kinds of roles, too, but had broken out into dark, psychological work. The movie he referred to was one in which he played a serial killer. Although proud of Brodan, Lachlan wasn't sure he could watch a movie in which his wee brother played a psychopath. "Are you okay?"

"I'm fine, honest. It was just hard going. Partied a little too much after to let it go. This next movie is a rom-com. Script is a bit ridiculous, but it's fun. A nice change of pace."

Deciding his brother did sound better than the last time he'd spoken to him, Lachlan let it go. "Okay. As long as you're all right. Your family misses you, though. Take a break after this movie, eh? Come home for a bit."

"Yeah, yeah, definitely. I have to go. Director wants us back on set."

"Where are you, by the way—"

The line went dead.

Sighing, Lachlan tucked his phone into his pocket.

For a long time, he'd felt more of a parent than a brother, but his dad had convinced him to take the break that was offered to him in Hollywood. So Lachlan had gone, and a part of him was ashamed to admit that he'd enjoyed no longer bearing the responsibility of raising his siblings alongside a perpetually distracted father.

Then everything changed, and Lachlan was all they had.

It didn't matter if there were very few years between them. He was the oldest, and it was his natural role to step in as patriarch.

Family mattered more to Lachlan than he could ever say, and there was a selfish part of him that just wanted everyone at Ardnoch, living their lives together. But if he couldn't have that, then he wanted his family to be close despite physical distance.

Yet somehow, he seemed to have only pushed his two youngest brothers away.

Movement outside on the drive caught Lachlan's attention, pulling him from his worries. At the sight of Mac walking alone, Lachlan cursed and hurried out of his room to find his friend.

It took him less than two minutes to race to where Mac was strolling as if he hadn't a care in the goddamn world.

"You want to explain what you're doing?"

Mac's head whipped toward him.

Lachlan sucked in a breath.

His friend looked wrecked. Haggard and tired. And there was no hiding the turmoil roiling in his eyes.

"What happened?"

"Robyn. We talked."

Guilt stabbed at Lachlan. Yesterday, after he'd kissed

Robyn (something he was assiduously trying not to think about), Lachlan avoided his friend. He hadn't wanted Mac to take one look at him and somehow know.

How selfish. "Oh Jesus, Mac. Did it go that badly?"

Mac started to walk again, slow but steady, staring across the estate, watching members play golf in the distance.

Lachlan waited.

Finally, Mac turned to him, his anguish palpable. "It was everything I was afraid of and more."

"I'm sorry."

"I don't know if we can come back from it. I've hurt her beyond bearing." He glared at Lachlan fiercely. "Never do that, Lachlan. Never break the heart of someone you love. It'll hurt you more that it will ever hurt them. Whatever Robyn's feeling, I think I must feel it a million times worse. And that's only right. I deserve it."

"No one deserves that."

"You weren't there. You didn't watch your daughter—a confident, bright woman—crumble into a wee girl and sob her fucking heart out because you broke it." Tears glistened in Mac's eyes, making Lachlan feel doubly shit and awkward. The last time he'd seen Mac this upset was over a decade ago. That had been about Robyn too.

He patted his friend's shoulder and repeated, "I'm sorry."

He found he didn't at all like the thought of Robyn breaking down. Feeling terrible for them both, Lachlan admitted apologetically, "I don't know what else to say."

"Nothing to say," Mac assured him. "I explained my part, my blame, but I took your advice and told her about the letters. I gave her the key to my cottage so she could collect them."

"Good. That's good, Mac. She'll read those, and they'll bring her a bit of peace. I'm certain you'll be able to move on from this. Finally."

"Aye, we'll see. And if we do … well, how do I be a dad to a woman who is almost thirty? She doesn't need me anymore."

Mac hadn't described a woman who didn't need her father anymore. "I think we both know that's not true. Robyn acts tough, but you're obviously her Achilles' heel. She still needs you to protect her soft spot."

His friend stopped, turning his body toward Lachlan.

Lachlan followed suit so they faced one another.

Tension knit across his shoulders at the look in Mac's eyes.

"Do I need to protect her from you?" he asked.

Fuck.

Lachlan shifted uncomfortably. "Mac, come on."

"You think I don't know what you look like when you want a woman? I've been with you for nearly two decades."

"I can't talk to you about this."

"What? That you're attracted to my daughter?"

"When *you* say it, it makes me sound like a perverted old man. She's twenty-eight."

Tense silence fell between them, and Lachlan forced himself to maintain eye contact. He felt like a little boy caught stealing sweets out of his mum's chocolate cupboard. Except this was obviously much worse.

Finally, Mac sighed. "You can have anyone, Lachlan. I'm not going to tell you not to go there because I don't feel I have the right. But think carefully before you do it. Because if it goes south and you hurt her and she needs me and wants me to pick a side … I won't let her down this time. I will choose my daughter."

Understanding dawned, and it was cold. A shiver skated down Lachlan's neck despite the gentle warmth of the spring sun. He nodded. There was no way he would lose his friend over a woman. Lachlan was closer to Mac than he was to two of his siblings. An attraction wasn't worth losing him.

Lachlan pulled his phone out of his pocket and dialed security.

"What are you doing?" Mac scowled.

"You shouldn't be out here alone. Or did you forget you're recovering from a knife attack?"

His friend rolled his eyes but didn't argue as Lachlan asked Jock where Mac's chaperone was. There was supposed to be security outside Mac's room at all times, which he sternly reminded his employee.

Not too long later, it was Jock himself who came out to escort Mac.

"I feel like a bloody child," Mac grumbled.

No, just someone Lachlan would do anything to protect. Someone he wouldn't lose.

As he marched inside to return to work, he saw the leaflet for the village ceilidh someone had left on the coffee table in the main reception. The ceilidh was held at the Gloaming a few weeks after Easter to celebrate Ardnoch's anniversary. Although the town dated back a thousand years, it became a royal burgh in 1630. That was the date the villagers used to celebrate. This year they were celebrating its 391st anniversary as a royal burgh.

Lachlan stared down at the leaflet. He attended the ceilidh every year because it was his duty to represent Ardnoch Castle and the Adairs. Arrochar also attended, and Thane if he could get a babysitter. Even some of his members attended when they felt like it.

Thinking it a fine excuse for a distraction from a certain American, Lachlan pulled out his phone and dialed a number he hadn't thought he'd be dialing again anytime soon.

After four rings, she picked up. "Hello, stranger."

Lachlan smiled at the teasing tone of Leighanne's voice. Good. She wasn't pissed off with him, then. "How are you?"

"I'm well. Busy."

He frowned. "Too busy to visit Ardnoch?"

She hesitated. "Visit Ardnoch?"

"I don't know about you, but I could do with some stress relief this weekend."

She laughed. "I see."

"And there's a ceilidh here on Saturday. Why don't you come as my date? It's all good fun. Free food and booze and then great sex afterward."

"You are a cocky one," Leighanne said, chuckling. "I'm sold. What time do you want me there?"

* * *

ROBYN

EXHAUSTION WEIGHED MY LIMBS DOWN, but I got to Ardnoch without driving the SUV off the road. This time, I drove to the mews, and Fergus came out to greet me.

In no mood for small talk, I did my best because he was such a jolly, friendly guy. We'd only spoken a few times, but every single time meant I pushed him further down my suspect list. He seemed devoted to the Adairs, appreciative of his job, which he loved, and that put a great big dent in his possible motive.

Unlike someone else.

"You look tired," Fergus said, brows pinched. "You all right?"

"Fine. Just a long night in a trailer during a storm."

He winced sympathetically. "I lived in a caravan for a

while. It's not so nice during bad weather. You should find somewhere else to stay. Somewhere safer in storms. That is … if you're going to be here a while?"

I shrugged a non-answer, thanked him, and walked out of the mews and down the gravel drive. It hadn't been just the weather that kept me awake all night. I hated to admit it, but I was too unnerved to sleep. Keeping the lights blazing through the trailer to ward off anyone who thought they could get the jump on me, I'd sat at the dining table instead. And I pored over the contents of the box I'd retrieved from Mac's.

Once I started reading the letters, I couldn't have slept if I'd wanted to. Most of the letters were short updates on his life. He told me about the places he visited with Lachlan; he shared funny stories about famous people but changed their names so I wouldn't know who he was talking about. Just like when I was a little girl, I found myself charmed by his stories. A true Scotsman, my father was a born storyteller.

As I read the letters, I could hear his deep voice narrating in my head.

He'd asked questions about my life; some of them my mom answered in the letters she sent him. She was terse but reassuring in her words—she basically made the point over and over that I was fine without him.

A low anger simmered inside me.

One day it would boil over if I didn't confront my mom about the part she'd played in separating me from Mac.

But she wasn't completely to blame. Mac had said so and reading his letters I concluded he was right. My dad had a wonderful life with Lachlan, and if he'd wanted to, he could have fought harder for me. It would've meant sacrificing his career, and ultimately he hadn't chosen to do so. He hadn't chosen me.

While I wanted to believe he'd come to regret that over the years, the pain was still there. Still fresh.

Yet, I had something new I hadn't had before.

In his letters, I found truth in his love for me.

Mac did love me.

I believed that.

Now I just had to decide whether that meant I forgave him enough to move on.

First, however, I wanted to speak to Sarah McCulloch. And it wasn't a delay tactic so I could put off speaking to Mac.

Someone came after me last night. And I would not be terrorized by the Ardnoch stalker. I wanted this whole thing over. Whoever the man behind the mask, I was beginning to think he was a puppet, and I wanted to chat with the person I suspected might be pulling his strings.

My plan was to find Lachlan and ask him to bring Sarah to me. As I stepped inside the main reception of the castle, its owner stood over the coffee table situated between the two sofas in the center of the space. He was on the phone and looked up upon my entrance.

His expression was unclear. "I need to go ... yeah ... see you then." He hung up and turned toward me. "Robyn."

I tried and failed not to like the sound of him saying my name. I'd been Ms. Penhaligon for most of my stay, and it made me feel like my mother. Ignoring how effortlessly sexy he looked, and always looked, in his white shirt and black suit pants, I walked toward him. "We need to talk."

He glanced over his shoulder and then back at me. "Not here. My office."

Before I could speak another word, he marched away. I hurried to keep up with his long strides as I followed him out of reception and toward the back of the castle into the staff quarters. Part of me worried he'd pull what he pulled yesterday—haul me into his office to have his wicked way.

This time I would need a little willpower because I was on a mission.

As soon as his door closed behind us, however, he turned to face me. He leaned against his desk and crossed his arms over his chest. "I'd like to say something first."

I mirrored him, crossing my arms. "Okay?"

He gave me an expression that I would come to picture in the future when I was at a boxing bag. Pitying and patronizing. "What happened between us won't happen again. Call it a moment of madness. Two moments of madness. But they're over. I kissed you against my better sense, and I won't jeopardize my friendship with Mac over ..." He gestured to me.

Over someone like me.

The rejection hurt. No lie. Rejection always stung. But there was no way I'd let him see it.

I rolled my eyes and dropped my arms to my sides. "Adair, as impossible as this may seem to you, I didn't come here to talk about you attacking me with your mouth. Twice."

He opened said mouth to argue, but I cut him off.

"I have more important things on my mind than you. In fact, I've already forgotten our not-memorable moments together." I savagely enjoyed the flash of anger in his eyes. "I'm here because I need you to bring Sarah McCulloch to me. It's past time I interviewed her about the stalker."

Scowling, he pushed up off the desk and took a few steps toward me.

I didn't retreat because it felt like he wanted me to.

"Sarah has been interviewed by the police and by Mac."

"She hasn't been interviewed by me."

"Why the sudden need?"

Lying about the threat that was left in my trailer went against my nature, but I couldn't trust him not to tell Mac. And I didn't want Mac to know for several reasons. "I've hit a wall with the evidence. I just want to make sure I haven't missed anything."

Lachlan studied me carefully. As if he didn't quite believe me. I held his gaze and tried to ignore the awareness that tingled across my skin. I could still feel the tickle of his beard, his hot mouth, his electric touch.

To my chagrin, I found myself unconsciously taking a step back.

Lachlan's eyes flickered down to my feet and back up again. Then he stepped away, creating more space between us.

I almost exhaled loudly in relief but managed to check it.

"Fine. I'll call Sarah in here."

"I want to talk to her alone."

He gave me a tight nod. "Then you may use my office."

"Very generous of you."

Lachlan threw me an unamused look but called house-keeping. It didn't take long to track Sarah, and together we waited in silence for her arrival.

We were locked in a staring contest that would probably be funny to an outsider, but not to me. My trailer got trashed because of this tosser (another British insult I wasn't quite sure I knew the meaning of, but I liked the sound of it), and my family was threatened, all because he couldn't keep his hands to himself. And yes, I kissed him back, but I wasn't the one who had insinuated he wasn't worth the hassle.

Though I certainly thought it now!

Suddenly his cool gaze dipped down my body and back up again, and his nostrils flared before he looked away.

Guess I won the contest.

Not that it felt like a triumph.

Some women might get off on a guy being attracted to her against his "better sense," but I found it insulting that anyone would think being attracted to me was a bad thing. I wasn't a big reader, but we'd read *Pride and Prejudice* in school, and it was one of the few books I reread every Christmas. In that moment, I got Elizabeth Bennet in a way I hadn't before. Her rejection of Mr. Darcy was so much more understandable now: *"I might as well enquire why, with so evident a design of offending and insulting me, you chose to tell me that you liked me against your will, against your reason, and even against your character?"*

Yeah. I get you, girl. It does not feel good at all.

"You don't have to wait with me," I said.

"Yes, I do. I need to explain to the member of my staff what is required of her."

"Ah, yeah, you do like to manage folks, don't you?"

"I'm not going to let you goad me today, Ms. Penhaligon."

So we were back to that, were we? "That wasn't goading. You remind me of a hen, clucking at her little chicks, pushing them around the pen so they're exactly where you want them to be."

As I knew he would be, Lachlan was affronted by the comparison. He opened his mouth, perhaps to retaliate, but there was a knock on his office door. Cutting me a dark look, he called, "Come in."

Sarah McCulloch opened the door, but I could only see her head. Her eyes were wide. "Sir?"

"Sarah, please come in."

The shy mouse pushed into the office but hovered near the doorway.

"This is Robyn Penhaligon. She's helping Mac with our little problem."

Little problem? Right. How would my father, the one

with the three knife wounds in his gut, feel about that description of the situation?

Having not slept because someone violated my space, referring to the situation as a "little problem" made *me* bristle.

"Ms. Penhaligon would like to ask you a few questions. Please take a seat, answer what you can. I'll leave you to it."

He was gone before I could speak, brushing past the blushing housemaid.

I studied her, thinking how awful it must be to be so shy and to have your every thought advertised across your face in a bright red flush. Giving her a small smile, I motioned to the chairs in front of Lachlan's desk. Unlike her boss, I would ask her permission first. "You're not required to do this. But if you want to chat with me, please have a seat."

Sarah nodded, wide-eyed, and sat. The housekeeping uniforms at Ardnoch were pretty modern, in contradiction to the other more traditional staff uniforms I'd seen. Lachlan's housekeepers wore jet-black tunics and black work pants. The tunic collar was red tartan, and the short sleeves had tartan cuffs. Sarah's dark blond hair was pulled back in a no-nonsense ponytail, and she wore very little makeup on her pretty face. Taking the seat across from her, I noted the way she twisted her hands nervously in her lap.

She did not give off murderous-stalker vibes, but I'd learned a long time ago not to be surprised by anything.

"How long have you worked at Ardnoch Castle, Sarah?"

"Um ... about three years now."

"And you enjoy it?"

She nodded.

"What age are you?"

"Twenty-seven."

Jesus, she looked a lot younger than that. "You're aware of the incidents that have occurred, including Mac's attack?"

She blanched. "Yes. I'm glad he's okay. Mr. Galbraith is a lovely man."

If she was lying, she was good. "Do you know anything about the incidents?"

"No. I already told the police that," she whispered.

"And there's no reason you know of that anyone would want to harm Lachlan or those close to him?"

Sarah shook her head frantically.

I pressed. "It's common knowledge there's bad blood between the McCullochs and the Adairs. Yet you took a job here?"

I noted the edge of defiance creep into her expression, and it gave me pause.

"That has nothing to do with me. I needed a well-paid job, and Mr. Adair offered me one. I wouldn't do anything to jeopardize that."

Deciding to use a different tactic, I relaxed back in my chair. "Yeah, it seems like a cushy position. Hanging out around famous people."

"Cleaning up after them, you mean."

There was that edge again.

Yeah, Sarah McCulloch had some hidden fire. Not surprising, considering who her grandfather was.

"Still, working for an attractive ex-Hollywood actor must be exciting." I stared at her pointedly, letting her know her crush was obvious without saying so.

She flushed a horrific orange-red that made me feel all kinds of guilty, but I was there to do a job. "I would never hurt anyone," she snapped, tears glistening in her eyes. "I wouldn't work here if I hated Mr. Adair. I don't care that the Adairs stole our land. It was centuries ago."

Catching the fact that she'd condemned the Adairs without proof, much like her grandfather, I leaned into her.

"Don't you mean *if* the Adairs stole your land? There's no evidence they did."

Sarah's nostrils flared. "I wasn't supposed to say anything. Forget it."

"Say anything about what?"

"Nothing." She lowered her gaze.

"Sarah, if you have something to say that's going to take you off my suspect list—"

"What?" Her eyes were round with shock. "You think I could do this?"

"I don't know you. I do know you just stated with absolute surety that the Adairs stole land from your family when there's no evidence they did. That to me is motive to screw around with Adair and this club's reputation."

She shook her head. "No, no. Mr. Galbraith already knows this, so I'm sure it's okay to tell you … The Adairs *did* take our land. Mr. Adair admitted it to my grandfather. Just ask your father."

I slumped in my chair at this news.

Well …

Shit.

* * *

I STORMED into my dad's room, and part of me was almost glad I had something to distract me from the letters and our family issues.

"Down here!" he called, having heard me barge into the suite.

I found him lying on the sofa in front of the TV, watching a soccer game.

He looked up at me, his expression hard to read.

"You didn't think I should know the Adairs *did* steal land

233

from the McCullochs? You didn't think that was pertinent evidence against Collum McCulloch?"

Surprise flickered across Mac's face. I knew it wasn't exactly the first thing he thought would come out of my mouth. Switching off the TV, he gestured for me to sit. I dragged a decorative chair from the corner and placed it in front of the sofa.

"Well? Adair lied to me. He told me there was no proof his ancestors stole McCulloch land."

"Don't be too hard on him, Robyn. He's protecting his family and his business."

"By stealing something that isn't his?" I was disappointed in a way that physically ached. For some stupid reason, I did not want Lachlan to be *that* guy.

"No, no, look"—Mac pushed himself into a sitting position—"Lachlan didn't know until about a year ago. He found letters in his father's belongings. Letters that dated back to his fourth-great-grandfather. And, yes, those letters suggested the land was acquired illegally from the McCulloch farm. But it doesn't outright state it, and it wouldn't hold up in a court of law. Lachlan felt bad enough about it to speak to McCulloch. I warned him not to, that the old bastard would not take kindly to it, but Lachlan wanted to offer him money. Reparation. McCulloch turned it down, but the relationship between them worsened."

I hated to admit how relieved I was to hear that Lachlan tried to do what was right for both families, but I was pissed that I hadn't known. "You didn't think I should know about this? I've met that man twice, and he could not make his hatred for Adair clearer. It isn't healthy, Mac. And that puts him right at the top of our suspect list. He has an *in* here, with Sarah. She can deny it till her cheeks turn purple, but this is *motive*, and you know it."

My dad gave me an appeasing look. "I thought it was

enough for you to know there was cause for grievance between them. And as for McCulloch's vitriol ... it's got less to do with the land and more to do with his sister's death. Believe me, that caused more bitterness between him and Lachlan's father than anything else."

Brain starting to hurt with frustration and lack of sleep, I leaned my elbows on my knees and cradled my head in my hands. It was on the tip of my tongue to confess about the trailer. About Sarah seeing Lachlan kiss me.

McCulloch was mad about land and grief-stricken over his sister's death. It didn't seem that far-fetched that he'd involve Sarah in his revenge and that Sarah, with her obvious crush on Lachlan, was happy to carry out the threats in light of his silent rejection of her. I believed the result they were looking for was Lachlan losing members and eventually having to close the club and sell the estate. None of that accounted for the man who attacked Mac, but the third player could still be connected to the McCullochs.

I found myself opening my mouth to tell Mac about the kiss and the trailer when my dad asked, "Did you read the letters?"

This brought my head up. I sank back into my chair, holding Mac's anxious gaze. "I did."

I interpreted his silent, "Well?"

Drawing in a breath and then exhaling slowly, I replied, "My mom was definitely to blame for some of it. But you still chose your career over me."

"I never ..." He leaned toward me. "I never gave you those letters to try to manipulate you into thinking this was all your mother's fault. I take full responsibility for my part."

"She still is to blame, too, though," I muttered. How was I to face her after this?

"Robyn, I hurt your mother more than I realized. I think

she was just trying to protect you from the same. Don't judge her too harshly."

"There wasn't a time when I was little that you weren't there for me or good to me. She had all the evidence in the world that you weren't going to break my heart like you broke hers."

"Until I took a job that meant leaving Boston," he reminded me. "I think she saw that as the beginning."

Huh.

I hadn't thought of that.

His perspective on it soothed the burn of my emotions.

All evidence suggested that the man my father had become was a very good one. A compassionate one. Kind. And fair. I wanted to get to know him.

I guess that meant my mind was made up.

"I want to try," I admitted. "To have a relationship with you."

A slow grin spread across my father's handsome face. He looked so boyishly happy, I couldn't help but return his smile. "Really?"

I chuckled. "Really."

He reached out a hand, and I shyly lifted my own. Mac clasped it in his. "Thank you. It's more than I deserve."

"Stop. If this is to work, I can't keep blaming you, and you can't keep blaming yourself. We're moving on."

"We're moving on," he repeated.

My dad looked down at our hands, and he tenderly rubbed his thumb over the top of mine. "How long can you stay?"

"I'm allowed to stay as long as six months, but if I need to stay longer, I've got that whole dual citizenship going for me … I'm here until we catch the fucker who stabbed you."

"You don't need to. I don't expect it."

"I don't care how many years have separated us, some

asshole stabbed my dad. And I'm going to make sure we find him."

He grinned. "You grew up fierce. I'm so very proud of you."

My chest ached at his words. They were words I'd longed to hear from him for so long.

"Come to the ceilidh with me this Saturday?" Mac released my hand but sat up straighter in his chair.

Surprised by the abrupt subject change, I asked, "What's a ceilidh?" He pronounced the word *cay-lay*.

"It's a social. We gather at the Gloaming and we drink and eat and dance to Gaelic folk music. There will be bagpipes and tartan and haggis. It's Scotland vomited up into one big room."

I laughed. "That is a charming description."

"Och, it's a good laugh. The council asks Gordon to host it every year to celebrate the anniversary of Ardnoch becoming a royal burgh."

"And what is a royal burgh?"

"A town founded by or granted a charter by the Crown. It was abolished in the '70s, but it used to be a big deal. Ardnoch was founded around a thousand years ago but became a royal burgh in the 1630s, and that's what the celebration is for. In actuality, it's just a bloody excuse to spend council money on a giant piss-up."

I chuckled, but I wasn't sure Mac was ready for a raucous social event that involved Gaelic dancing. "Should you be attending a ceilidh?"

"I'll stay seated most of the time," he promised. "I just need a wee breather from this castle. A night out and some good company. I want you to come and meet the locals. Get a better sense of the place."

It actually sounded fun. "What do I wear?"

"Something bonny. Everyone gets dressed up for it."

Considering I'd only brought casual clothing, I'd have to find a store or express online shopping. Maybe Lucy might be able to help me out. "Okay. I'm in."

Mac's eyes warmed. "Good."

A little while later, after chatting over sandwiches Mac had called down to the kitchen for, he walked me to his door, even though I told him not to.

"I need to keep exercising," he assured me.

"Just don't push yourself."

"I won't." As he opened the door, he looked down at me, serious. "I'd like you to think about moving into the castle. I've already talked to Lachlan, and he's fine with it. It's better than paying out money for that caravan."

"I can't afford Ardnoch," I joked.

"You know we wouldn't let you pay a thing."

"Mac, I don't know." Thinking about my trashed trailer, I did have to wonder if it might be safer here.

"I know you like your independence. But please think about it. For me."

"Okay. I'll think about it."

As I was making my way downstairs, I spotted Lachlan talking on the gallery with actor Marci Robbins. It was then that I made up my mind about staying at the castle. As per usual, I tried not to react to seeing a famous person. It was the first time I'd seen Marci, a British actor with multiple awards under her belt and a reputation of greatness few achieved. She was a class act from head to toe. In her late sixties, she'd aged with grace. She had the kind of bone structure and full lips that meant she'd always be pretty. But even more impressive was her ability to master the most complicated characters and always give a unique performance. For the first time, I felt truly starstruck.

I dragged my eyes from her to Lachlan so I wouldn't react to her presence. He looked up from chatting with Marci, saw me approaching, and his face closed down. Without even a nod in my direction, he turned to his guest and murmured something that made her laugh.

I walked past, stiff and outraged.

He'd completely ignored me.

That rude son of a bitch.

What a moron I was to have even let his mouth near mine.

As for living under the same roof, well, I was sorry to disappoint Mac, but it would be a cold day in hell.

20

ROBYN

$\mathcal{S}$taring at my reflection in the mirror, I veered between awed and disconcerted.

Never in my life had I ever looked this glamorous. Most of my twenties had been spent in uniform for work or barhopping in jeans styled with a cute top. Yes, I'd worn a prom dress senior year, and on the rare occasion I was invited to a wedding, I'd put on a dress. Nothing like this, though.

This was red-carpet worthy.

A huge part of me liked that I could still surprise myself. I'd never felt this overtly sexy before. Since arriving in Scotland, I'd experienced hurt, anger, confusion, fear, frustration, and I'd felt bruised, vulnerable, cautiously optimistic, and emotionally drained. I'd worn a detective's hat, an abandoned daughter's shield, and a literal and metaphorical pair of boxing gloves.

A sexy dress to feel nothing but sexy in was a nice change of pace.

Still, I worried I was overdressed for a ceilidh.

Or *under*dressed.

My legs looked particularly long in the short dress I'd borrowed from Lucy, and they had a shine to them because Jazelle from the salon had smoothed on some kind of oil. "The dress is too short, right?"

Lucy appeared by my side in the mirror. She wore a knee-length dress as tight fitting as mine. Except hers showed less leg. But way more cleavage. It was a dark green, perfect for her coloring, while my dress was black. "Gorgeous, you have the best pair of legs I've ever seen, and I've summered on the French Riviera. I'm kind of pissed at you for hiding them."

I chuckled and fidgeted. "Dresses and heels aren't my thing."

"I don't know why. You walk around in those like you were born to them." She gestured to the strappy, high-heeled sandals Lucy's stylist had shipped overnight for me. Unlike her dress, I couldn't borrow shoes because hers were all a size too big.

"If this dress is short on me, how short is it on you?" She was about three inches taller than I was.

She grinned wickedly. "Daringly so, gorgeous. Daringly so."

I laughed and then abruptly stopped because the glamorous laughing woman in the mirror was almost a stranger.

"Okay, stop looking at yourself or you might get stuck," Lucy teased.

"I'm sorry ... I'm just ..." I flicked a hand at the mirror. "I'm worried I'm overdressed, and I barely recognize myself."

"Well, I think you look just like your gorgeous self, except with more makeup. And, of course, those legs that have been hidden all these years like the century's greatest travesty. And you're not overdressed. If you're overdressed, so am I."

"But you can get away with it. You're Lucy Wainwright."

She cut me a strange look. "I look presentable, right?"

241

Shocked she even needed to hear it, I nodded. "Of course. You look phenomenal."

Lucy preened. "Good. Come on, everyone will be waiting."

Throwing one last look at the mirror, I turned, my high ponytail whipping around with the movement. The ladies at the estate salon did our hair and makeup for this evening. And since I was getting ready at the castle, it only made sense that I travel to the ceilidh tonight with Mac, Lucy, Eredine, and Lachlan.

Lucy handed me the clutch she'd loaned me. It was black, unadorned, and matched my dress, which was modest, except for its short hemline. The dress had long, tight sleeves, contoured to my body and a straight, high neckline. I didn't wear any jewelry. I wasn't a jewelry kind of girl.

"You look amazing," I said to Lucy again, hoping I hadn't upset her by not offering her the compliment in the first place. I'd just been so taken aback by my own reflection. Now I felt a little self-involved.

The girls styled Lucy's luscious hair in vintage waves, and she'd paired gold stilettos with her green dress. Earrings that sparkled in the light hung from her lobes, and I was pretty sure they were real diamonds and emeralds.

I couldn't imagine walking around with something worth that much money on my body. Which was why I didn't ask her the value of the dress I wore.

"Thank you, gorgeous." Lucy melted at my reassurance and caught me by the elbow. "This has been so much fun today."

"For me too. You've been such a good friend to me. I appreciate it."

"Which is *why* I'm being such a good friend. Appreciation is a dying sentiment."

Not only had Lucy helped style me for my first ceilidh,

she and Eredine also tried to teach me Scottish folk dances while streaming music on Eredine's phone. We'd laughed our way through the session, and I'd come to the conclusion that there was no way I would remember the steps nor could I even *contemplate* a folk dance in this dress.

"I wonder if any other members will attend tonight?" I mused as we walked out of her luxurious suite.

Lucy shook her head. "No. I asked around. Looks like I'm flying solo."

"I thought they'd love getting into something as traditional as a ceilidh."

"They do. But Lachlan hosts them here at the club. One for summer solstice and another at Christmas. As much as they love Ardnoch, they come here for the privacy, remember."

"So do you, but you're attending."

Lucy shrugged. "I guess because the village feels like home too. Everyone treats me like an ordinary person. It's great. And I love hanging out with Lachlan's family."

"Arrochar and Thane will definitely be there?"

"Should be. They usually are. Unless Thane can't get a babysitter." Lucy's expression softened. "But hopefully he does tonight. I like coaxing him into a dance or two."

Something about her tone caught my attention. Something … tender. "Thane, huh?"

My friend rolled her eyes as we descended toward the second floor. "Stop it."

"I'm serious. Do you have a thing for Thane? I mean, I'd get it. If I had to choose, he's the sexiest of the male Adairs."

Her hand tightened on my arm, and she stiffened a little. "I'd advise against it. Thane deserves someone who is going to stick around."

Wait. What? Was she … jealous?

"Oh, Lucy, I'm just making an observation. I'm not interested in Thane." In fact, I'd had plenty of Adair interaction for one lifetime. I was still sore over Lachlan ignoring me two days ago and had studiously avoided him since.

"I know that."

"So … you and Thane?"

Before she could reply, director-and-actor couple Merriam Burbanks and Jack Loman strode up the stairs toward us. I'd seen them around the castle but hadn't interacted with them.

Jack murmured, "Evening," and nodded his head in appreciation. Merriam commented, "You look beautiful, ladies. Enjoy your night."

"Thank you, Mer," Lucy called gaily as we passed on the staircase; I nodded my thanks, trying to act cool.

Laughing to myself at how surreal life was, it took me a second to catch up after Lucy said, "There is no me and Thane."

"Okay…"

She flicked me a sad smile. "Thane lost a wife he loved."

"How did it happen?"

"One morning he woke up, and she was dead next to him in bed. She'd passed away in her sleep. Brain aneurysm."

Emotion clogged my throat. I couldn't imagine how devastating that must have been for him. "God, that's heartbreaking."

Lucy nodded, eyes bright. "Thane's life is those kids. And it should be. It would be nice to see him find someone else, but that lucky woman will need to commit to being a good wife and an even better mother. Thane is … well, he's just wonderful." The forlorn quality to her voice upset me. "But I'm not cut out for settling down. I have my career to think about. However"—she beamed again, but the smile wobbled a little—"I am committed to making the man enjoy himself now and then by forcing him to dance at social gatherings."

Even though I knew she was right, that Lucy's career meant she was not the ideal candidate to be the perfect stepmother, I couldn't help wishing things were different. As strong and seemingly content as Lucy was, I worried about the shadows in the back of her eyes, the ones that appeared when she thought no one was looking. I worried my new friend was lonely, and considering how good she was to everyone else, I hated the idea of her feeling alone.

My concerns about her well-being were halted as we descended the main staircase into the castle's reception area. Lucy squeezed my arm, drawing me from my thoughts.

Mac, Lachlan, Eredine, and a woman I didn't recognize were waiting for us near the sofas at the fireplace.

Eredine looked willowy and elegant in a spring-colored maxi dress with cap sleeves. She'd left her gorgeous hair loose, and it tumbled around her shoulders in dramatic curls.

As beautiful as she was, there was a casualness to her dress that made me feel self-conscious. I wasn't used to self-consciousness and didn't like that I was experiencing it in front of Adair. "Okay, we're overdressed."

"Maybe a little," Lucy admitted with a shrug. "But life is too short not to dress up for it."

Groaning under my breath, my gaze moved to Mac, Lachlan, and the unknown female.

I almost stumbled on the last step.

The woman was a pretty blond, dressed in a chic jumpsuit the same color as Lucy's dress, and she clutched Lachlan's hand.

His date?

A strange sensation moved through my stomach. I'd experienced a similar sensation on a vertical roller-coaster ride. It had taken us to the top of the almost two-hundred-foot structure, only for it to hang suspended for a moment before plummeting.

So Lachlan brought a date.

What did I care?

Pushing my odd feelings aside, I concentrated on the fact that Mac and Lachlan wore kilts.

I tried not to stare at Lachlan, in particular, and failed.

A tall, rugged Scotsman in a kilt was definitely something to see.

Mac and Lachlan wore matching tartan—a dark green plaid with red, black, and white accents. Clearly a clan tartan. But while my dad wore a black suit jacket, matching waistcoat, and white shirt, Lachlan wore a dark gray waistcoat, jacket, and white shirt.

They each wore a matching sporran over the kilt, but my father's long knee socks were black on black with his dress shoes. Lachlan's socks were dark gray so the laces of his dress shoes were visible, wrapped around his calves.

And his calves … wow, those were powerful calves.

My eyes drew up his legs but unfortunately, the kilt obscured his thighs.

Oh my God, I was ogling the devil.

In front of his date, no less.

Shit.

"Jesus, he brought Leighanne. What was he thinking?" Lucy muttered under her breath just loud enough for me to hear.

Leighanne. The fuck buddy from Glasgow.

Wow. His point could not be any clearer.

I wrenched my attention from the bastard and his lovely date to my dad. Mac crossed the reception to greet us.

"You look beautiful, ladies," he said, throwing Lucy an appreciative glance before coming to me. He pulled me into his arms, disentangling me from Lucy, and I stiffened in surprise.

Mac was hugging me.

My dad was hugging me.

There was still a part of me that wanted to keep my guard up. Ward off his affection until I could trust him more. Yet I found it impossible to separate the dad from my childhood from the man in front of me. I couldn't *not* put my arms around him to return the embrace. "Hey, Dad."

At the word, Mac tightened his hold for a second before he pushed me gently away to study my face. "Sometimes I can't believe how grown up you are."

Looking at his handsome face, I acknowledged, "If it's weird for you, it's weird for me too. I'm calling a man who looks barely ten years older than me 'Dad.'"

"It's weird for us all," Lucy announced, laughter in her voice.

I threw her a look that made her chuckle before she sauntered off to join Eredine.

Turning to Mac, I said, "You feeling okay?"

"I feel good."

"You're walking like you're not feeling any pain."

"I'm not," he reassured, stepping to my side to loop my arm through his. "It's only if I push myself that I start to feel it."

"Okay, well, no ceilidh dancing, then."

"Promise."

"The cars are waiting," Lachlan announced before leading Leighanne toward the main entrance with Lucy. He hadn't even bothered to introduce me to his date.

In fact, he hadn't looked at me once. If that was the way he wanted things to be, then I could accommodate.

Eredine waited for me and Mac, and we exchanged compliments.

"Lucy tricked me into dressing for the red carpet. Said everyone would be dressed like this."

"Not quite as glamorous." Eredine gave me a reassuring smile. "But who cares? You look wonderful."

"She's right. Just enjoy yourself." Mac patted my hand in comfort.

"Will all the men be in traditional dress?" I asked as I tried to get into the back of Lachlan's seven-seater Range Rover without flashing anyone. Lachlan was already up front next to one of the estate chauffeurs. Lucy and Leighanne settled in the first row of the back seats, and Eredine took the spot beside Lachlan's date. I noted the smaller Range Rover in front of us that housed Jock and several security guards and experienced a flutter of apprehension at the reminder we required bodyguards simply to attend a village social.

"Not all, but most," Mac replied to my question as he climbed into the vehicle. I noted his slight wince as he sat beside me in the back row.

"You okay?"

"Just a twinge. Nothing to worry about."

Taking his word for it, I let it go. We chatted amiably on the short drive into the village. He asked me about my day, and I told him what Lucy had put me through.

"Put you through?" she turned to mock glare at me through the seats. "You make it sound like a punishment."

"I'm kidding. It was a great day. Though we started on the champagne a little early."

"And soaked it all up with Guy's amazing afternoon tea. We were delightfully pampered by Lachlan's staff."

I shifted uncomfortably because she was right. And I hadn't paid for any of it.

Mac nudged me with his shoulder. "You deserve some pampering."

It was becoming clear that my dad was weirdly intuitive and perceptive. At least when it came to me. "I should pay," I murmured.

"I heard that." Lucy scowled over her shoulder. "Get over yourself, gorgeous. Today you were my guest. Plus, you're Mac's daughter."

"Right." The problem was, I didn't like taking anything from Lachlan. If it were my dad's estate, I would've happily indulged in a little nepotism and freebies.

Taking freebies from Lachlan was a whole other ball game.

If he was listening up ahead, I wouldn't know as he appeared to be in conversation with his driver.

"I'm Leighanne, by the way." The Scottish woman's pretty face appeared between the headrests. "Lachlan didn't introduce us. I'm his friend from Glasgow." Her eyes moved to my dad. "Nice to see you again, Mac."

"You too." My dad was polite, but he lacked his usual friendliness.

Huh.

"I'm Robyn. Mac's daughter."

"Lachlan said Mac's daughter would be here, but I have to admit, I was expecting a child." Leighanne seemed incredulous. "I can't believe Mac's old enough to have had you. You're what ... my age?"

"No," Lucy answered for me. "Robyn is only twenty-eight. And she doesn't look *thirty-five*, Leighanne." There was a definite edge to my friend's tone.

"Oh right, of course. I didn't mean to insinuate you did." The woman seemed genuinely worried she'd offended me.

"It's cool. Mac had me young." I nudged my father, teasing. "We get that a lot."

"And of course, you don't look thirty-five," she hurried to assure me.

"Neither do you." And she didn't.

She beamed. "I'm a makeup artist so I know all the best

skin care regimens. I'll recommend my favorites later when we have a moment."

Her tone was sincere, friendly, and eager.

Leighanne was nice, and I wouldn't hold her choice of sex partners against her.

It felt like we'd barely left the estate when we pulled up to the parking lot in the center of the village, opposite the Gloaming. The parking lot was full.

The driver and Lachlan got out first, the former helping Eredine out of the vehicle while Lachlan helped Lucy and Leighanne. Dad got out and tried to assist me, but I didn't want to put any weight on him. Instead I hopped out with ease, despite my five-inch heels, and he chuckled.

Remembering his hug and the way he'd taken my arm, I decided to be brave, to lower my guard and attempt to trust him. If we were going to do this, I needed to show Mac I was ready to be comfortable and affectionate around him too. This time, *I* looped my arm through his and hugged into his side. Dad looked inordinately pleased by it and patted my hand on his arm as we said good night to the driver and followed the others into the hotel.

Jock and two security guards had already arrived, and I noted they, too, wore kilts to blend in. Lachlan exchanged a few words with them. One of the men stayed outside while Jock and another strode into the hotel ahead of us. I assumed they'd take positions from inside, pretending to be guests while they kept a watchful eye.

Energetic folk music blared onto the street from inside. People milled about in the reception area, and they called hello as we walked in. Our companions turned left into the dining room where more people lingered and then took a right through a doorway that led into the back of the hotel to a large room I hadn't visited during my stay.

The music was loud from the band on the low stage at the

far end. A woman sat at a harp while two men played accordions, a man and a woman each played a flute, and a female fiddler accompanied them. There was a drummer in the back and a bagpiper who currently wasn't playing.

It was a heady assault of fairy lights, tartan, thistles, raucous but charming music, fluttering skirts, and flying kilts as guests danced to a well-known folk dance. The scent of whisky, food, and something smoky filled the air. Chatter, laughter, and singing supplemented the joyful cacophony.

Round tables had been set up around the room's edges for people to sit and eat and drink. Two long buffet tables sat against the wall near the entrance, blanketed with an excess of food. There was a door to my right that led down a narrow corridor to a bar beyond, a bar that heaved with people waiting to buy drinks.

I met Mac's stare and grinned with pleasure. The atmosphere was fantastic.

He returned my smile and gave my arm a squeeze.

"You made it!" Arrochar sashayed toward us, a stocky man following at her back. Lachlan's sister's gaze was firmly fixed on my dad. She beamed. "You look great!" She rose on tiptoes to press a kiss to his cheek, and I noted the way Mac automatically reached out to give her hip a squeeze.

As the striking blond pulled back, she and Mac exchanged a private look before Arrochar focused on me. "Robyn, you look amazing."

She hugged me, and I returned the embrace. "Thanks. You too."

And she did. Because I'd only seen Arrochar in sweaters and jeans and muddy boots with very little makeup, it was interesting to see her dressed up. Her smoky eye shadow made her pale eyes even more stunning, and she'd slicked her hair into a high ponytail much like mine.

It seemed the Adair men weren't the only ones with lethal

sex appeal. I'd previously noted Arrochar's unique beauty, but I hadn't really paid attention to the way she carried herself. Confident. Self-assured. And with her way of staring like she was seeing right through you, I imagined she might intimidate some people.

"It's good to see you two together." She touched Mac's arm, looking up at him without hiding how happy she was for him.

My God.

Couldn't everyone else see it?

Pulse racing, not quite sure how I felt about what I sensed between them, I was thrown even more when the man at Arrochar's back cleared his throat.

"Oh." Her smile was sheepish as she retreated from Mac and put an arm around the man's shoulders. In her high heels Arrochar was about five eleven, six feet. The guy who I assumed was Guy Lewis, the castle chef, was a little shorter than Arro was in her heels. He was pretty-boy handsome with a small nose, pouty lips, and long-lashed eyes, but there seemed to be an effort to dilute his prettiness with his unshaven cheeks and unkempt dark hair.

"Robyn, this is my boyfriend and the chef at Ardnoch, Guy. Guy, this is Mac's daughter, Robyn."

"Nice to meet you," he said in a thick Aussie accent. "I've heard a lot about you. Can't believe Mac's old enough to be your dad, though."

I flicked Mac a look, and we shared a smirk. I guess we'd just have to get used to everyone saying that to us.

"Yeah," I replied, reaching out to shake Guy's hand. "It's nice to meet you too."

Guy cut Mac a quick look before glancing away to take a swallow of the pint in his free hand.

Arrochar shifted uneasily and threw me a strained smile. "Well, we better go say hello to the others." She dragged her boyfriend away to greet Lachlan and company, who I noted were surrounded by people.

Mac watched Arrochar walk away. When he eventually turned back to me, he found me staring at him in silent curiosity. I didn't ask. I didn't pry. I just squeezed his arm and said, "I'm starving."

He grinned, his shoulders relaxing. "Then let's feed you, wee birdie."

* * *

A FEW HOURS LATER, I was a little sweaty, full of food, and tipsy from the cocktails Lucy fed me. I wasn't a big drinker, so I still had two untouched old-fashioneds sitting at the table we'd claimed farthest away from the band.

Lucy, Eredine, and Arrochar talked me into ceilidh dancing, and I'd done what I could without flashing my underwear at everyone. It was great fun. But not wanting to leave Mac at the table alone all the time, I made excuses to rejoin him. It turned out he was never alone. Thane, who did get a babysitter, barely left Mac's side, and they sat talking, drinking, and laughing together most of the night.

A couple times, Lucy coaxed Thane up to dance, and as soon as he was gone, Arrochar was at Mac's side, their heads bent together as they chatted and laughed. In those moments, I searched for Guy but couldn't find him.

Lachlan and Leighanne danced a few times, with each other and with our friends and the villagers. Lucy was right —the villagers treated her and Lachlan like ordinary people. Lucy's grin was so wide, her cheeks must have ached. It was wonderful to see her like that.

I wandered around the room with my phone because I didn't have my actual camera, but the photographer in me itched to capture the evening. In between snapping photos, I spoke with villagers I knew—Suveer and Moira from the chocolate shop, Morag, and Janet.

Suveer introduced me to a Polish woman called Zuzanna and her Scottish husband Prentice. They owned the outdoor clothing and sports store in the village. Suveer also introduced me to Chen and Wang Lei who owned a Chinese restaurant and takeout that several people had already told me I needed to try. Chen was second-generation Malaysian, and Wang's family had owned the restaurant in Ardnoch since his grandfather emigrated to Scotland in the 1950s. The fact the restaurant had been in the village that long was impressive and telling. I couldn't wait to try his food.

I chatted awhile with the couple, and Wang offered me some great insight into places I might want to photograph in the Cairngorms National Park. When he and Chen were dragged away into conversation by another villager, I continued to walk around the ceilidh with my camera phone.

Taking candid photos of folks, I got some great shots— Lucy and Eredine laughing so hard at something, they were bent toward each other, mouths open, eyes almost shut, clutching their bellies in a way that was almost cartoonish; Mac and Arrochar smiling intimately into each other's eyes as if they were alone on a private island, not surrounded by a joyful rumpus; Thane standing with a few villagers I didn't know, clapping his hands in time with the amazing fiddler; Lachlan standing off to the side, watching Lucy and Eredine enjoy themselves with a subtle but undeniably affectionate look on his face.

"Put the phone away and come dance."

I glanced up and found Gordon, owner of the Gloaming and my trailer, standing over me. He was a big, burly Scot with hardly any hair on top of his head but a massive, bushy gray beard. His kilt was a different tartan from the Adairs' and Mac's, and he'd rid himself of his dress jacket. Sweat glistened on his jolly face as held out a big hand.

I grinned. "I'm not very good."

"Oh, it's not about being good. It's about having a good time!" he boomed.

Chuckling, I nodded. "Let me put my phone away."

I hurried to return my phone to my clutch and left it with Mac and Arrochar, who grinned as Gordon took my hand and practically hauled me onto the dance floor.

"This, somewhat appropriately," he yelled over the music as we joined the dancers, "is called 'The Gay Gordons'!"

Laughing, I let him maneuver me, watching the others so I could grasp the steps. We stood side by side while Gordon held my left hand in his left hand down at our sides, and my right hand over my right shoulder in his right hand.

"Forward one, two, three, four, and reverse!" he instructed, and I stumbled, laughing as we turned to avoid colliding with the couple in front of us. We did this a few times, and then Gordon boomed, "Spin!" We stopped so I could do just that before I was whisked unsteadily around the large circle in a polka embrace.

Thankfully, that was pretty much the pattern of the dance, so I got it down quickly.

All the skipping around wasn't easy in a short dress and high heels, but I gave it my best shot.

Afterward, Gordon bowed like a gentleman and led a now-sweaty me back to my table where he leaned over Arrochar and asked her for a dance.

I'd seen the hotel owner dancing all night. The guy had stamina!

"You look like you're having fun," Mac observed as I grabbed a bottle of water from an ice bucket in the table center.

I nodded, noting he'd finished his pint. "Another drink?"

"Do you mind?"

"Not at all."

"Let me pay."

"I got it." I patted his shoulder and, clutch in hand, made my way through the crowded room to the equally crowded barroom.

Ten minutes after shifting through the crowd, I leaned on the bar, waiting for my turn to be served. There were three bar staff, but they were rushed off their feet.

Aware of someone new pushing in at the back of me, I tried to shimmy to give them space but couldn't. There was no space to give. Apparently this person ignored that, because I felt the warm press of a body against mine. *Yeah, it was crowded, but a little patience and adherence to personal space would be nice.* I glanced over my shoulder to see who Mr. Impatient was, and tensed.

Lachlan leaned against the bar, our sides pressed tightly together, his blue eyes hot, his pupils slightly dilated from alcohol. "Enjoying yourself?"

Treating him how he'd treated me, I turned away, willing one of the bartenders to appear.

After a few seconds, I felt his elbow nudge against mine.

I ignored that too.

He did it again.

I cut him a filthy look.

Lachlan frowned. "You're honestly going to ignore me?"

Letting out a huff of disbelief, I replied, "I thought that's what we were doing now. I'm just following your example."

When he flinched, I knew he knew I wasn't just talking about tonight but about the way he'd given me the cut right in front of Marci Robbins at the castle.

"I'm sorry." He shocked the shit out of me. "That was unforgivably rude."

Lachlan clearly wasn't drunk, but he'd had a few. I could

only assume the alcohol accounted for the apology. And I took advantage of his lowered defenses. "Why?"

Again, he knew what I was asking. Lachlan blew out a breath as he ran a hand through his hair in agitation. He searched my face and said, "Mac knows there's something between us."

Dismay caused my pulse to skip.

"And he made it clear that while it's none of his business ... that if whatever was between us went south and you got hurt ... he'd choose you, and I'd lose his friendship."

Wow.

Emotion clogged my throat.

Mac said that?

I stared unseeing at the bar, trying to wrap my head around that, until I felt Lachlan's hand on my lower back. My gaze shot to his as his touch brought an immediate reaction. It was as if he had the key to my sexuality. I wanted to melt into him, wanted his hand to slide lower, down over my ass and under my dress.

It was ridiculous and frustrating.

Why him?

He molded his hand deeper into my spine, his fingers grazing the top of my ass as he leaned into me. "I thought ignoring you was the best way to avoid temptation."

My lips parted in surprise. "Are you saying you can't control yourself around me?"

The question was meant to be dry, teasing. It didn't exactly come out like that.

And he didn't respond to it with humor.

Instead, his hand flexed on my back before he jerked it away. Glowering, he bit out, "Apparently, I can't." And before I could respond to his unsettling confession, he disappeared, leaving me at the bar.

Reeling, it took all my concentration to wait at the bar,

get Mac's drink, and return it to him. Knowing he was perceptive enough to see something had rattled me, I told him I needed to use the restroom and left him with Eredine. A quick glance at the dance floor revealed Lucy and Thane slow dancing in murmured conversation. Whatever he said made Lucy laugh, her eyes sparkling with happiness.

Jesus, they looked good together.

The Adairs seemed to have a way of getting under a person's skin, I thought somewhat morosely as I made my way through the hotel's ground floor to the restrooms.

There was a line outside the ladies', of course.

So much for a moment to myself.

I wasn't waiting long when a voice said behind me, "Oh good, someone I know."

The Glaswegian accent made me tense, but I refused to show any outward discomfort as I turned to Leighanne. "Hey. Enjoying your night?"

She slumped against the wall at her back, fanning herself. "Aye, but it's so warm in here."

"Yeah."

"You?"

"Yeah. My first ceilidh."

Her eyes widened. "What do you think?"

"It's great fun," I said truthfully.

She leaned into me conspiratorially. "It's amazing how all the locals treat Lachlan and Lucy like they're not famous."

"It is. I know Lucy appreciates it."

Leighanne wrinkled her nose. "Hmm, she's hard to get a read on. I think she's jealous of me and Lachlan."

"Lucy's my friend," I warned her.

"Oh, I mean no disrespect. I like her ... but I think she definitely has a thing for Lachlan."

"No, I can assure you she doesn't."

Leighanne seemed to want to argue but dropped it. "Not that I have anything to worry about."

"Because you're just casual?"

She shrugged, a secretive, intimate smile on her face. "I think we might be more than that. I mean, it's obvious he's not interested in anyone else. He called me up here because he's had a long dry spell. So even though we don't see each other for weeks, I now know he hasn't even thought about touching someone else. I can just … tell"—she grinned giddily—"that it's *me* he wants. Not just sex."

Oh dear God.

Guilt and concern niggled me. "Um …" I couldn't let her go on thinking that. Lachlan would break her heart. "I … maybe you should discuss this with Lachlan. Like … right away."

Leighanne narrowed her eyes. "Why?"

"I think you might have your wires crossed."

"What do you know?"

Why did I feel so guilty? I shrugged, apologetic. "That he and I have made out a few times, and he's made it clear he'd like"—there was no other way but to be blunt—"to have sex … if the situation weren't so complicated with Mac. I'm not interested," I hurried to assure her with an outright lie, "but I thought you should know so he doesn't hurt you. I'm sorry."

She reared back like a wounded animal.

"I *am* sorry."

Leighanne gave me a sad, bitter smile. "Better coming from you than mortifying myself in front of *him*." She turned on her heel and marched away.

I closed my eyes and cursed under my breath, wondering if I'd done the right thing.

And if I'd done it for the right reasons.

*L*achlan seethed.

Kelvin Sutherland, a nephew of Morag Sutherland, who lived in Tain and according to Arrochar
was newly divorced, slow danced with Robyn.

His hands were too close to her arse.

Jealousy.

Lachlan couldn't remember the last time he'd felt jealous
over a woman.

Ever?

But he couldn't deny the burn in his gut or the agitated
way his fingers curled into fists as he watched Kelvin flirt
outrageously with Robyn.

The woman had been driving him nuts for weeks, but
coming downstairs into reception tonight dressed in that
fucking dress, she'd almost unmanned him.

His eyes drifted down her perfect ass to her long,
sculpted legs, and Lachlan felt the heat building in him, heat
that had started to simmer at the top of the evening, now
beginning to boil over. He could kill Lucy for lending that
dress to Robyn. It left little to the imagination but just

enough to taunt him into a fever. The neckline might have been modest in comparison to the hemline, but the material contoured her body, molding breasts that were obviously more than a handful.

Fuck, fuck, fuck.

It wasn't just that Robyn had an amazing body.

It never was about that.

There was something about *her*.

He'd never wanted inside a woman so badly in his life, to watch and listen and feel her come around him. The need was madness.

And the dress ... well, the dress just tipped him over an edge he'd been teetering on for weeks.

"Do I have to intervene?" His brother's voice sounded at his ear.

Reluctantly, Lachlan dragged his gaze off Robyn and Kelvin to find Thane at his side.

His brother smirked at him.

He scowled. "What?"

Thane nodded toward the dance floor. "You're making it pretty obvious."

Lachlan clenched his jaw. "I don't know what you're talking about."

"I'm talking about the fact that you've been prowling around Mac's daughter all night and while she might be oblivious to it, the rest of us aren't. Including your date."

"What?" Lachlan blinked. *Shit. Leighanne.* He glanced around, searching for her. "Where is she?"

"Last I checked, sitting in the empty reception room, staring sadly out the window." Thane clapped him on the shoulder. "Think you might have gotten this one's hopes up, brother. I suggest you go apologize for some hurt feelings. That way we won't have you brawling with Kelvin Sutherland over Robyn."

Feeling defensive, Lachlan brushed Thane's hand off his shoulder without a word and went in search of Leighanne. It took a lot of self-control not to look back at Robyn, but he was a grown man. A slightly drunk one, but he had enough of his faculties together to remind himself he didn't want people gossiping that he was mooning over the woman.

Finding Leighanne exactly where Thane said she was, at the other side of the hotel in the small, empty sitting room off reception, Lachlan took a seat beside her on the sofa.

"You okay?"

She picked at an invisible thread on her purse. "I wondered when you'd notice I wasn't there."

Despite the fact they both knew this was just a casual thing, it was still bloody rude and hurtful of him to not pay attention to the woman he'd invited as his date. "I'm sorry."

"You know, I thought she might be lying because she had a thing for you ... but then I watched you ... and she's right. It's not her, it's you. You can't keep your eyes off her."

"What are you talking about?"

Leighanne guffawed. "Oh, come on, Lachlan, it's so obvious you fancy the pants off Mac's daughter. It wasn't to me at first, but then she told me you kissed her, that you propositioned her—"

"What?" he bit out angrily. What the bloody devil was Robyn playing at?

"That's what she said. Was she lying?"

No. But what right did she have to tell Leighanne?

Unless ... she was jealous too?

The thought filled Lachlan with satisfaction, just as much as it pissed him off that she'd interfered with him and Leighanne.

"I think we should end this, Lachlan, before my feelings become any more involved."

He shouldn't have invited her to the ceilidh. Thane was

right. He'd sent the wrong message by doing so, and it was selfish of him. "I'm sorry, Leighanne. You deserve better."

She shrugged. "You never made any promises. And it was fun while it lasted. That's what I'll take from it."

"Then you're a better person than I am." He pressed a sweet kiss to her cheek. "Thank you."

She patted his hand and stood. "Do you mind if the driver takes me back to the castle so I can collect my things?"

"Stay." Lachlan stood too. "You can drive back in the morning."

"No. I'd like to leave," she said, chin set stubbornly. "I haven't been drinking."

He knew that. Leighanne was teetotal. She'd never said why, and he'd never asked. "Then at least let one of my men drive you back to Glasgow. It'll make me feel better."

"I'm a big girl, Lachlan. I can drive myself home."

Sensing he wasn't going to win the argument, he said, "I'm coming back with you to the castle."

"No!" She winced and softened her tone. "I just want to be alone. Stay. Enjoy the rest of your night."

He sighed. "Let me know when you get home safely."

Leighanne smirked. "Okay, Dad."

Seconds later, Lachlan watched from the hotel's main entrance as his driver, Dave, pulled away with Leighanne in the back of the Range Rover. Upon removing his phone from his sporran, he dialed security at the castle. Explaining the situation, he offered overtime to one of his men to follow Leighanne back to Glasgow to make sure she arrived home safely. After hanging up, he stared out onto the empty Castle Street, lit only by the old-fashioned streetlamps and the moon above in a clear, starry sky.

Guilt was a feeling Lachlan hated. He suffered enough of it on a daily basis because of his brothers; he did not want to feel it over a woman. Especially when his words hadn't chased off Leighanne.

Robyn's had.

If left to their own devices, Lachlan could've had a nice evening with Leighanne and then let her down gently in the morning. Now she would drive all the way back to Glasgow during the bloody night just to get away from him.

The jealousy seething inside him mingled with anger and frustration toward Robyn.

Determined not to make a scene, to wait until morning to tell Robyn off for her interference, it was like the fates had other ideas. When Lachlan turned around and strode back into the hotel, Robyn strolled out of the dining room and collided with him.

He steadied her, the feel of her warm and supple in his arms.

And any thought of leaving this confrontation until morning fled his mind.

Robyn startled and opened her mouth to speak when her eyes widened ever so slightly at his expression.

"Come with me," he demanded, guiding her toward Gordon's office, down the narrow corridor by the reception desk to the end of the hall to the left.

"Where are we going? I can walk on my own, you know," Robyn protested.

Lachlan didn't reply. He wasn't thinking straight. Instead, he reached Gordon's office, prayed it was open, muttered a cursed thank-you as the door swung inward, and after quickly checking over Robyn's shoulder to make sure no one was around, he pulled her inside and shut the door.

"Lachlan," she said hoarsely as dark surrounded them.

He could feel her body heat, smell her perfume.

"Turn on the light, please," she clipped out.

The edge in her voice had him reaching behind her for

the light switch. She sucked in an audible breath as his body brushed against hers, and he couldn't help his smirk of satisfaction.

Light flooded the room. Gordon's office was small—just big enough for a desk and some filing cabinets.

Robyn blinked up at Lachlan and then looked around. She moved past him to stand near the desk. "Is this Gordon's office?"

"Yes." He turned to face her.

"We shouldn't be in here." She took a step toward the door, and Lachlan stood in her way. "Are you kidding me?"

"We need to talk."

"About what?"

"About your obvious jealousy over Leighanne." He was baiting her; he didn't know how to stop himself.

Just as Lachlan knew she would, Robyn guffawed. "Oh, I don't think so."

"Did you or did you not tell her about our kiss?"

She scoffed, "Yes, but not for the reason you think."

"Explain it to me, then."

"I don't have to explain anything to you."

"Then I'll stick to my jealousy theory."

Her eyes narrowed. "Fine. I didn't want Leighanne getting hurt, and it was obvious from our conversation that you two were on different pages."

"What did she say?" he asked curiously.

"I'm not telling you that. It's her business, and you don't need to know it."

"Well, she's gone."

"Because of a stupid kiss that didn't mean anything?"

Agitation flared in his gut. "She thought we were heading somewhere we weren't."

Robyn nodded as if she already knew that. He assumed

that's what she meant regarding her conversation with Leighanne.

So it wasn't jealousy?

Robyn glared. "You didn't treat her very well. Are you like that with all your women?"

He took offense. "She knew the rules. I would never mislead a woman."

"Whatever you say." She began to walk by him to the door, and a sudden panic seized him.

And so Lachlan took hold of her upper arm.

Robyn flushed angrily and jerked away. "What are you doing?"

Let her go, let her go, let her go.

But Lachlan couldn't think straight when she was this close, her lush mouth just a bend of his head away. Want. That's all he could feel and think.

He kissed her.

His nostrils filled with the scent of her perfume, his tongue the taste of whisky. And Robyn.

Groaning, he released her arm to pull her into him, and it took him a moment to realize her hands were on his chest pressing him away, not toward him.

Fuck.

Lachlan released her, panting hard from just a kiss.

Robyn's cheeks were flushed; her eyes, now a dark blue-gray beneath the harsh ceiling light in Gordon's office, were bright with confusion. Her lips glistened as they parted. But no words were forthcoming.

Disappointment and rejection ate at Lachlan as he removed his hands from her hips.

"Fuck it," she whispered as she hooked a hand around his nape and pulled him down to crush their mouths together.

Relief and satisfaction flooded Lachlan as his mouth explored hers while his hands explored her supple body.

Needing every inch of her wrapped around him, he carried her to the desk until her arse was on it, and then he shoved the hem of her tight dress up her silky thighs so she could spread them.

"You know the rules?" He broke their kiss as he insinuated himself between her legs. He throbbed against her. "You know what this is?"

Robyn nodded, eyes low-lidded with desire, hips arching off the desk to push into him. "Just sex."

Just sex, he thought as he kissed her harder, deeper, as his hands caressed her body, frustrated by the material of her dress that kept him from bare skin. Not *just* sex. Mindless, exciting fucking.

Want.

Need.

Robyn.

Lachlan cupped her breasts in his hands, massaging them through her dress, rocking into her body with his desire to see her naked. There wasn't time. Not here.

Naked could come later.

For now, he just needed to be surrounded by her.

Fumbling in his sporran for the condom he'd half-jokingly put in there, he realized the sporran was in the way and unbelted it. Dropping it to the floor, he ripped at the condom packet with his teeth, staring into Robyn's lust-filled eyes.

A little smirk played around her lips as he rolled the condom on under his kilt.

"Not a true Scotsman, then?" she teased a little breathlessly, having caught sight of his underwear.

He grinned. "No one needs to see balls and cock flying everywhere during a ceilidh."

She laughed, and the sound pleased him more than he'd expected. The sound abruptly changed to an excited gasp when Lachlan slid his hands under her arse and jerked her to the edge of the desk. Curling his fingers around her silky underwear, he removed them quickly, dropping them to the floor on top of his sporran. Then he checked her readiness, fingers searching gently, slipping inside her with ease at finding her hot and wet. He groaned against her mouth before kissing her, licking at her tongue with his, desperate to deepen the kiss until she was breathless with need.

Robyn's fingers clawed at his back, trying to hold him closer, and Lachlan answered her silent request, guiding himself to her.

Nudging.

Then pushing in.

He grunted as her tight heat surrounded his tip, and the urge to see her face as he moved inside her overtook all else. Lachlan broke their kiss to watch her.

Robyn fisted his waistcoat in her hands, her inner thighs drawing up tight against his hips. Unfortunately, his kilt covered them both as he thrust the rest of the way into her so he couldn't watch, but the *feel* of her was enough to satisfy any man.

Her lips parted on a cry, her head falling back, and his hungry ardor became a desperate craving.

Anchoring her hips in his hands, Lachlan began to thrust. Hard, deep drives punctuated by Robyn's growing cries. Every sound of pleasure that fell from her lips drove him quicker toward climax. He imagined fucking her naked in his bed, watching himself move inside her, her breasts shaking with every pump into her body.

"I'm close, I'm close," Robyn panted.

Satisfaction, and not a little smugness, thrummed through him, and he increased the power of his strokes, each one pushing him closer to orgasm.

Then Robyn stiffened, her eyes grew round, and her back arched.

She throbbed around him in powerful waves of climax that along with her loud yell of pleasure was the equivalent of a tight-fisted tug.

His own climax hit him with unexpected force, and he shuddered almost violently as he came.

Chest heaving with the strength of it, Lachlan came down from the orgasm to realize he leaned on Robyn, his forehead resting on her shoulder.

It took him a minute to gather his thoughts.

They'd just had sex on Gordon's desk.

In a public place.

It was a quick fuck.

Fantastic.

And not nearly enough.

At the slight pressure of Robyn's hands on his chest, Lachlan reluctantly withdrew from her.

She wouldn't meet his eyes.

He watched her warily as he dealt with the condom, finding tissues on Gordon's desk so he could wrap and flush it. He wasn't going to leave the thing in the man's bloody rubbish bin.

Goddamn it. He'd had sex in Gordon's office like an irresponsible teenager.

And yet he wouldn't change it for the world.

Would she?

Still not looking at him, Robyn found her underwear and shimmied into them. Lachlan was amazed to find the blood rushing south again at the sight of her long, gorgeous legs. He wanted to kiss every inch of them, make his way upward to her inner thighs until he could bury his head and lick and suck until she begged for more.

Definitely not enough.

"Come back to the castle with me." The words were out of his mouth before he could stop them.

To his shock, Robyn shook her head.

This bloody woman ... "We both know that wasn't enough."

"I know." She surprised him. "But no overnight stays. Just sex. Remember."

And before Lachlan could say anything else, she strutted out of the office as if they'd merely had a little chat.

He grinned at her power play.

Christ, she was fun.

22

ROBYN

Out of sheer exhaustion, I finally had a full night's sleep in the trailer. For the last few nights, I'd barricaded the door and drifted in and out of consciousness but never fully succumbed to the dream plane. Thankfully, between getting ready for the ceilidh, having sex with Lachlan and the event itself, coming to terms with my new relationship with Mac, still trying to uncover the identity of his attacker while also avoiding my mom's phone calls ... let's just say no wonder I'd been distracted enough to deal with the horrible nights in the trailer.

There hadn't been any new creepy incidents, but I think it was probably the long day I'd spent on a solo photography adventure that pushed me to exhaustion. I walked around Inverness in the morning, taking artistic shots of Old Town. Then I crossed the river to photograph the castle and made a note to return at sunset to get more atmospheric images of the proud, turreted structure. It made me question if Lachlan might let me photograph Ardnoch, but I shivered just thinking his name, so I shoved him right back out of my head.

Unfortunately, I wasn't successful in locking him out entirely. Throughout the day, as I drove toward Aviemore, he entered my thoughts, memories of two nights before eliciting a heated physical response. Only the majestic peaks and valleys of the Cairngorms National Park could distract me. The reflection of the trees and cloudless sky across the lochs was mesmerizing and soothing.

Dressed in hiking boots I'd bought from Zuzanna and Prentice, I'd decided to head into the park for the stunning photo opportunities Wang had promised. When I mentioned his recommendation to Arrochar during the ceilidh, she'd told me there was a place called Lochan Uaine, a so-called fairy glen situated within the park. Despite being fairly tipsy, I remembered our conversation and looked it up, along with information on the best spots within the lochs and Munros of the Cairngorms. After a morning in Inverness, I ventured forth.

It was a good two-hour drive from Scotland's most northerly city. Well, it was for a person driving below the speed limit as she tried to navigate south on the left side of the road. Following the A9 road was fine-ish. It was a perfectly normal road.

But soon, I was driving along roads much like I'd discovered north of Ardnoch. They were single track with little bump-outs here and there called passing places. Afraid of meeting someone head on, I took it much slower than the cars I came upon while trying to get to the fairy glen.

It was worth it, though. The scenery was breathtaking.

Lochan Uaine was picture perfect. The tree-dotted mountains swept dramatically down toward the water, and the loch itself was green, a stunning emerald green that turned jade as the sun moved across its tranquil waters. Arrochar told me it was that spectacular green most likely due to the reflected light of the surrounding trees. That was the logical answer.

Legend had it, however, that Lochan Uaine was that color because fairies washed their clothes in it.

As I balanced on my haunches capturing images of one of the most beautiful places I'd ever had the privilege of seeing, I decided I liked the legend best. Honestly, the glen had something about it, something magical and ancient.

Feeling brave, I'd driven around, stopping when I found a lot to park in so I could follow the hiking trails. Sometimes I came across hikers who would give me the heads-up for places in the park that were particularly beautiful. It was all stunning—a smorgasbord of natural beauty that seduced me for hours.

I took so many photos and couldn't wait to upload them to my laptop. And I didn't miss a thing behind my camera. I knew when to lower the piece of equipment and just experience where I was. I sat my ass down on the rocky shore of a loch, the spring breeze whispering over my skin, as I processed the surrounding majesty.

A sense of peace that was difficult to explain wrapped around me in those moments.

I had no idea a place could do that—bring such a sense of serenity that all my worries, no matter how big, were forgotten. Even Lachlan.

Though he eventually bulldozed his way into my thoughts on the almost three-hour drive back to Ardnoch. Despite my confusion over the man, by the time I'd returned to the trailer that evening, I was physically exhausted in the best way. My phone showed missed calls from my mom, Seth, and Mac. I texted Mac and promised I'd see him in the morning.

And that was the plan. After waking up refreshed post adventure, I showered and changed into workout gear to meet Eredine and Lucy at the studio. However, as I was leaving the trailer, my cell rang in my hand. It was Seth.

Frowning in concern because it was pretty early in the morning back home, I answered. "Is everything okay?"

Seth exhaled. "Thank God. We were worried when you didn't answer your phone yesterday."

"I'm sorry. I didn't have a great signal where I was, and by the time I got home, I was exhausted. Is everything okay?"

"Got home?"

"What?"

"You said 'by the time I got home'?"

Did I? I shrugged it off. "It's just a turn of phrase. Is everything okay?"

"Why aren't you answering your mother's calls or emails?"

My stomach lurched as I yanked open the door to my SUV and got in. As I switched on the engine, my phone connected to the vehicle. "I've been busy."

"Too busy for your mom?" Seth's admonition boomed out of the car speaker, and I quickly tapped down the volume.

"Seth, I will talk to Mom when I'm ready to talk to Mom."

He sucked in a breath. "I knew it. Mac told you, didn't he?"

"About the letters."

"Yeah."

"So you knew." I shook my head in disgust and tried not to gun it backward out of my parking spot.

"Don't let him skew the narrative. There's more to it than just your mom returning some letters. He's not blameless."

"No, he's not, and Mac has been very honest about that. He and I are working through our issues. But Mom lied. *You* lied. And I'm not okay with that because it wasn't about me. It was about her. And you cannot possibly tell me any different."

My stepfather sighed. "No, I can't. It was selfish. She knows that. But you have to talk to her, Robbie. You can't shut her out."

"I'm not shutting her out. I'm just not having that conversation over the phone. We'll talk when I get back." I sought to change the subject. "Is Regan okay?"

"She needs you."

"Why? What's going on?"

"It's complicated. But she's dating this shady character your mom and I don't approve of, and she won't listen to us."

"Is she safe?"

"Yes. For now."

"Is she happy?"

"I don't know."

"Is she doing drugs?"

"What? No, of course not."

"Robbing a bank?"

"Robbie—"

"I'm not in Scotland just twiddling my thumbs, Seth. I'm here to reconnect with my father, and I'm sorry if that isn't as important as Regan hanging around some guy you don't approve of, but I'm not dropping my life to hurry back to Boston because you want me to parent your daughter."

"Shit, Robyn, that's not fair."

The truth was my parents weren't perfect. Whose parents were? Mine were good people who loved me and my sister. But Mom had always mothered and worried about Regan in a way she never had with me, and she'd shown favoritism over the years. She'd continually prioritized Regan's problems over mine, and in doing so expected me to worry and mother over Regan, too, even if I had my own issues to deal with. When it became apparent I had a much higher success rate in talking my sister around or out of something (e.g., asking her to quit dating a twenty-year-old biker when she was sixteen, suggesting she give up slacker friends who got her into pot when she was seventeen, leaving high school to pursue acting in New York when she'd never shown an interest in the profession her entire life, or dropping out of college before graduation, etc.), my mom and stepdad leaned heavily on me. It was something I'd naturally do as a big sister, but it didn't mean they were unburdened by the task of parenting her. And I was done.

After discovering those letters, I was so done doing what was best for everyone else but not for me. "I'm not coming home anytime soon. Unless Regan is in danger, abusing substances, or breaking the law, don't ask again. And tell Mom to stop calling me. We'll talk when *I'm* ready to talk."

"You don't sound like yourself, Robbie. I'm worried."

"Why? Because I'm putting myself before everyone else for the first time in my life?"

Seth was silent so long, I thought he'd hung up. Then, "That's fair. That's absolutely fair. And I'm sorry. You do what you have to do with Mac. Even though it might not seem like it, I'm glad you're getting the chance to connect with him. I just don't want him turning you against us."

"He's not. That's not who he is."

"No, I guess it's not."

I turned left toward the gates of Ardnoch Estate, and the sadness in my stepfather's voice chipped at my resolve. "Are you okay, Seth?"

"I'm good," he promised. "Just worried about my girls."

"Well, don't worry about me. Trust me, I'm where I'm supposed to be right now."

"Okay, Robbie. I'll let you go."

"Get some sleep. I love you."

"Love you, too, darlin'."

Despite my determination to let my parents deal with their own insecurities and worries, I couldn't help the niggle of guilt in my gut for being so harsh as the security cameras tagged my license plate and the gates swung open a few seconds later.

Fergus wasn't at the mews, so I left the SUV outside and walked down the gravel drive toward the path through the golf course that led to Eredine's studio. Two actors and current heartthrobs of our generation appeared out of the main entrance with a golf caddy leading the way. They stopped at the sight of me, and I gestured for them to continue.

One of them, a sexy Michael B. Jordan look-alike, grinned at me. "Never. Ladies first."

"Thank you, gentlemen." I nodded with a smile, pleased to discover manners still existed in the world. Unable to resist, I glanced over my shoulder as they walked toward the golf course and the Jordan look-alike stared back with a certain glimmer in his eyes.

It was nice to be admired.

It was also a nice distraction from my guilt.

Almost at the path that led toward Eredine's studio, I felt a tingling sensation on the back of my neck. Glancing over my shoulder again, this time at the castle, then seeing nothing out of the ordinary, I almost turned around when movement in a large, top-floor window stopped me.

A shiver tickled down my spine when I realized the window had the same aspect as the one from Lachlan's room.

Was he watching me?

I turned away, walking sightlessly toward the studio as the memory of two nights ago came at me in flashes of heat and musk. The sound of Lachlan's groan of release, his taste, the tight fullness of him thrusting inside me, the scratch of the wool of his kilt on my thighs—

"Stop it," I muttered to myself.

He'd insinuated we'd have sex again. He'd wanted to right

away. Yet I wasn't sure it was such a good idea. Mac complicated everything. Besides, I'd never been a casual sex kind of girl.

Lucy and Eredine greeted me as I strolled into the studio. They chatted about the ceilidh and things said and done by this person and that (names I didn't recognize because I still didn't know everyone all that well), and I laughed here and there, but my mind was elsewhere.

Last time we'd had a session together, I was trying to teach them dirty boxing, a style of fighting for when you were caught in an opponent's clinch. It was a combination of wrestling and boxing. Somewhat distracted, I decided to show them ground and pound. It was a great technique for a woman against a stronger opponent because it enabled them to grapple their attacker to the ground and then incapacitate with chokeholds and joint locks.

I'd suggested the girls get back into position to try it again, but my mind wandered to the owner of Ardnoch and whether I'd see him today. Or whether he was going to do what he was good at and avoid me.

He *was* slightly drunk when we had sex.

Did he regret it?

My cheeks flamed as I remembered our quick and furious interlude in Gordon's office.

Oh my God, I had sex on that poor man's desk.

So rude.

Not that I'd been thinking clearly in the moment. Obviously.

One minute we'd been arguing, as per usual, and the next minute, the man was inside me and I was so turned on ... I was almost embarrassed by how quickly I'd ignited.

"Robyn, am I doing this right? I think Eredine's turning purple. Shit, sorry."

Thankfully, I'd acted cool as a cucumber after the sex and

walked out of the office with my head held high. And I'd rejected his offer for more.

I was pretty pleased about that.

Especially since I'd wanted more.

"Robyn? Earth to Robyn?" Fingers snapped in front of my face.

I flinched.

Lucy stood before me while Eredine got to her feet, rubbing her throat.

Oh damn. "Are you okay?"

"No, she's not. Our coach was off in la-la land, and I did the chokehold thingie wrong. Or a little too right." She patted Eredine's shoulder. "Sorry, sweetie."

"It's okay." Eredine gave her a reassuring smirk. "But Robyn isn't."

I blinked owlishly. "I'm fine."

"No, you're definitely distracted."

"I'm fine," I insisted. There was no way I was talking to Lucy about this.

Lucy crossed her arms over her chest and jutted out a hip. "Wrong answer. It was clear from the moment you walked in here, you have something on your mind. Does it have anything to do with you disappearing from the ceilidh at the exact same time as Lachlan?"

She noticed that, huh?

"I'm not discussing this with you." I crossed the studio to grab my sports bottle. I'd barely worked out, but I was instantly overheated.

Eredine and Lucy followed, their gaze interrogative. Ignoring them, I said, "Why don't we just do some yoga today?"

"Need to relax, do you?" Eredine teased. "Something on your mind?"

"Oh my God, you two, stop."

"Not until you confide in us. We're pretty sure what happened, anyway, because Lachlan has been very close-mouthed." Lucy grinned. "And usually I can break him in minutes."

I couldn't help but laugh. "What did you ask him?"

"I asked if something happened between you two. Leighanne left. Then you both disappeared at the same time, which Ery and I noted, and then *you* came back for, like, two minutes before leaving with Mac. And Lachlan was brood-ing-no-fun-guy for the rest of the evening. When prodded, he wouldn't say a word. He avoided me all day yesterday—I'm sure of it."

Part of me wanted to talk to them about it. Ask their opinions. Get an outsider's perspective. I was too close to it, my hormones warring with my common sense, on the brink of winning. Yet, I didn't want things to be weird with Lucy. I said as much to her.

Lucy waved off my concern. "Robyn, Lachlan and I are not a thing and were never a thing when we were a thing. We're just friends. You can talk to me about this."

Reassured, I confessed what happened in Gordon's office.

Eredine's eyes widened, a scandalized grin stretching her mouth. "I thought you'd say you made out … not that you had sex. On Gordon's desk!"

Groaning, I buried my head in my hands while they laughed.

Someone tugged on my wrists, and my hands were forcefully removed from my face. Lucy, though still looking like she was struggling not to smile, asked after my well-being.

"He's Mac's best friend and boss. It's complicated. Is it worth making it complicated for just sex? I don't think so. It shouldn't happen again, right?"

"Just sex?" Eredine pushed.

"Well, amazing sex. There's no denying it's hot between us."

"But just sex," Lucy replied to Eredine before turning to me. She was no longer laughing, a little pucker of concern between her brows. "When he said that to you, you have to know he means it."

"I know he means it. It's just … physical. But it doesn't matter because it's not happening again."

Lucy shrugged. "If you're both on the same page, then it won't get complicated. If you start to feel like you're slipping off the page onto a different one, then extract yourself. Immediately," she warned, "or he'll break your heart."

I didn't think I was in danger of having my heart broken by Lachlan. Turning to Eredine for her opinion, she said, "I've never been good at casual, but if you can separate emotional entanglement with physical pleasure, then go for it. You're both grown-ups. You wouldn't be hurting anyone."

"What about Mac?"

"A daughter's sex life is never her father's business," Lucy answered.

We chuckled, and I nodded. "Okay, okay, let's move on to other things. Like yoga or something. I promise I won't be distracted anymore."

* * *

THE CASTLE WAS quiet as I made my way upstairs toward Mac's room. I passed Wakefield at reception but no other guests were around on the stairwell. Figuring they were at lunch, the very thought made me hungry. Eredine had guided us through the toughest yoga session I'd ever experienced, and I was sweaty and in need of fuel.

I thought perhaps Mac might want to go out for lunch. While considering places we might go, I didn't hear Lachlan until he was hurrying downstairs onto the second-floor landing. My eyes widened as he marched toward me, stern determination on his face. Like a moronic deer in the head-lights, I just stood there.

Then my hand was in his, and he hurried me upstairs toward the third floor.

My body throbbed in anticipation.

This was ridiculous!

I didn't argue or stop him. I just let him lead me by the hand to his room like a goddamn caveman.

Heart pounding, breathing shallow, I allowed him to drag me into his room. He kicked the door shut with his foot and then was on me like a starving man.

I kissed him for a few seconds before I felt his palm on my damp nape. Pushing him back, I panted, "I need to shower. I'm all sweaty."

Lachlan's eyes were fixed on my mouth. "You're about to get sweatier so there's no point showering just yet."

My lower belly clenched at the thought.

This was madness. Pure madness.

Any thought of stopping this thing between us went out the window as soon as he touched me.

"Makes sense," I murmured, reaching for his mouth again.

Lachlan, however, had other ideas. His fingers slipped under my sports bra, and I barely had time to lift my arms above my head before it was gone. Desire hardened his features as he pushed me toward the bed, gaze scorching my skin. I lay back, lifting my hips to help him pull off my yoga pants and underwear.

The pulsing throb between my legs grew insistent as I laid sprawled beneath his hot eyes, watching him undress.

Expression fierce, his voice was hoarse as he admitted, "I've been imagining fucking you all weekend. To have you naked, nothing between us."

I shivered at his intensity and enjoyed the view of his muscled physique as he quickly unzipped his suit pants. His shoulders were wide. I'd known from the way they strained his shirts and jackets that he was built. I also knew from having seen him half-naked in movies. But having all that finely honed gloriousness towering over me was beyond exciting.

And of course, I'd never gotten an eyeful of what was between his legs until now. I'd had him inside me, but I hadn't seen him because of his kilt.

"Whoa." I licked my lips, wondering how he'd fit last time.

"It's been like this since the ceilidh," he admitted, giving me a roguish grin as he reached for my right leg, lifting my ankle to his lips. "And as much as I want to jump on you like a wild thing, we will be taking our time."

"But I'm supposed to be meeting Mac." I sighed, melting into the bed as Lachlan trailed shivery kisses up my calf. I thanked God I'd shaved that morning.

"Mac can wait."

It took me a minute to gather my thoughts again.

"I'm not sure he—" I cut off my delayed response with a low moan as Lachlan's mouth reached my inner thigh and his hand caressed my stomach, fingers tantalizingly close to where I wanted them. My breath hitched as he licked the crease of my leg. The bristles of his beard tickled sensitive skin as he scattered kisses over my stomach and down my other thigh.

Deliberately avoiding the spot.

Frustrated, I arched my hips. "Lachlan."

He lifted his head, eyes full of mischief. "Problem?"

I grunted in irritation. "Stop torturing me."

"I didn't realize I was," the bastard lied, and then pushed my thighs wide, eyes a smoky cerulean with lust as he bowed his head between them. "Is this what you want?"

I nodded, trying to push up into his mouth, but he had my hips pinned.

"Say it."

I flushed at the demand. None of my sex partners had ever been particularly loquacious in bed. "I want your mouth."

"Is that it?" His breath whispered over me, increasing my excitement. "No special instructions?"

"I'm pretty sure you know what to do," I huffed, growing more agitated. My fingers fisted into the bedsheets.

Lachlan laughed, and then I was in heaven.

As he worshipped me, his hands smoothed up my stomach to cup my breasts and squeeze. I was overwhelmed by him, writhing on that bed, lost in nothing but passion. My moans grew to groans and cries, no longer cognizant of anything other than him and the pleasure he wrung from my body.

I came on a loud, hoarse cry of release that echoed around his room as he moved up my body, mapping it with his kisses. Still breathless, blown away by the best orgasm of my life, it took me a minute to realize that Lachlan was paying particular attention to the three scars on the right side of my chest: one near my right collarbone, another close to it just above my breast, and the third lower down just beneath my breast.

But then he was distracted by my nipple, for which I was grateful, and I wrapped my legs around his back to encourage him to come closer. My fingers worked through his thick, silky hair and moved down his back, touching and exploring him as he sucked at my breasts, taking his sweet time until both nipples were swollen and sensitive. I wanted him inside me. I could feel him throbbing against my stomach, and I kept trying to hitch my hips to bring him where he was currently very much required.

Lachlan chuckled at my efforts, his bearded cheeks grazing my breasts as he caressed my hips and ass and continued loving me with his mouth.

His head dipped downward again, and I thought I was going to get a second orgasm via his tongue when his kisses did a U-turn.

Back to my lowest scar.

He kissed it tenderly.

And then lifted his head to study it.

The scars were easy to hide with clothes, but I only hid them because I didn't want people to ask questions. I wasn't self-conscious about them, and I didn't think they were ugly.

While what happened had put me in therapy, it was also one of the things I'd done in my life that I was most proud of. I'd saved my friend's life, and the scars were my badges of honor.

Still, what did Lachlan think of them? Running my fingers through his hair, I asked him.

"I know what they are," he said, meeting my gaze. "I've seen bullet-wound scars before."

I nodded, hoping the mood wasn't about to be spoiled.

His brows puckered. "What happened?"

I shook my head, trying to signal with my body that I just wanted to have sex. When he didn't catch on, I said, "I don't want to talk about it."

A muscle ticked in his jaw. "At least tell me Mac knows."

"He does."

"Then I guess that's what matters," he bit out, seeming pissed off before his mouth took mine, his kisses hard, searching and breath stealing.

He broke the kiss only to grab a condom from his bedside-table drawer. Suited up, Lachlan caught me under the arms and hauled me farther up the bed as if I weighed nothing. Then he was over me, one hand braced at the side of my head, the other curled around my thigh.

He glided in, eased by my desire, and I gasped at the delicious, full sensation of him.

Lachlan held my gaze as he took his time, gentle, slow, deliberate flexes of his hips as he built a torturous friction between us.

"More," I demanded, dragging my nails down his hard chest, my thumbs catching on his nipples. "Lachlan, more."

In answer, he took hold of my hands and pinned them at either side of my head.

The sensation was unexpectedly erotic, and he bared his teeth in a savage, satisfied grin as he felt my reaction and kept up the slow lovemaking that was driving me wild with impatience.

Just when I felt my climax nearing, Lachlan stopped. He held himself over me, not moving.

"What are you doing?" I gasped in outrage.

In answer, he kissed me, lazy, sweet, sexy kisses that had me canting my hips in the hope of restarting the good stuff. But Lachlan withheld all but his mouth. I whimpered in exasperation, pushing against his hold on my wrists.

Lachlan groaned and to my utter relief began to move.

Breaking our kiss, Lachlan watched me as he started his torture all over again.

There was no other word for it but exquisite torture because just as before, as I hovered on the peak, he halted.

My protests were swallowed in his kisses, holding everything but his lips still as he explored my mouth and then trailed slow, hungry kisses down my neck to my breasts. When I tried to push my hips into his, he nipped lightly at my collarbone and shot me a warning look.

"You're a bastard." It would've sounded more convincing

if it hadn't ended in a moan of pleasure as he covered my nipple with his mouth.

What was he doing to me?

I found myself murmuring gibberish, pleading, begging for him to keep moving.

He did.

But then he repeated his cycle of torment.

Finally, my body could take no more. I was strung so taut, I was almost on the verge of tears, something I'd never experienced before. My body trembled with the need for release, and I wasn't alone. Lachlan's expression was harsh with need, the muscles in his arms straining as he held me down.

"Please," I whispered, vulnerable beneath his hot eyes. "Please, Lachlan."

Whatever impressive control he'd mastered snapped and he began to thrust. Hard, powerful drives. Savage, desperate, his face etched with fierce want.

Each drive tightened the need inside me, tighter, higher, the tension a coiling promise of bliss.

Then I shattered.

The single most out-of-this-world orgasm exploded through me.

I screamed with release as I came around him, my inner muscles rippling in wave after wave after wave …

Lachlan's hoarse yell of climax thundered around the room chasing my cries, and he collapsed over me, releasing my wrists as he shuddered and groaned into my ear.

The room was silent except for the sounds of our heavy breathing, but I could still hear my scream and his yell in my head.

What the holy heck was that?

I slapped a hand over my forehead as I tried to recover from the extreme pleasure.

Sex with anyone else was officially forever tainted by this moment.

That wasn't good! This was temporary! I glared at his ceiling as he pressed a sweet kiss to my shoulder. I did not want to get addicted to sex with someone who was temporary.

Remembering my pleas, the vulnerability, of being putty in his goddamn hands, enjoying the bastard holding me captive beneath his powerful body and talented hips, I stiffened.

Scrambling for the best reason to end this now, I gently shoved Lachlan onto his side to get him off. But he wasn't ready to detach, his hands reaching for me, touching me, caressing my stomach, my breasts ... and making it very difficult to leave his bed.

I glowered at him, confused by my warring desires.

His expression was soft with satisfaction, but his eyes were alert. "What is it?"

I fought hard against the impulse to just lie back down and let him continue touching me. Instead, I took hold of his hand at my breast and pushed it away.

Lachlan scowled, repeating his question silently as he sat up.

"This is too complicated. We should stop," I said.

The man huffed with disbelief. "Eh, pretty sure neither of us have come harder in our lives. Why stop now?"

Pretending I wasn't affected by his confession (though secretly delighted I'd given that to him too), I replied, "Because of Mac. I don't want to come between you two."

"I thought we went over this? It's just sex. If we're both on the same page, then it won't be a problem. Unless we're not on the same page?"

No, it was just sex. For now. But even sex could be addictive, and I didn't want to be constantly comparing him to my future lovers.

Think that ship sailed an orgasm ago.

Okay, I conceded that was most likely true.

If this was just sex, though, then I planned to avoid the guy outside the bedroom. "You're right. We're both on the same page. Just sex." I patted him on the shoulder. "This was great." And rolled away from him to get out of bed.

Lachlan hauled me back into his chest, and his wandering hand dipped between my legs. "Oh, I'm not done with you yet."

"I can't," I groaned, leaning back into him, my body übersensitive.

But then his fingers worked their magic, and pleasure flooded me. I arched into his touch, seeking more.

"Oh, but I think you can," he murmured darkly in my ear.

23

LACHLAN

G uy was discussing the estate menu. The head chef had come to Lachlan's office to go over his ideas, and his boss heard the words *seasonal*, *lobsters*, *cockles*, *sea bass*, *kale*, *asparagus*, and *leeks* … but they had no meaning.

Because Lachlan wasn't bloody paying attention.

In fact, Lachlan had found it difficult to focus since yesterday afternoon. Despite his wish to stay in bed all day with Robyn, Wakefield called up to his room with a problem, and he'd known it was time to get to back to work. He shouldn't have been screwing around during the day, anyway. He wasn't just the owner but the estate manager. While he had department managers and supervisors, he was still a required presence until he decided to appoint someone in his stead.

Yet, he knew if his butler hadn't called his room, Lachlan would've attempted to keep Robyn with him all day and through the night.

Unfortunately, she'd seemed almost relieved to escape him.

Not something he was used to.

After he'd convinced her to share a shower (the memories of which would keep him warm during cold, cold nights), Robyn had gone to Mac and barely given Lachlan a second glance as she'd left.

Of course, she wasn't the first woman to be unconcerned with their casual arrangement. Most of the women he entered into short-term affairs with were on the same page, Lucy among them. She came and went as she pleased and placed no pressure on either of them.

It hadn't bothered Lachlan a bit.

He was always relieved when a woman left his bed with no fuss or clinginess. Even if that did make him a bit of a selfish bastard.

But no one had ever wanted to run away from him afterward. Until Robyn.

It bothered Lachlan.

Why was she glad to be rid of him? He knew she loved the sex. There was no denying that the two of them were a combustible pairing. Fuck, but the woman turned him on. And vice versa.

Maybe that was it.

The sex was addictive, and it bothered him she didn't seem to want to stick around for more when he found it hard (literally) to let her go. And he'd been contemplating when they could find time to do it again since the moment she'd left. He'd barely considered anything else. Not Mac, not the estate.

Jesus. The last time he'd been this consumed by sex, he was a teenager.

"So rhubarb is good, yeah?" Guy asked.

The word pulled Lachlan's head out of his arse. "No. What? No … I mean, what?"

His chef raised an eyebrow. "Rhubarb. It's seasonal.

Excellent at the moment. I was going to incorporate it into the new menu."

"No." Lachlan abhorred the stuff. "No rhubarb. Ever."

"*Okay.*" Guy crossed the word off his notepad. "Then I'll need to rethink part of the menu."

"Everything else sounds good."

"Great." Guy stood but seemed to hesitate.

"Anything else?"

The man appeared uncomfortable, and Lachlan understood why when Guy said, "I hate to ask, but ... well, Arro isn't answering my calls. Can you call her and get her to call me back?"

His immediate thought was, *why isn't she answering your calls?* Those protective instincts raised his defenses. "What happened?"

The chef startled at Lachlan's almost bark. "Oh, nothing. It was just a stupid fight after the ceilidh. I was drunk and said something I didn't mean. You know how that is. I want to apologize."

Despite the chef's sincerity, Lachlan's concern was for his sister. Arrochar wasn't a huffy woman. She didn't know how to hold a grudge. Unlike her brothers. In fact, Arro had always been the voice of reason in their family, the practical but softening feminine influence they'd be lost without.

"I'll call my sister, but not for you." Lachlan stood, keeping his tone neutral. "I have no problem with you dating Arrochar, but while you are in chef whites under this roof, you are my employee. I'd prefer you maintain that distinction at all times."

Guy couldn't hide his frown, but he gave Lachlan a jerk of his chin and muttered a "yes, sir" that sounded anything but deferential.

Lachlan let it go and waited for the chef to leave his office before calling his sister.

When she didn't answer on his third try an hour later, Lachlan's concern became an anxious tug in his gut. Arrochar rarely didn't answer her phone, and she always called back.

As a forest engineer for Forestry and Land Scotland, Arro's current task kept her close to home at Blairnie Forest. They were timber harvesting, and it was Arrochar's job to plan every aspect of the process. While she worked mostly in an office, he knew she was currently in the field to implement solutions to some logistical problems they'd had with equipment and loading.

Her worksite was only a thirty-minute drive from the castle. Lachlan checked his watch, noted his sister would most likely still be on-site, and decided to find her for himself. It was a good distraction from a certain American consuming his thoughts. Or the fact that he hadn't seen Mac since he'd slept with his best friend's daughter.

That sounds very wrong.

"Damn the man for having a kid at sixteen and making it weird for everybody," he muttered dryly as he left his office.

Stopping in at security, he informed Jock where he'd be.

"All right, sir," Jock replied. "A quick update, though. Our geofence disabled a drone. McHugh has gone out to collect it."

The news irritated and concerned Lachlan. "The paparazzi already? They usually hold off until summer."

"Could just be a local who got too close to our perimeter."

"Or our little problem is trying to find a new way to scope out the estate." He referred to his stalker and the fact that the estate's security system was no longer vulnerable to the hacker.

"I wouldn't assume so, sir. It's an isolated incident. We'll check the drone for prints and keep you posted."

Grateful for the efficient team Mac had put together,

Lachlan thanked Jock and moved to leave when the guard said his name again. He glanced over his shoulder. Jock looked a little uncomfortable.

"Mr. Galbraith was here earlier this morning. When our system detected the drone."

"And?"

"He inferred that he would be returning to work this week." Jock winced, clearly hating the position he'd been put in.

Lachlan tried not to show his agitation at his friend's restless impatience. "I'll have a word with him upon my return."

The security deputy seemed relieved.

Not looking forward to a discussion about postponing Mac's return to work, Lachlan threw the thought out of his head for now and jumped into the Range Rover Fergus had brought around from the mews.

The thirty-minute drive to Blairnie Forest passed in a blur as Lachlan veered between concern for his sister and wondering if he should visit Robyn or give her time to adjust to their affair.

He liked to think of himself as a fairly patient man, but she brought out this fervent covetousness. With her, he was greedy to the point of craving.

Definitely a bloody addiction.

Turning off at the site Arro told him she was working from, he noted the parked cars of the site crew and the fact that Arro's Defender wasn't there. Seeing her colleague Marcello, a project manager, Lachlan got out of his vehicle. The Italian spotted him and moved away from the two colleagues in construction hats to meet him halfway.

"Lachlan." Marcello held out his hand in greeting. "Good to see you."

The Italian wasn't just a coworker of Arro's; he was a

friend and had been invited to a few family dinners with his fiancée in the past. They had a young daughter who regularly played with Lachlan's niece, Eilidh.

"You too. I hope you're well."

"Fine, fine. Is all okay with Arro?"

Lachlan stiffened at the question. "That's what I came to find out." He gestured to the site.

"Oh." Marcello frowned. "She called in sick two days running. Said she had food poisoning."

Scowling at this news, he replied, "I better check on her."

Marcello's brows drew together. "Tell her I'm asking for her. It's not like her. I've seen Arro try to work through flu."

It was true. His sister was always on the go, driven by a need to be useful, and she despised being ill to the point where she would deny it until her family stepped in to force her to take care of herself.

Bidding the manager goodbye, Lachlan jumped into his SUV and tried not to race to her house.

Something was wrong. He felt it in his gut.

Arro's home was a midcentury bungalow on the northern outskirts of Ardnoch. He'd offered her Adair land to build a home on, just as he'd offered his brothers, but Arro and their youngest brothers were holding out on their dream homes until they were ready to settle down. He'd teased Arro about the house she'd bought with her inheritance. In a quiet, nice neighborhood, the bungalow wasn't exactly fashionable. However, it was spacious enough for her library of books and the collection of inherited family objects Lachlan granted her permission to remove from the castle. Plus, she was surrounded by good neighbors. That's all his sister cared about. To be surrounded by family and friends. And books. Lots of them.

Seeing her car in her drive, he relaxed marginally, but it

didn't show in his charging strides as he hurried to the front door and pressed the doorbell.

Lachlan's calm did not come when minutes later she still hadn't answered the door.

He tried the bell again.

Stepping back from it, he stared into the front windows, searching for movement. Nothing. Following the paving stones around the house, he made his way into the decent-size back garden that Arro had spruced up with decking and a seating area off the kitchen. Designated veg, fruit, and potato patches had been planted in the back near the greenhouse.

After knocking on the kitchen door, he peered into the patio windows and was dismayed to find no sign of her. Then he noted the open laptop on the kitchen table next to a half-eaten sandwich and a cup of coffee.

She was in there.

Well enough to eat and work.

But not answer the door?

Truly concerned, Lachlan tried the doorknob and was relieved and annoyed in equal measure when it opened. Arro lived alone. Her doors should always be locked. Yes, they resided in one of the safest villages in Scotland, but (1) she was an Adair, and (2) he had a stalker after him willing to try to hurt—or kill—those he loved.

Once he'd given her a rollicking for worrying him, he'd lecture her about locking her doors.

"Arro!" he called as he moved through the kitchen. "It's Lachlan!"

He heard a shuffling and followed the sound out of the kitchen toward the bedrooms at the back. "Arro!"

"I'm here." Her voice was muffled through her bedroom door. "I'm sick. I don't want to infect anyone."

Frowning at the obvious lie, he stopped at her door and

tapped his knuckles lightly against it. "Arro, what's going on, sweetheart? I'm worried."

"I told you. I'm not well. Flu."

"Flu? You told Marcello it was food poisoning. What's going on? Why are you hiding and not answering your phone?"

There was silence on the other side of the door. Then ... "If I come out ... you have to promise you won't fly off the handle. That you won't do anything stupid."

"Arro," he said, a warning in his voice.

"Promise me, Lachlan."

"I promise," he bit out.

Yet, when she stepped out of her bedroom, it was hard to remember the promise over the roaring in his ears.

"What the goddamn fuck?" His words were low but rough with fury.

His sister, his precious, wouldn't-hurt-a-bloody-fly, wee sister was sporting a black eye, bruised cheekbone, and a cut lip.

Someone is going to die today.

At his expression, Arrochar's eyes widened, and she held up her hands as if to placate him. "Calm down, Lachlan. Please."

"Not until you tell me what I'm looking at."

"First, you have to know this has never happened before." Her voice trembled, and he could see she struggled not to cry. "This is the first time, and I broke up with him. I promise."

He stumbled back from her, his rage building. "Guy did this?"

That fucker was over.

Storming toward the front door, he felt a tug on his arm and whirled to shake off his sister when the sight of her flinching back, afraid, put out his surface anger like a bucket of ice water.

Emotion thickened in his throat as he took in Arro's battered face. "I would never hurt you."

Tears brightened her eyes. "God, I know that. But please calm down. Please."

Struggling to slow his breathing as his heart thundered in his chest, Lachlan attempted to, for her sake. He held out his hand to her like she was a frightened animal.

Arro walked into him, burrowing against him in a way she hadn't since she was a wee girl.

He felt a burning in his eyes as he embraced her, knowing he probably held her too tight but was unable to loosen his arms. Someone had beaten his sister, and not only had Lachlan not been there to protect her but he'd had a civil conversation with the bastard that very morning.

Yesterday he'd been screwing around with Robyn, and his sister was holed up in her house.

Scared.

And beaten.

"Tell me what happened," he whispered against her hair.

Arrochar eased away from him, eyes lowered to the ground as she motioned to the kitchen.

Lachlan tried to be patient as she forced him to wait until he'd made a fresh pot of coffee.

"It was after the ceilidh," she finally divulged as she sat down with him at the dining table. "He seemed fine at the Gloaming. Drunk, but fine. But he was quiet on the walk back to my place. Then it all just came at me as soon as we stepped in the house."

"What did?" He tried not to imagine it. His sister alone with that bastard, no clue what was about to happen. That there was no one there to protect her.

Arro licked her lips nervously and stared past him out the

window. "Apparently, I spent all night flirting with Mac, which is ridiculous. It's Mac, for goodness' sake. Guy has gotten it into his head there's something going on between us. Can you believe that? He started yelling about my behavior when Mac was attacked. I told him he was wrong. It's Mac. He's … he's … family. And I'd never cheat." Now she looked at him. Right in the eye. "I'd never cheat, Lachlan."

He knew she wouldn't.

Disloyalty wasn't in the Adair blood. "I know, sweetheart."

Anger flooded her features. "I called him an arsehole and he pushed me into the wall. I lost my temper and pushed him back and told him to get out and never call me again. Then all this rubbish started pouring out of him, how I always made him feel like an outsider, like he wasn't good enough, that I thought I was better than him, that I was an untouchable Adair." She blinked back tears. "I don't even know what that means. It was like listening to a petty little boy on the school playground trying to tear me down because he was jealous of me. Ridiculous and immature. My reaction wasn't very nice. I laughed at him and said he was pathetic … and that was the wrong thing to do."

Lachlan studied her face, hot blood causing a haze in his mind that he was trying very hard to beat back. "He hit you."

She pressed a tentative finger to her cheek. "Blindsided me. Hit me so hard, it took me down, and then he climbed on me to hit me a couple more times. He only got the other two hits in because the first had shocked me, dazed me. But I got my faculties together, spotted the paperweight on the table, and managed to shove him off me long enough to grab it. When he came at me, I cracked him over the head with it.

"The drink, the hit, it knocked him out but only for seconds. When he came to, it was like he was a different person. Like he couldn't believe what he'd done. He tried to

plead with me, told me he loved me"—she guffawed angrily
—"but I told him to get out or I would call the police."

"You should have called the police," Lachlan said, trying
not to raise his voice.

"I was ashamed." Her face crumpled and she sobbed, cries
that tore through his gut.

Getting out of his chair, Lachlan pulled his sister up and
held her while she cried, reassuring her she had nothing to
be ashamed of, nothing to worry about, that he'd take care of
everything.

When he finally felt her cries slow and her body relax, he
eased her into her chair and set about making her a cup of
the chamomile tea she liked.

"Sorry." She smiled wearily at him. "For crying like that. I
just … I feel stupid. That I didn't see he had that in him. I
should have."

"Don't do that to yourself. People have a way of hiding
their true selves."

"Still. I'm sorry."

"You never have to say sorry." He brought the hot mug
over to her. As she took it in both hands, he said, "You do
have to report this to the police, though."

"Oh, Lachlan, no." Her denial was instant. "Every time we
go to the police with something, we open up the chance of
the press finding out. That's the last thing the club needs
right now."

"Fuck the club," he bit out. "What if he does this to
someone else?"

"Don't put that on me." Her lips quivered. "Don't make me
feel bad for not wanting anyone to know about this."

"Well, I can't let him get away with it."

"Lachlan—"

He held up a hand to cut her off. If he couldn't have the
bastard arrested, he'd dole out his own form of justice. "I'm

firing him and making it clear he needs to leave the Highlands. Preferably on a plane back to Australia."

Arrochar nodded. "That works for me."

Her bruising was starting to yellow, meaning it was healing. Lachlan reached out to caress her cheekbone. "I'll let everyone know you have a flu bug and that I'm taking care of you. Everyone except Thane."

"Och, Lachlan—"

"I'm not keeping this from him."

Her brows furrowed with fierceness. "You're a pain in my arse. And if you even think about telling Mac—"

"I won't," he interrupted her again. "Mac would lose his goddamn mind and try to kill Guy, and while that might be fun to watch, Mac's not completely over his injuries."

Relaxing, she sank into her chair. "What are you going to do about a chef?"

He shrugged. "That's not anything you need to worry about. For now, I just want you to take it easy. I need to see to Guy, and then I'll be back tonight with a takeaway. What do you fancy?"

"You don't have to."

"It's not for you, it's for me." And he wasn't lying. He needed to be with her. Make sure she definitely was all right.

Arro gave him a soft, loving look. "Thank you for keeping your cool for me. It means a lot. And for firing him."

"I'd do anything for you, sweetheart."

Her eyes brightened with fresh tears, and she slapped playfully at his arm. "Go, before you have me blubbering again."

He nodded but didn't make a move. Instead, he suggested, "Perhaps you might find time to ask Robyn for some self-defense tips."

Arro raised an eyebrow.

Lachlan smirked. "I've seen her in action. She's impressive."

His sister considered him a moment. "You admire her, don't you?"

Admired Robyn? She irritated him, excited him, pissed him off, and turned him on ... but admiration? It never occurred to him before but yes, he did. He admired her bravery in coming to Scotland, he admired her independence and self-sufficiency. And he admired her physical and emotional strength. He admired a woman who laid beneath him and dared him with her eyes to find the scars on her chest anything but something she should be proud of.

And goddamn was he itching to know the story behind them.

"Yes, I do." He reached over and squeezed his sister's wrist. "She's trained in mixed martial arts."

Arro cocked her head, contemplating. "It would never have been my thing before now, but I have to admit, it would be nice to know I could handle myself without a paperweight."

Ignoring the humor in her voice—Lachlan was not ready (and never would be) to laugh at the situation—he got up and kissed her forehead. "I'll talk to Robyn."

"No, let me. Once this," she said, gesturing to her face, "looks better, I'll catch up with her. I keep meaning to have dinner with her, anyway." Arrochar stood to follow him to the front door. "Is something going on between you two?"

"Why would you ask that?" he asked blandly, glad his back was to her.

"Just the way you kept watching each other at the ceilidh."

"She was watching me?" he threw over his shoulder and then almost rolled his eyes at his idiocy.

Arrochar's lips twitched, but she did him the favor of not laughing. "Oh, it's that way, is it?"

"It's nothing serious."

"Does Mac know?"

"Like I said, it's nothing serious. We're both on the same page."

"You can have nothing serious with anyone. Why her? It's not like you to put sex before your family, and Mac is family."

Her admonishing tone chafed. "Arro, I love you, but I'm not discussing this with you. I'll be back tonight. Lock the door behind me, and lock your bloody kitchen door. None of us should have our guard down right now. Especially not you. And if that bastard comes here after I boot him off the estate, you get straight on the phone to me." Something occurred to him. "Does he have a key?"

"No. I would have changed the locks if he did."

"Still ..." Lachlan's brow furrowed. "How would you feel about relocating to my place until I can get the locks changed? Just in case. If the arsehole can hit you, he can go behind your back to have a key copied."

"You're so paranoid."

"For good reason."

At his implacable stare, she threw up her hands. "Fine. But I'll need to grab some things."

*　*　*

AFTER FOLLOWING his sister to his coastal home in the tiny settlement of Caelmore, just outside Ardnoch, happy she was secure inside, Lachlan didn't just call a locksmith to change out Arro's locks but arranged for a security company to update her standard house alarm.

He didn't care if it was overboard.

Then as he was driving up to the castle, he called Jock to prepare some men to escort Guy off the estate. He didn't explain why, and Jock didn't ask questions.

The rage that he'd dialed down to simmering began to boil over, but his promise to his sister kept it under control as he stormed through the trade entrance and into the castle kitchen.

Guy was there with his sous chef Rafaella and four junior chefs.

"Everyone but Guy out of the kitchen. Now," Lachlan barked.

The chefs startled, hesitating for a moment before Rafaella clipped at them to remove themselves. She followed, throwing a curious look at Lachlan over her shoulder as she left.

Lachlan turned to his sister's ex-boyfriend and his soon-to-be ex-employee and knew the bastard knew that he knew.

Guy dropped the large kitchen knife in his hand and walked toward Lachlan with his hands raised defensively. "Whatever she said, let me explain."

Lachlan raised a finger, pointing at him. "Stay the fuck there. Take one more step toward me, and this conversation will end less civilly than I promised Arro."

The chef abruptly stopped. He swallowed hard. "Lachlan—"

"You're fired. No ifs, buts, or maybes about it. I want you off this estate immediately."

Guy had the audacity to look shocked. "Do I get a reference at least?"

A red mist crept into the corners of Lachlan's vision. He seethed, holding it back. "You *beat* my sister. You're lucky I'm not calling the police."

The man didn't seem to understand the peril he was in. "If you don't give me a reference, my reputation is ruined. I left a five-star hotel for this job!"

Lachlan counted to five in his head. Then, "Not. My. Problem."

"This is my career! And over what? Your whore of a sister!"

The word *whore* hit Lachlan with the impact of a punch to the face. He bowed his head, glared at his feet, tried to count again, got to three—

He lunged at Guy with a downward swing of his fist that knocked the piece of shit to the ground. Blood sprayed across the side of the stainless steel island from the force of the blow to his nose.

Groaning, Guy pushed up off the floor, and Lachlan helped him to his feet, hauling him by the front of his chef whites so the fucker dangled off the ground. Out of the corner of his eye, Lachlan saw Jock stride into the room with two men at his back. Blood dripped down Guy's nose and mouth, the former of which was already swelling up. "If I ever see you near my family again, I'll end more than your career. Do you understand?"

Guy glared at him.

"Do you understand me?"

The arsehole nodded, and Lachlan shoved him at Jock, who caught and pushed him at the men at his back. The security guards each took one of his arms.

"Escort him so he can gather his shit, then get him off my estate. Make sure he never sets foot in Ardnoch again." The men nodded. "Jock, wait a minute."

Guy didn't struggle against Lachlan's men as they manhandled him out of the kitchen. He waited until they were gone to say to Jock, "I want it made perfectly clear to him that he's not welcome in Scotland. Understood?"

His man understood. "On it."

Once Jock was gone, Lachlan finally felt the pain in his knuckles and hissed as he flexed his fingers. Grabbing a bag of ice from the large walk-in freezer, he then went in search of Rafaella. He found her and the junior chefs in the small staff room off the kitchens. They looked a little pale-faced, and a lot concerned.

Lachlan didn't explain, even though they all noted the ice pressed to his knuckles. "Rafaella, you've just been promoted to head chef. We'll start interviewing for a sous chef next week, if that works for you?"

She nodded, wide-eyed. "Absolutely."

"Good. Any problems adjusting to the new schedule, let me know." He turned to leave, throwing over his shoulder, "There's blood on the side of the island. I'd disinfect the whole thing and the floor and get rid of any food prep that was out."

"*Okay*," she replied in a tone that suggested he was a little crazy.

He felt a little crazy.

In fact, he was practically buzzing with animal energy that needed release.

Pulling his phone out of his back pocket, he dialed Robyn. She didn't answer.

Fuck.

Ten minutes later, he'd changed into workout clothes and was beating the shit out of a boxing bag in the gym.

Sex with Robyn would've been his first choice, but apparently his American wasn't as keen to see him as he was to see her.

It was probably for the best. He was due home to Arro in a few hours.

Just the thought of his sister and what she'd gone through had him hitting the bag so hard, a crack opened in the ceiling.

24

ROBYN

A gentle Scottish mist attempted to cool my skin as I ran along the perfect golden sands of Ardnoch Beach. It was firm beneath my feet as I stuck close to shore, the water of the firth an arcadian soundtrack to my exercise. Lucy usually ran with me in the mornings and distracted me from scenery I knew I'd never get used to or take for granted.

Alone, I could revel in its beauty. I'd never seen sand like it and never thought I'd find it in Scotland. Miles of it stretched before me, a guide along the water as dark green hills loomed in the distance where the earth jutted out into the sea. Sunbeams cut through gray clouds, spilling angelic rays of champagne light across the water.

I'd needed this.

Some alone time.

Lucy had texted yesterday to tell me she would be in Edinburgh for a few days so to run without her. I'd texted her back but ignored the several missed calls I had on my phone.

One from my mom, and an unopened voicemail.

And two missed calls from Lachlan yesterday afternoon.

I also had a text message from Arrochar reminding me we needed to set a date for dinner together.

Life was starting to feel a little out of my control. Mac and I seemed to be speeding ahead into a relationship, and there was a part of me still terrified he would hurt me. Despite my feelings toward my mom, I also hated that we weren't on good terms and wouldn't be until I had the chance to speak with her face-to-face.

And Lachlan.

Jesus, I didn't know what to do about him. My heart warily suggested one thing while my body urged me to throw caution to the wind.

My body was pretty loud about it too.

Ever notice how it's always the moron who's the loudest in the room?

And then there was, of course, the glaring, startling reality that Mac's attacker and Lachlan's stalker had still not been caught.

The run on the beach allowed me to shrug off my worries and just let myself be. But it didn't take long for all my concerns to propel themselves back to the fore. Deciding the run was over, and to return to the trailer so I could proceed with my plans for the day, I upped the energy.

There was one person I hadn't had a chance to talk to. He hadn't been at the ceilidh. No surprise there since Lachlan was in attendance. Yesterday, I'd taken Mac for a drive, and we'd chatted about everything and nothing, including the case, and I'd asked about McCulloch and the land issue.

According to Mac, Collum McCulloch owned a small farm north of Ardnoch. But the family had insisted for centuries that they used to own land south of Ardnoch that bordered Adair land. It wasn't a huge piece of property, but it was coastal.

It was Adair land now, and Lachlan's members had homes on it.

The farm still existed northwest of the village, and it was where I planned to go.

Taking a quick shower and throwing on the nearest clean clothes I could find (not having on-site laundry was a pain!), I jumped into my SUV in investigation mode.

I thought on what a great day I'd had with my dad and how afterward when I returned to the trailer, I'd begun to feel anxious about it. Dad and I were cut from the same cloth. I noticed things about his personality that I recognized in myself. For instance, he had to know about my affair with Lachlan, but he didn't lecture me about it. In fact, he didn't even mention it. That was so like me. If I thought someone might be sensitive about something, I left well enough alone until they wanted to talk about it.

As we drove and he talked about his life with Lachlan and all the traveling they'd done, my wanderlust envied him. Mom had always been perplexed by my desire to journey to different places, but now I realized I'd inherited it from Mac. I just hadn't been able to afford to do it.

Our taste in music was the same. When I turned on my car, I switched the radio to a rock channel and throughout the day, I'd hear him murmuring the lyrics to the songs I loved too.

While he peppered me with questions about school and work and friends and past boyfriends and everything he'd missed, there were also moments when I stopped the car to take photographs of the scenery, and Mac stood at my side in easy silence. Comfortable silences that existed between fathers and daughters who'd been in each other's lives from the moment she first opened her eyes.

We had it. In spite of all the crap between us ... we had that easiness.

And it scared me.

It didn't make sense. The whole point of coming here was to see if I could salvage my relationship with my father. Yet now that I knew it was possible, I was anxious.

It worried me because that bond between us could break my heart all over again if Mac decided he wasn't interested in maintaining a relationship with me. While my gut said he wouldn't do that to me again, that he was enjoying reconnecting just as much as I was, I couldn't quite rid myself of the fear, though I was determined not to give into it.

Then I remembered a particular part of my conversation with Mac yesterday that had moved me.

"So ..." I'd studied Mac as we stood at the side of the road in among hills and valleys. I'd caught sight of a stag on the hills not far from the road, and the majestic beast had allowed me a few shots before he took off. It was then I found myself wondering whether I was allowed to ask Mac about his love life. I was curious. And he *had* asked about mine. "There's never been anyone special in your life? A girlfriend you thought about settling down with?"

My father had shrugged, apparently not uncomfortable with the question. "Not really, no."

"In all your forty-four years, you haven't been in love?"

He raised an eyebrow. "There's a distinct difference between those two questions."

Aha! So he *had* been in love, just not with someone he dated. "What happened?"

"A number of things. I suppose fear got in the way."

Surprised, I replied, "I can't imagine you being afraid of anything."

"Does reality disappoint you?"

"No," I promised him. "I just ... I'm sad that was the reason. And continually blown away by your honesty." Not a lot of men, especially not a lot of men perceived as tough-guy bodyguards, would admit to feeling fear over anything, let alone love.

Mac searched my face. "Everything you've told me about yourself, everything I can see for myself ... I bet you've never run away from anything because you were frightened."

I considered this. "I guess ... and I'm not saying this to hurt you because that's not my intention. This is just the truth. When you left, the pain was ... I imagine it was a lot like grief."

He flinched and I continued, ignoring my guilt for inflicting damage, because Mac wanted the truth. "And I realized that terrible things happen, things that hurt so bad, it's almost debilitating, but in the end, you get through it. Time, if not a healing agent, is kind of a numbing agent. Almost everything is survivable. Sad, frightening things happen in life, but I truly believe there's nothing more frightening than fear itself." I smiled at him. "Coming here proves that. Because I was scared out of my mind to do this, to meet with you, and I'm so glad I did."

My last words took the shadows from Mac's eyes, and we'd shared a soft, affectionate smile.

Then I'd pushed. "Do you want to meet someone, Mac? Have a family with her?"

Mac guffawed. "I'm a little old for that now."

"In what reality? You're forty-four. There's still time for all that."

"I'm happy as I am. Bachelor for life." He nudged me with his elbow. "And I already have a family."

Sensing he no longer wanted to pursue the subject, I'd let it drop.

But I thought about what I'd said to him, how there was nothing more frightening than fear itself.

Lachlan popped into my head.

Maybe I needed to remind myself of my own philosophy.

Maybe I was *avoiding* him. Not running. Just avoiding. For now. Until I could figure out if our affair was a good idea.

Telling myself to focus as I followed directions on Google Maps to McCulloch's farm, I missed the entrance and had to wait until I found a passing place on the single-track road to turn back.

The entrance to the farm was another rough, single-track road flanked by fenced-in fields of rolling greenery. Farm buildings sat in the distance, and the closer I got, more animals appeared. There were sheep on either side of me. I knew from Mac that McCulloch owned sheep and cattle, so the cows had to be farther afield.

As I slowed and guided my SUV left into the farmyard, the road changed to packed mud, and I thanked God I'd put on my hiking boots instead of my sneakers.

I didn't see a farmhouse, so I gathered it was somewhere else on the land. What was here was an L-shaped building made of stone with small windows and doorways that suggested it had been here for a long time. To my left was a large, doorless structure made of corrugated iron walls that curved up and over in a semicircle. A hoop house. Inside were animal pens.

To my right was a massive barn loaded with hay bales and farm equipment, including a tractor. Behind the barn, beyond the buildings that faced onto the farmyard was another barn.

Opening the door of my vehicle, I was assaulted by the smell.

Well, it *was* a farm.

I'd just closed my door when a young man appeared out of the darkness of the hoop house and sauntered toward me. He looked to be in his early twenties and had a stocky build. Dressed much like Collum McCulloch, including mud-splattered work boots, I guessed the man was a farmhand.

Hadn't Mac said he wasn't aware of anyone working with McCulloch that fit the description of his attacker?

And as the young farmer neared me, my suspicions grew. He had the most beautiful, piercing green eyes I'd ever seen.

Eyes that were hard to forget.

Eyes someone might use colored contacts to mask?

"Can I help?" he asked abruptly, coming to a stop just a couple feet from me.

I studied him. He wasn't overly tall. Perhaps five ten, five eleven. Broad shouldered.

He fit the attacker's description to a tee.

"I'm Robyn Penhaligon. I just came to ask Mr. McCulloch a few questions. You are?"

The man crossed his arms over his strong chest, eyes narrowed. "Jared McCulloch. What do you want with my grandfather?"

Say what?

"Grandfather?" Sarah had a brother? "You're Sarah's brother?"

"Cousin. Now what do you want?"

"What do you do here, Jared?"

"I work—"

"Don't say another bloody word!" Collum McCulloch's voice boomed across the farmyard like thunder. I physically jerked with the surprise of it.

Apparently, Jared was used to it because he didn't flinch. He did, however, shut up.

I braced myself as McCulloch marched across the yard, face red with fury. "You get off my land!"

What had *I* done? "Excuse me?"

He reached us and jerked his chin at his grandson. Understanding the silent communication, Jared strode away without a backward glance. I glowered at McCulloch. "Hello to you too."

"Ach, don't give me that, lass." He scowled ferociously. "You can't come onto my land, interrogating my grandson with no right to do so. I know why you're here, and the police have already interviewed us. We've got nothing to do with whatever mess that man has landed himself in. Now get off my land."

"What have I done to deserve such a welcome?"

"No Adair interlopers are allowed on McCulloch land."

I flinched. "I'm not an Adair."

"You're as good as."

"Because I'm Mac's daughter?"

McCulloch curled his upper lip. "No, because you succumbed to that prick like every other bloody woman does."

My cheeks grew hot. He didn't mean what I thought he meant.

He nodded knowingly. "Oh aye, everyone watched the two of you at the ceilidh, and you were spotted leaving Gordon's office seconds before Adair."

Oh my God.

"And gossip travels fast."

The thought of Gordon knowing Lachlan and I hooked up in his office was mortifying, but I pushed through it. "You listen to gossip?"

"Sometimes … when it's true." He pointed to my car. "Now get gone before I *make* you get gone."

Something in his tone made me think he'd have no qualms manhandling a woman into her car, and I bristled in outrage. However, facts were facts. This was his land, and I was trespassing.

"I think you have something to do with what happened to my father," I stated, expression hard. There was no way I'd let this man think he scared me. Once upon a time, he'd had my sympathy, but not now. "And you can try to mess with me and my trailer, but you should know I've faced bigger and badder things in this world than a troubled old man who can't let go of the past."

His eyes flashed dangerously. "Get the hell off my farm."

Anger simmered in my gut as I got into the SUV. Driving away from the farm, my fingers curled tightly around the wheel with impatience.

Because there was no one else who fit the profile of the stalker and attacker better than McCulloch and his grand-children.

Like I said: Occam's razor.

The simplest explanation is usually the right one.

Now I just had to prove it.

he noise broke into my dreams.

My eyes flew open, and I saw nothing but dark. Heart pounding, I struggled to hear over the rush of blood in my ears.

Something had woken me.

A crash.

My pulse leapt in my throat as realization dawned.

The suitcase. The suitcase I had stacked against the door of the trailer had been knocked over.

My ears pricked. It might have just been part of my dream. My subconscious—

Footsteps tapped softly across the trailer floor.

Blood whooshed in my ears.

Someone was here.

For a moment, fear paralyzed me as I heard the gentle creak of the floor moving.

Someone who didn't want me to know they were here.

Move, Robbie, I hissed inwardly. *Robyn, MOVE!*

Escaping the cage of terror that imprisoned my limbs, I thrust off the bed covers, got onto my haunches, and waited as I listened through the thundering beats of my heart to the intruder's movements.

They'd stopped outside the bedroom door.

The edge of the bed was less than a foot from the door.

The door was made of cheap wood, but more importantly, it swung outward into the trailer, not into the bedroom.

Balanced on the bed, hands holding the walls at either side of the doorway for support, I took a deep breath, pumped myself up, and then swung my knees up with force so I could drive my legs out into the door.

I threw my whole weight behind it and the door blasted open, hitting the resistance of the body behind it. A muffled but masculine curse preceded a clatter and then a thud.

Pushing out through the door, I almost tripped over his feet.

I'd knocked the fucker on his ass.

Slamming my palm into the light switch on the wall, I lit up the trailer and stared down at my would-be attacker as he stared up at me, gaze stunned.

Dressed all in black, black pants, black hood, black gloves, black ski mask, I could see nothing but his dark eyes. A gleam of metal on the floor caught my eye.

A push dagger.

My stomach somersaulted. First Mac, now me.

He'd obviously lost hold of it when I'd kicked out the door.

I instinctively lunged for the weapon, but the bastard grabbed my ankle and I lost my balance. My head whacked against the kitchen counter, momentarily dazing me.

There was a male grunt before I felt the heat of his body, trying to force me to my stomach on the trailer floor. Panic would finish me. If I let him pin me there, I'd have a hard time getting out of it.

My training cleared my mind and before he could grab my right arm, I twisted backward, elbow out, and smashed it into his face. It missed, but he flinched backward to avoid it and loosened his grip. I lunged forward and snatched up the dagger. He climbed over me, grappling me for it.

I needed to get him off me or this was over.

I slammed my head back and felt the pain of it connecting to his chin.

He fell off to the side, and I slid out from under him, swiping the dagger as I got to my feet.

The attacker scrambled to his feet to face me, his hands up defensively as I held the dagger expertly in my hand, body in fighting position.

If the attacker knew me, and I was pretty sure he did, then he'd know I could defend myself. Maybe he'd underestimated me because I was a woman.

Moron.

I had to hope the idiot hadn't clocked the block of kitchen knives on the counter behind him.

"Who are you? Huh?" I yelled. "Is that you, Jared? Huh? Coward!" I swiped the dagger at him, showing my intention to maim, not kill. A push dagger was called a push dagger for a reason. It had a T handle designed to be grasped in the hand so the blade protruded from your fist. People also referred to it as a punch dagger.

That's what Mac's neighbor saw happen to my father. He thought someone was punching Mac in the gut. Instead, it was this asshole stabbing him.

Rage flooded me, and I swiped at him again.

Mac was right. His eyes were an unrealistic purple. Contacts. He bowed back against the counter, and his alien eyes flew to the door that lay partially open, suitcase collapsed in front of it.

Oh no, he was not getting away. I wanted this over with.

"Don't even think about it, you fucker," I hissed, blocking his path. "You're going to stay right there, and I'm going to call the police."

His eyes narrowed.

Who are you?

Then he did what I feared and turned to remove the largest kitchen knife from the block.

I bent my knees, lowering into a defensive position as he mirrored me. Then he lunged with the knife with a lack of skill that told me he had no clue what he was doing. I swerved to my left to avoid the blade, grabbed his biceps with one hand, and brought the push dagger down through the inside of his upper arm at the same time. He yelled in agony, dropping the kitchen knife, and I tugged out the dagger with mean satisfaction, ready to take him to the ground.

But his fighting inexperience had lulled me into a false sense of security. I'd expected him to crumble under the pain of his wound.

Instead, he shocked me by slamming his fist into my face.

Throbbing pain exploded across my cheekbone, blinding me, and I stumbled back.

It was only seconds of distraction, but it was enough for him to lope over the suitcase and shove open the door. I roared in fury and dove for him, my fingers grasping the hood of his sweater. He grunted as I tried to haul him back, but I tripped over the suitcase, the trailer door slammed back toward my face, and I lost my grip on him as he took off.

Kicking the suitcase out of my way, ignoring the pain of my pinkie toe catching a metal buckle on the damn thing, I pushed open the trailer door, letting it slam against the side of the caravan.

Swiping up the kitchen knife, I checked left and right outside my temporary home and saw nothing.

No moving shadow in the distance.

No sound of gravel underfoot.

"Coward!" I shrieked my rage into the night.

Aware now of the adrenaline shooting through my body, I tried to control it as I hurried back into the trailer and grabbed my cell. Minutes later, the emergency services operator told me the police were on their way.

Hands shaking, I called Mac next.

He answered after four rings.

"Robbie?" he asked, sounding groggy with sleep.

The fear I'd felt when I'd heard the man breaking in came back, and I stared anxiously at the open door of the trailer. "Dad ..." I rarely called him that. Then I told him what happened.

His worry was palpable as he ordered me to find a neighboring trailer. But I didn't want to endanger anyone. "Stop arguing with me!" He sounded panicked.

"I'll lock myself in my car," I compromised.

"Fuck!" he bit out. "I'm on my way. I will be there in minutes."

"Don't kill yourself trying to get here."

I did as I promised. I yanked on some socks and hiking boots, shoved my phone inside my left boot, armed myself with the dagger and a kitchen knife, and wrapped ice in a tea towel. I then hurried out of the trailer and into my rental car.

The bleep of the locks didn't make me feel all that safe, but it was better than being a sitting duck in a tiny, static trailer.

* * *

I was wearing only a camisole and shorts, and the adrenaline was wearing off. Between that and the ice pressed to my cheek, I chittered in my car.

Until a black Range Rover pulled in behind my SUV a mere seven minutes later. The castle was fifteen minutes from the caravan site.

Staring into my wing mirror, I waited until the driver's door opened.

Lachlan got out.

Great.

Mac rounded the hood to join him as they stalked toward my car; I finally opened my door.

I'd barely cleared my left foot from the vehicle when Mac hauled me into his arms.

"I'm okay," I reassured him, holding on tight as I felt the tremble in his arms. Lachlan stood behind Mac, countenance fierce, a muscle ticking in his jaw. "I'm okay."

Moonlight lit his blue eyes, illuminating his disquiet. "What happened?"

Mac released me, brushing his thumb over my cheek. "He hit you."

"Lucky punch," I promised. "Hit my cheekbone, missed my nose, that's all I care about."

"Tell us everything."

I opened my mouth to do so when Lachlan unexpectedly embraced me. My lips parted on a sharp exhalation, but I returned his hug, caressing his strong back. That's when I realized we weren't alone.

Over his shoulder, I spotted Jock and three security guards.

"Really?" I eased out of Lachlan's arms. "You didn't need to bring your men. The police are on their—"

I was interrupted by the kick of gravel and blue-and-red flashing lights dancing across the dark end of the trailer park. They parked up behind the Range Rover and we waited as the officers approached.

After introductions, I stood inside the trailer with the two police officers, Mac, and Lachlan. A fresh tea towel filled with ice pressed to my cheek, I told them what happened, hearing my father's and Lachlan's indrawn breath as I described the fight.

The police took my statement and promised the detective inspectors working on Mac's case would be in touch to interview me. The officers asked me if I required an ambulance, as had the phone operator, but I shook my head. My face had gotten the worst of it, and I'd have a nasty shiner for a few days, but it would heal. Physically I was fine.

My attacker wasn't, so there was hope he would go to the hospital. The officers promised to put out an alert to the local hospitals for a man seeking medical attention for an injury matching the one I'd given him. They bagged up the bloody push dagger and kitchen knife and took those with them, much to my annoyance. My attacker wore leather gloves, but there was always a chance there could be prints on the dagger, and I'd wanted Mac's forensic lady to run prints first. Moreover, this was the first time we had DNA. I hadn't considered that when I'd called the cops.

When the police left, silence reigned in the trailer.

Lachlan opened his mouth to speak, but I beat him to it.

"This isn't the first time," I confessed.

"What isn't?" Mac asked.

I knew they would be mad at me for withholding information, but it was better they had the whole truth now. After all, I would have to tell the detective inspectors when they came around to interview me. "Lachlan and I were caught … kissing outside his office by Sarah McCulloch and Agnes. That night I came home and found the trailer trashed and all my evidence for the case ripped to shreds. They left a threatening note."

The men lambasted me before I even finished saying the word *note*, their questions and lectures rightfully incensed.

But I'd already had a shitty night, my head was pounding, and I needed quiet. I raised my hands and yelled at them to shut up.

To my gratification, they both closed their mouths.

"The message said, 'Kiss what's mine and I'll kill what's yours.'"

"Fuck," Lachlan bit out.

"Why didn't you say anything?" Mac was not only furious but I could tell he was disappointed, and his injured expression informed me he was also hurt.

Guilt churned in my gut. "I assumed the message was a threat against you. No one could get to you at the castle, so you were safe, but I knew you would both tell me to back off the case. Maybe even ask me to leave. And before you suggest I do either of those things, I think I know who's doing all this."

They leaned subconsciously toward me.

"This morning I went to talk to McCulloch. The fact that Sarah saw us"—I gestured vaguely to Lachlan, not wanting to keep bringing up the physical aspects of our affair in front of Mac—"you know … it got me suspicious about them again. It niggled at me. She's always hovering in the background. And McCulloch's history with Lachlan's father is clear motive. So I went out to the farm today."

I winced as they threw another round of agitated questions and curses at me.

This time I waited for them to calm themselves before I continued.

"Did you know McCulloch's grandson Jared is working the farm?"

They exchanged looks and shook their heads. "As far as I'm aware," Lachlan replied, "Jared is his daughter's son. His daughter lives in the Lowlands. They aren't close, and I've never seen a grandson around Ardnoch."

"Well, he's here now." I crossed my arms over my chest. "Jared fits the description of Mac's attacker, as did my attacker. And his eyes …" I explained about their brilliant green. "Easy to identify a criminal in a small village with eyes that color."

"Jesus Christ." Mac ran a hand through his hair. "I honestly never thought for a second it was him behind this. And to pull in his grandchildren to help?"

"We have no evidence of this," Lachlan reminded us. "And as enraged as I am right now, I won't go around accusing a man who has already been hurt by my family."

"I won't either," I promised him. "Not until I have concrete evidence."

"McCulloch isn't a stupid man," Lachlan mused. "Why send someone to attack you the very same day you paid him a visit about the investigation?"

"Counting on me not having told anyone?" I shrugged. "Assuming it wouldn't matter because I'd be dead after they were through with me?"

Mac flinched, and Lachlan's eyes blazed with some indecipherable emotion. "You're not staying on this case." He stared at me aghast when I silently dared him to stop me. He looked at Mac. "Tell her."

Mac took one look at me and sighed heavily. "She's a grown woman. And as terrifying as tonight was, she handled herself. Better than even me," he said, gesturing to his stomach.

"I had time to react, Mac," I said, ignoring Lachlan's mounting ire.

"I won't order you off the investigation," my dad continued, "but you're not staying here now that you're a target." He flicked a piqued and pointed glance at Lachlan. "The only place you're safe is the castle."

"No arguments," Lachlan commanded before I could speak.

I bristled at his tone. "I'll stay there because it's the right decision, not because you think you're my boss."

Tension crackled between us as he held my gaze. We shared a silent conversation.

The words weren't clear, but the message was. He wanted me to do what I was told. I had no intention of taking orders.

The wordless argument crackled with contentiousness and not a little hint of sexual tension.

Mac cleared his throat. "Right, then. We'll wait outside while you pack your things." Grabbing the sleeve of Lachlan's jacket, he forced Adair out of the trailer.

I stared around the place.

The trailer door was fine, so the intruder must have picked the lock.

Moving toward the bedroom, I bit my lower lip at the damage to the door. I'd have to pay for the repair work.

Once I'd packed all my stuff and hauled the bags to the exit, Lachlan reached in to take the luggage from me. I carried my pin board. As if reading my mind, he said, "I'll talk to Gordon about the caravan. He can invoice me for the repairs."

"You don't have to do that," I murmured.

His tone was arctic. "Yes. I do."

Mac insisted on driving my rental, and the Range Rover followed us to Ardnoch Estate. It wasn't the first time I'd driven up to the castle at night, but it still took my breath away to see it lit up. I'd noted the lights situated innocuously around the perimeter and discovered their purpose one night when I departed later in the evening than usual. Soft, golden light enveloped massive areas of the sandstone, leaving the rest in shadow, and the overall effect was atmospheric, ghostly but enticing.

"I wish I had my camera out right now," I murmured.

Mac gave a small huff of laughter. "That's what you're thinking about?"

I smirked. "I'm not going to mope over this. Nearly dying messed with me for a while, but it didn't crush me. No bastard will ever get inside my head like that again."

He slowed the vehicle to a stop outside the mews, pride glowing in his hazel eyes. "My daughter is fearless."

"Not fearless," I whispered, remembering my fear clearly less than two hours before.

"No," he agreed. "Wrong word choice. My daughter is courageous."

I was unable to hide my smile as I opened the passenger door. "Okay, I'll take that."

Hearing his chuckle relieved me. I didn't want Mac to fret about me while he still healed. Mental well-being was as much a factor in recovery as physical health. He was nearly recovered, and I didn't want anything to get in the way of that.

After retrieving keys to a room, Lachlan and Jock insisted on carrying my stuff upstairs, and I found the time to ask the man who was filling in for Mac if he ever went home to his husband and child.

"I *was* at home. We live in the village. Mac called me."

I frowned but my dad explained, "Nearly everyone is a suspect until proven otherwise. We trust Jock, Pete, and Kyle because they've been with us the longest."

Pete and Kyle were the two men who had accompanied Jock in the back of the Range Rover.

Lachlan led us to a room on the third floor.

The room opposite his.

Mac's brow furrowed, presumably about this arrangement, and to be honest, I was pretty disconcerted by it myself. Why would Lachlan want me this close? *Other than for easy access, of course,* I thought wryly. But surely, the guy didn't want me in his space all the time.

I wanted to ask for a room near Mac when my dad beat me to it. "Wouldn't it make more sense to put her in a room on my floor?" he said as I stared around the opulently furnished space. It was a nice step up from the trailer, that was for sure.

"Why would it?" Lachlan said, dumping my suitcase by the antique wardrobe.

"Because you already have security watching the floor."

Lachlan pointed toward the door. "There are cameras on this floor too."

Unlike the security cameras outside, the interior cameras dotted around the castle's common areas were discreetly hidden so the members didn't feel like they were being watched. Most bedroom corridors didn't have cameras on them, but Lachlan had a camera installed on his because of the stalker and one on Mac's for the same reason.

"But a key card is required to access my floor," he insisted.

"This will do," Lachlan maintained.

See, this was why Lachlan and I were not a good idea.

"This is fine," I assured Mac. "Thank you for coming to get me."

Sensing my desire to be alone, Mac hugged me tight, kissed the cheek that wasn't swollen, and told me he'd see me in the morning. Jock patted my arm in a friendly, "I'm glad you're okay" gesture, and they walked to the door together.

Mac looked over his shoulder at Lachlan who hadn't moved from his spot near the wardrobe. "Are you coming?"

"In a minute." Lachlan gave him a reassuring nod, a long look passing between them.

My dad glanced at me, expression unreadable, and then reached for the handle and closed the door as they departed.

I'd understood that look between Lachlan and Mac.

Despite our earlier silent conversation, Lachlan was breaking things off. The truth was in his gentle, apologetic look.

Why, when only seconds ago I'd concluded our affair was a bad idea, did I feel pissed and hurt?

And rejected?

"You don't have to say anything." I gestured to the door. *You can leave now.*

He strode toward me, and the urge to go to him, to forget the whole horrid incident through his drugging kisses and touch, was so strong, I wanted to retreat. I worried if he came any closer, I'd lose myself to this addiction for him.

Crossing my arms over my chest, I wore a mask of indifference as he stopped less than a foot away.

Lachlan studied me, the regret in his eyes making me feel like crap. "I'm sorry this happened to you. More sorry than I can say."

"It's not your fault."

He snorted bitterly.

"Adair."

"Back to that again?" he murmured.

"Aren't we?"

"I suppose so. We have to end this, for your safety."

The sensible thing to do was to agree, to watch him walk out of the room, and move on. But all I kept thinking was, why did he put me in the room across from his if he didn't want me anymore? "I'm not the kind of person who allows herself to be bullied by the actions of others. This is what these people want."

"Christ, Robyn, I'm not worth your goddamn life," he snapped, running a hand through his hair as he turned from me.

"Oh, get over yourself, Adair. It's about more than that. I refuse to be pushed around by these assholes. I do not make decisions based on fear. Ever." I motioned to him as he turned back to me, glowering. "But clearly you do."

"How dare you," he said gruffly. "This person or persons are after me, but it's the people I care about who are being tormented. Mac, Eredine … and now Mac's daughter."

Mac's daughter.

I wasn't a person he cared about.

I was just the woman he wanted to fuck but who happened to be the daughter of a person he cared about.

Message received.

"I put you in danger, and if anything happened to you because of me, it would destroy Mac. He'd never forgive me."

Wow, the hits just kept coming. I laughed bitterly. "So if anything happened to me, it wouldn't matter to you other than it would hurt Mac. Good to know."

His anger dissipated. "I didn't mean … but this was just sex. We agreed."

"We did. And believe me, the more I get to know you, the more the attraction remains physical." His eyes flashed dangerously, but I didn't care if I hurt his feelings. He was pretty adept at hurting mine. "But I guess, before this conversation, anyway, I assumed that even though our affair was casual, there was a level of care and concern for one another simply as two human beings."

"Robyn—"

"But if all I am to you is something to stick your dick into, then, no, you are definitely not worth my life."

Lachlan's face darkened. "Something to stick …" He gave a huff of unamused laughter. "You always assume the worst in me, don't you? You take my words and twist them."

"No. I just listen to what you *don't* say." Suddenly exhausted and sad and disappointed, I waved wearily to the door. "Can you just leave?"

"What do you want me to say?" he bit out as he crossed

the distance between us, leaning into but not touching me. "That when Mac told me you'd been attacked, I felt like I was coming out of my skin, and if I find the bastard, I will kill him? You have no idea the day I've had, Robyn. Women I care about were hurt by men that I should have protected them from!"

Confused, I shook my head. "Wom*en*? What—"

"And you"—he scowled ferociously—"making me feel like a piece of shit because I want to keep you safe. What the hell is that?"

God, he was such an asshole! "What the hell is that?" I yelled back. "It's me, reacting to you being a total and utter coward! Ending something you *want* because someone threatened you. Ending something you *need* because you're afraid of my father. And doing it like I mean *nothing* to you."

"I'm not afraid of Mac. And I don't need you," he said flatly.

I smirked unhappily. "Blue Eyes, you need me more than anyone I've ever met."

He flinched like I'd slapped him.

"I don't want anything from you that you don't want to give. I'm not sleeping with you in the hopes of snagging myself a rich, famous husband. Or because I see you as some kind of trophy or notch on my belt. And I'm not going to put up with your shit or stroke your ego or do any of the things that you *don't* need."

Lachlan studied me thoughtfully. "But you think I need you?"

"I think you need to lose yourself in someone who doesn't want more than you're willing to give. To forget all the crap that's going on outside these doors. To admit that you care about me as a human being without being concerned I'll think it's a declaration of some kind." I shrugged as I confessed, "I lied before. I do like you. I admire you, Lachlan.

I admire the way you look out for your family. I admire the way you care about Mac. Yes, you piss me off, but honestly, I couldn't let you touch me if I didn't like you. I'm not that woman. I don't do hate sex."

Something lightened in his expression.

"But it doesn't mean I want anything more from you than sex. So … there you are. My cards on the table. If you want to let those fuckers tormenting you win, then on you go." I gestured to the door. "It's over. Mac won't let our affair come between you two. I'm sure of it. But if you aren't, I understand, and again, you can leave." My gaze dropped to his sullen mouth, my skin heating with the memories of what he could do with it. "If you can get over all that and want to stay"—I looked into his eyes now—"then stay. But don't stay if I'm just another warm body to you. Stay because only my body will do. Stay because you need it to be me."

His silence was unreadable. We both breathed a little heavier, as if struggling to catch our breaths. But I had no idea what he was thinking.

And then his hand was on my nape, my body jerked toward his, and his mouth slammed down over mine. I moaned into his desperate, hungry kiss and clung onto his shoulders as he swung me into his arms. Seconds later, I was on the bed and he was stripping me of my shoes and pajamas as quickly as he could. His clothes were next, his face harsh with desire as he hurried out of his jeans.

"I'm clean," he offered as he climbed over me, nudging between my legs with hot need. "Got a health check when we started this thing. You? Pill?"

I hesitated. Did I trust him enough for unprotected sex?

"Robyn?"

Looking deep into his eyes, certainty flushed through me. This man was one of the most overprotective guys I'd ever met. He wouldn't endanger me. In any way. And he had just as much to lose by trusting me. "Me too. And yes, I'm on the Pill."

He slipped his hands between my legs, and they gleamed hungrily. "Ready for me."

"Arguing with you turns me on." I snorted, not able to make sense of it.

Lachlan grinned as he braced himself over me. "Back at you, Braveheart."

I raised my eyebrows, opened my mouth to query the endearment, but as he surged into me, all that came out was a cry of relief.

Yeah, this was what I needed. Wanted. Craved.

Craved.

Caressing my hands down his back to his ass, lust rippled in my belly at the feel of his powerful, muscular body beneath my fingertips. I wanted more. I didn't want to be loved. After the night I'd had, I wanted to be screwed into oblivion.

Squeezing his ass, I arched into his thrusts, pulling him deeper into me.

It was fast, furious, sweat coating our skin as our bodies met with wild abandon. Lachlan came first, and the orgasm seemed to surprise him.

I barely gave him a chance to catch his breath before I used a grappling move to reverse our positions. Straddling him, his expression still ragged with his climax, I undulated on him. I lost myself, became this sensuous, uninhibited creature, displaying my body for him, touching myself until I knew he was ready again.

Then I rode him.

I rode him hard until he bucked beneath me in a hoarse yell of pleasure. Seeing him lose control took me over the edge, and I cried out his name like a plea.

* * *

LACHLAN DIDN'T LEAVE.

I'd expected after our animal passions were spent, he'd leave my bed and return to his own. Instead, he pulled me into his embrace as the clock on the bedside table told me it was nearing sunrise. I should have been exhausted. Only a while ago, I was. Now I felt wide awake again.

Letting him hold me, trying not to read anything into it, I noted his knuckles for the first time.

They were swollen.

His words from our earlier argument came back to me. *Women he cared about were hurt by men today.* My good cheek to this chest, I reached out to stroke a finger over his bruised knuckles. "What happened today?"

Lachlan heaved a sigh beneath me. Then he told me about Arrochar and Guy.

I tensed with outrage. "You've got to be shitting me."

"Unfortunately not."

"Is she okay?"

"I left her sleeping at my place a few hours before I came back to the castle to check on things. She seems to be handling it well." He rubbed a hand down my arm. "I asked her to think about training with you. Tonight proved unequivocally that you can teach her to defend herself."

"I'd be happy to show her some moves." I sat up to search his face. "Are *you* okay?"

"Shit day," he admitted, concern open and clear for me to see in his expression. "But fuck, am I glad you *can* defend yourself."

In other words … I was always more than a warm body to him.

"I said some things I shouldn't have."

"It's done."

333

"I'm sorry." I stroked his chest.

"You were attacked because of me, Robyn. You're not the one who needs to apologize."

"I presumed some very not-nice things about you." I began to move down his body.

He raised an eyebrow. "Where are you going?"

I smiled saucily at him. "Words are just words," I whispered huskily. "An apology has more impact in action."

As my lips closed around him, Lachlan arched his neck and hissed with pleasure. "Fuck, woman," he panted as I continued to apologize with gusto. "On second thought," he huffed, curling his fingers lightly in my hair, our hazy, desire filled eyes locked, "apologize away."

When I was finished apologizing, Lachlan decided he owed me an apology too.

Coming down from orgasm, the beautiful Scot climbed back up my body and collapsed at my side. "Now I could sleep all day," he muttered, snuggling in beside me.

I didn't reply.

I was already drifting off, wonderfully satisfied, the horrendous events of the night forgotten in this mercurial man's arms.

The tender stroke of Lachlan's fingertips up and down my arm made me feel drowsy and content.

Another night in his bed. Another night he pulled me back into it when I made a move to leave.

"You're not what I expected," I whispered.

"What did you expect?"

"I don't know. I guess what I thought you were at first: an elitist, pretentious Hollywood star."

He grinned at my brutal honesty. "*Ex*-Hollywood star."

I returned his smile but continued, "Other than creating an elite product"—I gestured vaguely to the room, inferring the entire estate—"you understand this place, this lifestyle, isn't what matters."

The last three weeks had taught me this truth about Lachlan, more than the combustible weeks that led to the beginning of our affair. After my attack, once the police interviewed me and reinterviewed McCulloch and proved useless in procuring any evidence, or using the push dagger to find our man, things had gone quiet at Ardnoch again.

Stalker/attacker-wise.

As soon as she discerned I was okay, Lucy departed Scotland to meet with several producers and directors about potential future projects. But more members had descended on the castle. It was May, closing in on summer, when the estate was at its busiest. It was still strange to see famous people wandering around, working out in the gym, trailing caddies on the golf course, indulging in the spa, but I was getting a little used to it now. Besides, they weren't all famous "faces." There were a few writers and directors who I may have heard of in passing but couldn't pick who they were out of a lineup.

It kept Lachlan busy while I produced photographs he'd commissioned for the castle. I was a little blown away that he'd asked, but he told me Arrochar had shown him my Instagram, and he genuinely loved what I could do. That meant a lot. During the hours I wasn't adding to my portfolio, I still worked out with Eredine and added in one-on-one self-defense lessons with Arrochar in the early evenings.

There was an earthiness to Arrochar that Lachlan didn't have. That wasn't a bad thing. Not like I used to think. He just had this aura, this polish and self-assuredness that made even the most confident person feel a little intimidated by him. It didn't help he wasn't the easiest man to read, and he didn't always give much away beyond base feelings or what was going on in the moment.

Lachlan rarely talked about his past, his parents, or life before the club. Arrochar, however, chatted to me about what it was like growing up with a bunch of boys after their mother's death. Vivien Adair died from a blood clot after giving birth to Arrochar. Apparently, their father, Stuart, struggled after their mom's death, and his sister, Imogen, helped raise the kids for a year before he got himself together, but she'd remained as a mother figure in their lives. They had no grandparents on their mother's side, but their paternal grandparents handed over their right to Ardnoch Estate and disappeared to South Australia to live a warmer, simpler life.

Arro was four when their Aunt Imogen died in a hiking accident, sending their father into another deep depression. Their grandparents returned for their daughter's funeral but left Ardnoch behind for good afterward. They hadn't seen them since, though they did send a Christmas hamper every year.

Lachlan, being the eldest at only eleven years old, took it upon himself to parent his siblings. She said it was a role he never shook off.

He took a break from it to go to college and then pursue his Hollywood career, but Arro said, despite his protests that he wanted to retire as an actor, she always thought there was no coincidence that it aligned with their father's death. Arro was with their dad when he died. They were out walking her father's dog on the beach when he just collapsed. One minute he was there, the next minute gone. Heart attack.

So much death and sadness for their family.

Lachlan had yet to mention any of it to me. Not that we didn't talk. While we had lots of sex, it unexpectedly wasn't *just* sex. I didn't know if it was what I'd said to him the night of my attack, or if it was just a natural thing we'd fallen into, but after sex, I'd make to leave, he'd stop me, and we'd talk about our days before drifting off to sleep.

That first night in the castle in my bed, I'd woken in the morning to find Lachlan had returned to his room. Understanding the act for what it was, I returned the favor. I'd slip out in the morning before he woke up, and he'd not asked me to stop, so I took that to mean he appreciated that little nod to maintaining some kind of casual distance between us.

"Family," he murmured after what felt like a long while. "Family has always mattered the most."

"Was that something you learned from your dad?"

"Mum, actually." He surprised me.

I'd already done the mental calculations. "You were only seven when she died."

Lachlan leaned up, resting his head in the palm of his hand. "Yes. Seven. But I still remember conversations with her. By the time I was born, both her parents had died. She was an only child and had always wanted brothers and sisters."

I smiled thinking about it. "So she made sure you had plenty."

"Exactly. Mum fell pregnant with Thane three months after giving birth to me, so we grew up almost as close as twins."

"Three months? Ouch." I winced at the thought.

He chuckled. "She didn't seem to mind. I don't think."

"Then there was Brodan?"

"He came a few years later. I was three when he was born. Then Arran was a year after Brodan."

"That's a lot of babies in a short space of time."

His expression grew solemn. "Dad told me when I was older that the doctor suggested they stop after Arran. Mum was thirty-seven, and she'd put her body through a lot. But she wanted a wee girl. One more time, she'd said to Dad. I want my wee Arrochar." Pain glistened in Lachlan's beautiful eyes. "I think Dad blamed himself, but the doctors said the blood clot was just something that happens. Rare, but it happens."

I reached out to stroke his cheek, feeling the welcome soft bristle of his beard against my fingertips. Lachlan caught my hand and brought it to his mouth to press a sweet kiss to the back of it. When he released me, I couldn't resist the urge to brush my fingers over his mouth.

Drawing my thumb down his lower lip, I said, "I'm sorry about your mom."

He took my hand again, curled his around it, and rested it against his chest. A heavy silence fell between us.

Wanting to ease the tension, I asked, "Where does the name Arrochar come from? It's so unusual."

Lachlan seemed grateful for the subject change. "It's a place in Scotland. In Argyll. Dad said Mum just always liked the name. Arran is a Scottish place name too. That's why it's spelled with two *r*'s."

"I'd like to see both. I'd like to see everywhere here."

"Scotland's in your blood."

"It is," I admitted.

"You're glad you came?"

We hadn't spoken about my feelings regarding Mac. We'd talked about the time I spent with Mac, which was less now since my father had gotten his way and returned to work. Yet Lachlan seemed wary of broaching the subject of Mac. In fact, I got the distinct impression his and Mac's relationship had become somewhat superficial these last three weeks. I wasn't sure what was going on there, but I did know it was about me, and that did not sit well. I knew I should end things with Lachlan. Every time I'd made up my mind to walk away, he'd touch me. And then I was lost.

"Of course, I am," I replied. "It's not easy to forgive him for not trying harder, but knowing that he *did* try makes all the difference. And it's ... we have a connection. There's no denying the bond, and there's no denying that I haven't felt like a complete person until I came here to fix things with him."

"And now you've fallen in love with Scotland. I can see it in your photos."

I grinned. "It's difficult not to be seduced by this place."

"Well, you are easily seduced," he teased.

"I can be unseduced." I pulled my hand out of his hold and he laughed. Shaking my head at his nonsense, I continued, "In all seriousness, how could you leave this place for Hollywood? How did that happen? You don't talk about it."

Lachlan sighed, tucking his arms underneath his pillows to relax into them. "Not because of any particular reason. I just assumed it was all out there for everyone to know because I've done so many interviews."

"I'm not the type who watches celebrity interviews."

He grinned again. "No, I suppose not."

"So, how did it happen for you?"

"It was an accident. I was a second year at St. Andrews Uni, a prelaw undergraduate, and I hated it. The best part was being on the rugby team and getting student discounts at the local pubs."

"Your first time away from family?"

He nodded. "It was strange. Felt like I was abandoning them but at the same time, I ..." Guilt flashed across his eyes.

And I got it. I understood that feeling completely. "You felt free."

Lachlan's expression tightened. "I was young."

"I don't have that excuse. I felt like a third parent to my sister for so long, and finally I'm doing what I want to do and it doesn't revolve around my mom and Seth or Regan. So I get it."

His gaze softened. "I fully enjoyed the experience, let's say. And one of my suite mates was an aspiring actor. He'd gotten wind that Kevin Pierce, the director behind the comic book movies, was filming scenes for the latest one in Edinburgh, and they were looking for extras. Somehow I got roped into going with him, and the producer picked me out. She liked my look. Asked if I could fake a right hook. Afterward she gave me her card."

I guffawed. "Just like that?"

"I know," he said, laughter in his voice. "Actors who have been working for years to get noticed hate that shit when they hear it. I'm not well liked in that regard. But the producer was actually serious. Wanted me to audition for another movie."

"She wanted to have sex with you."

He looked away.

"Oh my God, I'm right."

"It wasn't tawdry sexual blackmail. I would have gotten the work without it."

"But you had sex with her, anyway?"

"She was an attractive, confident older woman."

I chuckled. "So you had sex with her."

His eyes lit up with humor, and he shrugged. "It led to some smaller bit parts here and there, and I liked it. I enjoyed being on a set. Got myself an agent, some acting lessons, and honestly, it all happened so fast. The next thing I knew, I was in New York filming as a young action hero lead in a sci-fi movie. It was ... surreal."

"But you enjoyed it?"

"For a while," he admitted. "I spent my twenties traveling the world, working hard, playing just as hard, and making a lot of money. But I missed home, and I missed my family."

"The Hollywood allure wasn't enough?"

"I never liked Hollywood. There's a smell of desperation in the air."

"Don't you miss it, though? Acting? Top-level fame?"

"I didn't pay attention to the fame when it was happening."

"How can you not pay attention to that?"

"Because for someone like me, it would just have constantly pissed me off to pay attention to it. Some celebrities feed off that shit. They need it. That was never the reason I decided to get into acting. And tabloids are bastards.

At the height of my career, I was constantly followed by the paps. They took a photograph and spun it into absolute bull-shit that the public bought into. You can't let it get to you, so you learn ways to ignore most of it. My agent and publicist were constantly on my back to go online and nurture my fandom, but I only had to talk to friends and acquaintances who were doing that to see how quickly it could turn on them."

"What do you mean?"

"It's why I'm still not online. There's this eagerness to condemn someone for their actions no matter the severity, or lack thereof, without examining or attempting to under-stand the circumstances. It's depressing. I mean, if we applied that lack of compassion and bloodthirsty attitude to real life and the law, Western civilization would still be hanging people for stealing fruit."

I had to admit, I didn't think he was wrong. "I *have* to be online."

"I don't mean you," he said. "You're on there for your business, not to assume the worst in people."

"Maybe I assumed the worst in you, though." I shimmied closer so our noses almost touched. "I needed someone else to blame for the distance between me and Mac. I'm sorry I put that on you."

He studied my face. "You don't need to apologize to me. I was a prick to you, Robyn, and you didn't deserve it."

We shared a soft look and then I reached up to caress his lips with mine. A whisper of a brush.

There was a heady sensation building between us that threw me off-kilter. So I tried to bring some levity to the conversation. "Favorite color?"

"What?" he asked, bemused.

"I'm getting to know you, and while I'm sure you've answered these everyday questions in interviews over the years, I just told you, I don't read or watch celebrity interviews. Not since I was thirteen and obsessed with Cam Gigandet."

He wrinkled his nose. "I didn't need to know that."

"Hey, it could have been you if I didn't dislike you so much for stealing my dad," I teased.

"Let's not talk about you having those feelings when you were thirteen."

"Spoiling the mood?"

"Uh, just a bit."

I chuckled. "Then answer the question. Favorite color?"

"I don't know. Blue, I suppose."

"Blue, you suppose?"

"Yours?"

"Turquoise. Like the ocean around Fiji."

He smiled. "Have you been?"

"I'd never been anywhere outside the States until I came here. I can't wait to travel. Where's the best place you've ever visited?"

Lachlan considered it for a few seconds. "I don't know. It's a toss-up between Vietnam and Canada. Abraham Lake in Alberta is one of the most beautiful sights I've seen outside the Highlands."

"Really?"

"Yeah, you should visit. Get some cracking shots for your business."

"On my list, then."

"Top of your list?"

"Italy."

"All of Italy?"

"Pretty much. Positano, Lake Como, Rome, Venice, Florence ... yeah ... all of it."

He grinned. "I've been to nearly all those places, except Florence."

"Show off," I teased, though I was a little jealous he'd seen so much of the world. "Okay, favorite movie?"

Lachlan groaned. "Oh, that's the worst question you could ask."

"Why?"

"Because people either expect me to say some dumb action movie or some film student, cult classic like *Metropolis*."

"I don't have any expectations," I promised. "My favorite movie is *Green Book*."

"Good bloody movie."

I waited.

He sighed heavily. "*Saving Private Ryan*. I remember going to see it when I was fifteen and being shell shocked by the opening scenes on Omaha Beach. I'd never seen a war movie like it. It had such an impact, and when I looked around at everyone else in the audience, one woman held her hand over her mouth in horror, and an old man had tears in his eyes. It was the first time I realized the power of film."

I caressed his chest and whispered, "I guess I need to watch it now."

"You've never seen *Saving Private Ryan*?"

"Nope."

"Great bloody movie. Other filmmakers copied the style, but when it first released, I remember everybody talking about how it felt like the first truly realistic war movie. Unsettlingly so."

"You do love movies, don't you?"

"Of course. Just don't have a lot of time for them these days."

"What made you give up the movies? Come back home?"

He considered this. "Truth? It wasn't just Dad dying. I missed home and my family. And growing up, the sense of taking care of our family legacy was instilled from birth. I mean, the castle as you see it now isn't what it was when we lived here as a family."

"It wasn't?"

"No. We had no staff, and many parts of the castle were in disrepair. We were what you called land rich but cash poor. Not poor as in poverty, but so much of what my parents had was shoveled into keeping this grand old lady alive." He gestured around us. "Growing up in a castle isn't as glamorous as people might think. It was cold and drafty and damp. I knew when I inherited her that something drastic needed to be done. So not only did I invest some of my earnings but I also searched for investors for the club. We returned the castle to her former glory and expanded out onto the estate."

"That must have cost a fortune."

"It did. Took us several years to recoup it. But we're already in the black."

"That's amazing. You're amazing."

He shrugged, and sensing his discomfort with my praise, I changed the subject. "What else do you like? Favorite food, book, pastime, and band?"

Lachlan chuckled. "Do we have time limitations that I'm unaware of?"

"Rapid-fire questions are a great way to get to know someone."

"Or panic them into giving bullshit answers," he joked.

I laughed. "You've never been panicked in your life."

"Wrong." He smirked but continued. "*Bánh xèo*." He pronounced it *boon say-oh*. "Vietnamese pancake, and delicious. I read a lot as a kid, and my favorite book when I was a teen was *One Flew Over the Cuckoo's Nest*. Cliché maybe, but it's a classic for a reason. Don't have time for pastimes, and my favorite band is Oasis."

"Oasis?"

"Some of us grew up in the nineties, remember."

"And some of us were only just born then, old man."

He narrowed his eyes. "Watch it, minx. Now your turn."

"Hmm, let's see … favorite food is pizza. I know. Unimaginative, but it's true." I wrinkled my nose at the laughing glint in his eyes. "Hey, I could have made something up but I'm being real here."

"Pizza. Okay. Nothing wrong with pizza. But I think we need to introduce you to some *bánh xèo* in the future."

"That works for me." No arguments there, especially if I got to try it in Vietnam. "Book: not a big reader but I do love *Pride and Prejudice*. We're equally cliché in our literary tastes, but sometimes lots of people like the same thing because it's good."

Lachlan nodded, grinning. "Amen to that. Pastime? Band?"

"Pastime: kicking ass and taking names," I said, referring to my martial arts training. "Band … the Eagles." I lifted my head to rest my chin on his chest. "Stupidest thing you've ever been asked in an interview?"

His brow furrowed as he stared up at the ceiling in thought. "Hmm … Mostly, I was just asked the same boring shit over and over again."

"Like?"

"Who was I dating? Who was my ideal woman? What was my workout routine? What did I eat? Did I manscape?"

"Those are shittier than my favorite-color question."

Lachlan chuckled and reached out to brush his thumb over my lip. "Then ask me something else."

I contemplated this and then tried to hide my smile. "What do you want most out of the person sharing your bed?"

His lips twitched, and I was glad he heard the teasing in

my voice and didn't take me too seriously. But then he surprised me with his answer. "To make me laugh."

I couldn't help my smile this time. "Good answer, handsome."

"I'm glad you came here, Braveheart," Lachlan admitted, his voice low, almost hoarse.

I felt a sudden increase in my heart rate as the thought occurred to me that at some point, perhaps even soon, I would no longer get to lie in bed and just talk with this man.

That wasn't our future.

A desperation came over me, and I kissed him, hungry with intention as I pushed him onto his back.

His strong hands gripped my waist as I found him with my hand and guided him where I needed him.

If this was all I ever got from Lachlan Adair, I was going to make the most of it.

* * *

"I HATE WAITING AROUND," I muttered, biting into the sandwich I'd brought from Morag's. I referred to the fact that our would-be killer had disappeared off the face of the planet.

Mac sat in his office chair, long legs up on his desk, chewing on the sandwich I'd bought him. My dad wasn't too keen on me leaving the estate on my own, but I'd go insane if I couldn't have some freedom. I liked wandering around the village and walking along the beach. I did him a favor and took my morning runs on the strip of coastline that belonged to the estate.

However, I'd just bought a drone so I could do some aerial photography while in the Highlands. My drone shots from New York and Boston were among my most popular, and it seemed a waste not to do it here. It would have to be outside the estate, though, because when I told Lachlan I'd

347

ordered one, he warned me his geofencing antidrone technology would disable it if it was on or near the perimeter.

"Considering my daughter was the latest victim of the stalker's attacks, I'm quite glad for the quiet," Mac replied sardonically.

Because Mac and I had been the two most seriously affected by the crimes at Ardnoch, the detective inspectors started painting their own picture of the investigation. They believed the threats against Lachlan were a different case altogether. That there was someone who had a beef with Dad and me that was the greater threat than the stalker.

Their decision to not connect the dots back to Lachlan meant their investigation was as stalled as ours.

But at least we'd connected the right freaking dots.

"Yeah, but it would be nice to not have this hovering over us anymore."

Mac considered this. Then, "Will you leave? When it's over?"

I swallowed my bite of sandwich, meeting his hazel gaze. "Probably." The thought made my chest tight. "I need to work things out with Mom. Make sure Regan is okay."

He lowered his eyes. "Have you spoken with them?"

"I've emailed Mom. Just casual checking-in stuff. Regan still won't answer her phone, but Seth assures me she's fine. Still dating some loser, but fine." Clearly, my sister wasn't talking to me, but considering I'd done little to deserve that, I wasn't going to chase her. She'd come to me when she pulled her head out of her ass.

Mac nodded. "I could … I could come visit."

I smiled, relieved at the offer. "I'd like that. And I'll be back, Mac. I love it here. I love spending time with you."

My dad beamed. "Me too, wee birdie."

"I'm thinking of traveling. On a shoestring budget, of

course. But the preorders for my Highland photos prove it's worth it, business-wise. I'll be a travel photographer."

"That sounds great, Robyn." His brows pinched. "Will it be forever ... or do you think you might choose somewhere to settle down?"

I heard the real query in his question, and it soothed something deep in my soul. My dad wanted me to come back to the Highlands. Permanently. "I don't know," I answered honestly. While I loved my dad, this was a small community with little chance of meeting someone I'd want to settle down with. Lachlan's smile popped into my head, but I threw that thought out right away. "I just want to try the traveling thing first. I might hate it. I mean, until these past few months, I'd lived in Boston my whole life."

"You *should* do it," he assured me. "You'll regret it otherwise. Don't ever have regrets in life, Robyn. I don't want them for you."

A knock at the door halted my answer, and I craned my neck as Lachlan strode into Mac's office.

He took us in, his eyes glancing from me to Mac and then to the half-eaten sandwich in my hand. He crossed his arms over his chest and said, a little disgruntled, "You've already eaten."

"Kind of."

"Give the rest to Mac," he ordered.

I raised an eyebrow. "This is a Morag sandwich."

Lachlan's lips twitched. "Trust me, I have better planned."

Brows furrowed, I eyeballed my delicious club. "Nothing's better than a Morag sandwich."

Mac chortled while Lachlan gave a beleaguered sigh. "Sandwich. Mac. You. With me."

Huffing under my breath, I stood and handed over the rest of my lunch to my dad who took it eagerly, eyes filled with humor at my less than happy expression.

"This better be good."

"I can kill him for you if it isn't," Mac teased.

"No need. I'll do it myself." I glared pointedly at Lachlan as I crossed the small room toward him.

"It's a sandwich."

"It's food. You should know by now not to mess with my food."

Lachlan grinned. "I have more food planned where we're going."

I looked back at Mac. "Shouldn't he have led with that?"

He laughed. "Enjoy yourselves."

Despite my teasing, I was not only delighted Lachlan sought me out during the day, I was happy to see he and Mac were a little more comfortable around each other. "What does Mac know that I don't know?" I asked, striding down the castle hallway at Lachlan's side.

"I'm taking the day off."

"Okay?" And at no forthcoming details, I added, "Is that it?"

He smiled mysteriously and placed a hand on my lower back to guide me out into the main reception. Two members on the sofas near the fireplace were glued to a newspaper and an e-reader, respectively. One looked up, and Lachlan murmured a good-afternoon to him. The other kept reading her newspaper.

Outside the main entrance, I stopped at the sight of the black Range Rover already pulled up.

"Get in." Lachlan opened the front passenger door for me.

Shooting him a narrowed look that amused him, for once I didn't argue and hopped into the SUV.

Glancing into the back of the vehicle, I noted the box with my new drone, my camera bag, and supplies. Next to them was a large picnic hamper.

"What's going on?" I waved a hand over my shoulder at the things he'd obviously procured from my bedroom.

Lachlan pulled on his seat belt and started the engine. "You wanted to take the drone out, right?"

"Yeah."

"I know the perfect place. It's a ninety-minute drive on mostly single-track roads through stunning scenery. Thought we could stop halfway, eat, you can take photos, and then we'll set up the drone near where I have in mind."

I felt a little fizzle in my stomach. Was this … a date? Pulse beating a little faster, I tried to sound unfazed as I asked, "Are you going to tell me the destination?"

"It's a bridge."

I frowned. "A bridge?"

"A sweeping curve of a bridge in a picturesque location. The scenery is beautiful, but you'll need aerial shots to get the true impact of it. I thought if we left a little later, you could get some shots in the daylight and then some during sunset."

His thoughtfulness was a total turn-on. It was also a little overwhelming. But Lachlan was acting so casual about the whole thing, I knew I'd ruin it if I made it a bigger deal than he obviously thought it was. "Sounds good."

He threw me a smile as we drove through the woods toward the security gates. "We could both use a day off the estate. Away from everything. And for once, the sun is shining."

I returned his smile. "True."

* * *

"YOU HAD AN AFFAIR WITH BRIDGET MENDEZ?" I gaped at Lachlan as he drove with relaxed confidence down single-track roads. As much as I was in awe of the scenic drive, our conversation about past relationships was distracting to say the least.

He grinned like a schoolboy. "I did."

I stared out the windshield, processing. Bridget Mendez was in her sixties now. At the height of her film career, she was an '80s pinup star. Not much of an actress, but iconic and considered one of the most beautiful women in the world.

"What age were you?"

"Twenty-three." He shrugged. "She likes them young."

"You're lying," I said, not believing he was lying for a minute.

Lachlan threw me a wounded look. "I would never."

It occurred to me that he had shared secrets the tabloids would have a field day over. He trusted me. The thought made me smile. "You couldn't tell anyone, could you?"

"Mac knew. I've told Thane." He grinned. "And now you."

"Well, I can't beat that." I waved at him. "Bridget Goddamn Mendez."

"What do you mean you can't beat that? You're sleeping with me."

I laughed uproariously at his cockiness. "You're gorgeous, but you're not a living legend."

"Hey, to some people, I am."

We chuckled together, and I shook my head. "You've had the weirdest life."

I felt him contemplate me a second before turning his attention back to the road.

"What?"

He gave me another considering look. "It doesn't bother you?"

"What doesn't bother me?"

"Me. Talking about the women I've slept with?"

I'd never been the jealous type. "You're not sleeping with them now, are you?"

"Of course not. I can barely keep up with *you*."

"See, that's what happens when you have sex with a woman ten years younger than you," I teased.

"I've had sex with younger women," he muttered, eyes flicking down my body before moving back to the road. "Age has nothing to do with it."

"Oh, and what has?"

"You." He slowed, hitting his turn signal to pull into a tiny parking spot off the road at a gate. Lachlan unclipped his seat belt, eyes hot. "You're wild."

I liked that description. "I do have stamina."

"That you do," he murmured thickly, attention on my mouth. Then he wrenched his gaze away and cleared his throat. "Wait here."

Wondering at his abruptness, I shook my head and watched as he got out of the SUV and opened the gate. When he returned, we drove down the single track where a couple of white cottages were situated beneath the shadow of a hill, or *beinn*, as they were called here. That's when I became aware of our surroundings. "Oh wow."

The cottages sat on the banks of a beautiful river. We were clustered in the valley of gently sloping, patchwork hills. The sun glinted off the placid river that cut through the valley like a stream of mirror, reflecting the greens of the trees and the gunmetal-tinged clouds in the blue sky above.

Following Lachlan out of the Range Rover, I noted he grabbed my camera gear and the picnic basket. "Where are we?"

"On the River Oykel."

"Are we trespassing?" I gestured to the cottages as Lachlan led me down a small slope near the river's edge where a fence of wood and chicken wire halted us.

"They'll move us if we are," he said, unconcerned. He carefully dropped the basket and my gear over the fence before climbing it with ease. Those long legs of his.

When he held out a hand to me, I eyed the obstacle he'd scaled with little difficulty. "I might not make it, and contrary to popular belief, it hurts there for us too."

He gave a short bark of laughter and then climbed back over the fence. Before I knew it, he swept me into his arms, and I squeaked with surprise.

Suddenly I was on the other side of the fence.

Lachlan jumped over it with impressive athleticism, and the only thing that distracted me from ogling him was the narrow stream of the river against the vivid greens of its banks. The muds, ambers, and chestnuts of the hills gave the Highlands texture, depth, and atmosphere. While a vibrant field of differing shades of green with a gentle stream running through it was pretty, the earthy ruggedness juxtaposed against it was what made the Highlands special.

I am gentle breeze, I am fertile. I am peace, I am tranquility. But I am mighty, I am storm. I am thunderous, I am valiant.

That was the Highlands.

A perfect dichotomy.

A swell of emotion weighed down my chest. "It's so beautiful. Words can't describe what I feel when I'm here. Do you ever get used to it? To its pure, unadulterated majesty?"

"Not if you're smart," Lachlan answered softly. "True beauty should never be taken for granted."

Feeling the heat of his eyes on my face, I turned to look at him and felt the breath leave my body at the intensity of his stare.

Seeming to realize what he'd inferred, he glanced down at the picnic basket. "I'm starved. Let's eat."

As Lachlan laid out a blanket and unloaded the basket of goodies Rafaella prepared for us, I got out my camera and took shots of our surroundings. And tried not to overanalyze his intensity.

When I glanced over my shoulder, Lachlan was settled on the blanket, legs stretched in front of him, ankles crossed, hands braced behind him, his head thrown back, eyes closed. Basking in the gentle spring sun. So goddamn handsome, I felt a flutter in my belly.

I couldn't help myself.

I held up my camera, caught him in my sights, and snapped a couple of shots.

Feeling a desperate need to kiss him, I returned to the blanket, carefully put my camera aside, and crawled over him.

Lachlan's eyes flew open and he sat up, but only so he could run his hands up my back. My mouth drew his immediate attention. "This might get us thrown off the land."

I didn't care.

I kissed him for bringing me here.

For thinking of me enough to plan this day.

He groaned, cupping my face but only to break the kiss. "We need to stop before we start."

I could feel how much we needed to stop beneath my ass.

Smug, I slid off him, and his look promised we'd finish later.

"What do we have here?" I kneeled over the array of snacks he'd arranged on real china. No paper plates for Lachlan. I smiled, amused.

After he'd explained what was in the little finger sandwiches, savory pastries, and sweet pastries, I helped myself. And moaned around the first bite of the cute, swirly little puff pastry I'd bitten into. "What is this again?" I asked after I'd swallowed.

"Bacon, Gruyère, caramelized onions, and horseradish *palmiers*."

"I have no idea what half of what you said is, but my God, it's delicious." I moaned around another mouthful.

Lachlan studied me, lips quirking, eyes smoky with desire. "If I'd known this would be the reaction, I'd have made Rafaella head chef sooner."

I rolled my eyes but didn't hold back as I sampled more of the chef's goodies.

"Better than Morag's sandwiches?" He watched me, seeming to enjoy my reaction to the food more than the food itself.

I nodded. "Don't tell Morag."

He flashed me a quick grin. "I will if you stop moaning."

"Making you hot?" I winked cheekily as I reached for a custard tart thingie.

"Considering you sound like you're coming, yes."

His words created a tingling warmth between my legs, and I leaned back on one hand, giving him a heated, low-lidded look as I bit into the tart.

We watched each other, sexual tension crackling between us as we ate.

Finally, Lachlan brushed pastry crumbs off his hands and asked, "Did you leave a man behind in Boston?"

"What makes you ask that now?"

He raised an eyebrow. "You did?"

"Do you think I'd cheat?" I scowled at him.

"Of course not. I just ... I meant an ex."

"I did." I drew up my knees, resting my elbows on them as I stared at the river. "Though I don't think you can call it leaving him behind. We broke up a while before I came here."

"Why?"

I turned to contemplate him. Lachlan had trusted me with some very personal things lately ... but he seemed okay with doing that while keeping our relationship casual. I was afraid if I gave him too much, I'd end up giving him everything.

How stupid would that be? Considering he wanted only a little more than nothing.

"It wasn't right." I didn't tell him that the shooting woke me up. Taught me to stop wasting time. "He wanted me to be someone I wasn't."

"What did he want you to be?"

"Ambitious in a different way than I wanted to be. He was a successful lawyer, and he wanted me to work my way up the hierarchy of the police force. He thought my photography business was a flaky and uncertain dream."

"Sounds like a prick."

I chuckled. "Yeah. Looking back on it, he was a prick." I'd thought Mark was good in bed because at least he made me come. But now I knew better. "You know, *our* time together has been very illuminating."

Lachlan's expression was curious. "In what way?"

"You're the most generous lover I've ever been with."

He raised an eyebrow. "Seriously?"

I nodded. Mark and the few lovers I'd had before liked to take but didn't reciprocate. "Until you, I just thought guys were selfish lovers. That it was just the way they were built." Lachlan had proven that theory wrong. He actually enjoyed giving. He got off on it.

"Jesus Christ," he huffed. "Men are arseholes sometimes."

"Now I know different." I grinned. "I have knowledge. Knowledge is key. When I do settle down, I won't be settling for a man who doesn't return favors."

I expected Lachlan to laugh, but he just stared pensively off into the distance.

At the sudden thick silence, I searched for a different subject. "I think Mac wants me to stay."

He looked at me sharply. "He asked?"

"Inferred."

"What did you say?"

"I have to go back to Boston at some point, fix things with my mom and Regan. And then I want to travel for my business."

"How did Mac take that?"

"He told me I should. Doesn't want me to have any regrets. But I'll visit, of course." I ignored the ache in my chest.

He studied me and then murmured, "So, when you say settle down with a man, you don't actually mean it."

"Of course, I do. I want that eventually," I said. "I'm not you, Lachlan. Casual sex won't satisfy me forever. I want true intimacy, someone to look after and be looked after by, a husband. And I want kids. I just want to see a bit of the world first."

The breeze blew back strands of hair that had come loose from my ponytail, tickling my nose. I tucked the strands behind my ear and waited for him to respond.

He didn't.

He just reached for another pastry and acted as if the river was the most fascinating stream of water he'd ever seen.

* * *

Lachlan's surprise destination was Kylesku (pronounced *Kyleskew*) Bridge. And he'd been right about the beauty of this place. The bridge swept around in a curve over two connected lochs on the northwestern coast of the Highlands.

Since no cars were behind us, Lachlan slowed as we crossed so I could take it all in. Hills that seemed to touch the clouds, others so tall they disappeared into them, reminding me of our altitude.

Water dotted here and there with little islands. Rugged rocks peeked through shrubs and grass and trees. Olives, emeralds, sage, burnt umbers, smoke, and ambers shone bright against clouds with mauve bellies. The loch was a still sheet of water reflecting the sky, unsure if it wanted to be blue or purple or gray.

"Lachlan," I whispered. I had no words. I desperately wanted to get my camera out.

"I thought you'd like it here." He turned left down a little slope into an empty parking lot. The man had barely stopped the car and I was out, hurrying to open the back passenger door so I could set up the drone. A few minutes later, I looked over my shoulder and saw him standing at the edge of the lot, snapping photos on his phone.

Smiling to myself, I returned to setting up the drone. Once I was ready to go, I walked over to stand at his side. "Dabbling in a little photography yourself?"

He smirked at me. "Sending some snaps to Lucy. She's always talked about coming here. Thought the pictures might give her incentive."

A little niggle of … *something* … something I hadn't experienced before when it came to Lucy and Lachlan took me aback.

It bothered me.

Because it felt an awful lot like jealousy.

And I adored Lucy. I didn't want to be jealous or insecure about her, and I didn't know why I was all of a sudden when I hadn't been before.

I frowned, trying to figure it out.

"We're just friends."

I was shocked that he'd assumed the right reason for my silence. "I know that." I said, unable to meet his eyes. "Good friends. You care about her."

"I do."

359

"Do you make friends of all the women you've slept with?"

"No. And not like Lucy. I think it's because we're alike. We both just wanted a distraction, an outlet. But nothing more. She's like you. She didn't lie about understanding the rules."

Oh, I understood the rules. He was right about that. And that's when it hit me, what bothered me about him and Lucy.

I was just another Lucy to him.

More than just a casual fuck. But in the end ... like Lucy, I'd be cast aside. Just friends.

Lucy was fine with that.

I ...

Swallowing hard, I set the drone down on the ground. "Let's do this."

It turned out Lachlan could be a very patient man. He pulled the blanket out on the lot and sat there, vacillating between silence while I worked and chatting amiably whenever I took the FPV goggles off that allowed me to see what the camera could see.

Cars came and went with tourists jumping out to take snaps of the bridge and the scenery as Lachlan waited with me for sunset.

"Are you sure you're not bored?" I'd asked a few times.

He'd waved the question away. "I like watching you work. It's relaxing."

As the sky began to change color, the brilliant golds, scarlets, and amber hues of the setting sun was quickly dwarfed by dark throbbing purples as heavy clouds that seemed within touching distance drew in overhead.

"Shit." Lachlan jumped to his feet. "Get your camera down."

Hurrying to do as he instructed, I'd just gotten the drone back and disassembled when the rain lashed down in violent jets that pounded and splashed off the ground. Our shouts of shock and surprise were barely audible over the plaintive sobbing of the sky.

In seconds we were soaked to the skin. Lachlan helped get my gear in the back seat and then we turned to each other.

Water streamed in my eyes as I stared up at him, shocked by the abrupt and capricious Scottish weather. It reminded me a little of the man before me, and I couldn't help but laugh.

Lachlan grinned and hauled open the passenger door. I climbed in and he slammed it shut in my wake. Teeth chattering with the sudden, drenching cold, I watched the blur of him through the water bouncing off the windshield as he rounded the hood and yanked open the driver's side to climb in.

"Fuck, it's cold," he announced, pulling the door shut behind him. "I'll turn on the heat."

"Push your seat back instead," I ordered loudly.

He stopped mid-stretch, hand hovering over the middle dash of the car where the heating controls were. Lachlan quirked a brow.

I pressed a hand to his chest, gently shoving him back as I moved into him. "I know a better way to get warm."

At his hesitancy, I froze. "Unless … you're afraid of getting caught."

In answer, he pressed a button at the side of his chair, the buzz of the electric mechanism filling the car as his seat moved back. I grinned and climbed over, straddling him. His shirt was so wet, his skin peeked through the white where it stuck to him. "What about your sterling reputation?"

Lachlan's eyes flashed. "Fuck it." He gripped my shirt hem and wrenched it upward as I raised my arms to help. The wet material hit the passenger seat with a slap that made me chuckle. A chuckle that died with a low moan as his hands moved up my damp waist to squeeze beneath my wet bra. I reached back to unclip it, uncaring we were in public. The rain concealed us, and honestly, the man just made me lose my mind.

"We seem to have a habit of getting caught in the rain," I joked.

"And needing to fuck after it," he said, but there was no teasing in his voice. Just lust. I noted his use of the word *needing*. Not want. *Need*.

I watched as he caressed my body with his gaze, hot on my hard nipples, then lingering on my scars. Something unreadable crossed his expression and then he stared into my eyes. "You're so beautiful."

His tender sincerity made me feel weirdly shy, and I was *not* shy. "Saying that while I look like a drowned rat, you must mean it."

But Lachlan didn't seem in the mood for joking. He drew me close, taking my right nipple in his mouth. I exhaled on his name as he sucked and laved. A whimper of need escaped me when he stopped. "Look at me."

I did, arching my back, pushing into the hard need of him beneath me.

Our eyes held, and my desire tightened as he gently squeezed my breasts, his thumb caressing my nearest scar. "You're the most truly alive person I've ever met."

I sucked in a breath at the compliment. "Lachlan."

A fierceness, something akin to anger, sparked in his blue eyes. "When you meet him, the man you want to settle down with ... make sure he's perfect." His voice was hoarse as he confessed, "I don't think I could live with anything else."

Emotion clogged my throat. At what he said. And what he didn't say.

Afraid of those feelings, I smirked, bent my head to his

and murmured against his mouth, "To hell with perfect. Perfect is boring." Then I kissed him. Hard. Hungry.

His big palm cradled the back of my head, holding me to him as he took over. Just as voracious, just as devouring.

And it was so much more than just a kiss.

27

LACHLAN

"You know, if you're going to brood, this is the wrong place to do it."

The familiar feminine voice jerked Lachlan out of his musings. He spun in his green leather captain's chair and smiled at Lucy leaning against the doorway to his stage office. "You're back."

She pushed off the doorjamb with a glamorous smile and sashayed across the room toward him. Her silk summer dress rippled with the movement, and he thought about how elegant she was in her high heels and how it wasn't quite as sexy as Robyn's athletic grace.

Damn.

He'd started doing that, and he wasn't quite sure how to stop.

Comparing every woman to Robyn.

"I'm back." Lucy sighed and settled her pert bottom on his desk in front of him. "And glad to be back."

"Kept your room for you."

"I noticed. Thank you."

"How did the meetings go?"

"Okay, I guess. Nothing sparked my passion."

"Maybe you should start screenwriting. Write something you want to star in."

Her lips parted. "I, uh … I actually already have started writing. You think I can do it? That I'm capable?"

"I think you're capable of anything you put your mind to."

She gave him a tender smile and then glanced back toward the door. Beyond it, they could hear members talking and laughing together. "The castle is busy."

"Summer approaches."

"Of course." She chuckled as she turned back to him. "I know busy is good for you, but I prefer it quiet."

Something in the back of her eyes, a shadow, caught his attention. "You okay, Luce?"

If it *was* there, it abruptly disappeared. "I should be asking you that, Mr. Broody. Is everything okay?" Her expression hardened. "Nothing bad happened while I was gone, right?"

"No. It's been quiet."

"That's good. How's Mac, the family, Arro … Thane?"

Lachlan wasn't stupid. He was aware of some attraction between his friend and brother. However, he knew Lucy. She wasn't the settling-down type. Didn't trust anyone long enough to do it. And for that reason, she'd stayed away from his brother. Lachlan couldn't say he wasn't thankful. Thane's heart had already been broken by his wife's sudden death. The last thing he needed was to become entangled with a charming but elusive American starlet with a mysterious past.

"Everyone is well."

"And Robyn? Or is she the reason for the brooding?" she teased.

Lachlan exhaled heavily. If he admitted what he was feeling out loud, it might make the inner turmoil worse. But he wasn't a stupid man, prone to bouts of self-denial. He understood his feelings, recognized them. He just didn't know what to do with them.

Lucy leaned toward him. "Hey, are you okay?"

"Luce …" He shifted uncomfortably and then pushed out of the chair. Restless. He strode over to the tall, narrow window adjacent to his desk and stared out at the golf course and woodlands beyond.

"You know you can talk to me if something is bothering you."

His pulse quickened. "Luce … remind me that I have no room in my life for a woman."

"And why is that again?"

Images of his childhood, of his father, flashed before his eyes. His mother's gravestone. Watching Thane grieve over the gravestone of his wife.

He remained silent.

"Or not." She gave a huff of laughter, but it sounded a little hurt.

Lachlan turned to her. "It's just not for me, Luce."

"I know. I get it. You know that." She strolled toward him, her heels clicking on his hardwood floors. When she stopped before him, she didn't have to crane her neck to meet his eyes, she was so tall in the shoes. "Why do you need the reminder?"

He gave a small huff of disbelief. "Robyn."

His friend's eyes widened with understanding. "Are you saying … oh my God, you're falling for her."

The idea made his heart pound, his skin flush, and he scowled. "No, I'm sure it's not that drastic," he denied. "But I do … I do have real feelings for her. Unexpected and real. I don't know how to move forward."

"You would usually end things."

"When the woman started to have real feelings, yes, but this has never happened to me before." Suddenly he realized who he was speaking to. "I mean, Luce, you know I care about you—"

She held up a hand, cutting him off with a tight smile. "I know what you mean." She sighed and crossed her arms over her chest. "I should have known Robyn would do this to you."

"Why?"

"You tell me. She has something, doesn't she?"

Yes, she did. And it was driving him mad. Lachlan wanted to be around her all the time. She never bored him. Her dry wit and no-nonsense attitude made him laugh while her sense of adventure and lack of inhibition ignited his blood. Yet it was her fearless honesty and soft compassion beneath the sexy toughness that most called to him. He'd told her things. About his family. His past.

It made the fact that she still wouldn't confide in him about the scars on her chest that much more disappointing. Lachlan wanted to *know* her. Even as it excited him to keep discovering her.

"Is it just the sex?" Lucy pushed.

He shook his head. It wasn't just the sex, although that was goddamn mind-blowing. He was addicted to the taste of the woman.

"What do you want me to tell you?"

"To walk away."

Lucy reached out to stroke his cheek, her fingers rasping against the bristle of his short beard. "Sweetheart, even if I tell you to do that, you won't. I can see it in your eyes. She's under your skin."

Fuck.

Luce was right.

He turned away to stare out the window at his estate. Only a few short months ago, all he had to worry about were his siblings and his business.

Now not even his mystery stalker overshadowed the top of his concerns.

Robyn.

His mind, his very blood, was filled with nothing but her.

It was aggravating and not a little terrifying.

"I'll leave you to brood." Lucy's heels faded away. "And Lachlan ... Robyn is wonderful, but she's made it clear this isn't her permanent stopping place. Don't be the guy who holds her back because he doesn't want her but he doesn't want anyone else to have her. She deserves better than that."

He scowled out the window. That wasn't his intention. Ever. He wouldn't do that.

He turned to say so, but Lucy was striding through the doorway.

"Oh! Jesus!" He heard her cry. "What are you doing skulking here?"

Hurrying toward the door, he heard Fergus of all people reply, "Sorry, Ms. Wainwright."

Lachlan stepped through the doorway to see Lucy skirting the mechanic. She glared at him and threw an exasperated look at Lachlan before she strode away toward the main staircase.

"Fergus?" The mechanic rarely came into the main rooms of the castle. "Problem?"

"Computer issue with one of the Rovers, Mr. Adair."

"Fergus, you can call me Lachlan when it's just the two of us," he reminded him. For God's sake, he'd grown up with the man.

"Right." Fergus grinned, but it was a preoccupied smile.

"Computer problem?" Lachlan prompted.

"Yes. It'll need to go in, I'm afraid. Wanted to check with you first."

The manufacturer always charged a fortune, but if Fergus

couldn't fix the issue, then there was nothing else for it. "Book it."

"Lachlan." Fergus tipped an invisible hat to him, a quirk he'd picked up from someone when he was a wee boy, and then sauntered in Lucy's wake toward the exit.

That restlessness made itself known as soon as he was alone again.

A walk.

A walk along the beach would do him good.

The castle was in order. If he was needed, they'd call his mobile.

And if he stayed there any longer, he would give in to the urge to track down Robyn.

Lachlan had to prove to himself that he could stay away from her. In fact, he wouldn't go to her tonight.

He dared himself not to.

* * *

REACHING for the phone on his bedside table for the millionth time, Lachlan tapped the screen and the clock lit up.

Three fifteen in the morning.

Sticking to his guns, he'd denied himself Robyn. Ate dinner with Arrochar at her place, stayed late into the night, and returned to the castle at midnight. If he was being honest, he'd hovered outside her door for a good five minutes before calling himself a weak-willed prick and then stormed into his room.

A grown man reduced to an addicted teenager by a woman a decade younger.

But what a woman she was. Lachlan groaned as he imagined from memory Robyn before him on her hands and knees. Never just receiving what he had to give but taking it, demanding it, bucking back into his thrusts with a savage, greedy lust. Just the memory of it made him painfully hard.

"Fuck," he muttered, throwing the covers off the bed. He sat up, running a hand through his hair, feeling his willpower ebb.

She was mere feet away, across the hall. His if he wanted. Why the devil was he denying himself?

Rat-a-tat-tat.

Lachlan looked up at the sound of the knock on his door. Robyn?

He leaned over to switch on a bedside lamp and then strode across the room to unlock the door. To his disappointment, no one was there.

What?

He popped his head out the doorway and looked to the right. The double doors at the end of the hall moved slightly, as if someone had just disappeared through them. An uneasiness settled over him as he finally saw the trail of red rose petals along the corridor floor.

"What the ...?" he murmured, retreating with the intention of putting on some clothes to investigate. White flashed against the oak door on his peripheral, and Lachlan jerked back from it to see a printed note pinned to his door.

His disquiet grew as he read it.

Your love is cold. Mine is colder.

Lachlan cursed under his breath and hurried across the hall to check Robyn's door. It was locked. Good.

He glanced down the corridor at the trail of petals. It was a clear sign that he was to follow it. And wherever it led, he didn't want Robyn near.

Rushing back into his bedroom, he threw on clothes and called down to security for backup. Within minutes, he heard the knock at the door and found Pete standing outside with Kyle, Xander, and Eccleston. "You were fast."

Pete wrenched his gaze from the note on the door, his expression grim. "Trail of petals leads all the way downstairs. We haven't followed it yet. We wanted to make sure you were secure first."

"Let's check it out." Lachlan closed his bedroom door behind him. "How did they get past the cameras?"

"Distraction." Pete looked pissed. "Sorry, sir. There was a disturbance at the front gate, and we were all focused on that."

"Disturbance?"

"Someone broke the cameras. McHugh went out to check them, but we haven't heard back from him yet. The rest of us were checking the perimeter of the castle when you called."

"Shit." They picked up the pace, following the petals without speaking so they didn't wake up the members. The trail led all the way downstairs and into the staff wing.

"The kitchen?" Pete deduced.

Sure enough, as soon as they walked into the kitchen, Lachlan halted abruptly.

The bright lights overhead flooded the kitchen so there was no missing the large pool of blood around the body of security guard Greg McHugh.

Pete rushed to the body as Lachlan froze in utter shock. "Secure Mr. Adair!" he barked at his men, and he felt the security guards surround him, guns out.

"No, no." Lachlan came out of his horrified daze as he watched Pete check McHugh for a pulse. "Is he ...?"

Pete looked up in furious grief. "He's dead."

His gut roiled with nausea. Forcing it down, he ordered, "Check the cameras."

"Not until you're secure." Pete stood, frowning as he spotted the trail of petals when Lachlan did.

They curved around toward the back of the kitchen where the commercial walk-in freezer was.

Your love is cold. Mine is colder.

"Oh my God." Lachlan was gripped with terror as he understood. "Robyn. ROBYN!" he roared, pushing his men off him and dodging Pete as he raced past his fallen security guard toward the freezer.

The handle was up.

It was closed.

"ROBYN!" He was sure she was in there. His fingers fumbled with the handle in his panic until another hand joined his. Pete.

Together they pulled, and the door opened with a breathy suction.

He saw her hand first as the freezer swung open, and his knees threatened to buckle.

Then she was revealed.

Her red hair covered her face.

"Lucy?" Renewed shock made him hesitate just a second. It wasn't Robyn. "Fuck, Lucy." He hurried into the freezer with Pete and together they lifted her cold, strangely heavy body out of the walk-in.

Laying her gently on the floor, he noted her worryingly blue lips and deathly stillness. Pete rested his fingers on her neck and sagged with relief. "Call an ambulance!" he yelled at his men. "She's still alive."

28

ROBYN

*I*t seemed like a nightmare, finding myself at the hospital for the second time since arriving in Scotland. Lucy's private bodyguards stood like towering human shields in front of her hospital room, and there was a buzz about the place that not even Adair incited.

Hollywood actor Lucy Wainwright was almost killed by a masked assailant.

The same man who murdered one of Lachlan's security guards.

I didn't know McHugh, but his death weighed heavily on my shoulders.

The bodyguards parted from Lucy's doorway and Lachlan slipped out, his features taut. While others might look at him and see stoic, I saw distress.

I wanted to go to him.

Mac's presence almost stopped me, but I thought, *fuck it*.

I met Lachlan halfway and embraced him before he could say a word.

It soon became apparent that his tense body wasn't

373

relaxing and his hands hovered lightly over my back, not fully embracing me in return.

Now feeling a little weird about hugging him, I stepped away. He didn't even seem to register he'd been in my arms. Barely meeting my eyes, Lachlan focused on Mac. "Lucy will be okay. She's recovering from mild hypothermia. They reckon she was only in there for about five minutes. Lucy can't remember anything."

Jesus. The commercial freezer operated at 0°F. "*Mild* hypothermia?"

He nodded but still didn't look at me. "They're keeping her overnight for observation, but the doctor said she'll be okay to return to the castle tomorrow."

Mac grimaced. "Lachlan, the members have been alerted, what with the police ... and McHugh." Anger burned in Mac's gaze at the mention of his man, and I reached out to squeeze his hand. "They've begun preparations to leave."

Lachlan took this news with no reaction. "I need to get back to Lucy. You get back to the castle."

"Can I see her?" I asked. "Eredine is out in the waiting room as well."

He shook his head. "You'll see her when she gets back to the estate. Take Eredine with you and relocate her to the castle. On our floor. I want her under guard too. Mac, have you checked on my family?"

Mac nodded. "Of course. Arrochar has been moved temporarily to Thane's. I have security watching the premises."

"Thank you. I have to get back." He turned and marched into Lucy's room without another word.

Unease settled over me, but when I looked at my dad, I shrugged it off. There was no time to stew over Lachlan's distant behavior. We had an estate to secure—and a killer to find.

374

***

AFTER KISSING Lucy's warm cheek, I leaned away from her and returned her soft smile. Hers was sleepy but at least it was there. "I'm glad you're okay."

"Me too, gorgeous," she murmured and closed her eyes.

I drifted away from her bed, my attention moving to Lachlan who stood at the footboard watching his friend, steadfastly not looking at me.

That niggle in my gut returned.

I was surprised Lucy hadn't upped and fled Ardnoch, but Lachlan said she insisted on staying, that no one was chasing her away while he needed her.

Did he need her?

Studying him watching over her like a grim guardian angel, I thought perhaps he did.

"I can stay," I offered. "Let you sleep."

He shook his head. "No. I'm good here."

There was an unpleasant twinge in my chest. "I could keep you company, if you need to talk."

Now he looked at me. "I don't. You should go. There are things to be done. Aren't there?"

He was so cold.

So far away.

I experienced another pained sensation. "Right. Well, I'm around if you ..." I trailed off and stalked out of the bedroom. Squeezing past Lucy's bodyguards, I strolled down the hall with my head held high.

If Lachlan didn't need me, that was fine.

Mac did. He was determined to find the bastard who killed McHugh. So was I. We had to figure this out together.

***

NOT EVEN A WALK along the beach with Mac could soothe me. The gentle lap of the water should have been calming, but all I kept thinking about was Lucy and McHugh.

"There has to be something we're missing from that footage," I said for the hundredth time.

Mac sighed at my side. "We've checked it over and over. So have the police."

While the security team was distracted by the cameras down at the gate, our masked assailant broke into the castle. We'd caught him on several cameras. From what we could piece together, he'd broken into Lucy's room. She had no recollection of the encounter, but we had him on camera, brazenly carrying her unconscious body over his shoulder through the castle down to the kitchens. McHugh was on his way to check the camera situation down at the gate when he heard something and followed the noise. From what we could ascertain from the footage, the assailant heard McHugh before he saw him, hid Lucy out of sight, and waited behind the kitchen door.

Studying it was chilling. I wanted to scream at the cameras, to warn McHugh to watch out.

But, of course, it was too late. McHugh walked into the kitchen, our killer stepped into sight much like he'd done to Mac outside his cottage, and stabbed the security guard several times in the gut before the man had time to react.

As a cop, I'd seen lots of horrible things. Even had them done to me. It didn't make watching that play out any less devastating. Unlike Mac, whose major organs were miraculously missed, the masked man used a long kitchen knife and stabbed McHugh six times, perforating his major organs. He had a wife, a baby boy. Now they no longer had a husband and a father because I hadn't stopped this bastard already.

"Stop blaming yourself, Robyn."

"I can't help it. We're not exactly dealing with a mastermind here, and yet he's left behind barely any clues. McHugh is dead. Lucy had hypothermia—"

"But is alive and well."

"And Lachlan's business is in jeopardy." Just as Mac had relayed to Lachlan that first morning after the murder, once the members found out, they started fleeing the estate. Adair called in extra security for both the club and his family. And not just because of the killer but because of the press. Someone leaked the story of Greg McHugh's murder, and it was all over the papers two days after the attack.

While paparazzi couldn't get onto the estate, they flooded into the village. They received ice-cold treatment from Ardnoch residents, many of whom "reserved the right not to serve them," but it didn't deter the paparazzi. Having them around was making us all uptight and anxious.

Plus, I couldn't forget the new evidence that landed in our laps, making everything all the more confusing.

When Lachlan called Brodan's head of security to inform them that the people he cared about were in jeopardy, he discovered Brodan's team was dealing with threatening messages too. That put a whole new spin on it. They sent us their received messages, which were less lovelorn but more vengeful with threats of ruin and misery. While they had a different tone to Lachlan's—and might just be a coincidence —we couldn't discount the possible connection.

"Maybe we're dealing with two people with vendettas against the Adairs, and they've joined forces. It would explain a lot."

"It is possible," Mac conceded. "But I wish it wasn't. It's bad enough trying to figure out who our masked killer is."

Killer.

How did we get here? We'd progressed from a high-level threat to red blinking lights and screaming sirens. My escape that night in the trailer took on an even more chilling edge than before.

"Do you still think it's McCulloch?" Mac asked.

The thought of the farmer taking it this far didn't sit right in my gut, but he was still the one with the clearest motive. "Grief is a strange thing, Dad. Who knows? It could be he started this and his only intention was to ruin Lachlan's business—mission possibly accomplished—and whoever he joined forces with has crossed the line."

"You don't think he's a murderer?"

"Do you?" I frowned. "I mean ... I do get very angry vibes from him, but I don't know. And I can't cross him off the list for an 'I don't know.'"

"If it makes you feel better, my gut tells me McCulloch isn't a murderer. But you're right. He could be working with someone who has gotten out of line."

"And the background check on his grandson came back with no red flags?"

"Right. Hardly anything on it. No criminal charges, no debt. Nothing of interest."

"Damn it," I whispered, frustrated beyond belief.

"How is Lachlan coping?" Mac asked. "I mean, actually coping?" At my questioning look, my dad shrugged. "He's not saying much, so I assumed he'd tell you more than he's telling me."

Wrong.

I stared stonily at the water. "I know as much as you."

Hearing my flat tone, Mac cleared his throat. "Do you ... want to talk about it?"

And say what? Admit that I was hurt? That I was a fool woman like all the other fool women who came before me? "Not really."

"What about that phone call from Seth?"

I tensed. We'd been in the security room going over

footage when Seth called five days ago. I'd cut him off twice and he kept calling, so I'd answered in front of Mac. My stepfather was worried about Regan again. She wasn't answering his calls, and he was considering filing a report. It wasn't the first time my little sister had done this. In fact, when she took off after my shooting, we filed a report, and then she finally got off her ass and called to tell us she was in Bali. Concerned, but pretty sure she was doing her usual irresponsible silent bailing-out on life, I'd explained to Seth the situation at Ardnoch but said I'd come home if he was certain she was in trouble.

He said he wasn't.

That his gut told him she'd just taken off again.

Seth was just being a dad. I got it. I understood. My stepdad told me he'd take care of it and keep me posted. Then he asked me to be careful and told me he loved me.

Yeah, I had all sorts of guilt riding my shoulders.

"What about it?" I answered Mac's question about the call.

"Regan."

"We have a killer to find. Kind of takes priority."

It took me a few steps, but I realized Mac wasn't at my side anymore. I stopped to look back.

He stood against the shore, hands in his pockets, a breeze blowing through his longish, salt-and-pepper hair. Fully recovered now, Mac was back in the gym daily, and it showed. My father was a big guy. Strong guy. Something about seeing the hurt on his face, that vulnerability, was worse than seeing it on anyone else. "You don't trust me."

I flinched at his statement.

"Even after all our time together, you still don't trust me. Not with the things that matter."

Bowing my head, I contemplated my feet and took a deep breath of sea air.

Mac wasn't wrong.

I clammed up. When it was about things or people I felt deeply about, I clammed up.

"Robbie, I don't know what else I can say or do to prove that I am a safe place for you."

Emotion burned in my nose and eyes. I looked up. His eyes, the eyes I'd inherited from him, were bright with mirrored emotion.

And abruptly, I was exhausted.

Not only by my guilt but by denial and mistrust and distance.

I didn't want that with Mac. "I'm sorry." I walked to him. The tight, cold mask my face had frozen into slipped. I let him see it all. "I feel like I'm failing."

He grimaced with sympathy and then pulled me into a hug.

Mac was right.

His arms felt like a safe place.

Trying not to cry, I curled my fingers into his leather jacket and just held on. The stalwart, comforting embrace of a father proved to have the soothing effect I'd been searching for. When I finally relaxed, I eased out of his arms and gave him a grateful smile.

He tucked a loose strand of my hair behind my ear and asked, "Do you want to talk about it?"

"Where do I start?" I began walking again, and Mac fell into step. "There's the case. McHugh."

"Again, not your fault." There was a shared bleakness in my dad's eyes. "We're all struggling with that one, Robbie."

His disconsolate tone made me feel selfish and short-sighted. I'd barely known McHugh. His death was so much worse for my dad. I reached out to squeeze his arm. "You're doing everything you can."

Mac ignored my reassurance and asked, "What else is buzzing around in that tough noggin of yours?"

Considering him a moment, I noted the determined look in his eye and let him have the change of subject. I smirked unhappily. "There's Regan."

"What's going on there?"

All the hurt I'd been harboring for a year burned in my gut. "I told you she went backpacking after my shooting. What I didn't say was that she abandoned me when I needed her."

"Abandoned?"

I nodded. "I told you how, my whole life, I've been a mini parent to that girl. Mom and Seth, whether they meant to, put me in the role. We're both adventurous, have a wild side, but mine is balanced. I feel responsibility. I understand consequences. I know where to draw the line."

"Regan doesn't," Mac deduced.

"No, she doesn't. And Mom and Seth got it into their heads when she was a goddamn toddler that only I could get through to her, and I just naturally took on that role."

"I'm not sure that's right, but who am I to judge anyone's parenting style?"

I snorted. "No one is a perfect parent, but you're right. This past year, I've realized how much I resent being put in that position. But maybe I wouldn't resent it so much if she hadn't taken off without me on the dream trip we'd planned together, just weeks after I got shot and nearly died." I wrinkled my nose. "Do I sound bitter? That sounded bitter to me."

"You sound like you have reason to feel bitter."

"Yeah, okay, I have issues with Regan. And she's done irresponsible things in the past. For instance, not telling anyone she'd taken off after I got shot. Now she's doing the same thing, but there's this small part of me that's like, 'What if she *is* in trouble?' I've left countless voicemails and emails and heard nothing back. I know she's been in contact with Mom and Seth, but now she's dropped off the face of the planet. I'm worried, but I'm not certain she's in trouble. So am I prioritizing myself and this case over a sister who needs me?"

"She's the Boy Who Cried Wolf."

"Exactly." I studied my dad's contemplative expression. "So what should I do?"

"What you're doing. Your sister isn't a wee girl anymore. It's not her big sister's job to teach her where to draw the line. She's a grown-up. She knows where the line is, Robyn, and crossing it or not crossing it isn't your responsibility. You can't control her, and you need to let go of the idea that her consequences are yours."

"I know. That's why I'm here still. But the guilt ..."

"Is just a part of who you are. You love her, you worry about her. That's natural. But you are not failing her, Robyn. All you can do is be there for her when she comes to you."

Tears pricked my eyes at his gentle advice, and I nudged him with my shoulder. "Thank you."

He nudged me back. "You're welcome, wee birdie."

We fell into a companionable silence for a few minutes and then he asked hesitantly, "Is there anything else on your mind?"

I sucked in a breath. Oh yeah, there was definitely something else on my mind. "Well ... there's Lachlan."

Mac waited for me to say more.

I made a face. "Do you want to hear this stuff?"

"I want to hear what's bothering you." He shot me a wary look. "But leave out the details."

Chuckling unhappily, I retorted, "What details? He was already Mr. No Future before all this happened, but at least we were having a good time together. I made it clear that I'm not some faceless woman in a long line of faceless women, and he seemed to agree. I thought we were friends. He told me things I wasn't expecting."

"Like?"

"About his family. His past. He trusted me with information I'm not sure he's trusted other women with."

"I can see him doing that with you."

I raised an eyebrow.

Mac gave me a proud smile. "You're an honorable, trustworthy person, Robyn. Anyone can see that."

Honorable. People didn't use words like that anymore. It was nice Mac saw that in me. "Thank you."

"You're welcome."

"I get it from you."

He sighed. "I'm not so sure about the honorable part. But I appreciate it. So … your relationship with Lachlan has turned into something more?"

I couldn't ascertain if that bothered Mac. He was excellent at remaining outwardly impartial. "It's confusing. He's trusted me, but I haven't felt it was prudent to trust him in return. Seemed dangerous to my self-preservation."

"You care about him?"

I eyed Mac. "I don't know when or how, but yes. Caring about him just sort of happened."

"You connected with him. Those kinds of connections come out of nowhere sometimes. You find them in unexpected places." He sighed heavily, wearing an expression of mournful frustration. Arrochar came to mind, and I wondered if he was silently referring to her. Had he unexpectedly connected with Lachlan's little sister? Was she the woman he loved and didn't pursue out of fear?

Part of me wanted to ask, yet I knew without really knowing that it was a topic very much off-limits. And I still wasn't certain how I felt about whatever was (or wasn't) going on between them.

"You shouldn't run from it if you've found something genuine with him. If anyone can pull Adair's head out of his arse, it's you." Mac continued, "And I hope any reservations have nothing to do with me. I will never stand in your way."

"I know. It's not that … The thing is … if I start giving more of myself to him, then it is going to hurt when he ends it."

"I think it's already going to hurt. Which means there's nothing left to lose in being honest, being yourself. That way, it might not have to end."

"You know him."

"I do." He nodded. "And it's true he is adamantly against settling down."

"See—"

"But …" Mac sighed. "Och, I don't want to say anything out of turn or get your hopes up."

My pulse leapt. "About?"

"I just … there's something between you that I've never seen between him and another woman."

I considered the possibility that Mac's observation had weight and offered, "Yet he's been distant since the murder."

"That's guilt. I know Lachlan. He blames himself."

I nodded, imagining that was true. But that didn't account for how he'd pushed me away but kept Lucy close.

"Robyn …" Mac touched my arm. "One of the most magical things about you is your bravery. You follow your gut, and you face your fears because, like you said, you realize the fear of fear itself is much worse than the actual fear. And believe me, regret, too, is so much worse than fear."

It was the abrupt reminder I needed.

Dad was right.

I had to stop holding myself back from Lachlan and just go for it. Whatever happened, at least I'd know I'd given my entire self to whatever was between us. Yet, there was still that little niggle in my gut. And the last few days, it had only gotten worse.

"I'm not a jealous type," I prefaced, "but I have to admit, it's bothering me how much time Lachlan's spending with Lucy. I know"—I held up my hands to stall his next words—"she's been through the ringer. But we're on day seven since the murder, and Lachlan is still spending every second with her and forgetting about everyone else who might need him."

Like me.

"Is it because it's Lucy, or would you feel the same if it were anyone?"

"Both. I'd be agitated by his distance during this time if it were anyone, but it's Lucy and ..."

"They have a past."

"Exactly." My cheeks flushed with embarrassment. "I don't know if this is the kind of thing you talk to your dad about."

"Let's just make our own rules." He nudged me again, expression tender. "And considering I've known Lachlan a very long time, I can promise you there's nothing going on between him and Lucy. If Lachlan wanted her, he'd never have broken off their affair."

"Maybe her attack has made him realize how he feels about her." That's how it seemed, anyway. I knew Lucy had almost died, and I was so thankful she hadn't, but Lachlan was hovering like a husband who was beside himself with worry.

"I think you need to stop thinking and just ask him. Be honest with him."

"Honest with him." My stomach erupted into butterflies at the thought. "Sure. Sounds easy enough."

* * *

SECURITY MET me at the estate gates. For several days, the paparazzi had blocked the entrance with their cars, making it hard to get in and out. The extra security created a perimeter to allow estate staff through.

When the paps queried who I was, Jock informed them I was an estate housekeeper and that had shaken the bastards off my back. But I got a sudden inkling into what life as a famous person might be like, and it was disturbingly claustrophobic.

It was a relief to watch the gates swing closed behind me and the armed security take up position in front of it again. I worried for Lachlan. I didn't know if members were demanding a return of fee payments, but I did know he was paying staff not to work as well as a shit ton of money for extra security.

I wanted him to talk to me.

He wouldn't.

Following Mac's advice, I didn't lock myself in my bedroom that night as I had the past seven nights. The estate had mostly cleared out, and Lachlan furloughed a number of staff members while the situation remained uncertain. Mac wanted to move back into his cottage but realized, given what had happened to McHugh and Lucy, he and I were safer in the castle. Especially now there were more men and women on the grounds patrolling and manning the security room.

Lachlan was determined no one would get in or out without his team being aware of it this time. Mac told me he'd even demanded Thane, the kids, and Arrochar move onto the estate, but his siblings refused to be sequestered with the rest of us. They accepted the security guards Lachlan put on them, not just for protection against the killer but against the paparazzi who were hounding them too. However, that was as far as they were willing to change their lives during all this.

I stood outside Lachlan's bedroom door, those butterflies back in my belly, and lifted my fist to knock. What was the worst that could happen?

He'd reject me.

As horrible as the thought was, I'd survive it.

I knocked.

The door swung open a few seconds later, and I could feel my skin turn hot at the sight of Lachlan. I'd missed him. Not just the sex (although I could've used some wild sex to dissolve some stress and tension this past week) but just being with him. I enjoyed making him laugh, the way he grinned at me with that boyish, wicked twinkle in his eyes that caused women all over the world to swoon in movie theaters. I missed lying in bed listening to him talk in his cultured Scottish brogue about his family, the tragedy, the joy, the strange but often wonderful life he'd led.

"Hey, Robyn."

I started at the voice and glanced beyond Lachlan into the room.

Lucy was lying on Lachlan's bed in a silk robe and night-gown, her impressive cleavage on display.

The intimate sight was a punch to the gut.

Feeling a little blindsided, it took me a minute to say hey back.

Lachlan moved away from the door and gestured for me to come in. He studied my face, but he didn't speak.

I took only a few steps inside and turned my attention to Lucy who showed no traces of having been through hell. In fact, she looked as glamorous as always. Like a '50s pinup, sprawled elegantly across Lachlan's bed. That's when I finally noted the TV was on. She had a tray of snacks on the bed in front of her.

They were hanging out. Watching a movie together.

Just like they'd been hanging out every second of every day since her attack.

I knew there was no reason to be jealous. This was Lucy. I was glad she had Lachlan to take care of her. And I suspected the brother she had actual feelings for was Thane.

But maybe that had changed.

Maybe, like I'd said to Mac, her attack prompted her and Lachlan to realize what they felt for each other was more than friendship.

"You okay?" She sat up a little straighter, her brows creased in concern. "You look a little tired, gorgeous."

At her endearment, I felt stupidly emotional. Lucy deserved someone like Lachlan. Who was I to stand in the way? They had history. I was a casual fuck. "I'm fine. I just wanted to make sure you were too?"

"I'm good." She grinned and gestured to the food in front of her. "I'm indulging. Do you want to hang out? There's plenty. And we're watching reruns of old British comedy shows."

I forced a smile at her offer but no way did I want to be a third wheel in this scenario. "Thanks, but I think I'm going to get a workout in before bed."

"Great, make me feel even more guilty," she teased.

I was pretty sure my smile was more of a grimace, but I didn't care. I just wanted out of there. Lachlan hadn't said a word. Not a surprise. I'd barely gotten a word out of him all week.

It occurred to me that I might have imagined his tender looks. Was I just a warm body after all?

My sudden insecurities riled me.

How dare a man make me feel this way?

I refused to allow it.

He didn't want me anymore. Fine! I didn't need him.

"Have a good night." I gave Lucy a wave and ignored Lachlan's existence as I let myself out.

Inside my bedroom, I also ignored my trembling fingers as I hurried into fresh workout gear. I didn't look at his bedroom door as I passed.

Because I wasn't out of line here, was I?

No matter what happened with Lucy, if you were having sex with one woman, it was beyond inappropriate to have another in your bed, even if it was platonic. How would Lachlan have felt if he'd walked into my bedroom to see a guy sprawled on my bed half-dressed?

"Probably wouldn't care," I muttered angrily.

It seemed Adair had the ability to cut people out of his life.

Guards on the grounds kept watch as I marched up the gravel drive to the gym. A guard at the main entrance opened the door for me with a friendly "good evening," and all the lights automatically came on as I walked in.

I was the only one there.

Good.

I wanted privacy.

After warming up on a couple machines, I pulled on my gloves and started beating the shit out of the boxing bag.

I was alone in the gym, and Lachlan didn't care.

There was the crux of it.

A murderer, one who tried to kill me before attacking Lucy and killing McHugh, had come after me. Now that said killer had proven himself a ruthless, sick bastard, Lachlan was nowhere to be seen. And while I didn't need a man to protect me, it was always nice to know that the one in your bed cared enough to want to.

That you were a priority to him.

"Argh!" My reverse spin kick sent the bag swinging so hard, I had to step back.

"Very nice."

The voice made me jump.

My pulse slowed when I whipped around to find Pete.

The security guard took a step toward me, gesturing to the bag. "Though we may have to reattach the thing to the ceiling."

I smirked at that. "Sorry."

"Don't be. I'm glad you can take care of yourself." Shadows edged the blue irises of Pete's eyes. The security guard refused to go on leave after Greg McHugh's death, even though Mac advised it. But Pete stubbornly remained. Like me, I think he was determined to be around when we caught the fucker.

McHugh's funeral was in two days. Mac told me Pete and Greg had been good friends. "How are you?"

Pete shrugged. "Glad to be working. Keeping busy. I saw you come in here, and I know we have a guard outside ... but you shouldn't be out here at night on your own. Does Mr. Adair know?"

"Yeah, he knows." I looked away. "Like you said, I can take care of myself."

"I'm obviously not as enlightened as Mr. Adair, then." Pete crossed the distance between us.

"What do you mean?"

"I wouldn't want my woman out here no matter how well she can take care of herself."

There was a sudden hollow feeling in my chest. "I'm not his woman."

"Pete's right."

I jerked at the voice. Jesus Christ, everyone was getting the jump on me tonight. Then it occurred to me the damn guard outside kept opening the door, so there was no beep from the security system anytime someone used their key card to get in.

I glanced over my shoulder at Lachlan. He glowered ferociously at us.

What. The. Actual. Fuck?

"You shouldn't be in here at night."

Pete retreated, the neutral mask of a trained security guard falling over his face. "Mr. Adair."

"You can return to your duties, Pete. Thank you for seeing to Ms. Penhaligon's safety, but I assure you, it's already in hand." There was a bite, almost a warning, in his tone that neither of us missed.

I bristled as Pete marched out of the gym.

How dare he come in here and try to pee around his territory.

I turned back to the bag and resumed punching it. Rapidly. Hard.

"Robyn." His voice was near now.

I refused to look up.

"Robyn."

Thump, thump, thump. Thump-thump-thump-THUMP!

My arms ached and sweat coated my skin, but I didn't care. It was the bag or his face.

Suddenly, Lachlan grabbed the boxing bag, pulling it out of my reach.

Breathing hard, I stepped back, scowling at him. "What are you doing?"

"You shouldn't be in here."

"I told you where I was going."

"Then left without looking at me. I deduced from your cold shoulder that the information wasn't intended for me."

"Then why are you here?"

Lachlan scoffed incredulously. "I don't know. Because I'm concerned." Then his expression darkened. "But I guess since you're not my woman, it's not my place to worry."

"I'm *not* your woman. That's not what we are."

He pushed into my personal space, his chest brushing mine. I had to arch my neck to maintain eye contact. "I thought it was clear that while we're having sex, we're not to have sex with other people."

I guffawed. "I was talking to Pete, not offering myself to him."

"He watches you too much."

If he did, I'd never noticed. "He can watch all he likes." *Free. Woman.*

Lachlan's eyes flashed. "I'm not playing this game with you."

"What game?" I pushed him out of my space, and he stumbled a little, nostrils flaring. "You do not get to come in here and accuse me of something when I just walked into your bedroom to find Lucy in her lingerie on your goddamn bed!"

Blinking rapidly, his shock slackening his features, Lachlan took a few more steps back only to be halted by the boxing bag. "You cannot be serious."

He wouldn't make me feel stupid about this. It wasn't stupid. "She's your ex. You have history. And I repeat, you were alone in your room for the seventh night in a row, and unbeknownst to me, she's in there in silk nightwear on your bed."

"You're making it sound as if it's something it's not."

"Yeah?" I took a step toward him. "I guess I'm making a big deal out of nothing, then. You won't mind if I invite Pete into my bed to watch movies while I'm wearing a silk nightie?"

His hot gaze ran down my body before returning to my face. "It wouldn't be the same thing. Lucy was almost killed. She's my friend."

"I'm sorry about what happened to Lucy. And I'm glad she has good friends who want to take care of her, but the man

I'm sleeping with does not invite another woman into his bed under any circumstances, so ... *this* needs to end." I gestured between us. "Maybe you don't see it, but there's something between you two, and I don't want to get caught in the middle."

Lachlan looked like I'd slapped him. "Are you fucking kidding me?"

"Don't." I snapped. "Don't act like I'm making this up in my head. Here are the facts: You are sleeping with me. This person came after me too. He actually killed someone. And I've barely seen you. I've been *alone* in my room every night since. While you were taking care of her."

He looked winded. "I ... I didn't think you needed anyone to take care of you. You're stronger than Lucy."

I laughed bitterly. Because that said it all. "Haven't I already told you? There's a difference between needing and wanting."

At his silence, I shook my head, unable to look at him. Instead, I grabbed my shit. "Go back to Lucy. I don't *want* you anymore." Heart pounding, chest aching, I marched toward the ladies' shower rooms.

I'd just opened the door when I heard his pounding footsteps. His arm reached over my head, his palm slammed into the door, and I was unceremoniously manhandled inside. "Adair!"

I dropped my gear, trying to maneuver out of his arms, but he caged me against the partition wall between the entrance and the showers. "Get off me."

"I. Don't. Cheat," he growled through gritted teeth, his nose brushing mine.

"I never said you did. Now get off me. I won't ask again," I warned him.

"I don't want Lucy. Not like that."

"Adair." I'd give him to the count of three.

Regret softened his expression. "It's Lachlan. And I'm sorry I made you feel like I'd abandoned you when you needed me. That wasn't my intention."

"I don't need you," I lied angrily.

"This isn't what I expected between us. But I shouldn't have left you. If anything had happened to you ..."

I pushed against his hold, but the bastard wouldn't let up. "Don't pretend like you care, Adair, just because you don't want to be a bad guy. It doesn't matter to me." Another lie. So unlike me. The truth? *Actions* mattered to me. And he'd made his feelings clear this week. Rejection, fury, and the image of Lucy happy and taken care of in his bed awoke something ugly in me. "*You* don't matter to me."

He had the audacity to look wounded.

Ignoring a flicker of guilt, I pushed, "Go back to Lucy. I don't care who you fuck now that it's not me."

He leaned in and whispered hoarsely against my lips, "Liar."

To my horror, I could feel the burn of tears in my eyes. "I swear to God, you've got two seconds to get out of my way or I will make you."

"You would have done it already. We both know you can leave whenever you want. So what do you want?"

"I don't want you!" I pushed with all my strength against him, and he stumbled for a second but only to recover and use his whole body to hold me against the wall.

"Liar," he snarled against my mouth. "You want me *and* you need me."

The tears were coming, and I hated the vulnerability. In front of him of all people! It was horrifying. I hated—

"I hate you!"

Fury darkened his expression. "You want the truth?" he hissed. "When I realized that fucker had locked someone in the freezer, I thought it was you, Robyn. I've never felt terror like it. And a sick, awful part of me felt absolute relief that it *wasn't* you."

I stilled, shocked to my core.

"I've been drowning in guilt all week."

Hence all the time he's spent with Lucy.

Oh my God.

"The truth is ..." His hungry gaze ravaged me. "I need and want and care about you. I have no idea what's happening to me. What you're doing to me ..."

His confession hung between us, heavy, throbbing.

I was a little breathless as I confessed, "I don't hate you ... I've ... missed you."

An almost feral triumph lit his eyes.

Then his mouth crushed over mine. He released his hold as I kissed him back with equal desperation. His hand curled around my right thigh, opening me, and I could feel every inch of hard desire as he thrust his hips against mine.

The madness of lust took over.

I steadied myself with a hand on his shoulder as he yanked off my sneakers and then almost tore my sport leggings and underwear, whipping them from me. Then my right leg was draped over his shoulder, his head between my legs, his mouth on me.

At the first touch of his tongue, I threw my head back against the tile and cried out in pleasure.

Yes, yes, this was what I'd needed.

His wicked mouth, his talented tongue, the tickle of his beard against my skin ... It didn't take long to ricochet me off the peak into an explosion. I panted hard from the orgasm as Lachlan stood and provocatively wiped his thumb over his lips. Smug satisfaction burned in his eyes, and I wanted to pay him back, make him lose his mind too.

Fumbling for his zipper, I pulled him into me. As soon as

he was free, he gripped my ass and lifted me up so I could wrap my legs around his waist.

He surged into me as we fell back against the wall, and I gasped at the overwhelming fullness I'd yearned for.

"I've been so empty," I confessed in my mindless longing for him.

Lachlan groaned against my mouth. "I'm sorry, Braveheart." His voice was gruff. "No women in or on my bed but you. No leaving you alone again." He kissed me tenderly.

I didn't want to believe his promise, but I felt it planting a seed of hope in me as I held on to him, as he drove into me in luscious thrusts.

My passion-filled cries echoed off the shower room tiles, exciting Lachlan, his lovemaking turning savage.

It wasn't just desire. Or want.

It was *need*.

And it soothed the ache in my chest as much as it inflamed the hot ache between my legs. Because he was becoming necessary to me.

And I wanted to become a necessity to him too.

29

LACHLAN

Those stunning golden, green, brownish, bluish, gray, ever-changing hazel eyes looked up at him as he moved inside her.

Robyn.

Something primitive, something base within him, recognized her as his.

She belonged to him.

But he was at war with that part of himself, even as he tenderly took her for the second time that night, now in the privacy of her bedroom.

Every time the warring side that wanted to run took hold of him, he'd hear her words again, see her hurt, feel it deep in his bones.

This person came after me too. He actually killed someone. And I've barely seen you. I've been alone in my room every night since. While you were taking care of her.

Robyn Penhaligon was the toughest woman he'd ever met. He teasingly called her Braveheart, yet beneath the banter of endearment was sincerity. But she wasn't invulnerable. The scars on her chest proved that.

And he'd abandoned her when she'd most needed to feel safe.

The thought was a painful scrape through his gut.

"Robyn," he murmured her name like a plea and kissed her as he reached between their bodies to torment her like she tormented him.

At the sight, sound, and feel of her climax, Lachlan couldn't hold back any longer. His hips jerked hard against hers, and he shuddered through his own release.

Spent, he fell onto his side but refused to let go of her. Despite their harsh argument earlier, Robyn turned into him. No barriers. No holding back.

She snuggled her face into his throat and while he liked her there, Lachlan needed more. Tipping her chin back, he kissed her again. Soft but deep.

Possessive.

Fuck.

He broke the kiss and swallowed hard.

Not since his father's death had he felt so lost at sea.

"I was shot by a drug dealer," Robyn announced randomly.

It took him a second, but Lachlan realized, no, it wasn't random.

His fingers trailed down over her chest to the scars.

She was offering … *herself*.

His breath caught.

Reject the offer and run? Or stay … for once?

Their eyes locked, and the thought of hurting her was worse than any war battling inside him. "When?"

"Just over a year ago. It's why I left the force."

Swallowing hard against a vision of some junkie bastard shooting her three times in the chest, he choked out. "Tell me."

And so she did. When she got to the part about her heart

giving out, dying on the OR table, his own heart nearly stopped.

"You left because a job you didn't love wasn't worth your life?" he guessed.

Robyn hesitated, and he tensed at the crack in her voice. "That's what I tell people."

Turning her face to him with a gentle prod of his fingers to her chin, his voice was like sandpaper as he asked, "What's the truth?"

Tears brightened her eyes, shocking him into utter silence. She looked heartbroken. "I killed the guy who shot me. His name was Eddie Johnstone. A drug dealer from East Boston. I'd never killed someone before, and although it was self-defense ... it took me a long time to work through. I'm not even sure I have properly. My therapist said it will take time."

A deep ache emanated from his upper chest. "Jesus, Robyn. I'm so sorry. But you must know it wasn't your fault. And he was a criminal."

"He was. He wasn't a very nice guy. But he had a sister and a mother who loved him, and I took him from them."

"He almost took you from your family." *From me.*

"I know." She reached up to caress his cheek through his beard. "I'm getting there. Slowly but surely. But I never want to be in that position again."

Lachlan realized she had been put in that position again—when the masked attacker broke into the trailer. He tried not to think too hard on that and asked, "You see a therapist?"

Robyn nodded and talked about the months after the shooting. Bending his head, he pressed soft kisses to her scars as she told him about her recovery, about the therapy, the nightmares she still had sometimes, and about her sister abandoning her when she needed her.

He raised his head and saw the pain of that abandonment

buried in the back of her eyes, and vowed he would never lose sight of that vulnerability in Robyn again. He knew better than anyone that often those who seemed the strongest buried their pain a little deeper than the rest. Sometimes those who seemed the strongest needed the support of others more than those around them ever realized.

Past boyfriends, Mac, Regan, even her mother ... they'd failed to make Robyn a priority.

Lachlan suspected it was the thing she craved most, even if she couldn't admit it.

"I don't want to hurt you." The words were out before he could stop them.

Instead of flinching from his concerns, Robyn reached up to stroke his cheek, her fingers rasping against the bristle of his beard. "Tell me why you don't want anything more than casual. Please."

It was something he'd never said out loud before.

Something he wasn't too proud of.

And to confess it to Robyn, the most fearless person he knew ... "You'll think less of me."

"Try me."

Pulse racing, the urge to remove himself physically from her was strong, and as if she sensed it or felt his increased heart rate, she slid her leg over his, her strong thigh trapping him.

It was hard to want to move after that. "I'm not you, Braveheart," he admitted. "I might have played an action hero on the screen ... but I'm afraid I'm a bit of a cowardly bastard."

"I don't believe that."

He huffed bitterly. "I ... I lost my mum. Then I lost my dad. He was there, but without her, he fell apart. He wasn't the man or the father he was before her death. Even though he got better over the years, he never moved on. People are supposed to move on, aren't they?"

"He loved her very much," Robyn whispered, emotion bright in her eyes.

"Half of him was here. The other half was with her. And then Aunt Imogen died before I lost Dad too." He squeezed her waist. "If that wasn't bad enough, I had to watch my brother go through the same thing. He's stronger than my dad ever was, but I'm my father through and through. And there's the fact that my great-grandfather lost his wife young in childbirth too. His father before him lost his wife to influenza only six months after they were wed. We Adairs seem cursed to lose the people we love." His grip on her tightened. "What a fucking awful existence my father had. I can't imagine anything worse."

Understanding dawned on her face.

"Lachlan," she whispered. Her lips parted as if she wanted to say more but didn't have the words.

That's because there were none.

His was a deep-seated fear and as much as this woman was under his skin … he wasn't certain the fear wouldn't win in the end.

"I'm a risk," he said, owing her that honesty.

"Then I guess I'm a risk too." She moved over him, pushing him back on the bed, straddling him. Her hair tumbled around her shoulders, tickling his skin, and he reacted instantly to the glorious sight of her naked body.

He was addicted.

"I can stay …" She pressed a kiss to his chest. "And rather than labeling ourselves something, we just see what happens." She looked into his eyes. "Or if you want me to, I can go, and I promise not to hold it against you. What do you want, Lachlan?"

His body betrayed him, his hands gripping her hips tight at the words "or I can go."

Staring at this brave, sexy woman who had taken over his life, he knew what she'd do. She would face her fear head-on. She inspired him.

He flipped her onto her back with such speed, she let out a cute squeak of surprise. Lachlan took hold of her hands and held her down. "Does that answer your question?"

Robyn grinned, and in a quick blur of movement, he found himself on his back again.

He stared up at the ceiling, dazed.

How the fuck did she do that?

As she moved over him, announcing it was her turn, Lachlan gave a bark of laughter and happily let her have at it.

30

LACHLAN

It was unlike Lachlan to feel nervous about anything, but as he stood outside Mac's office, he hesitated a moment to take a deep bloody breath.

The truth was, since his affair with Robyn had begun, he'd been avoiding his friend. Not just because it was complicated but because he wasn't sure he could give her up if that's what Mac wanted. And that seemed ungrateful at best, perfidious at worst, considering Mac's loyalty over the years.

Sucking it up, Lachlan knocked on Mac's door.

"Come in."

He strode in with purpose, ignored Mac's raised eyebrow, and decided to just come out with it. He closed the door and turned to him. "I know I should never have touched Robyn in the first place ... but I care about her and have long before I could even admit it to myself."

Mac relaxed back in his chair, hands over his stomach, contemplating him. "Christ, Lachlan, do you not think I know that? You would never have touched *my daughter* if it was just an attraction."

There it was. The truth Lachlan had denied for too long.

"I want to try something real with her," he promised his friend but was honest enough to add, "I can't promise it will work out, but I want to try."

"No one can promise that." Mac stood and rounded the desk. "I know you. I know you're a good man. And if you give Robyn another reason to stay, then I'm grateful."

Lachlan shook his head, feeling ashamed. "You're a better man than me, Mac."

The unspoken hung in the air between them.

Mac swallowed and looked away. "Does Robyn know?"

He nodded, studying her father. "Does that mean we're okay?"

His friend clapped him on the shoulder, smirking. "I'm happy for you."

"I don't deserve her."

"No, you don't." Mac chuckled. "But what man does? She's one of a kind … but if it has to be someone, then I'm all right with it being you."

It was the tepid blessing of a father who recognized how special his daughter was. Lachlan was okay with that. It was better than the opposite. "Thanks, Mac."

He nodded.

Awkward tension filled the space between them. Lachlan sought to break it. "Arrochar is insisting on hosting a dinner for us all. I told her the timing couldn't be worse."

"Maybe it's what we all need," Mac disagreed. "And the paparazzi have gotten bored and fled Ardnoch for scandal elsewhere."

Unfortunately, his members hadn't come back. Lachlan was in the midst of a PR nightmare on top of everything else. Truthfully, however, he felt less stressed about it than people might imagine. When someone had been murdered and the people you cared about were in danger, the material stuff didn't matter so much.

And he was certain, he and his PR team could turn things around once they caught the killer.

"You're right," Lachlan found himself agreeing. "I'll tell Arrochar to arrange it."

* * *

"You okay?" Lachlan asked as he and Robyn strode toward the dining table.

Arrochar's house was filled with the noise of his family chattering over one another.

"Mom was an only child," Robyn said. "She doesn't talk to her parents. Seth's parents live in Florida, his brother in Texas."

He raised an eyebrow in question.

She grinned. "Not used to big family dinners."

"Oh, this is nothing," he said, holding out a chair for her so she was between him and Mac. "When Brodan and Arran are here, usually with their flavor of the month, it's even noisier."

Seated around Arrochar's large dining table was his sister, Thane, the kids, Lucy, Eredine, and Mac. The table was overlaid with food because Arro loved to cook and was good at it. Lachlan wasn't too bad either. He'd had to be because his dad couldn't cook, and his brothers didn't want to try.

"This smells amazing, Arro," Mac offered.

His sister beamed affectionately at him. "Everyone dig in."

The next five minutes were filled with food talk. "Pass the potatoes." "Do you want the mac and cheese?" "Try to leave some beef for the rest of us, Lewis." "Someone put some salad on their plate, please, it's not just there as decoration." And so forth.

"You got enough?" Lachlan asked Robyn as he spooned more mac and cheese onto her plate.

She laughed, holding up a hand to ward him off. "More than. You trying to fatten me up?"

"I'll take you whatever way I can get you."

Robyn rolled her eyes, but he could tell she liked it. It made him smile harder and impulsively lean forward to kiss her, even though she was eating.

She laughed against his mouth, and he loved it.

When he pulled back, he caught Eredine's eyes; they twinkled with joy for him.

Feeling a strange heat rise on his neck, he turned back to his plate to eat.

This was Lachlan's happy place. Surrounded by family, the sound of their conversation filling his ears. With Robyn by his side, it felt more poignant.

It would only have been more perfect if Brodan and Arran were there.

"Uncle Lachlan?" a sweet, high-pitched voice asked.

Swallowing his bite, he looked down the table at Eilidh who insisted on being seated next to her favorite person in the world—Aunt Arrochar. "Yes, sweetheart?"

Eilidh bit her lip against a mischievous smile as her gaze moved to Robyn. "Is that lady your girlfriend?"

Robyn choked, and he covered his laughter with a quick cough. He glanced at Robyn as she took a drink of water. Patting her on the back, he asked, "All right there?"

At his teasing tone, she flicked him a dark look that only made him grin harder.

Turning back to Eilidh, he said, "This lady is Robyn. Remember?"

His niece nodded. "Is Robyn your girlfriend?"

"Yes."

Out of his peripheral, he saw water spray across the table.

Eyes wide, he stared down at Robyn as she spluttered and coughed.

Strangled laughter came at them from all sides.

"Did I say something wrong?" He caressed Robyn's back as she pulled herself together.

Even Mac chuckled at her side.

"No." She blinked up at him as she wiped tears from her eyes. "That bit of mac and cheese just went down the wrong way."

"*Right.*"

Her gorgeous eyes narrowed. "I swear if there weren't children at this table, I would fork you." She pointed said fork at him.

Lachlan leaned in, his lips brushing her ear as he whispered, "It's pronounced fuck."

He felt her shiver and smiled smugly. Easing back, he watched her struggle to contain a smile and pressed another kiss to her lips to feel it.

"This is weird," Thane said, breaking their locked gazes.

Lachlan looked at his brother. "What is?"

"You?" But Thane was openly delighted. "Lachlan Adair ... it only took him thirty-eight years, but he's finally someone's boyfriend. Can you be a boyfriend in your advanced years?"

"Fu—" He caught himself, glancing at the kids. "Shut up."

Thane snorted.

"Aw, leave him alone." Lucy nudged Thane playfully. "It's nice."

"Can we stop talking about it like we're teenagers and I'm his prom date?" Robyn pressed the back of her knuckles to her cheeks.

"Oh, do we have to?" Arrochar pouted. "We've been waiting on a woman taking him down forever, so we have years of gentle mockery stored up."

"Take me down? How do *you* know she likes to practice her wrestling skills on me?"

"Shut up." Robyn shoved him and he snorted, enjoying her discomfort. "My dad is right there."

"Yes, please shut up." Mac cut him an only semi-mocking dark look.

Lachlan pressed his lips together.

"What's wrong with that?" Lewis asked. "I like wrestling too."

Thane threw his brother a "will you watch what you're saying?" look, and Lachlan was sufficiently chastened. He nodded in apology but couldn't stop the smile prodding his lips.

Conversation resumed to subjects other than his and Robyn's relationship, and he enjoyed the way she easily fell into discussion with his family.

She was curious about Arrochar's job as a forest engineer and what it entailed and genuinely interested in Thane's work as an architect.

"I'll take you out to our homes," Lachlan said to her as they finished dinner and moved to the lounge to relax with drinks. "Thane designed his home and mine."

"I'd love to see them."

Lachlan slid his arm around her, pulling her down beside him on the couch as his family and friends surrounded them.

The kids had gone off to play in the garden; Lucy settled on the arm of Thane's chair, the two of them lost in conversation. Lachlan ignored the twinge of concern their closeness caused, knowing Lucy was just being friendly.

As Robyn continued to chat with his sister, Eredine, and Mac, Lachlan was content to just listen, pressed to her side while his hand rested on her opposite hip. It was a compulsion to keep her close, to touch her, to breathe her in as she laughed and teased and swapped stories of growing up in Boston with Arrochar's stories of growing up in a tiny village.

She didn't seem to mind his caresses, her own hand curled possessively around his knee.

Now and then, Arrochar would meet his gaze, and her genuine emotion and joy in what she observed made his chest expand with feeling.

In that moment, Lachlan knew he'd found something he hadn't even known he'd been looking for.

He just hoped to fuck he didn't ruin it.

"I feel like you're not taking this seriously." My hands flew to my hips as I looked down at Lachlan in mock irritation.

He grinned at me, his expression attractively boyish. "Braveheart, you're straddling me. I'm unable to take anything seriously while the blood is rushing out of my brain."

I tried not to smile and failed, the corners of my lips twitching. His eyes dropped to my mouth, and he grinned harder. "Stop it. We're training."

I'd offered to teach Lachlan some MMA and while I'd assumed he'd get all macho about being able to take care of himself in a fight, he'd been surprisingly keen.

Now I knew why.

Feeling him stir beneath me, I lightly slapped his chest. "You're insatiable!"

"It's this place." He threw his hands up defensively. "Every time I'm in here now, all I can think about is fucking you in the shower room."

Rolling my eyes, I slid off him and jumped to my feet.

"There are cameras in here. There aren't cameras in the shower room."

"True." Then he did a kip-up, an acrobatic transition from prone to standing, with ease and agility that didn't surprise me considering what he did to me in bed. *Show-off*, I thought, amused, and then he reached for my hand and dragged me toward the shower rooms.

"Uh, no!" I yanked on his hand, laughing.

Lachlan didn't let go, instead turning back to me with a coaxing smile, cuddling me against his body. For the past week, when we were together (which was a lot), he couldn't seem to stop touching me. I'd noticed it at Arrochar's dinner, and I couldn't say I wasn't enjoying it. He'd also been rapacious. Part of me thought it was just because the sex was fantastic, but another part of me thought he was using it as an escape. The day of McHugh's funeral, Lachlan practically kept me tied to the bed. He'd wanted to attend but knew his presence would only bring the paparazzi, and he didn't want to do that to Greg's family. Mac attended along with some of the men from the estate, but Lachlan was forced to stay home.

And bury his feelings inside me.

I let him because I knew he needed it, and I wanted to be the person he turned to when his emotions were too much.

Still … "We're not having sex in the shower room again."

"There's no one here." Lachlan bent his head to nibble on my ear.

A shiver rippled down my spine, and I lazily pushed against his chest with a moan. "Lachlan …"

"Hmm." He trailed his lips down my neck toward my cleavage, and his hands moved upward to cup me.

My back bowed as my fingers dug into the muscles in his back. "We're supposed to be working out."

"Sex is working out."

Remembering I couldn't even if I wanted to, I reluctantly slid my fingers into his hair and gently tugged.

He lifted his head from my breasts with a raised eyebrow.

"My period came this morning," I whispered. "Sorry."

Lachlan looked disappointed, but he didn't release me. Instead, he straightened, sliding his hands around my back to hold me to him. "You got your period this morning and you still want to work out?"

"My first day is always light. Second day is the worst." I frowned, realizing this might count as oversharing.

He squeezed me closer. "What is it?"

"Too much info, I guess."

"How so?"

I shrugged, running my hands down his damp T-shirt. Before I'd wrestled him to a mat and straddled him, we had actually been working out. "Guys don't want to talk about that stuff."

"In general, no ... but if you're having an off day, it'd be good to understand why. The last time you had your period, I barely noticed except for the no-sex part. No cramps, nothing? Energy still up. Do you have off days?" he teased.

I answered honestly. "I used to have horrible periods as a teenager, cramps that kept me in bed all day, migraines ... but my twenties have been a lot kinder. I can be a little snippy and impatient with mine. And I cry more at things I wouldn't normally cry at."

"Like what?"

Trying to ignore the butterflies incited by his seemingly genuine interest in everything *me*, I offered, "Movies. Christmas TV ads. When other people cry."

"I can't imagine you crying at a TV ad."

"There are lots of things about me you don't know."

His hands slid down my waist and over my ass, and my

skin flushed hot at the sensation. "I look forward to discovering them all."

"Are there lots of things I don't know about you?"

"Mmm." He bent his head to brush over my mouth.

"Like?"

"Those are for you to find out." He nipped at my lips. "That's the beauty of it, is it not?"

I chased his lips. "Lachlan."

Another nip.

Curling my hand around his nape, I pulled him to my mouth and kissed him hard. Our tongues licked at one another and within seconds, I was a blaze of need. "We have to stop," I whispered, trying to retreat. His kiss, his tongue, his taste, his hands squeezing my ass … "I'm so turned on right now, and we can't do anything about it."

"We can kiss," he disagreed and captured my mouth again.

I didn't know how long we stood there, making out in the empty gym, and I didn't care. How long had it been since I'd just made out with a man? Not since I was a teen. And God, I forgot how fun it was.

There was a vague sound of someone clearing their throat. I couldn't be sure, though, so I didn't bother coming up for air, and neither did Lachlan.

"Ahem!"

Okay, that was definitely someone.

We pulled apart, panting, burning eyes locking for a moment before we seemed to agree at the same time to look away. Lachlan focused over my head. "Lucy."

She stood beyond our mat, glamorous as always in a long maxi dress and A-line jacket made of supple, soft brown leather. High-heeled boots completed the casual but chic ensemble. She smirked at us. "So sorry to interrupt what was a truly spectacular show, but I need Robyn."

Lachlan reluctantly eased his hold on me as I turned to face her. "Everything okay?"

Thankfully, there'd been no awkwardness between Lucy and me since my confrontation with Lachlan. In fact, she wasn't even aware there'd been a problem. Lachlan didn't invite her into his bedroom anymore, but we hadn't abandoned her either. I'd kept up training sessions with her and Eredine, and Lachlan and I had eaten dinner with Eredine and Lucy a few nights during the past week.

I was perturbed that she hadn't left Ardnoch while her would-be killer was still on the loose, but she was taking precautions. Out of the corner of my eye, I noted her two huge bodyguards standing near the gym entrance. Her bodyguards were a team of six who alternated in shifts.

Lucy's smile slipped. "Eredine is feeling a little trapped."

I felt Lachlan tense behind me.

"Not anyone's fault." She rushed to reassure us. "But since I have the big guys"—she gestured to her bodyguards—"and the paps are gone … I thought we could take her to her place. She wants to move back in, and I'm happy to pay for twenty-four-hour security for her to do that."

I glanced behind me at Lachlan.

He was stone-faced. "She's safer here."

"Lachlan …" Lucy took a step toward him, her expression pleading. "You know Ery. She needs space and alone time, and her lodge is her happy place. She's … struggling. I think she feels less safe here at the castle than she does out there."

I nudged him. "There will be security on her."

He sighed. "Fine. If it's what she wants. Nobody's a prisoner here."

I rose up on tiptoes to press a grateful kiss to his mouth. His fingers slipped under my shirt to caress my bare waist in response, causing goose bumps to prickle my skin. I gave him another quick kiss and then announced, "I'll go have a quick shower and change."

"Great!" Lucy beamed. "I'll have a Rover waiting outside for us. Wait until I tell Ery."

"Can you ask Fergus to bring my car around?" I swiped my gear off the floor.

"Your car?" Lachlan asked at my back.

I nodded, turning to him. A few weeks ago, I'd reluctantly returned my rental when Lachlan offered me the use of one of the estate vehicles for free. It was a cheaper model SUV, not a Range Rover, and one of the reasons I'd hesitantly accepted his offer. The biggest reason being, I couldn't afford my rental any longer. "Yeah. I need some new shots, and Ery mentioned there's a small fairy glen not far from her lodge."

His eyebrows pulled together. "Then I'll need to put a man on you."

Brushing my hand down his arm in reassurance, I replied, "Lachlan, I can take care of myself."

"I don't want you out on a trail on your own right now."

I glared at him.

Lucy called as she departed, "I'll, uh … just meet you outside."

"Robyn, don't look at me like I'm being overbearing."

"You are a little, though."

His expression darkened.

"Hey." I held up my hands defensively. "I'm not stupid. I know the danger is still out there. But I'll mostly be in my car, tailing Lucy and her human shields who will be with us at Eredine's."

"Until you go off alone to take bloody photos."

Realizing he had a point, as stifling as his point was, I said, "Okay, compromise—I will only go if Lucy and her human shields agree to accompany me. If she can't, I won't go."

"Agreed. So you won't need your car."

"No, I still want to drive," I argued as we walked out of the gym. "It makes me feel a little freer. I'm safe in my car. Don't argue with me about it, please."

He released another heavy sigh. "Fine."

* * *

BACK WHEN I'D first met Eredine and interviewed her in the cabin not far from the studio on Loch Ardnoch, I'd thought the cabin was hers and she lived on-site. I'd soon learned, however, that Eredine's small home was a fifteen-minute drive northwest of the estate via mostly single-track roads.

I'd followed Lucy and Eredine to Eredine's lodge in the woods. It was exactly as I'd imagined. She was surrounded on three sides by trees, and the lodge was built on stilts with a wraparound porch, small but picturesque. She had a ton of colorful plant pots scattered here and there along the porch, though it looked like some were dying in her absence.

It felt utterly remote, and while I wasn't surprised it was to Eredine's taste to be out here alone, I was taken aback she'd want to be out here alone after what happened to Lucy and McHugh.

Yet, her whole face seemed to brighten as we escorted her into her small but chic home.

While we lounged on the sofa and Lucy on one of the armchairs in the open-plan living area, kitchen directly behind us, Lucy's bodyguards stood vigil outside: one out front, one out back.

"Isn't it weird taking them everywhere with you?" I asked, sipping at the coffee Eredine brewed.

Lucy shrugged. "They're usually with me all the time. I've just never needed them to be with me all the time while I'm at the club. One of the many perks of being a member. So, no, it's not weird, but it is annoying."

Remorse filled me. "We will find him, Lucy. One of these days, he's going to slip up."

"Oh gorgeous, it's not your fault, and you giving me big puppy eyes only makes me feel guilty." She waved her hand, her gold bracelets jangling. "And anyway, I don't need to be here. I could leave anytime, so staying is my decision."

"Why are you staying?" Eredine asked.

Looking comfortable and at home here, Eredine was snuggled up on the opposite end of the couch. While I'd spent lots of time with the young woman, I was still no closer to knowing her. I had no doubt of her kindness, compassion, and sincerity, but I'd also never met anyone so secretive. There were ghosts in her eyes, and I sensed Lachlan had some inkling as to what haunted her. Despite our intimacy, he refused to divulge much about Eredine, and honestly, I admired him all the more for it.

He was a loyal friend.

Lucy answered Eredine's question, "Because the people I care about the most are here, and I'd feel like I was abandoning them."

My smile was soft, affectionate. "We wouldn't think that. We'd be happy to see you safe."

"Well, that's how I feel about you. I can't leave. Not until I know Lachlan and you all will be okay."

"I think Lachlan is more than okay." Eredine shot me a big, mischievous smile.

I felt my cheeks heat. "Please stop."

"I can't. I have been dying to get away from the estate so I could ask you what is going on. I've never seen him like this. He called you his girlfriend."

I glanced from her to Lucy who looked just as curious.

"We're ..." I tried to sound more casual and less giddy than I actually felt. "We're giving it a real shot."

Eredine shook her head in amazement. "If I hadn't seen it with my own eyes, I wouldn't believe it?"

Laughing, I replied, "No need to sound so surprised."

"It's not a surprise he wants you," she hurried to reassure me, glancing at Lucy for help, who was contemplating me with an unreadable expression. "But Lucy and I have known him awhile, and he has always been about the casual."

"He has his reasons for that."

"They are?" Lucy asked.

"*His* reasons," I said gently but firmly, and she pressed her lips together, looking a little displeased by my refusal to share. "But we both agree there's something more between us, so he said he wants to try." I bit my lip to halt my smile.

"Oh my God." Eredine looked happier than I'd ever seen her. "I wasn't sure if he was kidding about the whole girl-friend thing so this is amazing news. Does that mean you're staying in Ardnoch?"

"We'll see. We don't want to pressure each other." My eyes moved to Lucy who still seemed to be processing what I'd relayed. Suspicion crept in. "You're okay about this, right?"

She cocked her head, brows together, a soft smile on her lips. "Of course, I am. I'm ... I am so thrilled Lachlan has pulled his head out of his ass ..."

"But?"

Lucy grimaced. "I care deeply for you, Robyn. I'm just worried about you."

Understanding, I nodded. "I know where I stand with him. And I know there are no guarantees. But ... he's worth the risk."

She considered this and then shot me that charismatic grin. "Then I'm happy for you both. If you weren't driving, I'd suggest a toast."

"We can toast coffees," Eredine said.

The three of us leaned in, holding up our mugs, and Lucy announced, "To Robyn and Lachlan. May our action hero be worthy of our real-life heroine."

I chuckled while Eredine *awwed* and we clinked our mugs together.

Discussion spiraled from there into girl talk, and we shared stories about past relationships. I say "we," but it was me and Lucy. As ever, Eredine was closemouthed about her past, and Lucy didn't broach the subject. Following suit, I left well enough alone. It was the first time in a while I'd seen either woman so relaxed, and I wouldn't ruin it by asking questions Eredine wasn't comfortable answering.

"Oh shit!" Lucy exclaimed as her eyes caught the clock on Eredine's kitchen wall. She shot to her feet. "I completely forgot I have a video meeting with a director in half an hour. Oh shit, shit, shit. Do you think they can get me back to the castle in time?"

"Of course." I hurried to my feet, grabbing the sloshing cup of coffee out of Lucy's hand. "It'll be cool."

"I'm interested in this part," she explained as she slipped back into her boots. "It's the first in ages that's sparked something in me."

"It'll be fine," I reassured her. "Go, go."

"What about you?"

"I've got my car."

"Maybe you should follow us back?"

In all honesty, it was nice to be off the estate. I was enjoying Eredine's company, and I still wanted to visit the fairy glen nearby. I said so to Lucy.

Her eyes darted to the clock, and she frowned in thought. "Promise me you won't go to the glen later than six?"

"It doesn't get dark for hours yet." This far up, the sun

didn't start to set until around eight thirty at this time of year.

"I know how lost you get in your work. Just promise."

"I already promised Lachlan I'd be back at the castle for dinner at seven. I plan to keep that promise."

"Good." She hurried over to give me a distracted kiss on the cheek, treated Eredine to the same, and then fled the cabin hilariously fast.

I flopped down on the sofa. "She's a complex lady, that one."

"How so?"

"I don't know. It's like she's two people. The woman who loves acting, loves the fame ... but then there's this other part of her that seems to crave the idea of home, family. I think that's why she spends so much time here."

Eredine gave me a sad smile. "Yeah. I think you're right. Sometimes she has these moods. She gets melancholy, and maybe it's because she doesn't know what she wants."

I'd never been subjected to Lucy's melancholy moods and was a little surprised to hear she suffered from them. "I wonder if what she wants is here in Ardnoch, not in Hollywood, and she's just in denial about it."

"By what she wants, do you mean someone in particular?"

Thinking of Thane, I shrugged. "Maybe someone here might have caught her eye, yeah."

Eredine considered this. "That would be nice. For her to stay, permanently."

The urge to pepper the young woman with questions about her own reasons for choosing Ardnoch was strong. "You like it here, don't you?" I said inanely.

"Of course. It's my home."

"But that accent tells me somewhere else was home first."

She smirked at my stealthy attempt to unearth her

history. "Nowhere has been home until here. But I am originally from Chicago, if that's what you're asking."

"How did you meet Lachlan?"

"In LA." Eredine stood. "Another coffee?"

Her tone said, "Don't ask me anything else." Like I said, I didn't push people. "Sure."

A knock at the door stopped her midway, and I held up a hand to halt her from checking it out. Instead, I did, peeking out the side window first and relaxing at the sight of one of Lachlan's security team. There were so many of them now, I didn't know them all by name (even though Mac had introduced me), but I knew this woman. At six two with a pretty face no amount of scowling or slicked-back hair could hide, the bodyguard was difficult to forget.

I opened the door. "Hey."

She nodded. "Just wanted you to know I'm here now that Ms. Wainwright has left with her private security." She gestured to the SUV parked out front. "I'll be sitting in there, on guard if you need me. Now and then, I'll take a walk around the perimeter too."

"Great. I'm sorry, your name again?"

The guard straightened to her full height. "Everyone calls me Ada."

"Thank you, Ada. I'll let Eredine know."

Ada nodded and turned swiftly on her heel, marching down the porch steps and across the drive to her vehicle.

I closed the door and turned to a bemused Eredine. In a creepy voice, I said, "Ada is watching over you. Don't be scared if you hear footsteps around the perimeter."

Eredine chuckled at my teasing. "Life is so weird right now."

I chuckled with her, even as I felt a twinge of guilt for making light of the situation. The problem was, if I didn't find ways to laugh at the absurdity of it all, I'd fall into a gloom of despair that a murderer was still out there, and the man ... well, the man I cared about was still in danger.

* * *

THOUGH EREDINE OFFERED to show me the way to the glen, I knew how distracted I could get while working, and I knew she was enjoying being home, so I declined. Instead, she gave me what seemed like straightforward directions, and I got in my car with a nod to Ada, who frowned like she hadn't realized I would be leaving the premises.

Vacillating between returning to the castle like I'd promised Lachlan if Lucy couldn't come with me and going to the glen anyway, the reddening sky of the early evening persuaded me it would be fine if I went. I wouldn't be long. The light was just too gorgeous to let it go to waste.

The glen was a mere five-minute drive from Eredine's lodge, but it was up the narrowest single-track road I'd encountered thus far. Tense behind the wheel, I kept a moderate speed in the event of confronting an oncoming vehicle. As I followed the switchbacks through forested hills, I began to doubt my decision. One, I'd made a promise, and two, it *was* foolish to go anywhere in the woods alone at the moment, no matter how capable I was.

"Shit," I muttered under my breath.

I needed to turn back.

Hoping to come upon a passing place to do a U-turn, I kept my eyes peeled. Just as I spotted one in the distance, a truck appeared ahead of me too.

It was going at speed, giving me no chance to get to the passing place first to wait for them to go by so I could do my maneuver.

Grumbling under my breath at the truck's reckless speed,

I waited for them to slow at the passing place so I could get by.

Instead, I heard the roar of their engine over the music playing from my radio, and my heart jumped into my throat as the truck with tinted black windows kept coming right at me. A bigger, sturdier vehicle than mine, I knew if it hit me …

The driver must be distracted, my frantic brain thought. I pressed my palm to the horn, blasting it.

The truck kept coming.

"Oh my God." Fear exploded through me, and I slammed my foot on the brake.

Then horrific understanding followed when I saw the ski-masked face behind the wheel of the truck.

He wasn't stopping.

Had no intention of stopping.

Instinct forced my hands to spin the steering wheel to the left, and I felt the ground give way beneath my tires as I soared off the embankment and down into the sloping valley of trees.

The sensation didn't last long.

A tree caught my fall.

The sound of crunching metal filled my ears as I flew forward in my seat and—

32

LACHLAN

T he road to Inverness flew past him at speed as Mac drove them to the hospital as fast as the law would allow.

Lachlan sat in the passenger side filled with a dread that made him physically ill. He had the shakes, clammy sweat coated his skin, and his stomach roiled with nauseating fear.

"Shit, Lachlan, you look like you're about to pass out." Mac's voice sounded far away even though the man was right beside him.

He cut him a look. Mac's features were taut, his own face peaky. "I'm all right," Lachlan managed. "Just keep driving."

All his life, he'd worried his family was cursed, and when Thane's wife died, that was it. Lachlan was sure of it. Adair men were doomed to watch the women they loved die. His grandfather was the only one in generations to escape that fate, but Lachlan found it hard to imagine he'd ever be that lucky. Perhaps it was punishment for the sins of his ancestors who, from all accounts, were ruthless, self-involved bastards. Many of the landed gentry were back then.

If Robyn died—

A harsh lurch of nausea had him rearing back in the passenger seat. He slammed his eyes closed and took a couple deep breaths. *Man up, Lachlan!* he yelled inwardly. If Robyn ... Mac would need him.

Tears of fury clogged his throat.

Who was he kidding?

If Robyn died, he'd want to die with her.

It was true.

He was just like his emotionally weak father after all.

"She's not dead," Mac bit out angrily, and for a moment, Lachlan wondered if he'd spoken out loud. "My daughter is not dead, so stop looking like you're going to her funeral."

Lachlan nodded sharply and tried to mask his feelings.

All he kept hearing over and over was Eredine's voice.

"Ada and I were worried, so we followed her. She'd swerved off the road. Hit a tree. The paramedics just got her out. She's unconscious. They're taking her to Inverness. Lachlan ... we passed a truck on the road, couldn't miss him on those tracks ... he was wearing a mask. That's what alerted us—"

The fucker.

"Coward couldn't fight her ... so he drove her off the road," he muttered darkly to himself.

"We don't know that yet." Mac heard him. "We'll find out when Robyn tells us. And she *will* tell us. I feel it in my gut, Lachlan. My girl is fine."

Please let his bloody gut be right.

When they pulled into a space at the hospital, Lachlan jumped out before the engine was off and then swayed against the car as the world tilted.

Jesus Christ.

"Lachlan, you all right?" Mac was at his side, bristling with concern and impatience.

Lachlan waved him off and pushed him toward the hospital main entrance. Attempting to shake off his debilitating dread, he followed Mac in, ignoring the nurse at the reception and her wide-eyed stare when he appeared at his friend's back.

"Uh …" She reluctantly dragged her eyes off Lachlan. "Let me check." She typed into the computer. "Robyn Penhaligon. Yes, she was brought in forty minutes ago and is currently in diagnostics." She gestured to double doors to their right. "Just give your name at reception and they'll let you know when you can see her."

"Diagnostics," Mac said as they marched toward the doors. "That's good. They're just checking her over."

Lachlan wouldn't get his hopes up until he saw her for himself.

They didn't need to give her name at reception. As soon as they walked into the waiting area, Eredine hurried across the room and threw her arms around him.

He squeezed her tight, grateful she was okay and that she'd had the sense to follow Robyn.

Eredine hugged Mac next, and one of his security team, Ada Renshaw, crossed the room to join them. "Sir, Ms. Penhaligon regained consciousness in the ambulance. They're just testing her vitals and have taken her in for an MRI."

Mac sagged at his side. "She's okay."

"Miraculously, it looks that way."

His friend slumped into a free chair next to Eredine, and Lachlan couldn't help but do the same. Limbs still trembling, he didn't feel a hundred percent.

A bag of salted peanuts appeared in front of his face at some point as they waited. He looked up and saw Mac holding it out to him, expression grim.

Lachlan scowled.

Mac waved the bag at him determinedly. "You had a

shock. And you're shaking. Your blood pressure more than likely dropped. Eat."

The thought of eating nauseated him, but he took the nuts because he knew Mac might force-feed him otherwise. A few minutes after demolishing the bag, he realized the bastard had been right when he started to feel less light-headed.

"Robyn Penhaligon's family?" a nurse said as she approached the waiting room.

Lachlan and Mac shot to their feet.

"I'm her dad." Mac moved toward the nurse.

She raised a disbelieving eyebrow. "Her father?"

Jaw muscle ticking with annoyance, he nodded. "Teen dad, at your service. Now can I see my bloody daughter?"

The nurse nodded, expression apologetic, then looked beyond him to Lachlan. "Lachlan Adair." She recognized him. "Oh. Well, are you related to Ms. Penhaligon?"

"She's my better half," he uttered hoarsely.

It was just a saying, something people usually called their spouses.

That's what the nurse took it to mean, unable to hide her shock that Lachlan Adair was seriously involved with someone and it hadn't been splashed all over the Scottish tabloids.

But he'd said those words because he meant them.

Robyn wasn't just under his skin. She made him whole in a way he hadn't been since he was a boy.

As the realization sunk deep into his soul, he followed the nurse and Mac, listening intently as the nurse said, "Your wife and daughter is recovering from a concussion, most likely caused by impact with the car's airbag. She's complained of tenderness in her neck and shoulders, her ribs, and there's some bruising on her shins from the impact with the dashboard, but otherwise she's in good health. The MRI showed no signs of intracranial bleeding, so all we need to do is keep an eye on her concussion. We advise an overnight stay for observation."

Robyn was alive and well.

He exhaled heavily, relief making his knees shake as they strode onto a ward.

"I'd like her moved to a private room." He found his voice.

"I'll need to check if we have any available."

"I'll pay extra."

The nurse grimaced over her shoulder. "Mr. Adair, this is an NHS hospital. If we need the private room for a sicker patient, they're prioritized regardless of who you are or what you're willing to pay."

Well, that was him told. "Give her the room, I'll pay for it, even if you have to move her out of it for someone else."

She nodded. "I'll see what I can do." Stopping at the last bed on the ward, the nurse pulled back the surrounding curtain, and there she was.

Robyn.

She looked up at them from the bed, no sign of damage except for a paleness to her skin and shadows under her eyes.

His knees almost gave out.

And then she opened her mouth and announced angrily, "That fucker drove me off the road!"

* * *

IT SEEMED to take hours for everyone to disperse from the private room he'd acquired for Robyn. While they waited for the police to arrive, Eredine and Ada were allowed in to see her so she could thank them for rescuing her.

Then the two detective inspectors from their case arrived to interview Robyn. She remembered what kind of truck their murderer drove, but she couldn't remember the registration number. At least they had something to go on this time. Lachlan wanted that piece of shit found more than ever.

And to Robyn's and Mac's relief, the DIs were again thinking the two cases were related.

Lucy arrived soon after the DIs, along with Arrochar. Lachlan hovered on the edges of the room while Robyn chatted as if she hadn't just been run off the road into a tree. Other than enraged the attacker had come at her in such a cowardly manner, she seemed in good spirits.

And her behavior was increasing the heat on Lachlan's simmering fury.

Eventually, Mac surmised something in Lachlan's countenance and stood. "I think it's time we give Robyn and Lachlan some privacy, eh?"

The women glanced over at him, and he ignored the raised eyebrows and murmurs and waited for them all to get out.

Mac was last to depart. He halted in front of Lachlan, a warning in his eyes. "Maybe save the lecture until after she's out of the hospital."

Lachlan made no promises.

With a sigh, Mac threw a tender smile at Robyn over his shoulder and exited.

As soon as the door swung shut behind him, Robyn raised an eyebrow. "Are you going to stand way over *there* or get over *here* and kiss me?"

His feet moved before he was even aware of instructing them to. He bent over the bed, cupped her face in his hands, and pressed a soft, relieved kiss against her mouth. Squeezing his eyes closed, he deepened it, tasting her, exulting in her being here and alive.

When he finally released her, Robyn gave him a charmed smile. "Now that's what I call a kiss."

What if he'd never gotten to kiss her again or have her smile up at him like that? To feel all that goddamn spectacular energy that emanated from the very essence of her? He hadn't lied that night in bed when he told her she was the most truly alive person he'd ever met. And her magic had almost been snuffed out.

Because of him.

He couldn't take it anymore.

If the curse was real, then every second Robyn stayed here, the greater chance he had of losing her. "You went to that fucking fairy glen alone," he snapped abruptly.

Robyn winced, raising a hand as if to touch him, but he retreated. She frowned. "Lachlan, I was turning back. I promise. I was trying to find a passing place to turn around when the bastard came out of nowhere."

"It was reckless, and you promised."

"I know." Her eyes flashed with irritation. "That's what I'm telling you. I realized that and I was turning back."

"A bit goddamn late to be sensible." He gestured to the hospital bed.

"Hey! I do not need a lecture right now."

Cursing under his breath, Lachlan reached out and hauled one of the visitor chairs closer to the bed. Slumping down into it, he bowed his head and tried to get his shit together.

A tickle caused a shiver down his nape and then he felt it again, more, as Robyn stroked her fingers through his hair.

"I'm sorry I scared you," she whispered.

He squeezed his eyes closed.

Fuck, but he never wanted to care this much.

Lifting his head, he took hold of her wrist and pressed a kiss to it, feeling her pulse beneath his lips. Their eyes locked, and it was as if she could see right through him. See his torment.

"I'm *so* sorry," Robyn insisted.

"I know. It's not your fault." He kissed her palm. "But there's something I need you to do for me."

"Anything."

"I'm going to book you on a flight back to Boston."

Her hand jerked in his, but he held on.

"Robyn, you've nearly been killed twice. It's not safe for you here. I want you in Boston until we've caught him."

"I can't." She frowned at him, seeming shocked. "Lachlan, this is *my* case."

"No, this is Police Scotland's case."

"And a fine job they're doing."

"They haven't much to go on. Neither have we. Now they have a truck, which is something we didn't have before. He's making mistakes now."

"And I want to be around when he makes his last one."

"No," he commanded. "You're leaving Scotland tomorrow. End of discussion."

Robyn ripped her hand out of his. "You can't order me to do that. You can't order me, period."

Lachlan took a deep breath. "Fine. Then do this for me. For my sanity and peace of mind. Because if you don't—"

"If I don't, then what?"

"It's me or the case, Robyn." His gut clenched at the ultimatum, but it was the only thing he could live with. He wouldn't get himself in any deeper with her when the risk of losing her was so high.

Her lips parted, and she made a noise as if he'd winded her. "Are you serious?"

"More serious than I have ever been," he replied grimly. He could live with hurting her, deal with soothing that hurt after, once this was over and he could fly her back to Scotland from the States.

But she didn't give in like he'd dementedly hoped.

Instead, an alarming flatness entered her eyes as she stared at him. "You don't know me at all."

He reached for her. "Robyn—"

"No." She jerked back from him, the flatness obliterated by her rising fury.

"Robyn, I'm asking you to do this for me. If you care about me, please."

"If I care about you?" She gaped at him, disbelieving. "Lachlan … if you care about me, you wouldn't dare ask me to do this. It's not about asking me to run away from this coward, to let him win—it's not about that. It's only slightly about you trying to wrap me up in cotton wool when we both know it'll suffocate me. What it *is* about is you giving me an ultimatum. Asking me to be someone I'm not, just to soothe your fears." Tears filled her eyes, gutting him. "That's not love. That's emotional blackmail."

Suddenly, it felt like rocks were piled on his chest. His breaths were shallow through the restriction. "I can't … I can't get in any deeper with you if I'm constantly worried about your safety. It'll drive me mad." Understanding dawned. Robyn was the worst kind of woman he could have fallen in love with. Her courage would always put her at risk. He stood up, pushing his chair back with force. "I'm sorry. This isn't going to work between us."

Her tears escaped as she stared up at him in hurt shock.

Lachlan couldn't stand it.

Cursing under his breath, he marched from the room. Every footstep that took him from her, he prayed she'd call out and change her mind, that she would prove to him she could be low risk when he needed her to be.

She didn't.

And he didn't stop walking away.

So.

That was that.

"Lachlan?" He heard Mac call his name, but he kept on.

He stormed out of the hospital and into chaos.

Camera lights flashed in his eyes as he was immediately set upon by bodies. "Adair! Is it true your stalker killed another woman?"

"Look this way, Adair!"

"Lachlan, can you tell us what happened? Who is the victim and what does she mean to you?"

"Is it true her name is Robyn Penhaligon? Who is she to you?"

Seconds from punching the bastards out of his way, they were forced back by Mac and Ada, and Lachlan was hauled into the safety of the reception area as hospital security ordered the paparazzi to remain outside.

Lachlan spun out of Mac's grip, searching the hospital for the nurse. "She told them," he spat, ready to take his rage and frustration out on anyone who would use him like this. They had Robyn's name!

"Lachlan, calm down, calm down." Mac guided him forcefully into the men's restroom.

"Get off me!" He shrugged off his friend.

Mac checked the stalls to make sure they were alone and turned to Lachlan, grim-faced. "It's very unlikely it was the nurse, Lachlan. There are a dozen people in that waiting room who heard you declare yourself for Robyn."

That was true. It didn't make him feel any calmer.

"I'll call security to come collect you."

"Put them on Robyn. They have her name." He considered something. "They'll connect the two of you. They'll harass you too."

"I don't care." Mac scowled at him. "What happened?"

Deducing his meaning, Lachlan turned away. "I'm not discussing it with you."

"I'm her father, Lachlan. Tell me or I make you tell me."

He looked back at him, eyebrow raised. "I'm your boss."

Mac narrowed his eyes. "Don't give me that bullshit."

"We broke up. All right? It's fucking over. You want to leave me, fine." It wasn't fine. None of this was fine.

It was so bloody far from fine, Lachlan felt like he was coming out of his skin.

"Explain."

He gave him the gist of it.

"Ah, Lachlan." Mac leaned against the wall, scrubbing a hand down his face.

His gut twisted in knots, and he glared at the restroom's tile floor. "Call the team. I need to get out of here. Put however many men you need on Robyn."

"You're making a mistake."

Exhausted, drained, and aching with misery in every part of his body, Lachlan stared unseeing at his friend. "It's my mistake to make. Now can you just do your job?"

With a heavy sigh, Mac pulled his phone out of his pocket to call the team.

33

ROBYN

$\mathcal{M}$ ac offered to pack up my room for me, but I wasn't about to run away now. Not after everything.

Instead, I told him to wait for me in his SUV outside on the castle driveway. He'd already returned to the cottage while I was in the hospital, so he had no packing today, just chauffeuring.

The castle staff were grim and subdued as I passed them in the halls. The very walls of Ardnoch seemed to have soaked in the gloom of everyone's emotions. There were few club members left, staff were still furloughed, yet there was security everywhere. It felt like a prison, not a luxury escape for the rich and famous.

I was sad for Lachlan.

Even as I seethed with hurt, grief, and fury, I could still hate that he seemed to be losing everything.

My pulse increased as I approached my bedroom door, and his. Hurrying inside, I felt jumpy and nervous as I rushed around the room to get my things together before I inadvertently bumped into the estate owner.

"I'm sorry I put you in danger."

I jolted with surprise at the voice, looking up with dread to find Lachlan standing just inside the room. His hands were in the pockets of his trousers, stance almost casual. But his expression was stern, and his bleak expression gave away his true feelings.

"Again," he bit out.

I lowered my eyes, closed my suitcase, and zipped it. "You didn't put me in danger." Grabbing the handle, I dropped the case to the floor and let the wheels take over. Blood rushed in my ears as I strode toward him. "The psycho messing with your life put me in danger."

I tried to pass him, but he reached out and took hold of the suitcase handle, his fingers brushing mine. His touch made me release it in instinct. Call it self-preservation.

"Let me." He took my case.

We walked in silence down the hall and then the stairway where he lifted and carried my suitcase with ease, even though it was twice the size it'd been before I left for Scotland. Once we reached the first floor, I held out my hand. "I can take it from here."

He wouldn't let me.

The bastard wouldn't go away.

My rage toward him built as I hurried to follow him outside to the SUV where Mac waited. Lachlan handed my case to the underbutler, Stephen, who put it in the trunk. I smiled my thanks, but I knew it didn't reach my eyes.

Wanting away from the man who'd destroyed all my hopes, I intended to get in the back of the SUV without another word. I could feel his gaze on me, could sense his longing... because I *knew* him.

And I'd never been so disappointed in anyone in my life. Not even Mac or my mom or Regan.

I turned and saw the anguish in his eyes and hated him

for it because it didn't have to be this way. And I knew his fears were so deep-seated that anything I said wouldn't make a damn bit of difference to him … but it would to me. *I* could walk away knowing I'd been honest. "I didn't even like you," I said harshly.

Lachlan flashed me a grin, but it was cold. Wounded.

"You were everything I thought I didn't want or need, no matter how physically attracted to you I was. But I came to see something in you."

A muscle in his jaw ticked as he glared at me.

"I saw how much you cared. About your family, about Mac, about Lucy and Eredine, and the people who work for you. I saw the weight of responsibility you carry on your shoulders, responsibility men like you don't need to feel."

"Men like me?"

"Men who can afford to pay others to shoulder that responsibility. But that's not you. I came to admire you, and because of that, I took a risk on you. And I know it was my risk to take. You even warned me … I fell, anyway."

His hands curled into fists at his sides.

"I'm in love with you," I admitted, tears thick in my throat. "I love you. And yet somehow right now, I hate you too."

Lachlan flinched.

"And even though you've disappointed me, hurt me … I know you can't help it. I don't want you to end up alone, Lachlan." I shook my head. "I know it's not me, but one day I hope you find the person you love enough to prioritize, to battle your demons for."

At his winded expression, I turned and climbed into the waiting SUV.

Mac looked over his shoulder from the front passenger seat. "You okay?"

I shook my head.

437

Not now. Not yet.

My chest felt like it was too full of air, painful pressure making it hard to think. Taking a few meditative, calming breaths, I sank back in the seat as the engine started and closed my eyes.

I wished for numbness.

For now, feeling nothing sounded so much better than feeling everything.

* * *

LACHLAN

"And even though you've disappointed me, hurt me ... I know you can't help it. I don't want you to end up alone, Lachlan. I know it's not me, but one day I hope you find the person you love enough to prioritize, to battle your demons for."

He watched the SUV drive away, a mounting panic knocking the breath right out of him.

If he couldn't get past his fears for Robyn, then it was never going to happen.

Because he loved her.

He loved that woman more than he knew it was possible to love another human being.

So what's worse? he wondered, agonized.

Throwing her away before they could build a life together?

Or risking the chance of building that life only to lose it?

Was a limited amount of time with the woman he loved better than no time at all?

He knew only one person who might have that answer.

* * *

ROBYN

Mac's neat guest bedroom looked cozy and warm. Soft, golden light blazed from the bedside lamps, my suitcase laid at the foot of the bed, and the robe I'd bought from a boutique in Inverness was draped across the bed. While I'd been downstairs in his kitchen, hugging a mug of hot coffee between my hands, Mac was upstairs readying my room.

My camera gear had been set up near the window with care. He'd even lit a few nice-smelling candles that I'm sure Arrochar or someone must have bought him.

The consideration of it pierced the numbness I felt.

Mac's arm slid along my shoulders, and he squeezed me against his side.

"You're sure I'm not intruding?"

He kissed my temple. "Wee birdie, you could never intrude. I'm delighted to have you here."

I looked up at him. "Are you happy to be home?"

"I am."

Sensing his answer was sincere, I decided not to kick my own ass about the fact that we were splitting security resources by moving out of the castle. But I couldn't stay there, across the hall from the man who rejected me when I was most vulnerable, when I needed him the most.

It was hard to reconcile my mind and my heart on this one. My heart was broken. Whether I'd meant to or not, I'd subconsciously been weaving a fantasy future for me and Lachlan, building my hopes for it on the idea that he was *it*. He was the guy I was going to spend the rest of my life with.

Two people didn't connect the way we had without knowing that it's special, that it's *it*.

Yet he wasn't my future. I wasn't *it* for him. And my brain kept telling me that I shouldn't mourn a man who would abandon me like this, who would cut me out of his life. My brain was right. My heart was just having a hard time accepting that truth.

34

LACHLAN

"*D*on't, Eilidh."

"I just want to say hello."

"He's sleeping."

"Oh … he smells funny."

"Eilidh, come on. Dad said not to disturb Uncle Lachlan."

"But I want a cuddle."

A weight spread across his chest. "Morning, Uncle Lachlan." He felt the whisper of breath across his neck.

He peeled his eyes open, the blurry ceiling the first thing he saw before the aching pound started in his head. Dark hair came into his vision, and he glanced down to see his adorable niece sprawled across his chest like a sea star. Her chin rested on his upper chest, her big blues locked with his.

She beamed up at him. "Morning, Uncle Lachlan," she repeated.

Despite the throbbing in his head and edges of the room tilting slightly when he moved, he couldn't help but grin at Eilidh as he wrapped his arms around her. "Morning, angel. Where did you come from?"

441

"Sorry, Uncle Lachlan." Lewis appeared at the side of the bed. "Dad said not to wake you."

He reached out to ruffle his nephew's hair. "It's okay. What time is it?" His mouth felt like it was filled with cotton wool balls.

"Eight. We're just getting ready for school."

"I thought I told you not to come in here?" Thane strode into his guest bedroom.

The house Thane designed was situated on Adair land outside Ardnoch in a small, barely populated area called Caelmore. While the other homes in the village (if it was big enough to be called such) were situated near the main road that led into Ardnoch, Thane's home sat above the sand dunes, overlooking the sea.

It was a contemporary structure, built with larch cladding and lots of glass.

He and the kids' mum, Francine, built it together while she was pregnant with Lewis. Thane also designed Lachlan's home—the one he never used, situated on the land next door.

"I wanted a cuddle." Eilidh pouted at her father, somehow growing heavier on Lachlan. He realized why when Thane tried to lift her off, and she refused to go without a fight.

"Eilidh," Thane admonished, sweeping her up before she could protest. "Uncle Lachlan's not well. Leave him alone."

She scowled over her father's shoulder but gave Lachlan a cute wave. "Feel better, Lach Lach."

He winked at her, and he saw her smile before she disappeared out the door with her father.

"You okay?" Lewis asked.

Always so serious, that one.

Like his father and eldest uncle.

Brodan and Arran had missed out on the serious gene.

While Brodan easily played the cocky, charming, laid-back Scotsman, Lachlan shrugged on the persona like a mask. He presented himself to the world in the way he wished he were.

But he wasn't that man.

Though he'd felt like him for real when he was with Robyn. She freed something in him.

"Uncle Lachlan?"

"Yeah, I'm okay," he replied, hoping there was a kernel of truth in it.

Thane strode back into the room. "Lewis, breakfast."

His son left without argument.

"Make sure Eilidh doesn't try to pour her own cereal," he called after him.

"Will do," Lewis called back.

Then Lachlan was the focus of his brother's attention.

Vague memories of the night before came back, shifting at the pounding bass in his skull.

"You owe me a bottle of Clynelish."

Lachlan smirked unhappily. "I gathered as much." Groaning, he sat up, swinging his legs off the bed only to let his head fall into his hands. "Fuck, I feel like I might owe you three bottles."

"Nah, just the one."

The bed depressed at his side, and he glanced out of the corner of his eye to look at Thane who sat beside him. "Did I get drunk in front of the kids?"

"No," his brother assured him. "They were already in bed."

They were silent as bits and pieces of their conversation last night returned to him.

As if reading his mind, Thane offered, "I meant what I said, Lachlan."

He met Thane's gaze.

His brother gave him a bolstering nod. "If I had the choice to go back and start a life with Fran knowing I'd lose her in

443

the end, I'd do it anyway. Not just because she gave me the kids but because she helped make me who I am today. And my life was infinitely better for having her in it." Thane placed a comforting hand on his brother's shoulder. "A decade of happiness is better than a lifetime of emptiness."

Emotion choked him.

His brother's strength was humbling.

Nodding, he patted Thane's hand and tried to get a grip on the thickness in his throat.

"Does that nod mean you're going to pull your head out of your arse and go to Robyn?"

Lachlan's pulse leapt at the thought. "Aye." He nodded. "Let's just hope she'll take me back."

"Well." Thane stood, grinning at him. "You'll have a better chance if you go to her not smelling like a distillery."

Lachlan grimaced. "Right. Food, shower, brush my teeth first."

And then he'd go to her.

Because Robyn was wrong.

She *was* the one worth fighting his fears for, and he refused to be another person in her life who didn't put her first.

* * *

AFTER ENDURING breakfast with his family (his head was killing him and as much as he loved his niece, she was going through a phase of shout-talking), Lachlan decided to cross the land between their homes and use his place for once.

Letting himself into the large home, he pictured Robyn there and wished he'd brought her to see it and made love to her in the large master that overlooked the inlet. While there was a large, open-plan living space from the front to the back of the house—the kitchen and lounging area set against wall-to-wall bifold doors that opened out onto a deck that looked out over the Ardnoch Firth—there were also smaller rooms behind the kitchen. There was a small viewing room with a giant picture window and window seat where you could sit, lean against the glass, and look out over the water.

Robyn would love it.

Hurrying upstairs to the master that sat above the kitchen with its own overhanging deck, he moved with urgency. *Shower, dress, get to Robyn.*

Two days was far too long as it was for her to think he didn't love her the way she loved him.

He shook his head in wonder as he stepped into the shower.

Robyn loved him.

How did he get so goddamn lucky?

It seemed implausible, but he wasn't going to question his good fortune.

In the walk-in closet, he chose clothes without his usual care for appearance.

In fact, he was so focused on Robyn, the sudden explosion of pain across the back of his head and the lights sparking in his vision came out of nowhere. Confusion was the last feeling to absorb him as he stepped into his bedroom, the floor the last thing he saw, coming toward him at speed, before everything went dark.

35

ROBYN

hile extremely cozy, Mac's cottage seemed to close in on me. In the sitting room, I stared around dazedly with hands on my hips. Outside, vigilant in a car, were two members of the security team. Guarding me. I flinched thinking how much paying for this had to be draining Lachlan's coffers.

But Mac wouldn't have felt free to leave me to go to work on the estate if his men weren't outside. And I'd promised I'd stay put today, a promise I now regretted.

I was not a person who lounged around the house.

Deciding I could work on uploading new shots to my website, I moved to return upstairs for my laptop when I saw the pile of get-well cards sitting on Mac's coffee table. Oh right. He'd told me those came through the letterbox for me from the villagers after they heard about the car acc—well, it wasn't an accident. The car *incident*.

I smiled at the thought, thinking how different it was living in a village compared to Boston. Growing up, Mom complained all the time how much things had changed since she was a kid.

"This used to be a community," she'd gripe. "Now my neighbors can barely look me in the eye long enough to say a goddamn good-morning."

But here, in Ardnoch, people cared enough to send a card to someone who'd only lived among them for a few months. Deciding to open the cards first, I brought the pile into the kitchen, made coffee, and sat at the table. There was one from Gordon and his wife. One from Morag and her husband. Chen and her husband Wang Lei, Janet from the tourist shop, Suveer and Moira from the chocolate shop, and even a bunch from villagers I didn't know well or hadn't even met. A card from Arrochar, and one from Thane and the kids. There was even one from Jock and his family.

I was just reading a cute little card from Fergus when something prodded the back of my mind.

To Robyn,

Hope you feel better soon.

Fergus

I squinted at the handwritten card with its succinct, straight-to-the-point message. What was so familiar about it? Irritated, I took another sip of coffee, but I couldn't tear my eyes off the words.

What was—

I tensed with dawning. "No way."

It wasn't the words that were familiar—it was the *handwriting*.

Suddenly, I was running through the cottage and only the tender scream of my ribs slowed me as I attempted to hoof it upstairs. *Damn it*, I huffed, irritated at my body. I still hurt from the crash.

Grabbing my laptop, I hurried downstairs and ignored the jarring pain of it against my bruised ribs. I was too excited to slow down.

Back in the kitchen, I reopened the card after opening

Lachlan's case file. I'd transferred it from Mac's laptop to mine weeks ago.

Zooming in on the photo of the Post-it Notes Mac was obliged to hand over to the police, a chill brushed down my back.

We missed it. We should have ordered all of Ardnoch's staff members to write something down for handwriting forensics to analyze.

I placed the get-well card up against the screen, my eyes bouncing from it to the Post-its bearing the message "Why don't you see me?" Those were the ones that had been placed all over Lachlan's stage office at the castle.

There was no mistaking it.

It was the exact handwriting.

Fuck!

I'd suspected the little shit weeks ago when Mac was first attacked, but I'd let his good-boy attitude and the Adairs' belief in him sway me from questioning him further.

The handwriting was something, but we would need more evidence. Fergus was working at the estate because it wasn't his day off and Lachlan hadn't furloughed him. Quickly checking the file I'd obtained from Mac with staff addresses, I memorized Fergus's.

I should call Mac. Yet I knew he'd leave me behind and go after Fergus without me. I wanted the satisfaction of getting the evidence to nail this prick. Call it stupid pride, call it vengeance, but this was personal. And it wasn't like I'd go alone. I couldn't.

There were two bodyguards waiting outside in a car.

Grabbing a few supplies, as ready as I could be, I locked up the cottage behind me and walked over to the car with the alert security guys. I slid into the back seat, and the two men turned to look at me.

"I'm Robyn," I introduced myself. "You are?"

"Gillies," the driver said.

"Smithy," the other replied. "Problem?"

"Yeah. I need you to take me somewhere."

"Okay." Gillies switched on the engine. "Address?"

I told them, and he popped it into his GPS.

Only a few minutes later, I realized we were driving toward Arrochar's bungalow. But then we veered off onto a quiet cul-de-sac with an ugly-looking, midcentury apartment block situated around a pretty courtyard. Arrochar's home was a mere few minutes from here.

Probably coincidental, right? There weren't a lot of places to live in a small village like Ardnoch.

"Don't drive any farther," I ordered as we approached and gestured to a spot outside a neighboring bungalow. "Park here."

Gillies did as I instructed, and both men looked at me over their shoulders as if to say, "What now?"

If they accompanied me, neighbors would definitely be suspicious. They looked like the Men in Black.

"Wait here."

"No," Smithy said flatly. "We're under strict orders to stay with you at all times."

"You're not exactly inconspicuous, and it's important that no one sees me. Now, I could have easily lost you by taking off through the backyard of my dad's cottage, but I'm not an idiot, I'm not at my physical best, and going anywhere alone right now would make me a moron." I leaned into them. "But where I'm going, no one is home. I just need to check some things out. I have my phone. If you give me your number, I'll call you from up there"—I gestured to the apartment block —"if I need you."

It seemed to take them forever to deliberate, but finally, Gillies took my phone and typed in his info, replacing Mac as my first speed-dial number. Irritating, but I'd fix it later.

"Great. I won't be long." I got out and forced myself to stride with relaxed casualness up to the building. I also tried not to look like I was checking out the building numbers while I actually was. If any of Fergus's neighbors were watching, I wanted them to think I'd been here before and was perfectly welcome.

Slipping my hand into my pocket as I strutted upstairs to the second floor, I pulled out the bobby pins I'd grabbed from my stuff back at Mac's. Following the concrete gallery around to the side of the building that housed Fergus's apartment, I pulled one of the bobby pins apart and hoped I could do this as fast as I used to be able to.

Heart hammering, I got to his door and took another bobby pin in hand and bent the entire thing at a right angle to create a lever.

Inserting it into the lock, hoping my back hid my activities from outside view and I just looked like I was turning a key, I took the other splayed pin, made a loop out of the end for gripping and began to pick the lock.

Sweating, because it took me longer than it should have, I forced myself not to look over my shoulder and sighed with relief as I heard the door click open. Removing the bobby pins, I pushed into the apartment and quietly closed the door behind me. My ribs ached from the tension.

Believe it or not, it was Regan who taught me how to pick a lock with bobby pins. She googled it when she was a teenager for a reason still unbeknownst to me. But I thought it was a neat skill that might come in handy one day.

Thank you, baby sister.

It was dark—the curtains over the front window were shut.

Letting my eyes adjust to the gloom, I tried to hear over the rush of blood in my ears.

Nothing.

Stealthily, I made my way through the small apartment, checking every one of the four rooms, including behind cupboard doors. The apartment was empty.

But the fourth room was behind a locked door.

My heart rate escalated.

A locked door was never a good thing, right?

Making quick work of the lock with my bobby pins, I pushed inside and fumbled for a light switch. It snapped upward, and light flooded the tiny room.

"Holy shit." A wave of nausea washed over me.

The room was obviously used for storage but scattered across the floor, as if he'd emptied the box and didn't have time to tidy it, were photo albums, loose photographs, and magazine clippings. Lowering to my knees, I opened the albums and inhaled sharply.

The Adair family.

With Fergus.

Photos of him as a little boy, growing up with them. Most of the shots were of him and Brodan. But there was a cluster of photos of him and Arrochar, and when I saw those, I sucked in a breath.

Were the Adairs that blind?

The way Fergus looked at Arrochar was almost the same as how he looked at Brodan.

Pure hero worship.

There was a photo of Fergus with Arrochar at the ceilidh weeks ago. His arm around her, beaming at the camera. He wasn't over her?

And the magazine articles were all about Brodan. Every single one of them. His face was blacked out with a marker in all of them.

Shit.

I lifted the lid on another nearby box and found more

magazines. Another box filled with every film Brodan had starred in.

Where Lachlan fit in, I wasn't sure. The messages were left for him, but … these boxes didn't say proud friend. They told me with absolute certainty that Brodan, in particular, was the focus of Fergus's obsession.

But why?

I yanked my phone out of my pocket because I had what I needed. We'd go to the police with the post-it notes and cards so they could use it to obtain a warrant to search Fergus's apartment. The evidence needed to be collected legally, which meant I needed to get out of there and get the notes to the police. Wanting to give Dad the heads up, I scrolled through my contacts trying to find him now that Gillies had taken him off my speed dial.

The phone burst into song in my hand as it rang, and I startled, cursing under my breath.

The number came up as unknown.

Usually, I'd ignore unknown numbers.

However, a strange sensation of foreboding shivered down my spine, and my thumb hit the answer button before I could think about it. "Hello."

There was heavy breathing down the line.

Chilled, I glanced over my shoulder, wondering if Fergus knew I was in his apartment.

"Hello?" I bit out angrily as I stalked out into the main living space, standing in the middle of the room so no fucker could get the jump on me.

"Is this Robyn Penhaligon?" a voice that was clearly masked using a voice-changing app asked. The accent was Scottish, however.

I swallowed hard. "Who is this?"

"I have Lachlan Adair."

My heart lurched in my throat. *No.*

"When I get off the phone, I'll text you directions to his location. If you want to save him, you'll shake your body-guards and come alone."

Fuck. I wanted to say his name. To say, I know it's you, you asshole. But the thought of putting Lachlan in further danger stopped me.

"I'm watching you, Robyn. I'll know if you step on this land with those men at your back."

He hung up.

Shaking with the rush of adrenaline, I tried to figure out how to get rid of my security. Then I remembered Fergus mentioned he owned a motorcycle.

I was rummaging through his drawers for keys when the text came in.

Pulling up my maps app, I tried to figure out where he was sending me.

From my guess ... oh shit.

McCulloch land.

Anger ripped through me as I stormed into the kitchen, wrenching open drawers to look for keys. It had been that old bastard all along!

Finding a key that looked like it could fit a motorcycle, I snatched it and let myself out through the French doors off the kitchen that led onto a balcony. The balcony overlooked the parking lot and was hidden from the street at the front of the building where Gillies and Smithy waited.

Ignoring my aching ribs, I climbed onto a drainpipe attached to the building and shimmied down the cold metal. Even that slight drop to the ground shot shards of pain into my ribs, but I didn't have time to take a breath.

My phone beeped in my pocket.

Another text. YOU HAVE TEN MINUTES OR HE DIES.

Hurrying across the lot to the old motorcycle sitting in the spot marked with Fergus's apartment number, I got on the bike and felt relief flood through me when the key slotted perfectly into the ignition and the motorcycle growled to life. I checked the text with the directions again and memorized them as best as I could.

Then I was off, the motorcycle wobbling beneath my feet because I hadn't ridden one since high school—and even then, it was a moped. I followed the road north out of Ardnoch, gunning the engine when I felt more confident.

The directions led me to a trail just narrow enough for a bike to traverse on the edge of McCulloch's land.

And because I wasn't a moron—and Fergus and McCulloch weren't masterminds—I called Mac and told him everything in one big rush.

"Stay put!" he yelled in outrage as soon as I was done.

"If I don't go to wherever it is they want me, they'll hurt him. They've come too far now not to. I'll get there and you find a way to follow me without alerting them."

"Robyn—"

"We're wasting time, Dad!"

"Fuck!" he bit out. "Fine. Forward me the text with the directions."

"Thank you. I love you."

"Don't say that to me right now … I could kill you for going off on your own."

"I'm not on my own. You're coming to get me."

He sucked in a breath. "I love you. I'll be there as soon as I can. Be careful."

"Yup." I hung up abruptly, second-guessing my decision. Maybe it was safer to wait for Mac.

There had to be a reason Fergus and McCulloch wanted *me* there too. Either way, they were caught … but that was the problem. Either way, they were caught. If I went, I put myself in danger along with Lachlan, but there was a chance I could save him.

If I didn't go and I waited for Mac, they would definitely kill him. They had nothing left to lose, right? And they hadn't exactly proven themselves the most rational people.

Rock, meet Hard Place.

Gunning the motorbike engine, I shot off down the trail, my fury spurring me on. I had no reason to fear getting lost from that point on. The trail led directly to a small shack in the woods, and the same truck that had run me off the road was parked out front.

I almost shook my head in disbelief.

This couldn't get any more cliché. Fergus had watched one too many movies about how to do this.

I stopped the bike near the little porch of the run-down wooden structure. There seemed to be no purpose for it, but then I didn't know enough about farming to understand why McCulloch would have this building on his land.

Getting off the bike, I froze at the sight of the door opening. It was crooked on its hinges and creaked as it swung into the dark of the little shack. No one stood behind the door.

Well, that's creepy.

Pushing through the fear that hit my knees like reflex hammers, I walked up the porch steps and—

"Lachlan!" I moved to launch myself through the doorway, but sense halted me.

He faced me sideways. Tied to a chair, blood trickling down his temple, pale and probably concussed, his hands handcuffed behind his back. A gag covered his mouth.

Lachlan looked toward me, and his eyes widened with horror. He shook his head as he shoved his body with all his might, moving the chair with the violence of his reaction.

"Stop it." A figure moved into view and pressed a gun to the head of the person I hadn't even noticed was knocked out next to Lachlan. "Or I kill her."

Lucy!

Lachlan froze, but he glared at me, and I heard his muffled shout for me to run.

I couldn't run.

Not now.

The masked man turned and looked directly at me. "Get in and shut the door or I blow her head off."

Fergus.

It was definitely his voice.

Aware that McCulloch might be hidden behind the door, I slipped into the room with my back scraping against the wall. Lachlan craned his neck, following my every move. Seeing his despair, I quickly looked away and reached out to catch the edge of the door to shut it.

To my shock, we were alone in the small rectangular, one-room shack. There were two small windows at opposite ends that let in very little light. Except for a low-watt bulb hanging from the ceiling and an unconscious Lucy and an injured Lachlan tied to metal chairs, there was nothing else in it.

And of course, Fergus.

No McCulloch.

"You might as well take off the mask, *Fergus*."

He shook his head. "Not the plan."

"What is the plan?"

"Following orders."

McCulloch's.

"And those are?"

"To get rid of you."

Goose bumps prickled over my skin. He said it so casually. "Why?"

He shrugged. "I just do what I'm told."

"No … *why?*" I gestured to him. "Why would you do this to the Adairs? I thought they were like family to you?"

His strange purple contacts brightened in the dim light. "Family? Family doesn't abandon each other."

Lachlan grunted.

Deciding the best plan of action was to keep Fergus talking long enough for Mac, his men, and the police to get there, I pushed, "You think they abandoned you?"

Fergus scoffed behind his mask. "Treated me like a pet they could cast aside whenever they felt like it. I was Brodan's best mate. Did you know that?"

I nodded.

"He was all I had. Growing up in a family like mine ... Brodan and Arrochar were all I had. And he fucked off to Hollywood and forgot about all of us, and she broke it off with me like what we had was nothing!"

"So you want them all dead?"

He swiped his head to the side, his gun hand wavering. "I just wanted them to hurt like I hurt."

I imagined him waiting outside my father's home and then gutting him, just like he'd gutted McHugh. Rage seethed beneath my surface. "Why Mac?"

Fergus lifted the gun and pointed it directly at me, and Lachlan thrashed against his bindings. "Stop it, or I kill her right now," the mechanic warned.

Lachlan desisted, but his chest heaved with panic.

Trying to block him out, I asked my question again.

"Because," Fergus answered, "he wants what's mine."

Oh my God.

I squeezed my eyes closed in understanding.

No wonder we couldn't put the pieces together. Mac's attack wasn't because he was close to Lachlan or investigating the case.

It was because Fergus noticed what I'd noticed.

There was something between my dad and Arrochar.

Fergus was still in love with Arrochar Adair.

Feeling so grateful that he'd failed in taking my dad from me, but so horrified for McHugh, my eyes flew open. "And Greg McHugh?"

Fergus's breath hitched. "A mistake. He caught me unaware." To my shock, I heard tears in his voice. "It wasn't meant. I'm sorry that happened."

"You're sorry you murdered a man?"

He shook the gun at me, and my hands flew up defensively as Lachlan roared behind his gag. "Don't judge me, bitch!"

"I'm sorry," I appeased him. "I'm just trying to figure this out, Fergus. It doesn't make sense to me ... bringing Lachlan and Lucy here. Why hurt Lucy?"

"That's for me to know."

I frowned because he'd been pretty forthcoming so far. That also meant he intended to kill us—the more we knew, the more we needed to die. But I had no intention of allowing that to happen. *Just keep him talking.* "Then what about me? Why attack me?"

"Him." He cut his chin toward Lachlan.

"You wanted to hurt Lachlan?"

"Not me." Fergus shrugged. "Lachlan's been all right to me. The only Adair to give a shit."

"So why would you hurt him?"

"Because I made a promise." He raised his gun again and pointed it at me. "I am sorry, Robyn. You're a good person."

"Do you think I didn't tell anyone I was coming here?" I blurted out, trying to stall. "I've been to your apartment, Fergus, and saw the room with all the boxes. They know it's you. The police are on their way."

His hand wavered. "No ... No ... I ..."

A deafening crack sounded milliseconds before Fergus's head snapped back. Blood and brain matter exploded out of the back of it.

My breath expelled from my body in a shocked cry as his body folded like a puppet whose strings had been cut.

Shocked to my core, I tore my gaze from him to Lucy who now stood, arm outstretched, holding the small handgun she'd just used to kill Fergus.

Holy shit.

Lucy looked at me, eyes fierce. "I started carrying after the freezer. Moron didn't even think to pat me down."

"Oh thank God." I wanted to slump with relief, but there was no time. "We have to get Lachlan out of these cuffs. I think McCulloch must be the one working with Fergus. We're on his land."

"Okay." Lucy nodded. "*He* has the keys." Her eyes widened on me, as if she'd just realized what she'd done. "I can't ..."

"It's okay." I gave her a reassuring, tremulous smile. "I'll get the keys. You stay there." I moved over to Fergus's body and avoided looking at his head as I bent to pat his pockets.

Something hot and hard pressed against the back of my skull, and I heard Lachlan's muffled yell of outrage behind me.

No.

"Stand up slowly. Don't make any sudden moves," Lucy ordered.

Oh no.

Tears clogged my throat.

I did as asked, the pressure of the still-warm gun painful against my head as I stood. I felt the heat of her at my back and then she grasped hold of my neck, nails biting painfully into my throat as she moved the warm muzzle to my right temple. She turned me to face Lachlan, and my horror was mirrored in his eyes.

"You were my friend," I whispered lamely. Because that's all I could think to say.

My mind screamed a huge fat fucking *NO*.

Not Lucy.

"Yes," she said softly in my ear. "And I hate that it's come to this."

Lachlan yanked at his arms, but they'd been entwined around the chair's back before they'd been handcuffed. His muffled shouts of Lucy's name over and over were breaking my heart.

"Shush, Lachlan, and stop moving." She pushed the gun into my temple so hard, my head pushed to the left.

He stilled immediately. I couldn't stand the bleakness in his eyes.

If she killed me in front of him, he'd never get over it.

But I had the sudden, horrifying realization that she *truly* planned to kill him too. There was no way out of it for her unless we both died.

Stall her. "Why has it come to this?"

"I didn't think it would," Lucy said, bitter sadness in her voice. "I promise I didn't think it would. At first, I just wanted him back."

Lachlan's eyes widened as I stiffened against her.

"You're the only one who deserved me, and I'm the only one who deserved you," she told him, affection clear in her tone. "I've been used and abused since I was a kid, and I naively thought escaping to Hollywood, becoming *someone*, would give me back my power. But there are always people with more power, more control, no matter where you go. They used me too. And I let them. It was only when we got together I realized I could deal with all of it, if I had you."

It was hard to know if what she said was true. Hard to believe anything out of her mouth because she'd played her part as our friend so convincingly.

I shuddered and realized I was going into shock. I couldn't let that happen. If I could just distract Lucy long enough, I could get out of her hold without losing half my head. A trained killer would have popped us both and gotten on with their plan. However, Lucy had proven herself the consummate actor, a lover of drama, and she'd want us to know why this was happening before she concluded her plans.

I had to keep her talking for as long as possible. "You told him you just wanted an affair."

"I lied. Like you lied. Like most of us lie. I thought he'd come around. See what I could see. I'm America's sweetheart. Royalty in my own right. And Lachlan is not just an actor. He's a gentleman with a pedigree few men in my life can match. The industry was falling all over themselves to be a part of his club, and that was the type of man I deserved to be with. But he couldn't see it like I could. So I tried to move on. But I chose wrong."

Her nails scored across my throat lightly, and I sucked in a breath. "Slept with a married actor, and his wife caught us. Ever heard of Rozette Donelly?"

Yeah, hadn't everyone?

Rozette Donelly was the head of one of the major studios.

"Yeah. That Rozette Donelly. I fucked her young husband, and she found out and blackballed me." Lucy laughed with an edge of hysteria.

How did we not know?

How is it possible we missed this?

"I haven't been taking a break or casually meeting with directors and producers. She killed my career!" Lucy yelled right at my ear, and I winced. I felt her body shudder as she tried to control herself. "Bitch killed my career. Every person I reach out to, she finds out about it and kills any chance of work."

There was no remorse in her voice for sleeping with Rozette Donelly's husband. She didn't see herself as anything but the victim in this scenario. And while what Rozette did was vengeful, I realized Lucy couldn't recognize her own blame.

Lachlan stared at Lucy like he'd never seen her before in his life.

I felt the same way.

She deserved a goddamn Oscar for her performance at Ardnoch these past few months.

"I thought if I could come back to Ardnoch, I could make Lachlan see that only he was equal to me. But he was so distant, off screwing that Scottish nobody down in Glasgow. I got angry. I thought maybe if I made things difficult at the club, he'd need me more."

"The creepy stalker notes."

"Exactly. I saw the way Fergus watched Arrochar, and I heard the bitterness no one else seemed to hear when he spoke about Brodan. So I slept with him to try to lower his defenses, get him to confide in me, and lo and behold, our little mechanic had a gambling problem."

"You paid him?"

"Yeah. I paid him very well to do all the dirty work. He killed the deer. Trashed the studio. Left the notes. I hired a hacker back in the States to infiltrate the security system on the estate. And everything was going smoothly until Fergus got it in his head to stab Mac."

I seethed at the reminder.

"Not only was it completely off plan, he pissed *you* off. Which derailed everything because our darling Lachlan got attached."

Lachlan's gaze locked with mine, a silent plea in his eyes. He wanted me to take her out. But I needed her fully distracted, or I could lose my head.

"Lucy..."

"Don't." She choked me lightly, pressing the gun muzzle deeper into my temple. Just as I was about to take the chance and wrestle out of her hold, she stopped choking me. "You ruined everything, Robyn. I thought if Fergus attacked you, you might go home, but that night in the trailer, you kicked his ass. I had to pay off a skeevy doctor in Inverness to stitch up the moron's knife wound. And that fucker is still black-mailing me. Not for long, though."

I didn't even want to know what that meant. Then something occurred to me. "You had Fergus put you in that freezer so you could get Lachlan back?"

"Very astute. Yeah, I did. It was a risk that didn't quite pay off." She said it like she was talking about wearing a risqué dress to the goddamn Academy Awards that got her slammed on the worst-dressed lists. "And I thought it was working. I thought you"—she spoke directly to Lachlan —"were coming back to me."

He glowered at her.

"I know." I could hear the sneer in her voice. "I'm disgusted with myself that I even thought a man could make things better when they have always made it so much worse."

"And Thane?" Was making me think she had feelings for Lachlan's brother just a manipulative attempt to keep me off her scent?

Lucy tensed at my side. "I didn't lie. I'm attracted to Thane, but he doesn't have Lachlan's clout. He may be from a good family, but he's just an architect."

I heard Lachlan growl beneath the gag.

"Still, it was quite clever of me to use him to make you think I had no interest in Lachlan, wasn't it?"

Clever? There was no word for what Lucy was. I'd never encountered someone with the ability to become whatever she thought she needed to be to achieve her goals.

"What's the plan here, Lucy?"

"It was always *this*. After McHugh's death—and Lachlan's defection after I put myself in a goddamn freezer—there was no other choice. Fergus wasn't the brightest bulb. He didn't see it, but I knew the trail would lead to him eventually. Everything spiraled out of control, and now I have to fix it. This is the only way. I had Fergus lure you here, knowing that all three of you would have to die to put everything to rights."

She leaned in and pressed a soft kiss to my cheek. I shivered with disgust. "I'll be the only one to survive the madman stalking the Adair family. He shot you and Lachlan first, and I managed to get free and wrestle him for the gun. Of course, I'll shoot myself in the shoulder to make it look more realistic … but I'll be alive. And I'll be global news. The person everyone is talking about. Hollywood will be desperate to make movies with me while this is fresh in people's minds. I'll be free publicity. There's nothing Rozette could do to stop me when I'm that bankable."

She was unhinged.

Completely.

"You're a damn fine actor, Lucy," I said, the words breaking with emotion.

She caressed my throat. "If things were different, we would have been best friends. I see what he sees in you, I do. I don't respect or admire many people as they're never quite good enough, are they? But you're an equal. I always wanted a friend like you. I hope you know that."

Tears slipped down my cheeks.

Not just from fear for Lachlan, for myself … but with utter sadness.

Because I'd cared about her.

And all along, I'd missed that she didn't think like other people thought. She didn't feel like other people felt.

All those shadows I'd seen and dismissed in her eyes.

"Don't cry, Robyn. I'll make it quick—"

The door to the shack blasted open, and the gun muzzle skidded off my temple when Lucy startled.

I didn't hesitate.

I grabbed her wrist and twisted it with my right hand and at the same time, I slammed my left elbow back into her nose, feeling it crunch beneath the power of the blow. She shrieked as I broke her wrist, the gun clattering to the ground. Then I spun around and threw my entire weight behind a short, brutal jab to her face.

Her head snapped back on her neck, and her eyes flickered shut before she tumbled to the ground. Assured she was out, I whipped around and scrambled for the gun, bringing it up only to find McCulloch standing in the doorway with his shotgun at his side.

He looked down at Lucy and then Fergus before his gaze met mine. "Looks like my services aren't needed after all."

I didn't lower my gun.

I'd been taken by surprise too many times today already.

McCulloch's expression hardened, and he threw his shotgun to the ground with a pointed look. He knelt before Lachlan and when he pulled out a penknife, I lurched toward them but was drawn short as McCulloch cut at the bindings around Lachlan's shins.

"Do you have keys for these handcuffs?" he threw over his shoulder.

Swaying a little with relief, I dropped to my haunches and checked Fergus's pockets, finding the set of small keys we needed.

I rounded Lachlan's chair, shaking violently with adrenaline, so much so that McCulloch gently moved me out of the way, took the keys from my hand, and released Lachlan.

The chair scraped back as he soared out of it and turned to me, ripping off the gag. "Fuck, fuck, fuck," Lachlan uttered hoarsely, crossing the distance between us to yank me into his arms.

I sank into his embrace, my fingers bunching the back of his shirt into my fists.

We didn't say anything.

We just held each other as we struggled to breathe.

Men led by my dad streamed into the shack, and Lachlan reluctantly passed me to Mac. Over my dad's shoulder, I watched Lachlan tentatively move toward an unconscious Lucy. He lowered before her. When he looked back at me, grief and rage mingled in his expression, and I couldn't stand his pain.

"One second, Dad." I pulled out of Mac's relieved embrace and crossed the shack to Lachlan. I crouched beside him and slid a palm across his hunched shoulders. "None of us could have known."

"I failed her," he whispered.

"No. Lachlan—"

"I'm sorry to interrupt," a deep voice intruded. I glanced up in the dim light to see one of the DIs who'd interviewed me several times before standing over us. His expression was grim. "We need to know what happened here."

What happened here?

Something neither of us saw coming.

I glanced over at Lucy who still hadn't stirred.

"You might want to put her"—I pointed to Lucy—"in handcuffs before she comes around."

36

ROBYN

The paramedics examined Lachlan where he sat on the open end of the ambulance. He answered their questions with irritated impatience, and my gut churned with the events of the day.

Forensics were all over the shack on McCulloch's land. The coroner had just taken off with Fergus's body.

Lucy was loaded onto an ambulance—with a police escort.

Mac stood near the shack porch talking solemnly with the DIs. Jock, Gillies, and Smithy watched me from their spot near two Range Rovers.

"You all right, lass?"

I jumped and cursed myself for it.

Hard not to be jumpy after the day I'd had.

I glanced up at the big man beside me. "I don't know what I am."

McCulloch nodded grimly. "It was quite the betrayal. From both of them."

"How did you know we were here?"

"Jared saw you riding up the trail. Came back to the farm

467

to alert me you were on my land. This used to be where the old farmhouse was. My father demolished it after he built the new one but left the shack, which used to be an old wood-shed for my mother. It was once furnished with her things. She liked to escape out here to read and craft. I kept it for sentimental reasons. Now I'll have to demolish the thing, tainted as it now is."

"I'm sorry," I whispered hoarsely, feeling guilty.

"For what?"

"For thinking it was you because of what happened to your sister."

The farmer exhaled heavily. "My only issue with Adair is the land. I let go of what happened to Maryanne a long time ago."

"You let it go?" I frowned. "Lachlan doesn't think so."

McCulloch's gaze pierced through me. "His father not only lost his sister, too, he lost his bloody wife. If that man did owe me a debt for what happened to Maryanne, he paid it twice over in grief."

I nodded, ashamed I'd gotten him so wrong.

He seemed to understand. "You followed motive. It's done. Move on."

Move on?

I found Lachlan again, his eyes downcast as the para-medic spoke to him. He looked haggard. Lost.

How did you move on from that kind of betrayal? How did you move on when you'd been so utterly deceived by someone you cared about?

How would he ever trust again?

37

LACHLAN

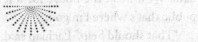

"*I* just can't believe this has happened," Wesley Howard said for what felt like the millionth time.

Lachlan nodded, face blank, at the computer screen. "I know."

"But we need to get our members back into the club."

As a top investor, owner of the most expensive home on the estate, and a board member, Wesley, though not entirely lacking in compassion, ultimately viewed the whole thing as a business situation. And Lachlan was glad for his attitude. The PR nightmare gave him something beyond sitting alone with his turmoil to focus on.

"I've spoken with Luther"—his actor friend and the other board member—"and if you're not opposed to it, we'd like to ask Marci Robbins to replace Lucy on the board."

Wesley scrubbed a hand over his thick beard. "Don't you think it should be someone younger, on par with Lucy?"

He shook his head. "You should see the other members around Marci, Wes. The word fangirling was invented for it."

His friend snorted. "I can see that happening."

"She has clout and respect. We're all about image. What

469

better thing to brag about than Marci Robbins approving you for membership to Ardnoch?"

Wesley nodded along. "No, you're right. Do it."

Lachlan just had to hope the legendary British actor wasn't put off by the scandal.

"I've got a break coming up, and the wife is missing Scotland. We'll be at the house for a few weeks, and I'll make it public that's where I'm going."

"That should help," Lachlan said. "I'm grateful."

"I'll contact Roman, pull a few favors, and get him to come too."

Wesley referred to Roman Bright, the son of Oscar-winning actor Garrett Bright, and an Academy Award-winning screenwriter in his own right. He'd canceled his annual May Stay after Mac's stabbing.

"That would be great." Lachlan clicked on his members' file. "We've already reached out to sixty percent of our members, and most of them feel assured the club is a safe retreat once more. But there are a few A-listers we need to convince, and I think you and Roman coming to stay will do that."

"Great." Wesley leaned into the camera. "I gotta go, Lachlan, but I hope you're doing okay, man. You look tired. Get some sleep."

After saying goodbye, relieved to be off the video chat, Lachlan slumped in his chair. He had no fear that his members would return to Ardnoch. They loved the drama and scandal Lucy had left in her wake.

Lucy.

Her name was like a knife in his mind.

The night of the event when she'd revealed herself as the culprit behind everything, he'd been in such a state of agitation, he could barely speak. Robyn stayed with him, and he'd experienced the most peculiar sensation of needing her near so he knew she was okay—and yet, he also wanted her as far from him as he could get her.

Never mind that one of his closest friends had betrayed him beyond imagination; he'd let Fergus, a man he could take out in a heartbeat, get the jump on him. Whatever he'd hit Lachlan over the head with, it left him with a bad concussion, and he'd had a headache for days after. The thought of Fergus not only doing that to him but dragging him downstairs in his own home and out to his truck, then into the shack and tying him to that fucking chair ... Lachlan should've woken up at some point before then.

If he'd only woken up, Robyn would never have been in that position.

It was a joke.

The great Lachlan Adair, once Hollywood's most bankable action hero, handcuffed to a chair, incapacitated by a concussion but aware enough to watch on in horror as the woman he loved faced her death.

What a bloody hero.

He flinched.

In the end, Robyn had saved them.

He hadn't been able to protect her.

Didn't deserve her.

But fuck, did he love her beyond bearing and was so goddamn grateful she could save herself. If he'd had to watch her die while he could do nothing to stop it, the death Lucy had in store for him would've been welcome.

"No one knew," Robyn said that night. "None of us had a clue, so stop blaming yourself."

"Shouldn't I have known? I'm the one who slept with her. Not to mention it's my business to know what's going on with my members' careers. I should have been paying more attention. If I'd known what was happening to Lucy's career, maybe—"

"Lachlan, Lucy was an amazing actor. We just didn't realize

she was acting with us. As for her career, I'm sure if any of your members knew what was happening to her, they also knew how close you two were and would very deliberately not gossip in front of you."

That was probably the truth. But it didn't make him feel any better. "What do you think will happen to her?"

"What do you want to happen to her?"

He thought on it carefully, trying to separate his rage from his guilt. "I want her to pay for what she's done here ... but I also want her to get the help she needs."

"Me too."

Lachlan gestured to her, and she'd crossed his room to slide onto the bed next to him. He pulled her against him and held her.

He'd held her all night. And in the morning, he'd gone into himself, trying to process the whole thing with Lucy. His distance hurt Robyn. Another thing he had to make up to her.

A knock at his office door brought his head up. "Come in."

Mac strode into the room, and Lachlan straightened in his chair.

Things between them had been strained after his and Robyn's breakup, and they hadn't quite returned to normal. Lachlan hated it. "Mac."

His head of security nodded and gestured to the chairs in front of Lachlan's desk. "May I?"

"Of course."

He settled in with casualness and studied Lachlan through his low-lidded gaze.

"What is it, Mac?"

"We had to call the police. A couple of paps scaled the front gate."

He raised an eyebrow. "They're getting desperate."

Lucy's attack and plot with Fergus had made the global

news. It wasn't the kind of worldwide recognition Lucy planned for, but she had it now, anyway. She wasn't granted bail by Police Scotland and was currently in jail until the case went to trial. Lachlan's (and now Robyn's) lawyer warned it was more than likely Lucy would either plead insanity or take a plea bargain to avoid going to trial. Robyn thought Lucy wouldn't want the world to know the details of the case —she wanted fame, not notoriety—and would take a plea bargain.

Lachlan wasn't sure about anything when it came to Lucy.

But the journalists and paps had descended on Ardnoch like vultures, trying to get the scoop on any bit of information about the case the world didn't know yet. They'd been hassling Brodan who was in a furor because he was contractually obligated to finish shooting his current film when all he wanted to do was come home to Ardnoch to make sure his family was okay.

The paps followed Arrochar and Thane again. Lachlan hated the bastards. Always had. They were one of the reasons leaving Hollywood behind had been such an easy goddamn decision.

"It'll die down," Mac said, reading his expression. "Something else will take their interest in a few days."

He nodded. "I'm sure you're right."

His friend narrowed his eyes at his flat tone. "You can't bury all this shit, Lachlan. You have to talk to someone about how you're feeling. Pushing people away will only make things worse."

"I'm not pushing anyone away."

"So how do you think wee Eredine is coping? Her close friend psychotically tried to murder a man she considers a brother and a woman she's come to care about."

Lachlan flinched at the word *psychotically* as much as the

thought of Ery, whom he had neglected. "We don't know if Lucy is psychotic."

"Fine. But let's not get off page here. Eredine won't leave her cabin. I finally spoke to Arrochar, and she's on her way there now to try to talk with her. If anyone can help her, it's Arro."

Feeling guilty for ignoring Ery, he could only nod.

"Speaking of your siblings, they're worried about you, and you won't talk to them."

"I've been busy trying to keep my club together."

"And what about Robyn?" Mac said her name with such sharpness, it felt like the crack of a belt across his skin.

Lachlan glared at his friend.

Mac returned the expression. "It's been a week. You've ignored her phone calls, avoided her when she's been on the estate."

He swallowed. "I just ... need time."

His friend heaved a sigh. "Lachlan ... I'm a man."

"I did notice that, thank you."

Mac ignored his sarcasm. "There was nothing any man, no matter how capable or strong, could have done after taking a blow to the head like that. And perhaps you could've gotten out of rope bindings, but he'd twined your arms through the metal of that chair before handcuffing you. Add to the fact that you had a bad concussion and your faculties weren't all there ... there wasn't a lot you could do."

Shame filled him, making him furious. "I think you better get out."

"Robyn didn't die, Lachlan," Mac said angrily instead. "She's living and breathing and here ... and so what if she had to be the one to rescue you both? All that matters is you both survived."

"I don't care that she saved us. I'm grateful she could."

"But you wish it had been you. That you could prove to her that you are capable of protecting her."

He looked away sharply, his cheeks hot with anger and embarrassment.

"She doesn't need you to protect her, man. She just needs to know that you care enough to want to."

Mac's words pierced through his pride, reminding him of the night in the gym when Robyn accused him of abandoning her when she needed him.

"Fuck," he hissed.

"Lachlan."

Something in Mac's voice drew his gaze, and he tensed at his friend's grim expression.

"She's leaving," Mac said, sadness darkening his eyes. "Her flights are booked. She leaves for the States tomorrow morning."

His panic was immediate and physically painful.

His chair rolled back into the wall as he stood abruptly. "Where is she now?"

Something like hope brightened Mac's face. "At the beach near the caravan site."

* * *

HEART POUNDING, Lachlan pulled his SUV to a stop beside the new one he'd provided after the other was totaled when Fergus ran her off the road.

That nightmare was over now, though.

And he needed to pull his head out of his arse.

Lachlan climbed from the car and kicked off his dress shoes and socks, placing them back inside. Rolling his trousers at the ankle, he strode down the dunes, letting the sand slide him down the slope and onto the beach. The golden stretch was a honey-wheat color from the rain that had fallen through the night. Compact and hard beneath his bare feet, the coolness of it felt good. Calmed him, even.

Looking left, he saw a few people in the distance with a dog bounding between them.

Turning right, he saw a couple not too far up the beach, and beyond them ...

His heart slowed.

Robyn crouched near the shore with her camera to her face.

Lachlan walked down to the shoreline and let the chilled tide reach his ankles, circling like icy fingers before they were pulled back into the water. The sensation moved up his body, causing goose bumps across his skin.

It was so invigorating, his mind cleared.

Sticking to the shore, he let the water sweep around his feet every time it rushed in, and he thought on what he would say to Robyn when he reached her. Lachlan still wasn't sure he deserved her, but *she* deserved to know his true feelings.

As he closed in, her profile came into sharp focus, and his emotions expanded like a physical thing through his chest. No woman was as beautiful to him as Robyn Penhaligon.

And the thought of losing her—

Fuck, it literally took his breath away.

Lachlan inhaled a gulp of fresh air, trying to quell his rising panic.

He watched as she stood, stretching those long legs as she lowered her camera so it hung heavily around her neck from its strap. She stared out at the water, lost in thought. The light breeze flicked at her ponytail while loose strands danced around her cheeks.

Every morning.

Every morning he wanted this woman's face to be the first thing he saw upon waking.

Sensing a presence, Robyn looked sharply toward him. A wary expression tightened her features, and he hated himself for making her feel that way about him. "What are you doing here?" she asked. He loved her voice. Low, mellifluous, with a slight rasp to it.

He couldn't imagine not hearing her voice every day.

For a moment as he stopped before her, Lachlan just looked, enjoyed memorizing every piece of her in case he didn't see her for a while. The only sounds between them were the lap of the water, the gulls above them in the sky.

Finally Robyn spoke again. "Mac told you I'm leaving."

He nodded.

"I wouldn't have left without saying goodbye," she promised.

He knew that. She was too honest, too honorable to just walk away without a word. Not that he deserved it. "I stayed away too long. I'm sorry."

Robyn looked away with a shrug. "I get it."

"I don't want you to get it. I shouldn't have stayed away." He took a step toward her and that not only brought her attention back to him but she retreated.

Fuck.

"Braveheart," he said hoarsely, "I am so fucking sorry."

"Stop apologizing. It isn't your fault."

"Not about that. Yes, about that … but I mean …" He gestured between them. "For pushing you away. Twice." He reached for her hands, and thankfully she didn't pull them away. "Fergus hit me over the head when I was on my way to come see you. To tell you I was sorry for the ultimatum … and that I love you."

Her eyes widened.

He forged on. "I love you, Robyn. I want you to stay."

The return of her wariness gutted him, as did the way she tugged on her hands until he had to release her.

"You don't believe me," Lachlan whispered, vacillating between self-directed fury and at her for her faithlessness.

"I don't know," Robyn answered, ever honest. "I don't know, Lachlan. And I can't stay even if I did. I'll have to return for Lucy's trial, but for now, I need to go back to Boston. I have to figure things out with my mom and Regan … I just … I have to figure things out."

The urge to argue, to persuade, bubbled inside him, but that little voice in the back of his head, the one that taunted him for being unable to save her, whispered maybe this was how it was meant to be.

Because you could love someone more than you loved yourself.

But that didn't mean you deserved them.

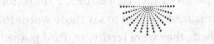

Children's laughter, ducks quacking, traffic passing in the distance were the soundtrack to the park as I strolled with my mom. It had been some time since I'd walked in the Public Garden, even before I'd left Boston for Scotland.

"Thank you for agreeing to meet me," Mom said.

The sun beat down on my bare skin revealed by my tank top. "I forgot how pretty this place is."

"Yeah." Mom sighed. "So … how are you doing after everything? You've been through the ringer, baby."

I shrugged, my tone masking the truth. "I'm okay."

"The tabloids kept phoning the house."

"Sorry about that."

"Don't be silly. Seth handled it. We're just worried about you."

I didn't know what to say to her. There were so many reasons I was reeling. One, because I never thought anyone could ever deceive me the way Lucy had. That messes with your head, questioning how you missed it. I'd considered myself pretty astute, but at no point did I ever suspect her.

That's scary.

It makes you doubt yourself.

It makes you doubt other people.

And I didn't want what she'd done to make me not trust people anymore.

Maybe I'd already let her win by not trusting Lachlan when he told me he loved me. I'd yearned, I think for far longer than I even realized, for him to say those words to me. Yet when he said them, they were terrifying. He'd pushed me away before, several times, and I couldn't live my life like that. Loving someone so much and having them love you back but on their terms, always holding you at arm's length. Never the priority.

That wasn't the kind of love I wanted.

And he'd only proved me right when he didn't fight it. When he didn't fight to make me believe. Maybe it was wrong to want him to. Maybe that wasn't love either.

I felt empty without him, though.

It was survivable.

But it was awful.

It was like waking up every day knowing that no matter what goodness the day brought, it lacked the joy of anticipation because the person you most looked forward to seeing would never be there.

I think that's what love is: the person you most look forward to seeing.

The person you looked around for when something funny happened and you wanted to share it.

I wondered if I'd ever really laugh again.

Not the sound or the action—those were easy. You just opened your mouth and out came the sound.

But real laughter came from the soul. Something that sparked true joy.

480

"I think I have a right to be worried. You're not yourself," Mom said, breaking through my dismal musings.

"I'm fine, Mom. Aren't I always?"

She considered this. "And are *we* fine?"

I looked at her, directly in the eye because we were the same height. Except for the fact she had cornflower blue eyes and mine were hazel, we were almost mirror images of one another. While Regan inherited Seth's red hair and chestnut eyes, I'd inherited my mother's hair (and of course, Mac's eyes). I'd also inherited her height and figure, though I always thought she moved with more femininity than I did. I blamed my no-nonsense stride on my athleticism. Mom wasn't into physical activity beyond a stroll in the park. She was more of a creative. She liked reading and fashion and gossip rags. Regan was more like her than I was.

I loved my mom.

But I was Mac's.

There was no denying it.

And I missed him already.

"I'm mad at you," I answered honestly. "I'm hurt."

"If this is about those letters—"

"Don't make excuses, Mom. It'll only make things worse. Mac has accepted his blame in all of this, and he and I have worked through that … but we could've worked through it long before now if you hadn't made it so hard for him to see me."

She strode away and sat down on a rare find—an empty bench overlooking Duck Island. I followed, contemplating the petulant twist to her mouth and trying to tamp down my answering irritation.

Thankfully, Mom took a few minutes to gather herself before she spoke. "I just didn't want you to get hurt."

"Wrong."

Her head whipped around, her hair flying around her

shoulders. Blue eyes snapped fire at me. "You don't believe me."

"I think you've confused *you* not wanting to get hurt."

"I was protecting you."

"You were protecting yourself." I was impressed by my neutral tone. "What you did was selfish, and I lost sixteen years with my father because of it."

"I knew it," she hissed, eyes narrowed. "I knew he would turn you against me. You're so like him."

I glared back. "Mac didn't turn me against you. Mac didn't even lay blame at your feet. He gave me the facts, and I drew my own conclusions. And you can either be a grown-up and admit that you fucked up and hurt me ... or ..."

"Or what?"

I shrugged miserably. "Or we go on as before."

"But?"

"What do you want me to say, Mom? That I can just forget this and forgive you for lying to me for sixteen years?" Tears filled my eyes. "You stood by and watched my heart break and you could have done something to stop that. But *your* feelings were more important."

Tears spilled down my mom's cheeks and she swiped at them, embarrassed. Looking away from me, I heard her harsh breathing and knew she was trying to get herself under control.

We sat in silence for what felt like an eternity, staring at the water.

Finally she looked at me. "I'm not a perfect person. And I'm sorry if you think I put myself before you when it comes to your father. My only excuse is that he was the first man to break my heart, and it scarred me. I wasn't thinking straight. Even when Seth tried to tell me I was doing wrong by hiding those letters and gifts from you ... I was so sure I was right."

She licked her lips nervously and surprised me by whispering, "I'm so sorry I did that to you."

Relief I didn't even know I needed swept through me.

Yes, people could shock the hell out of me.

But sometimes that might be a good thing.

I reached for my mom's hand and held it between mine.

Hope lit her eyes.

"I forgive you," I whispered. "I forgive you, Mom."

Her lips trembled as she covered my hands with her other.

We both knew it wasn't quite as simple as that. That forgiveness was a complex concept and it didn't work alone. Forgiveness was inextricably connected to time. But I had to trust that with time, my love for her would chip away at my resentment.

As we watched the ducks, I vowed to let go of the past. Mac was back in my life, after all. And he wasn't going anywhere.

When he'd dropped me off at Inverness Airport, he'd hugged me so long, I thought we might meld together eventually. I hated how desolate he'd looked, like he thought I wasn't coming back.

And while the thought of being anywhere near Lachlan Adair was a knife in the gut, I'd experience that pain as long as it meant seeing Mac again.

"I have to go back to Scotland once the trial starts," I told Mom.

She nodded. "And to see your father."

"Yeah. I want to spend time with him. Annually if possible."

"What happens after the trial?"

"Traveling. For my business. The travel photographs are selling well."

"They're beautiful." Mom patted my hand, pride in her eyes. "Seth has his eye on one for our anniversary present."

I grinned. "Mom, you can have any picture, anytime you want."

"It'll be nice as a present," she assured me.

"How's Regan?" I asked tentatively.

Mom sighed wearily. "Who knows. I got an email from her last week and she said she's in Rio."

"As in Brazil?"

Mom's lips turned down at the corners. "I assume so."

"Do you want me to try calling her again?"

"No." She shook her head. "Seth and I had a chat about that too. You have enough on your plate with this Lucy Wainwright case. Your stepfather and I will handle Regan."

A slow smile prodded my lips.

Mom's brows furrowed in curiosity. "What?"

"Nothing." I rested my head on her shoulder and watched the people in the park. "It's just sometimes ... change is good."

Change is good, I repeated to myself, thinking how Lachlan was now little more than a stranger to me.

Change is good.

And one day, I hoped I'd feel that way about him too.

39

LACHLAN

The rain battered against his body as he jogged along Ardnoch Beach. He didn't care. The pelting sting of it bouncing off him was satisfying. For four weeks, he'd felt numb, going through the motions, doing what needed to be done.

Members were returning to the club in dribs and drabs, but the suites and lodges were fully booked over June, July, and August. Things were returning to normal.

And what a miserable existence it now was.

Gunning it up the sand dunes at speed to make it to the top, Lachlan jogged onto the trail that led past both estate lochs and up toward the castle.

Through the blurry precipitation, Lachlan saw a figure waiting near the path that led from Loch Ardnoch to the castle. The platinum-blond hair gave her away.

Arrochar.

Slowing on approach, he noted despite outfitted for the weather, her hair was drenched and the rain lashed off her rain jacket. "What are you doing?" he called to her. "Get back inside!"

She ignored him and he halted before her, aggravated. "You'll catch your death, Arro, what are you doing?"

"What are you doing?" His sister scowled. "You thought going for a jog in this weather was a good idea?"

Actually, he did.

"Inside." He put a hand on her shoulder, turning her toward the castle. "Come on."

Together they ran toward shelter, pushing into the side entrance.

A memory of another day like this, following Robyn into the same doorway, flashed through his mind, and he forced it back out until he felt nothing again.

"You can use one of the rooms to dry off," he said to his sister. "Why were you out there?"

Arrochar stared at him incredulously. "Because I'm worried about you."

Ignoring that, Lachlan strode into his office to his desk phone. He hit the button for Butler and Concierge, and Wakefield answered. "Mr. Adair, how can I be of service?"

"Ms. Adair requires the use of a room. Make sure there are fresh towels, a robe, and tea laid out for her. And I'll need someone to obtain dry clothing from her house."

"Lachlan, I don't need people to do that for me," his sister argued.

"Bring the key to her room to my office."

"Yes, sir. Right away."

Lachlan hung up and turned to his sister. She was a sopping mess. "Take off the raincoat at least." He gestured to her to throw it over the armchair.

"I didn't come here to be pampered. It's a bit of rain, for goodness' sake."

He leaned against his desk, crossing one ankle over the other, folding his arms over his chest. "And yet I got the distinct impression you were ready to lecture me for running in it."

Arrochar scowled as she yanked the zip of her jacket down and shrugged out of it. Luckily, knowing how to dress for Scottish weather, her raincoat kept her sweater dry underneath. She threw the coat over a chair and then rested her hands on her hips. "I don't care about you running in the rain. I care about the fact that I said I was coming over to share lunch with you, and you deliberately made sure you weren't here."

Shit. He shook his head apologetically. "Arro, I forgot."

"Did you?" she said disbelievingly. "Or are you just avoiding everyone who loves you?"

"Arro," he warned.

"No. Every time someone tries to bring it up, you snarl at them like a big beast and we all back off. Well, I'm done backing off."

"It's been a month. Give me a chance."

"Why? So you can screw up your life even further by waiting too long to fix things?"

"Arro … I mean it."

His sister lifted her elfin chin in defiance. "Let me ask you something, and I want an honest answer."

He sighed impatiently.

She forged ahead anyway. "Do you love Robyn?"

Agitation screamed in his nerve endings.

"Jesus Christ, Lachlan." Arrochar shook her head at him. "As well as I know you, I can't tell what you're thinking half the time. But whatever you feel for Robyn is so big, you can't mask it. I say her name, and the way you feel is right there for everybody to see."

A walking wound.

Pride pricked, he glowered.

"If you love her, why are you not on a plane as we speak,

heading to Boston to get her back?"

"I tried to get her back," he snapped. "I told her I loved her, and she made it clear she didn't believe me and she left."

"And you let her?" Arrochar looked aghast and not a little disappointed in him.

That was all he needed. "Bloody hell, Arrochar, dig the knife in deeper, why don't you?"

"Oh, I bloody will." She stepped toward him. "The Lachlan I know wouldn't just give up. He goes after the things he wants. He always has. He's a man I have always hero-worshipped and respected."

"Well, maybe I'm not him," he barked. "Maybe that man never existed. Playing a hero on the screen doesn't make me one, Arro. I'm just a man. As it turns out, a bloody ordinary one at that. Has it ever occurred to you that maybe I just don't deserve her?"

His sister looked stunned.

Then understanding softened her expression. "Lachlan."

"Just leave me alone, sweetheart," he whispered hoarsely. "Please."

"No." She shook her head. "No, not if that's the rubbish you've got percolating in your head right now ... Do you know what one of my best memories is?"

He didn't answer.

"I was ten, and it was the school Christmas dance. Shannon Wright slowly turned our group of friends against me. Sniffing at me like I smelled of BO, telling people she'd seen lice in my hair ... stupid mean-girl stuff that was way worse for me in primary school than it ever was in high school."

"She was jealous of you."

"I didn't know that then, though. And back then, it was the end of the bloody world. I didn't want to go to the dance, but Dad said I had to because it was the Christmas ceilidh and as leading members of the community, the Adairs always had to represent. Like I knew what that meant at ten." She smirked.

Lachlan's lips quirked. He remembered his father giving him the same speech throughout his childhood.

"I was crying in my room that day," Arrochar went on. "And you came in and found me and asked me what was wrong. I told you about Shannon and about Dad making me go, even though everyone hated me. And you, a seventeen-year-old boy, broke off a date to escort me to the dance." Her eyes brightened with sentiment. "I walked in there with my big, handsome brother, and they all thought it was so cool that you came for me, that I had a brother like you. All my friends had mega crushes on you, and you were nice to them for me, even though they'd been horrible because you knew I just wanted things back to normal. Shannon was completely forgotten.

"And there's more. When Dad died, I couldn't get watching him die out of my head. And it was you who pulled me out of that black hole, Lachlan. You wouldn't leave my side. You reminded me every day that I wasn't alone. My big brother always coming to my rescue. Whether it was a stupid wee school dance or when I was in the darkest place of my life—or when I was ashamed because a man I trusted hit me.

"I don't think of myself as a woman who needs taking care of, but everybody needs someone in their lives who makes them feel safe, who makes them feel like they're not alone and who makes them feel important." She crossed the distance between them, resting her hand on his arm. "You are that person for me, and for all of us. No matter if we're here or on a film shoot or fuck knows where," she said wryly, referring to Brodan and Arran, "knowing our big brother is always there for us, is always our safe harbor, is always the one who cares, it makes all the hard days so much easier."

Emotion clogged his throat. "Christ, Arro." He grabbed at her hand, curling it into his chest.

"I know what happened has affected you more than any of us can understand … but I never want you to doubt the man you are. You are a man confident in who you are, the good you have in you, the things that are important to you, and the things you are capable of. Don't lose that. You're my hero, Lachlan Adair, and I defy anybody to say otherwise."

Chest aching with his sister's words, Lachlan tugged at her hand. "What if … what if she left me because I'm not that person for her?"

Arrochar shook her head. "Do you honestly believe that's who Robyn is? That she would think that of you?"

Swimming against the tide of the dark insecurities Lucy's betrayal had stirred, Lachlan pushed them aside and found the truth. Arro was right. That wasn't who Robyn was. "Then why did she leave?"

"Probably—and I say this with as much gentleness as I can because I love you and don't want to hurt you—because you let her leave without a fight."

He flinched.

"Words don't mean anything, Lachlan. I think we both know Robyn respects action over words. You can tell her that you love her until you're blue in the face … but until you actually get up off your arse and *show* her what she means to you … she's never going to believe you."

His numbness had slowly thawed over the last few minutes, and now he felt it fall away entirely. Pulling his sister into his embrace, he hugged her hard. "Thank you, sweetheart."

"It's just payback, big brother," she whispered. "Time for us to have your back"—his sister eased from his arms and grinned up at him—"while you go after what you want."

40

ROBYN

Sitting on my parents' back porch, I watched Mom as she pottered around in her garden. Their house was a small colonial revival in Dorchester. Regan and I grew up here and cursed the nineteenth-century aging beauty for being cold in the winter, for having wobbly floorboards, and for generally being a pain in the ass because Seth was always having to do something to it.

But we loved it. Coming home to the blue-and-white house was nice. It was weird to be living at home again, but so far it was good. Knowing it was only temporary helped a lot. Mom and Seth graciously offered up my old room when my landlord announced a week after my arrival that my lease was up in two weeks and he wasn't renewing it. Jaz and Autry offered me a spot on their couch, but my old bedroom was a much better solution.

Though I loved hanging out with them. I didn't realize how much I'd missed them all. In fact, I'd just come from a morning of soft play with Jaz. The girls were great, but an afternoon of peaceful chill-out time on my parents' porch was exactly what I needed after a raucous, chaotic morning.

Feeling Seth's eyes on me, I glanced to my right where he sat on the other porch seat, sipping a cold beer.

My stepfather was of Cornish stock, thus the name Penhaligon, and a prime example that my mom had a type. Although not as tall as Mac—because who was—Seth was six two and broad-shouldered with rugged, handsome features, chestnut eyes, and thick hair that was once a copper red but was now faded through with gray. When he smiled, dimples creased each cheek, and to my everlasting envy, he'd given those dimples to Regan. Seth was ten years older than Mac and looked his age in a way my father didn't. But he still had that big, commanding presence and sense of capability that always made me feel safe growing up.

"What are the plans now, darlin'?" Seth asked.

I shrugged. "Hang around for a while. Get all my preorders mailed out. And then I'm going to travel for a bit."

He nodded, but there was a little furrow between his brows. "You'll keep in touch while you travel, right?"

I'd known from the moment I'd come home that Regan's behavior was affecting my stepfather more than he let on. He was unusually quiet, stuck in his own head, and clearly worried sick about my little sister. I could kill her. Despite Mom's assurance she and Seth would deal with Regan, I'd tried calling her every day, to no avail.

"Of course, I will."

He nodded again but looked away, taking another sip of his beer.

Feeling more than a pang of guilt for being so distant while I was in Scotland, I reached over and curled my hand around his arm. Seth looked at me. "Things were crazy in Scotland and I was going through a lot, but I promise to keep in touch while I travel."

My stepfather patted my hand. "I know."

Despite what I'd found with Mac, a natural bond that I

was immensely grateful for because it completed a part of me I didn't know was missing, I realized I would never give up what I had with Seth. I also realized I had never made that clear. "You know I love you, right?"

He gave me a curious look—we weren't the type of people to throw "I love you" around. It was just implicit. "I do. I love you too."

"I've never thanked you for being my dad. I couldn't have asked for a better one, and reconnecting with Mac doesn't change that."

To my shock, Seth's eyes brightened with emotion and he swallowed hard, blinking as he looked away. It took him a minute to get himself together before he looked at me again, his love clear in his eyes. "You're my kid, blood or no."

It was my turn to get choked up.

"What are you two whispering about?" Mom broke the moment as she strutted up the stairs, whipping off her dirty gardening gloves. "Darlin', give me a drink of that beer, will you?"

Seth held out his beer with a small smile and watched her nearly empty the thing.

"So?" She handed him back the beer as she settled on his lap. His arm wrapped around her waist, pulling her against him. "What's the chat?"

"Just telling Seth what an amazing dad he is," I answered honestly.

Mom looked proud of me. "Isn't he, though?"

"Right, you're embarrassing me." Seth snorted. "Subject change."

As if on cue, we heard the faint ring of the doorbell.

"I'll get it." Mom popped up and hurried through the porch door into the house.

"More shoes?" I asked Seth.

Mom had a small shoe addiction.

"Who knows."

Only a minute later, Mom stepped back out onto the porch, her eyes on me, worried. I understood why when a tall man appeared behind her. I barely heard her say, "Robbie, there's someone here to see you."

Knees goddamn shaking, I stood up, a sense of unreality coming over me to see Lachlan Adair standing on my childhood back porch next to my mother.

"You're Lachlan Adair," Seth said, and his tone broke through my dazed state.

My stepfather actually looked starstruck.

"I've seen all your movies." Seth held out his hand to my ex-lover, and his words reminded me who Lachlan was to the rest of the world.

Sometimes I forgot.

To me, he was Lachlan. The man I loved (and hated a little too).

Heart pounding, I watched on as Lachlan shook Seth's hand, amiable, telling him how nice it was to meet him.

Then all eyes were on me.

"What are you doing here?"

Lachlan stared at me in an emotionally hungry way that didn't do anything to help the speed of my pulse. "Can we talk? Alone?"

"Seth"—my mom practically yelled my stepfather's name—"why don't we go to the grocery store and get what we need for dinner tonight? Are you staying, Lachlan? We'll get extra."

The big Scot shrugged uncomfortably. "I'm not sure."

"We'll get extra, anyway."

Then my mom guided Seth into the house with such haste, my stepdad almost tripped over the kitchen doorway.

It might have been funny if I wasn't so confused.

"What are you doing here?" I repeated.

"May I?" Lachlan gestured to the porch chair Seth had vacated.

I nodded dumbly and sat in my chair, much to the relief of my wobbly knees.

There we were, sitting next to each other, just a small table between, and the breeze blew the scent of his cologne my way. Longing pierced me. Damn, he looked good. A little tired, maybe, but it did nothing to mar his rugged handsomeness.

"You're wearing jeans," I said inanely.

Lachlan smirked. "Yes. Is that a problem?"

Just that you look insanely hot and I miss you so much, I feel like I'm splitting in half, and I hate that you can do that to me.

"'Course not."

A tense silence fell between us, and my right knee bounced with nervousness.

Lachlan's eyes dropped to it and he frowned. "Robyn—"

"What are you doing here?"

His gaze flew back to mine. "Mac told me you'd moved back in with your parents while you figure out your next move."

"I meant here in Boston, not here at this house. Although that too."

His eyes washed over my face, seeming to caress every minute aspect of it, and blood rushed to my cheeks. "Fuck, I've missed you," he confessed hoarsely.

My stomach fluttered. Since the moment he'd stepped onto the porch, hope had risen within me. Was it possible that Lachlan Adair did love me? "You came all this way because you missed me?"

"I came all this way because I was scared that if I didn't follow you here, you'd make up your mind to not come home."

His words hit my chest, expelling a shocked exhalation.

"Home? Is Ardnoch my home?"

He pushed up off the chair and knelt at my feet. He reached for my hand and placed my palm against his chest. I could feel his heart pounding hard beneath it. "Braveheart, I want your home to be where I am because *my* home is wherever you are."

Tears filled my eyes at his beautiful words.

But he wasn't done.

His expression turned fierce. "I am so sorry I let you walk away. That I ever allowed you to think that my love for you isn't real." His grip on my hand tightened, pulling me toward him. "So many people have failed you, made you feel like you aren't a priority. I don't want to be one of those people. Not when you are the most important person in my life. You consume me. You are beyond a priority at this point. You're … fuck, you're everything. Robyn, I don't know if I deserve you … but I can promise you, no man will ever try harder than me to be worthy of you."

My tears, tears of pure relief and joy, spilled down my cheeks as I threw myself at him, almost taking him off his knees. Lachlan grunted and regained his balance as I peppered his face with kisses. When my lips met his, his laughter filled me, and then he was kissing me back, his arms strong, tight bands of steel, not letting me go.

But I didn't feel caged.

I felt bound by belonging.

"Does that mean you'll come home?" he broke the kiss to demand gruffly.

I stared up at his face, a face I'd come to love more than any other and asked, "Is that where you'll be?"

He nodded, grinning that mischievous, boyish smile I hadn't seen in weeks.

I beamed, so happy, I could die from pure bliss. "Then that's where I'll be."

41

ROBYN

T

he whir of the automatic blinds prodded through my consciousness, followed by a stream of light tickling my eyelids.

I groaned, peeling my eyes open and blinking against the sunlight streaming into the master bedroom. One wall of the room was made entirely of glass bifold doors. The fitted blinds were on a timer to rise at six o'clock. Lachlan was happy to change it so I could sleep longer, but I liked getting up at the same time as him, not wasting the day.

I reached across, feeling the warm but empty spot next to me in bed. He was already up. I heard the fall of the shower in the bathroom and imagined Lachlan standing under it. From memory. We'd had plenty of shower sex these last three months.

Remembering Lachlan called last night to say he'd be home late and that I'd fallen asleep before he returned, I felt a tingle waking between my legs. The club had been unbelievably busy over the last three months, and there were many late nights for Lachlan, but he promised things would wind down soon before the winter guests descended.

I could go join him in the shower, which would be better for him, but I couldn't get my ass up off his mammoth, comfortable Low Tokyo bed.

Not his, I reminded myself.

Ours.

Anytime I called something his and not ours in the house, it pissed him off.

"If you don't start referring to it as such," he'd said one day, belligerent, "I will sell everything in here so you can pick out new furniture, if it means you claiming it as yours."

I'd tried not to laugh because he was genuinely put out. "I claim you as mine—isn't that enough?"

Lachlan liked that, but he still wanted me to feel like the gorgeous home looking out over the water, next to Thane's, was mine too.

And it was slowly but surely coming to feel like it. It would even more so with the special building Lachlan erected next to us for my business. The structure itself was complete. Soon the interior would be, too, and for the first time, I'd have a dedicated space for my photography business. That, and the fact the house was a mere five-minute drive from Mac's cottage, made it as perfect as anything could be.

While Mom and Seth took me leaving hard (though they promised they were happy for me), I'd left with the assurance I'd return to Boston for the holidays.

I'd left with the utter certainty that Ardnoch was my home.

Lachlan was here.

Mac was here. Mac, who was over the moon to have me back so we could continue getting to know each other.

My new life was here.

I still wanted to travel, and in fact would need to if I wanted to grow my business. Lachlan was talking about hiring a manager for the estate so he could travel with me. For now, everything was on hold while we waited for Lucy's trial to start. In the three months since I'd moved back to Scotland, the process against Lucy had been slow. But being a cop who'd once dated a lawyer, I already knew that it would be.

Lachlan and I had some things to distract us from the case, beyond our seemingly never-ending appetite for one another. I'd gotten to meet Brodan, for one. Lachlan's middle brother returned from filming to check on Lachlan. As tall as his brother, he was less rugged. Brodan was good-looking in more of a Scottish Captain America way and had a devil-may-care attitude that came more naturally to him than it did to his big brother. He flirted with me and any woman in his vicinity, other than Eredine, whom he treated with a measured respect that made me like him even more. But Brodan's eyes held shadows that I knew Lachlan saw and worried about. His brother insisted he was just exhausted, but instead of recuperating at home, he'd left as soon as he could.

It felt like he was escaping the people who knew him best.

Lachlan suspected it, too, and my overprotective guy brooded for days after Brodan's departure.

Arran finally contacted Lachlan as well, but he didn't make any promises to come home. He was in Thailand, working at a bar, doing his thing. He was fine. Maybe he'd be home at Christmas, he said.

I had a low opinion of Arran. Who didn't come home when a family member was almost murdered?

Suffice it to say I felt the same way about Regan, but I couldn't think about my sister.

It hurt too much.

Instead, I focused on my new life as much as I could, trying to push through the fact that Lucy's fate was still unknown. There would be no plea bargain for her because there was so much evidence regarding Fergus's murder. Her part in stalking Lachlan and in McHugh's murder was harder to prove, but she was facing a lengthy prison sentence for killing Fergus, kidnapping Lachlan, and attempting to murder us both. At present, Lucy's defense team had brought in forensic mental health professionals to evaluate whether she was a candidate for the insanity defense.

I wasn't a psychologist—and wouldn't be so bold as to diagnose Lucy with a personality disorder—but it seemed likely considering her extreme behavior, narcissism, and fixation. We didn't know if the abuse she'd spoken of really happened or if it was all part of her manipulation to make us see her as the victim, but no accusation of abuse should be ignored, and I hoped the mental health professionals assigned to her case helped her as much as they helped the police look into it. A part of me was incredibly sad for Lucy, despite the terror she'd put us through.

I didn't know how the trial would play out. I just knew I wasn't looking forward to it and couldn't wait for it all to be over.

Maybe then Lachlan would find his trust again.

While he trusted me and made that clear by confiding every part of his life to me, he'd grown more aloof with club members. In a weird way, I think many of that crowd kind of got off on it. The mysterious owner of Ardnoch Estate. Moreover, after all his years as a playboy, he'd chosen to settle down with an "outsider." That always garnered interest. We'd been hounded by the press for a while, but it thankfully died down. I knew it would all flare again when the case went to trial. It was strange seeing my face plastered across tabloids and the internet. And at Lachlan's wise advice, I avoided reading any commentary about our relationship.

I'd come to realize, however, I could put up with a lot of

bullshit as long as I ended up right where I was. Hauling my ass out of bed, I sauntered into the bathroom, my body tightening delightfully at the sight of my boyfriend naked and glistening in the shower.

Lachlan gave me a heated look, his lips quirking at the corners.

I winked and then walked right past him to brush my teeth.

If I had time to brush my teeth before sex, I was absolutely doing that.

I could feel him watching me.

Looking into the mirror above the sink, I discovered I was right.

He'd stopped washing. Just stared at me like a starving man.

Hard to pass up that invitation.

Wiping my mouth on a hand towel, I replaced it with deliberate slowness. And then, eyes locked to his, I curled my fingers beneath the hem of my tank top and lazily drew it up off my body.

My naked breasts bounced with the movement, and Lachlan's hot gaze dropped to stare at them.

Feeling smug at the yearning on his face, I removed my shorts and underwear with equal slowness.

"Get your arse in here," he demanded, eyes on said ass.

"Ask nicely." I turned to lean against the sink, letting him look his fill.

Lachlan narrowed his eyes. "My darling Robyn, will you please get that fantastic arse of yours into the shower so I can say good morning properly?"

Smiling, I pushed off the sink and sashayed over to the large shower that was open to the room, making it more of a wet room. Before I'd closed the distance between us, Lachlan reached out, grabbed me by the waist, and hauled me into his arms. I was instantly wet from the rainfall head, his body, and well … *him*.

"I missed you last night." I ran my hands up his chest as he sought to touch every inch of me.

"I know." He breathed harshly against my lips. "As soon as we can, we're traveling somewhere far, far away where no one will bother us and we can fuck like monkeys all day, every day."

I laughed, the sound caught in his kiss. He pressed me against the wet tiles, and his strong hand wrapped around my left thigh, opening me to him. With those deft fingers of his, he stroked me to readiness, until I was on the cusp of shattering with the tension.

My cries of approaching orgasm echoed off the walls, stuttering when his hand fell away. "No, don't stop." My fingernails bit into his back.

Lachlan grunted and then he was there, pushing inside me.

"Oh yes!" My head fell back against the tile at the delicious fullness of him.

"Eyes open," he murmured.

I did as asked and kept his gaze as I held on tighter while he moved inside me with a steady, controlled rhythm that was driving me crazy.

Feeling my nails dig into his muscle again, he picked up the pace, his hips driving with more power. I needed more. I hopped into his arms, wrapping mine around his neck, and he caught me. Our lips met, and I kissed him hungrily.

His groan of need was followed by the sensation of moving, the water from the shower no longer falling over us. I broke the kiss, realizing he was walking us out of there.

"Where are you going?" I asked breathlessly.

"Bed," he grunted.

"We're wet," I protested.

"Then I'll change the sheets."

Before I could argue further, my back was on our bed and Lachlan was braced on his knees, hands on my hips, and he was pumping into me at an angle that blew my mind.

Sometimes, Lachlan's self-control was frustrating because he was so good at hiding his emotions from people, but in bed ... oh boy, was it amazing. I came twice before he followed me into bliss.

One of my favorite things in the world was the feel of him shuddering against me. I loved caressing his back, soothing him as he lost himself to me, the sound of his climax echoing in my ears. Just remembering the noises he made as he came turned me on, sometimes at the most inappropriate times.

Bemused at the sound of his chuckling as he fell to his side on the bed, I smiled uncertainly. "What?"

"I need to shower again."

"Worth it though, right?"

His smile died, a solemnity falling over his features. Pulling me into his arms on the now-damp bed, Lachlan brushed his mouth over mine and whispered, "You're worth everything."

Romantic bastard. I grinned, pleased, snuggling into him. "Don't go to work today. Let's just stay in bed."

"Okay."

I lifted my head, surprised. "Really?"

"Do you want me to?"

"I don't want to keep you from work."

"Do you want me to stay with you?" he pushed.

In truth, yes. We hadn't had a full day together in weeks. "I want you to stay with me."

"I want to stay with you too. I will always want to be where you are over anywhere else in the world. All you have to do is ask."

"You're very romantic this morning," I teased.

Lachlan smiled. "Have you read the news? I'm madly in love with an American photographer."

I shimmied with giddiness, unable to hide it whenever he said it to me. The man had the ability to turn me to jelly. It wasn't fair. "I did read that somewhere. I also read that she's madly in love right back."

"Good," he said gruffly, trailing kisses down my neck.

"So you're taking the day off?"

He raised his head and answered, "Well, let's see. Deal with a myriad of queries from staff and members or spend the day making love to my w—" He cut off, looking surprised.

"What is it?"

"I ... I almost called you my wife."

I grinned, unable to contain the explosive feeling that moved through me. "Really?"

Lachlan's blue eyes turned a lighter shade of azure as he studied my reaction. "It sounds right, doesn't it? It never sounds right calling you my girlfriend. That sounds impermanent." He scowled. "Wife is better."

The caveman quality to the way he grunted it made me snort. "Is that a proposal?"

Lachlan's eyebrows rose. "Is that a yes?"

"I don't know. I haven't been proposed to."

"I thought you'd think it was too soon."

Deflating quickly and miserably, I shrugged, easing away from him. "Of course."

Refusing to accept my retreat, Lachlan rolled on top of me, straddling me as he gently held my arms down above my head. I felt a renewed flush of heat between my legs. He stared at me, amazed. "You would marry me?"

"You haven't asked," I repeated.

His expression darkened with something beyond desire.

"I would ask you in a heartbeat. I didn't want to rush you into anything."

The joy that blossomed before began to bloom again. We'd talked so much over the last few months about what we wanted in life, I had no doubt that our wants and needs aligned. Lachlan never thought about having kids, but now that he'd found me, he seemed eager to get started on that whenever I was ready. Being a decade older than I was, I knew he didn't want to wait too long, so we wouldn't. We'd travel a bit first, and then we'd start a family.

I could see it playing out in my mind.

And it was more gold than I ever imagined I'd mine from my life.

With Lucy's trial hanging over us like a dark cloud, the thought of planning beyond that filled me with the kind of anticipation I didn't realize both of us needed.

"I want to spend the rest of my life with you," I promised him. "And you know when I make up my mind about something, I don't fuck around."

Lachlan smiled, a smile I'd never seen on him before.

It erased every shadow in the back of his eyes, every cynical line between his brows.

It took my breath away.

As did his next words. "A man should plan a proposal better than this, and I promise there will be a grander one with a ring and all the traditional stuff … but I can't leave this bed without asking now. Without knowing I leave it with a promise. Robyn Galbraith Penhaligon, will you do me the great honor of becoming my wife?"

I bit my lip to stop the stupid girlish squeal from escaping and nodded frantically.

Lachlan laughed. "Was that a yes?"

"Yes!" I yelled and then escaped his hold and grappled him onto his back. I peppered his face and chest with kisses and said, "Yes, yes, yes, yes!" feeling him shake against me with laughter.

And I didn't care about a ring or him planning a romantic dinner or whatever people were supposed to do when they proposed. All I cared about was this feeling. This laughter and joy between us that came from deep within our very souls.

EPILOGUE

LACHLAN

For a moment as Lachlan contemplated his companions, he smirked at the thought of what the tabloids would do to get their hands on a shot of his stage office right now. He would have used his real office, but it was too small. Instead he'd shut the door of this one, with one of the footmen, Gerard, standing guard outside in case a guest came knocking.

It was a rare occasion when he had all of his board members in one place.

Wesley, Luther, and the newly appointed board member Marci Robbins sat in casual relaxation in his suite of chesterfield chairs around his coffee table.

If it had been up to Lachlan, he would've spent the entire week in bed with Robyn after she agreed to marry him. But the day after, unfortunately, was this scheduled meeting with the board.

Not just to discuss the five spaces that had opened up on the membership list but to look over candidates he wanted to interview to help him manage the estate. Now that he and Robyn planned to marry, travel, then settle down, he needed to start training someone to take over whenever he wanted to be with his family.

Still reeling with contentment, Lachlan was afraid to say he'd missed half of what the board members had said in the last fifteen minutes. He hadn't known a person could reel with contentment. It had always sounded like such a tepid adjective before now. But, in fact, Lachlan discovered contentment was far more powerful than mere happiness. Happiness could still be tinged with anxiety and insecurity because, in his experience, it often came hand in hand with fear—fear of losing it.

Being with someone like Robyn made it impossible to let fear of the future dictate his future.

"I think Murphy is a wild card." Marci's exquisite, upper-crust English accent cut through his reverie. "We would be better with Davina Dunhaven. Her reputation is stellar."

"All of your candidates are women." Wesley smirked at Marci, deliberately trying to ruffle her feathers. "Your feminism is showing, Robbins."

"Oh, heaven forbid." She widened her eyes in mock horror. Then she nudged Luther. "What do you think?"

"I agree about Murphy." Luther nodded. "But I think Taron Mathers is a better option."

"Because he's Cockney like you?"

He flashed her a bright white grin. "No, love, because he's Lachlan ten years ago."

It was true. Taron Mathers was a young, up-and-coming action star, but he'd proven he had bigger acting chops than just his ability to throw a believable punch. "He's better than me." Lachlan leaned forward and moved Taron's photo forward. "He has my vote. He'll bring a youthful credibility to the club."

They'd just agreed on their first new member when a knock sounded on his office door. "Come in."

He straightened when Mac strode in, expression unusually tense. He didn't acknowledge Lachlan's guests, which wasn't like him. "Sir, may we speak in private?"

Lachlan always chafed when Mac called him *sir*, but now it felt worse since they were actually going to be family. Last night, Robyn called her father while Lachlan called his siblings to tell them they were engaged. Mac was happy for them, stopping by the house this morning to congratulate them. And while they joked about Mac becoming his father-in-law, it was actually bloody weird.

Though not weird enough to stop Lachlan from marrying his daughter.

At Mac's strange tension, Lachlan excused himself and strode out of the room with Mac to find a private corner in the main reception. "What's going on?"

Mac heaved an exhale. "I've just called Robyn up from Eredine's studio."

She'd gone there to join Eredine's class that morning. Ery had grown distant with everyone since Lucy's betrayal and refused to talk about it. Lachlan was frustrated and beyond concerned at this point, but Robyn insisted on patiently worming her way into Eredine's trust. Arrochar, being closest to Ery, had agreed that it was the only way to play it. She needed time, and all they could do was show her they weren't going anywhere while she processed what had happened.

"What's going on?"

"Security was called out to the gates. By Regan Penhaligon."

Jesus Christ.

Lachlan scrubbed a hand over his face. "She's here?"

"Jock's escorting her cab up to the castle as we speak."

Lachlan strode toward the main entrance, and out of his peripheral, he noted Wakefield hurrying across the room to get to the door before he could. He nodded at the man as Wakefield pulled one of the doors open to let him and Mac pass.

The gravel kicked beneath his feet as he saw the vehicles approaching up the long drive.

Movement caught his attention, and he turned to see Robyn jogging up the path from the direction of the studio. He and Mac hurried to meet her.

"My sister?" she asked Mac without preamble as Lachlan pulled his fiancée into his side.

Mac nodded. "Got visual ID. Definitely Regan."

Robyn exhaled a deep breath, eyes glued to the cab as it followed a Range Rover.

"You okay?" Lachlan asked, pressing a kiss to her temple.

She nodded, patting his chest in reassurance. "Relieved, worried, anxious, furious, concerned, ragey, curious ... plus a million other complicated feelings I can't get into right now."

"Why do you think she's here?" Mac asked.

The cab rolled to a stop.

"I guess we're about to find out," Robyn murmured.

The back door of the cab flew open abruptly; a foot encased in a spiked, bright blue stiletto appeared first. The body that followed belonged to a beautiful redhead dressed in a bright blue dress with a conservative neckline and a very unconservative hemline.

Her copper-red hair hung around her shoulders in stylized waves.

She stared at the three of them for a second and then one hand flew to her hip. She cocked it and grinned, revealing two appealing dimples.

There was something wild in Regan's smile.

Knowing what he knew, Lachlan braced himself.

He had the sudden sense of foreboding that Ardnoch's peace and tranquility was about to be disturbed.

"Hey, sis." Regan winked at Robyn. "Did you miss me?"

THERE WITH YOU

THERE WITH YOU

THE ADAIR FAMILY SERIES #2

For Regan Penhaligon, there's no better place to run to than
the exclusive Ardnoch Estate in the remote Scottish
Highlands. Her impulsive behavior has finally caught up with
her and Regan's visit with her sister, Robyn, is an
opportunity to hide from someone who has grown
dangerously obsessed with her.

Determined to make amends for her mistakes, Regan plans
to repair her relationship with Robyn by staying close. And
when an offer of help comes from Thane Adair, Regan
gratefully accepts.

Widower, Thane, needs a new nanny housekeeper for his
two young children and when they bond with Regan
Penhaligon, he offers her the job. But as the weeks pass and
the complex American reveals who she really is, Thane
struggles with his growing attraction to her.

Regan never expected to feel so intensely for Thane, but she
can't deny her passion for him or her love for his children.

When someone from Thane's past threatens his family, Regan wants to be his pillar of support. However, his continued inability to trust her might just destroy their chance at future happiness… and the person who drove Regan to Ardnoch might snuff out her chance for any future at all.

OUT AUGUST 23rd 2021
PREORDER NOW

ACKNOWLEDGMENTS

Here With Me has been several years in the making. The Adair siblings came to me not long after the *On Dublin Street* series finished, but it seemed it wasn't our time back then. However, the Adairs never left me, demanding that I introduce them to my readers. When the time finally came, I can say with utmost honesty that Lachlan Adair and Robyn Penhaligon swept me into their fictional lives and didn't let go long after I wrote the last word of their book. Living in Ardnoch with them has been a beautiful escape from a difficult year, and I hope it provides a wonderful escape for my readers too.

For the most part, writing is a solitary endeavor, but publishing most certainly is not. I have to thank my wonderful editor Jennifer Sommersby Young for always, *always* being there to help make me a better writer and storyteller.

And thank you to my bestie and PA extraordinaire Ashleen Walker for handling all the little things and supporting me through everything. I appreciate you so much. Love you lots!

The life of a writer doesn't stop with the book. Our job expands beyond the written word to marketing, advertising, graphic design, social media management, and more. Help from those in the know goes a long way. A huge thank-you to Nina Grinstead at Valentine PR for brainstorming with me, for your encouragement, your insight, and for going above and beyond. You're amazing, and I'm so grateful for you.

Thank you to every single blogger, Instagrammer, and book lover who has helped spread the word about my books. You all are appreciated so much! On that note, a massive thank-you to all the fantastic readers in my private Facebook group, Sam's Clan McBookish. You're truly special and the loveliest readers a girl could ask for! <3

A massive thank-you to Hang Le for once again creating a stunning cover that establishes the perfect visual atmosphere for this story.

As always, thank you to my agent Lauren Abramo for making it possible for readers all over the world to find my words. You're phenomenal, and I'm truly grateful for all you do.

A huge thank-you to my family and friends for always supporting and encouraging me. In particular, a heartfelt thank-you to my dad. Writing Robyn's emotional story with her father reminded me how lucky I am to have a dad who always prioritizes me, is always there for me, and is one of the most honorable, trustworthy people I know. I'm so grateful you're my dad.

Finally, to you, thank you for reading. It means the world.

ABOUT THE AUTHOR

Samantha Young is a *New York Times, USA Today* and *Wall Street Journal* bestselling author from Stirlingshire, Scotland. She's been nominated for the Goodreads Choice Award for Best Author and Best Romance for her international bestseller *On Dublin Street*. *On Dublin Street* is Samantha's first adult contemporary romance series and has sold in 31 countries.

CPSIA information can be obtained
at www.ICGtesting.com
Printed in the USA
LVHW101754131121
703258LV00020B/2071